Let Me Go

A novel by Hazel Myer

First Printing: 2018

ISBN 978-0-244-06185-2

Lulu Press, Inc

Raleigh, North Carolina, United States

www.lulu.com

A note to the reader,

This novel contains explicit reference to the presentation and treatment of a person diagnosed with an eating disorder and other mental health conditions throughout. Some readers may find content within this book disturbing or distressing and are encouraged to not continue reading if they find it so.

This book does not in any way promote eating disorders, associated behaviours or the consequences of them and has the sole purpose of supporting those affected and educating people about one individual's struggles to overcoming this life-threatening illness.

This book is based on a real person's experiences. Their name, certain dates, places and specific personal details and qualities have been changed to protect their identity. All other characters are purely fictional and any perceived similarities are entirely coincidental and unintentional.

~ Let Me Go ~

Dear Friend,

It's been a long time since I last wrote to you. Do you remember all those letters I used to keep tucked away beneath my mattress? I wrote to you diligently every day, half-believing that a miracle would happen and one day I'd receive a reply in the post. It took me a long time to accept that none was coming, that you would never reply because you can't read; there's no address that can reach you.

It took even longer for me to let go, to scatter the letters into the fire and watch hours after hours of my pleading scrawl burn into the night and as the smoke carried my words away in the wind. I buried the ashes. It's been a long time, but I feel I'm ready to speak out now. I have a story to tell, a story that you played a large part in, a story that irrevocably changed my life in more way than one. A story that I feel is ready to be told. You might not like what I'm writing, dear Friend, I must admit I've never been this honest before, but it's the truth, and truth changes everything.

At the time, as you're well aware, I didn't fully understand what was happening to me. The nature of my illness meant I didn't have the capacity to understand, not when I reached that point before my diagnosis. I always wonder, and perhaps will continue to for the rest of my life, what would have happened if the doctor had recognised my symptoms earlier? If they had realised and given me help sooner, educated me on what was happening inside my head and given me the tools I so desperately needed to see the light that had all been distinguished, would it all have happened? I guess it's something that I will continue to puzzle over, there's no answer for the past.

But now let's begin. The 'official' start of the story is not until my admission to Intensive but if I started there I'd be lying to myself. Things started before that, with events that you're not aware of, things that happened before I ever met you. Things that led to your arrival and the things that started this whole circle.

Before

I've never really noticed the mirror before, and if I have then it's never meant anything to me. Just a reflection and a reversed one at that, but I'm looking now. I scrutinise the remains of my rounded, childhood cheeks that used to make dimples when I smiled, memories of a past life that time is rapidly forcing me out of. I stare at my school uniform, no longer the checked blue of a primary school dress, but a harsh cloaking of black that serves as a constant reminder of how much time has passed and how it isn't too long until I reach adulthood.

I look at my body that has begun to shape and change in ways that I don't feel entirely comfortable with and a niggle of doubt creeps like a fog into my mind. I look deeper into the depths of the mirror and a monster looks back.

'I'm not fat,' I tell myself. 'My family have always said I'm pretty and have a nice figure.'

'They're just saying that,' it purrs. *'I think you should lose a bit of weight, just a little. A little won't hurt and you'll feel so much better afterwards. It will make all of your problems disappear!'* The monster smiles and bares its teeth.

I consider its words. It's true that I am officially 'depressed' and am developing a rather poor body image and an internal hatred for myself, the doctor had said as much in his stuffy office on my last visit. I'd sat for my allocated fifteen minutes and answered his questions about my general life and 'how it made me feel' until I was handed a diagnosis on a piece of paper and referred to the Child and Adolescent Mental Health Service (CAMHS).

It's also true that the bullying has got worst.

Much, much worse.

For instance, no matter the sport, it's a well-known fact that I'm consistently picked last for P.E. It isn't being last that bothers me… it's the bickering and the squabbling that goes on between the two teams as they fight over who should have me, a feat that the teachers will allow to carry on for a few seconds that drag on

~ Let Me Go ~

like hours until my torture is ended and I'm presented with a team and met with the frosty stares and curled lips of displeasure from my temporary group. But that's not the worst. The worst is being shouted at and followed in the corridors, by students above and below me, chasing after me and throwing their insults until I feel each one stabbing like a knife into my back as I run.

The worst is being kicked at in the corridors so I have to watch the floor wherever I go and skip over the legs that fly out to trip me, or not being fast enough and landing sprawled on the ground, pressing my face into the floor and hoping desperately for the earth to swallow me whole. The worst is when the boys in my classes steal my stationary and put it down their trousers and down another garment as well, before thrusting it back at me so that I feel tainted, violated and tearful and have to throw it away before indulging in a large squirt of hand sanitiser. The worst is when people refuse to talk to me or roll their eyes dramatically whenever I speak, and only seem to want anything to do with me when they're in bigger groups with their friends behind them. That way any interaction with me looks like a comical joke and an attempt to provoke yet another embarrassing social moment for me to stew over for the next few weeks. The worst is walking to lessons and older students spitting out their chewing gum onto my bag, and me not realising it until I've returned home in which time the greying lump had stuck fast and buried into the fibres.

But the worst of the worst?

Nothing can compare to the way it makes me feel about myself. 'Yes,' I answer back. 'I'll go on a diet. I'll practise 'healthy eating' and put in a nice exercise routine. This won't get out of hand; it's just a little diet.'

The monster smiles and maliciously rubs its paws together as I turn from the mirror. I am mere putty, putty that is to be moulded into a better person than the failure I am at present.

3 months later…

I stare at the mirror, twisting my head slightly to the side to scrutinise my appearance from a different angle. It all depends on how you 'look' at the mirror to see from the perspective you want. My eyes range over my prominent cheekbones, the chapped lips that were my long-lost smile and the sunken pits that are my eyes with their shadow of black bags beneath them. A broken soul. My eyes travel further, see the sharp points of my collarbone and the ribs that you can count through my papery skin, the sudden jar of my hips that burst from my waist in jagged points to the joints of my knee caps which are becoming wider than my thighs.

I twist and the skin stretches, stretches to the point where I can press my fingers into the wasted muscle, push them up until I can put my fingers behind my ribs, feel their smoothness and the way they press against me. I travel along the rough bumps of my spine as it traces its way up my back, the mottled purple bruises and scabs stretching alongside like some perverse artwork, created from spending hours a day sitting on the plastic chairs at school. I look at myself, at the 'self' I have become, and it isn't enough.

I tilt my head the other direction and, like a flicked switch, a sudden change of light, my complexion alters completely. I stare at my thighs, my lips curling back in unrestrainable disgust. They bulge and swell before my eyes, growing until I can see the layers of fat swarming beneath my skin, multiplying and spreading outwards through my body. The bones vanish, become replaced by rolls of blubber until, if it isn't for the fact I lack the blue skin and fins, I'd assume myself to be a whale.

I curl my hands into fists and fight the urge to smash through the mirror and strangle the girl behind it who has the nerve, the audacity to stand there in this state. I imagine her melting, melting until all that is left is a viscous pool of fat on the floor, seeping into the carpet and tainting the room with its filth. How dare she? How dare I? I pinch painfully at my skin, imagine tugging and pulling until the fat comes off and spills out of me like some toxic poison.

No fatty, there will be no dinner for you today.

~ Let Me Go ~

Dear Friend,

You may think I'm being harsh by putting everything down to the bullying, pointing a finger at the individuals who made my school life such a misery and saying in an all-powerful voice 'it was you. It was your fault that I got sick, your fault that my desire to be accepted almost cost me my life!' and I suppose, that to some extent at least, you'd be correct to think so. Naturally, I had other characteristics that made me more prone to the development of the illness, such as being a perfectionist, a high achiever and having issues with my body confidence in response to puberty.

The monster, you remember it, don't you? It was the monster that fed me the lies about myself and the world around me. It was the monster, coupled with the comments from the bullies that made me feel like I had no place in the world and the stress of exam season at school that made me only able to get through the days by focusing on my diet. A diet that quite literally wore me away until I was nothing because you can't hate what's not there to hate. You can't spend your time with feelings of self-loathing if there's nothing or no one left to loathe.

My illness reduced me to a shell, empty on one hand and yet with the potential to be full of something I was not on the next. At times I would be empty, a forgotten ghost of the girl I used to be. The characteristics and personality that used to give me an individual spark to my eyes and a sense of identity consumed by the illness until all that remained was my outer skin. But at others, I would be full, full to the brim with the threat of bursting with the monster and its plans. I had still lost the main element that was me but, rather than remaining empty, I had been filled with a new 'personality'; I guess you could call it. I think that's what made it worse, both for me and for my family who had lost their little girl. The urge to diet, to exercise and to lose as much weight as possible became prevalent in my mind, no matter the consequences.

I no longer cared about my grades at school or the impending dates of my exams that had previously left me studying for the vast majority of my evenings. I no longer cared about my hobbies. My love for music and playing the piano became lost; my fingers grew stiff and forgot the keys they had so frequently played.

It was this that led to my admission through A&E to a paediatric ward with heart problems. The doctors had told me previously of the damage I was doing, and the charts and test results all pointed to a complication, but I don't think I could have stopped even if I was aware of what would happen. I was so consumed with the monster and hatred for myself that I failed to see what it was doing to me and I didn't understand that my condition was now classed as 'life-threatening'. I failed to see the physical damage that was being done, the damage that I was so unknowingly causing to myself.

Chapter One

The sharp stench of disinfectant stings my nose with each breath I inhale. The ward is silent, apart from the steady beeping of my monitor and the gentle squeaks of the nurses' shoes as they move up and down the corridor. I lift my sleeve to my nose and sniff, attempting to inhale at least some vague remnant of home, something that doesn't burn with each breath. It's become so encompassed within my skin that I can practically feel it bubbling beneath the surface. But there's nothing left. I must have sniffed it so many times over the past two weeks that all trace of scent is long gone, a memory carried away on the breath of the wind.

I don't understand why I'm here.

My bed is in a room with three others, none of which are currently occupied at the moment. There's another room next door with a half dozen or so beds in, they shift me from room to room like it's some perverse game of musical chairs – or beds I guess would be the more appropriate word. I'd rather be in here than in the room next door, there're older teenage girls in there whose boyfriends visit throughout the day. To them I'm just a kid; a nobody. Their over-bed tables and cabinets are piled high with a whole magnitude of calories, boxes of chocolates, fizzy drinks and other items. They all look at me with a vague sense of suspicion and interest whenever I'm moved in there and I can tell by their eyes that they're questioning why my table is piled with books rather than sweets, and why I become so vocal and non-compliant when it comes to meal times. I asked originally if I could go into a private room, but the doctors swiftly refuted this, saying that I needed to be under close medical observation, hence the reason why my bed is in the empty room directly opposite the nurses' desk. The doctors are due up onto the ward within the next few minutes; I'm hoping that today will be the day of my discharge. I don't hold out much hope, though, considering I ask for this each day and the answer is always the same – a monotonous 'No' followed by some explanation such as I'm 'too weak' or am 'too much of a risk to myself'. They'll run out of excuses eventually, once they come to terms with the fact that there is no cure for my illness, and even if there was I wouldn't take it.

I turn as I hear the jingling of keys and a flurry of footsteps as a swarm of doctors hurry pass; they'll start at the top of the ward first in the room where all the younger children are before they come and see me. I give my area the once-over, checking that nothing is out of place, that my bed is neatly made and the bloodied tissues are carefully hidden out of sight. Little things matter when it comes to the doctors, if they see that I'm organised and prepared then maybe they'll deem me sane enough for release.

Besides my neatly occupied area and the remaining three beds in the room, the adjacent wall is compiled of shelves stacked high with board games, books and magazines. There is a sink in the corner alongside medical waste bins and a narrow mirror above it in which the monster has taken up residence.

I expect the doctors to be a while in the first room; there was an admission in there last night. Considering I've had to spend the past two weeks either sitting in my chair or lying in bed, I have a fairly good understanding of the way things are run here. I have nothing better to do than observe the staff and patients, even reading my books gives me headaches after a while. The whole ward runs like some well-oiled machinery, ticking repressively like clockwork. One shift starts and then another, beginning with the doctors doing their rounds at precisely ten fifteen every morning and ending with the evening handover at eight. Everything works… except for the patients themselves.

I've seen it all. There are three types of patient; the broken and injured, the ill and damaged, and the ones like me who don't fit into distinct categories but remain snugly in the middle. There are the children who come in with their raggedy stuffed animals, too loved to be a distinct shape any more for their weekly session of chemotherapy, babies with fevers and unusual rashes that cry pitifully throughout the night, sports fanatics with broken bones who are waiting for them to be pinned and the ones who have jumped from heights or necked bottles of bleach in an attempt to leave everything behind. And then there's me.

I know what my diagnosis is, I'm not stupid, I just don't understand why I'm here. I was admitted after a particularly distressing meal. I hadn't had anything to eat or drink all day and, in my moment of weakness, had consumed a small portion of vegetables and a half-slice of bread for dinner. The ending result was not one that was pretty. I had run up and down the stairs in a vain attempt to burn off the sixty-two calories I had consumed, but I kept slipping on the way down and falling the remaining stairs because I was too weak for the exercise. I picked myself up and continued on, despite the fact that my breath was coming in painful gasps and that the edges of my vision were blurring. My parents tried to block the stairs to stop my progress, but I pushed past them and continued, falling down again and again.

I threatened to leave the house to go on a run; my parents weren't having any of that so they called the Crisis Team. The Team didn't hesitate in telling my parents to take me to A&E for an emergency admission. I remember that my bag was already packed at the foot of my bed (I had been in and out of hospital so frequently that I had neglected to bother unpacking) and I was sent on my way with Mum. I was seen within two hours of my arrival, had an ECG which was deemed 'abnormal' and failed to have any blood drawn considering my levels of dehydration. I was admitted to the paediatric ward with a weak heart, severe malnutrition and dehydration as a result of my eating disorder. Believe me; it's as fun as it sounds.

I can hear the group of doctors hurrying back down the corridor and watch as they re-group in front of the nurses' desk. They always do this after visiting a room; they make a note on the relevant files and update the nurses on the patients they've just seen. They'll be with me in less than two minutes. I briefly contemplate setting the timer on my phone to see just how accurate my guess is, but they'll probably deem that rude if the bleeping goes off and announces their arrival. Are manners a sign of sanity? I barely have time to consider; they're coming my way. I cross my fingers under my blanket and send a silent prayer to whoever may be listening; please let them send me home.

The curtains whip shut around my bed, enveloping me in a filtered pale blue light and my blanket is immediately crossed with bars from the pattern. The doctor looks briefly over his chart before introducing me and the reason for my admission to the other doctors, who scribble on their pads with such an intensity that I'm surprised they don't go right through the paper. The nurse on duty stands to one side and looks at me sternly down the length of her nose as this morning's breakfast experience (in which I had told her quite clearly where she could stick my *Weetabix*) is obviously still playing on her mind. "Good morning, Bethany," the doctor says, in a rich Polish accent, wafting his coffee breath over me as he continues to swiftly scan through my notes from the previous day. "The nurses have told me that you've refused almost half of your meals and fluids since my last visit. Why is that?" I glare at his over-polished shoes – isn't it obvious? Why would I want to eat and drink when there are calories in everything?

Truth no.1 – Calories are everywhere. They spread through the air so that, if someone in the same room as you eats something, you inhale all the badness as well.

After a moment of awkward silence in which it quickly becomes obvious that I've no intention of answering, he addresses the other doctors once more. "Bethany has been here for two weeks and has remained fairly uncompliant with her treatment plan. She has weekly sessions with her psychotherapist on the ward and we are in close contact with her psychiatrist. Following his last visit on Tuesday, it's been highly recommended that, should Beth continue to be uncompliant and irrational with her cognitions and behaviour, then a bed in a specialist Psychiatric Unit is to be found." I repress a sigh. He's told this to a different group of doctors almost every day this week and has been threatening Inpatient since my admission. They have no intention of doing such a thing, firstly because I'm too fat to be admitted for anorexia and secondly because it will cost the government a fortune, even deep down they all know I'm not worth it.

He motions for me to lie on the bed and proceeds with my daily physical examination. I feel his warm fingers press onto my concave stomach before he tuts quietly and mutters something to the nearest doctor who scribbles furtively onto their clipboard.

"When was the last time you emptied your bowels, Bethany?" he asks.

I blush a deep crimson. Does he seriously expect me to answer that in front of all these strangers? I know the line he's going down though, due to a lack of food and fluid, constipation is a common ailment for people with eating disorders. "This morning," I lie easily.

"From what I can feel of your stomach, you haven't been for at least a week. It's of no use to you lying to us and telling us what

you think we want to hear," he warns smoothly.
I scowl. It's of every use to me, it might get me out. He pulls a
stethoscope from the deep pocket of his blazer and listens to my
heart. "Breathe for England, Bethany! Breathe for England!"
I breathe.
He shakes his head sadly again and I overhear him murmur to
the doctors "her pulse is weak. Order another forty-eight hour
ECG monitor." I grit my teeth and glare angrily at the ceiling. I
honestly don't understand why I'm here and why I am being
treated like some fragile, china ornament that might shatter at
the slightest touch. If there's one thing being sick has taught me,
it's how to be strong. I hate it that people treat me like I'm a
small child who can't comprehend what's happening to them.
The doctors have already told me that I 'lack the capacity' to
make informed and rational decisions any more. It's not just the
staff here in the hospital that treats me like this, it's my family
too. I overheard the nurses telling my parents about my 'delicate
state of mind' so that everything I am now told has been watered
down to a degree that I can supposedly 'cope' with. I don't
understand why I am being so closely monitored and subjected
to numerous treatments that I don't need when there are many
more sick and injured children on the ward who need much
more help than what I do.
The nurse wraps her arm around my back and pulls me gently
into an upright position so that the doctor can listen to my back.
He presses the stethoscope to me for a minute and I make a
conscious effort to breathe in a deep and regular manner. He
pulls away and I lean back against my pillows, attempting to
conceal how those few minutes of sitting unsupported have tired
me.
"I'm going to prescribe you another bag of saline fluids, you're
showing sure signs of dehydration given the cracked lips and
lack of toileting," says the doctor. The nurse begins nodding and
I can see the faint movement of her lips as she recalls his
recommendations for later. "Observations will continue as
normal, with two vials of blood being drawn first thing in the

morning and last thing at night. Your blood glucose is looking low, so I'm going to suggest this is monitored every two hours rather than every three. I'll also be ordering another forty-eight hour ECG monitor to be worn on your chest because your heart is still concerning me; I will also be booking you in for an ultrasound as soon as possible to see if there's anything more serious going on.

In regards to your weight, you've lost three and a half kilos since your admission, which is unsurprising considering your intake has been minimal. I'll put it in your notes that you're to be weighed first thing tomorrow; we'll see if there's been any change. I'm going to ask our dietician to come up and speak to you about an increase in calories, and I'm also going to highly recommend that you take your meals on the play-tables in front of the nurses' desk so that your intake can be monitored." He pauses and looks down at my charts once more; making sure that he hasn't missed anything. "If you remain uncompliant and a threat to yourself, then other methods will have to be considered for your own safety and wellbeing. Do you have any questions for me or the nursing team?" he asks.

"Yes. Can you discharge me now, please?"

***

I smell the food long before I see the caterers carrying the trays up the ward. I bury my nose into my pillow; I'd rather inhale the burning fumes of disinfectant than calories. I squeeze my eyes tight, hoping that for once the caterers will forget to bring me the meal that has already been decided for me by the nursing team, but deep down I know that's not going to happen. A nurse with a kind smile and a pile of greying ringlets balanced haphazardly upon her head taps me gently on the shoulder and I jump, my nose jerking from the pillow and I instantly smell a concoction of various microwaved dinners. "Come on, Beth," she says kindly. "You know what the doctor said this morning. We've laid out your lunch on the little red table." I look the other way and pretend that I haven't heard her. Eating is bad enough, but at least when I eat alone I have some chance of hiding a large proportion of it.

"Come on," she encourages, wrapping her arm around my waist to help me stand. "You know what will happen if you don't try."

I nod and allow her to lead me over to the red table that has been set aside for me. I sit in front of the tray and raise the lid uncertainly, speculating uneasily about what may be lurking beneath; a plate of white rice, some sort of casserole, broccoli and a pot of ice-cream by the side. Do they honestly expect me to eat all of this? The nurse goes back behind her desk and sits down comfortably, before looking at the computer. She looks past the screen at me, not taking her eyes off of me for longer than a few seconds at a time.

I gulp as I look back down at the plate before me. I stand very little chance of successfully pretending to consume it if she's going to watch me like a hawk.

I pick up the knife and fork and hold them uncertainly in my hands. I stare down at the food, watching as it begins to expand before my eyes. I can see the nurse staring at me out of the corner of my vision; there's no way I can hide this or get rid of it. I begin to panic and my breath catches in my throat. How many calories are on this plate? I don't know. "Beth, can you make a start please?" says the nurse encouragingly. "If you can't manage it then we can give you a replacement of Fortisip if you'd prefer?" No, I would not prefer Fortisip; I would prefer to not have anything at all. I look down again at the plate, immediately trying to calculate the calories and how much I can get away with leaving. I start with the broccoli; that's the lowest thing there by far. I eat it slowly, cringing as I chew and swallow, feeling as the calories cling to my teeth and the inside of my mouth before being swallowed down into my stomach. I cut the pieces into tiny amounts, so tiny that the vast majority of each forkful is air.

~ Let Me Go ~

Truth no.2 – If you cut food up small enough then some of the calories seep out.

I want them to think I'm eating more than what I actually am. I keep stopping to put down my fork and take a sip out of the beaker of water they've given me, placing my head in my hands and trying to stifle the urge to fling the plate as far away from me as possible. After finishing with the broccoli, I pause once more to analyse the casserole and rice, moving my fork aimlessly to and from my mouth in order to make it look like I'm still eating. What's in the casserole? I don't know, I can't tell by looking at it whether it's a ready meal or been home-cooked, I don't know the ingredients and I don't know the macros. I can't eat this.
I glance subtly at the nurse who has been tasked with watching me eat, she's looking properly at her computer screen now, she must have seen me eating my broccoli and thought I'd just carry on.
Using my fork, I push all of the food into a corner of my plate, mashing it into place to decrease the volume and make it look like some is missing. I then use my knife to smear some of the sauce around to make it look like I've made some attempt to eat it. Satisfied with my newly-created artwork, I rest the cutlery back onto the tray and call to the nurse that I'm done and can't possibly eat any more. She comes across and looks down at my plate with suspicion. "Are you sure you can't finish it up? You've made a good start," she asks. I repress a smirk, I haven't even touched it. "No," I reply smoothly. "I can't eat any more." She removes the tray from the table. "Go on back and sit down then, love, I'll bring your replacement over once I've put this away."
"It's not a full replacement, is it? I ask nervously.
"Oh no, you've eaten about half of this so I'll only give you a half replacement."
I nod and shuffle slowly back towards my bed, no longer able to repress a smile. Even if she was going to replace all of it, it still wouldn't make up for what was on that plate. There're only two

hundred calories in a bottle of replacement, they really ought to read the label

Chapter Two

I lean back into the pillows as the doctor finishes my physical examination. It's been twenty-four hours since the ECG monitor was put on my chest. I am not allowed to shower or even wash in case I get it wet and I'm self-conscious that I smell. "Bloods show low levels of sodium and potassium, it takes multiple times to draw the required blood due to dehydration. ECG shows signs of concern so I think we'll be putting at least another twenty-four on after tomorrow." I repress a sign, although wearing a monitor is a pain, it's not me I feel sorry for, it's the poor person on the second floor tasked with the job of watching my heart-trace for a full twelve-hour shift until the next person takes over.

"Her weight this morning has decreased by another kilo and she's been refusing the vast majority of her meals and fluids," the doctor continues as the others take hurried notes on their clipboards. "I'm going to prescribe another bag of saline fluids and will be informing Beth of what was discussed earlier, as I think those methods are now appropriate considering the severity of the situation at hand." I gulp, that really does not sound good. He turns back to me as the doctors finish up their writing. "Do you have any questions?" he asks. He asks me the same question every day, as is required by protocol. He seems to know exactly what's coming through, considering I ask the same thing each day too. "Can you discharge me now, please?" I ask quietly, trying to kid myself into believing that I have at least some chance of him agreeing. He shakes his head dejectedly and motions for the others to leave. Once the curtain swishes back into place behind them, he turns to look at me, a sad expression on his worn face. "You know I can't do that," he says slowly. "You are very sick and we wouldn't be doing our job if we just let you go, it also doesn't help that I know you have no intention of following your treatment plan in the community, considering the consequences of that are what caused you to be admitted in the first place."

"I'll follow it, I promise!" I say earnestly.

He smiles sadly. "My dear, if that was even slightly true I might begin to consider it. We both know that's not the case, however, and it's prudent that you receive the help you need before it's too late." I look down at my hands, and try to conceal the look of disappointment that must clearly be written all over my face. "You've been here for almost two weeks and there has been no progress, if anything your physical health has declined. You know as well as I do Bethany that you are very physically compromised at the moment. You're the healthy weight of a nine year-old and you're sixteen. By not complying with your treatment plan you're putting the staff and most importantly yourself into a very difficult situation." I gulp, but continue to stare resolutely at my hands. If I can just pretend hard enough, then maybe this won't actually be happening. I'll be at home and left to my diet in peace. "I have a suggestion, well more of a definitive actually; I want you to be fitted with a nasogastric tube. It will be inserted into your nostril, down your oesophagus and into your stomach so that when you refuse to eat and drink, you will be pumped with the nutrients you require to survive. If you refuse, then you will get weaker and weaker until, in roughly a weeks' time, you will be transferred to the Intensive Care Unit and the tube will be fitted anyway. It's your choice." I sit there in silence as he lets the words sink in. "We all want what's best for you, and with the appropriate support and treatment I believe you'll make a full recovery," he says quietly. I shake my head and a traitorous tear glances off my nose and lands on my hands. "It's your choice," he reiterates before leaving and pulling the curtains wide open behind him so that my bed is clearly visible from the nurse's desk once more.

That's no choice. That's no choice at all. I feel like a small animal; caged, frightened and cowering in the corner in a vain attempt to be left alone. They want to put a tube down my throat. They want to pump me full of calories. I feel trapped, backed into a decision that I don't want to make. I pick up my phone and swipe shakily through my contacts, my finger hesitating over Mum's number. I want Mum; I need her to come and get me and take me back home, I don't want this eating disorder any more and I don't want to be here. The urge to call her is overwhelming, but Mum is at work. If I call her and tell her about the tube there's no doubting that she'll leave immediately and rush to my bedside. She'll panic, cry and perhaps plead with the doctors to consider another option. But there isn't another option.

If I refuse this then I'll be transferred to ICU and they'll insert the tube anyway… no matter what decision I make. I click my phone off and bury it under my pillow, shielding my family from the choice I'm about to make… the decision the doctor knew I would make when he told me. I wipe the tears from my face with the back of my hand. If I'm going to have it done, I'll have it done under my own terms and most definitely not on ICU. Nothing says brave more than standing up and fighting, especially when they believe you'll do the opposite. I'll consent, but just because I'll have the tube fitted doesn't mean I'll let them pump me. That decision will still remain my own. They can take my dignity, but they can't take me.

~ Let Me Go ~

***

My legs shake beneath me as I follow the group of nurses into the treatment room at the end of the ward, threatening to collapse beneath me with each step I take until I have to throw out a hand and grip the wall for support along the way.

They unlock the door and motion for me to climb onto the table whilst the senior nurse goes into the medication room to collect the necessary equipment. The other holds a polystyrene cup of water with a straw before my face and the remaining grips my hands firmly.

"This is likely to be very uncomfortable for you, Bethany," says the senior nurse as she re-enters the room wearing plastic gloves and carrying an impossible length of tube. I feel my heart pound painfully against my ribcage, fear claws up my throat and I feel like I'm going to be physically ill. I fight down the urge to run and hide from what they're about to do to me. I searched it on my phone beforehand, a mistake I'm now deeply regretting. Each of the faces in the images I found were unnaturally contorted with pain, eyes squeezed tightly shut and tears streaming at the tube protruding from their noses. They didn't use anaesthetic.

"We'll try and get this fitted as quickly and easily as possible, but you will need to help," she continues briskly. "Now, I'm going to insert this tube into your right nostril and feed it down your throat and into your stomach. The stiller you are, the less painful it will be. When it reaches the back of your throat you may feel the need to gag, so you'll be sipping this cup of water to help swallow the tube down. If you resist the tube then it will only take much longer and be more painful for you. You've consented to this treatment, but you can tell us to stop at any time. If we stop then the doctor will be told. Do you understand?" I nod my head shakily, two tears escaping down my cheeks that I can't reach to wipe away. If the doctor is told, then I'll be sent to ICU for sure, I can't let this beat me.

~ Let Me Go ~

I shut my eyes tight and imagine that I'm far, far away.
Somewhere where children don't feel the need to starve
themselves to be accepted, that aren't admitted to paediatric
wards and unable to attend their school proms because their
weight is too low. Children that can't go outside without being in
a wheelchair because their legs can't carry them any more, that
aren't having an NG tube fitted when they just want to go home.
I can feel the pain and tickle of it inside my nose; my eyes stream
with humiliation and pure fear at what is being done to me. I feel
the raw scraping of it against the back of my throat and my body
automatically curls in on itself to protect me from the sudden
invasion. The nurse's hands tighten around my own; I'm not
sure whether she's trying to be supportive or trying to hold me
down.

"Sip the water, Beth, there's a good girl!" says the senior nurse as
she twists the tube further down my throat. I gag and pull
forwards, instinctively cowering from the plastic that should not
be there... because this isn't real, this can't be happening. Their
grip on me tightens. "Stop it!" I shriek, my voice screeching out
of my mouth before I can stop it as I struggle to pull away from
their iron grip. "Stop it! You're hurting me!"

"Nearly there! We've got past the throat now!"

The nurse pushes the tube further until I feel it slide down inside
me. She pushes faster and I watch as a whole length of it
disappears until all that is left is the little pink plastic clip on the
end. "There we are, that's much better now, isn't it?" I gasp and
retch again. With each movement of my neck and head I can feel
the tube twisting inside me, pulling and choking, rubbing and
catching until I gag once more.

The senior nurse goes into the adjacent room and returns with a
plaster in the shape of a teddy-bear which she uses to stick the
tube firmly to the side of my face. I tuck it hesitantly behind my
ear. "There we go; we'll tell the doctor that you've had it done.
Well done, I know that can't have been pleasant, but at least it's
all over now."

I climb down from the table and automatically say thank you, although I'm not sure what I have to be thankful for. The nurse who held my hands puts her arm around me and leads me back to my bed. My legs shake with the remnants of shock and fear and my breath stings sharply in my chest. It feels so unnatural and plain wrong; I want to pull the tube out of my stomach and pretend that it never happened.

"Do you want me to call your Mum and tell her about it?" she asks gently as I sit back in my chair. I shake my head; asking someone else to tell her will be a copout. She'll see soon enough anyway when she comes in to visit me after work, there's no point in upsetting her now. "Ok, well give us a call if there's anything we can get you or if you'd just like someone to talk to," she says. "I'm going to give you some space; I can tell that you're still in shock. You were really brave, Beth." I pull my jumper out of my cabinet as she leaves; I keep it in there to protect it from the stench of disinfectant and fear - it's the only thing that still smells of home.

***

My parents freaked when they first saw the tube, and after I explained why I had it they immediately stormed up to the nurses' desk and engaged them in what I assume was a very heated conversation. For the rest of the week, I only eat half of my meals and drink only a limited amount of calorie-free fluids. The little I do manage to consume is painful to swallow, making the experience even less pleasurable for me - if that's even remotely possible. No matter how much I chew, the food still manages to catch on the tube as I swallow. It makes me gag as I feel the tube get pulled down with the food until being released once it's in my stomach.

So far, my tube has not been used. After each refusal, staff tell me that they're going to give me a replacement through the tube, they've said that I can choose between having it fed through by gravity in which a nurse manually filters it down, or pumped into me via a machine, every time I go for the option that's not given, neither. Legally, I have every right to refuse treatment. Despite the fact that I am aware, on the one hand at least, that I am underweight and in desperate need of sustenance, on the other I feel so hideously fat that my immediate response to eating is a straight 'no'. I can't help but want to lose weight, despite the warnings from the staff, the discussions with my psychotherapist and the pleading from my parents. It's not just about what I want; it's about the monster too.

Every morning I can hear it talking to me from its place in the mirror. It tells me how proud it is of me and how much progress I'm making in becoming a better person. It tells me how the bullies at school will leave me alone and that everything will be ok if I can just lose a couple of pounds more. It tells me that, despite the staff wholeheartedly believing they're doing the right thing in trying to help me; I shouldn't listen to them because they don't understand the burning intensity of which I have to lose weight. I feel invincible.

I've settled as best as I can into my little corner of the ward and have established a well-practised routine. Each morning I wake an hour early and, whilst the night staff believe I'm still sleeping, indulge in one hundred squats, one hundred sit-ups and thirty minutes of jogging on the spot to kick start my metabolism for the day.

Truth no.3 – Exercise burns those foul calories before you even eat them so that they die as soon as they're swallowed.

I then take a shower at the lowest temperature it will go until my fingers and toes turn a pale blue and I shake so hard I worry that I'll fall and get caught. I spend the rest of the day reading in my chair and make as many attempts as possible to walk up and down the corridor for various things, before another cold shower, a repeat of the exercise routine and then bed. I know that I'm not helping myself, but every time I see the number creep down the scale I feel so exhilarated and as if I have some point to my life; the monster in the mirror smiles and tells me how well

~ Let Me Go ~

I'm doing and that I mustn't give in to the doctors. But despite what the numbers might say I'm still fat and have much more to lose; I'll only stop when there's nothing left of me.

***

Despite the magnitude of additional blankets piled on top of me, I can't seem to get warm. I bury deeper under the covers, pulling them up and over my head to create a warm cocoon and to block the noise of the little child crying in the other room.

I feel an incessant pulling at the edges of my mind, it's been happening all day, but I didn't want to say anything in case the doctors thought there was something more seriously wrong with me and I'm kept in here for longer.

It's the monster, and it's trying to get in. I don't mind the monster, sometimes it even keeps me company and there's no denying that it's definitely helped me to lose weight. But that doesn't mean I like having it inside my head, I like the privacy of having my brain and my thoughts to myself. I close my eyes tight and visualise a large rock, which I roll into the forefront of my mind to prevent its entrance. I imagine nailing planks of wood over the cracks around the edges until not even a breath of air can get in.

The pulling gets stronger until I can practically feel the monster's clawed fists hammering against my mind, searching for a way inside.

I strain as I fight against it, but I should know there's no hope. With a mind as damaged as my own, it won't take long until my resistance comes crumbling down. With a final pull, my metaphorical barriers crack and the rock becomes lost in the rubble. My mind floods with the monster as my thoughts alter to coincide with what it wants me to do. My previous longing to lose weight is suppressed by an irrefutable and overwhelming desire to do what the monster wants and waste away completely. I have to lose weight and fast.

There's no point in me managing a few meals to satisfy the

~ 25 ~

nurses and stop them from doing anything else; there's no point in anything at all. I want to be emaciated. If I stop eating and drinking completely my weight will plummet, the doctors will see there's no point in keeping me here because treatment isn't working and I'll be sent home to lose even more. The monster's right, I was kidding myself before by eating some of those meals and drinks. I don't deserve to eat and feel well; I don't deserve to live at all. I deserve every ounce of pain that is possible to inflict upon myself and what better way than starvation? The monster's smile becomes my own; I am determined to make it proud.

Chapter Three

I twist my head painfully to the side and look at the rain streaking like tears down the window, my heartbeat increasing in response to the movement. Four days have passed since the monster got me. Four days in which nothing has passed through my lips, apart from the continuous refusals to eat and drink. I don't feel that it's my choice any more, despite the nature of the illness causing me to fear food; I am genuinely hungry and can't stop thinking about eating. It feels like every waking thought is about food, I even dream about it, so that I wake even hungrier than before.

I'm flopped on my bed, my head raised by a stiff pillow as I'm now unable to support it on my own. My mattress has been replaced with a special air covering which hums continuously in order to protect me from developing sores from my protruding bones. I cannot walk; I cannot move. Even breathing is an effort. I am so physically and mentally tired that I'm desperate to sleep, but nobody tells you how much prolonged starvation hurts. The pain leaves me unable to rest so that I'm desperate for some kind of distraction, only I don't have the concentration to do anything and my eyes won't focus to read. No one ever tells you about the physical pain an eating disorder causes.

My parents sit around my bedside. The doctor called them earlier this morning to tell them that their daughter is now at risk of death before urging them to come to the hospital as soon as possible. Mum holds my bony fingers in hers, stroking my cracked hand delicately as if she's worried that the slightest touch may break me. She thinks I'm bordering unconsciousness and, as I'm barely able to move or speak to tell her otherwise, I watch through half-closed lids as she lets the tears she's been holding in for weeks flood down her face. She doesn't wipe them away.

Dad paces before the window, too distressed to sit still, his eyes trained on my chest and the monitor beside me convinced that each weakened flutter of my heart, each rattled breath, will be my last. My heart breaks. I never meant to hurt anyone, just myself. I don't understand how everyone is so upset to see me like this, it's just me, and it's not like I matter nor have any place in the world. I'm better off dead; it would make the world a much better place if I, the monster and my illness weren't in it to hurt everyone who gets too close.

The doctor came to visit me once again this morning. He'd sat down in the chair by my bed and, after reading through my notes and charts, told me sternly, "Miss Thomas, you are now at risk of death. Do you understand? Your body has begun to shut down, you are dying. If you don't eat or drink something in the next twelve hours then you will die," he repeated, hoping desperately that it would sink into my fogged mind and bring me back. "If you continue to refuse your care-plan then certain measures will be put in place. We can force-feed you, Miss Thomas, a total of three times until we will have to legally contact the Mental Health Team to assess and potentially Section you. Do you want to be Sectioned?" I try to shake my head, but I can't manage it. I want to cry and scream that this isn't my fault and that I didn't ask for this, but I have no energy and no tears

left inside me.
Even after an hour's reflection before the arrival of my parents, I
still firmly believe that he doesn't understand … no one does.
They can't force-feed me or Section me. There's nothing wrong
with me.

***

There is a limit to everything. The average person can hold their
breath for roughly a minute before losing consciousness. The
cheetah's maximum speed limit is around 120 km/h and, as it
would turn out, there is also a limit to the amount of hunger you
can feel before it's impossible to feel any more.
As it would turn out, upon reaching this point at precisely one
o'clock that afternoon, I no longer feel hungry. I feel empty, but
that's a different thing entirely. Whenever I look into the mirror,
I can see the monster smiling back at me. It keeps telling me how
pleased it is with my progress, how much better I look now that
I've stopped all intake completely. It tells me how the doctors
don't properly understand my condition and that, despite it not
being malignant or malicious in any form, them trying to make
me gain weight will be obstreperous rather than for my own
good. It's a relief to not have the clenching pain in my stomach,
the pounding headaches and nausea that comes with starvation,
it's like a magic wand has been waved and the pain has all but
disappeared. I can finally move again, not to the extent in which
I can do jumping jacks or sit-ups, but enough to function. If it
wasn't for the residual beeping of my heart monitor, I would
have questioned whether I am still alive.
My heart is still beating but, according to the doctors, only just.
They've explained to me that, due to the fact that all other muscle
and fat supply has been largely depleted, my body has begun to
effectively 'eat' my heart as a final means of requisitioning
energy. Despite the fact that, even though the mere suggestion of
this should scare me into complying with whatever plan they put

in place, the monster has told me to not be overly concerned. And what reason do I have for doubting the monster?

Truth no. 4 – The monster is my friend, despite how controlling and irritating it can be at times. It tells me the absolute truth and I trust it, quite literally, with my life.

If it's telling me not to worry about my heart decreasing due to it being used for energy, what reason do I have to worry? It says that as long as the number on the scale goes down, nothing matters anyway. It's all about the goal, not how you get there. I glance towards the basin mirror in the corner of my room and see the monster looking back at me. It smiles wide, bearing its fangs and its eyes glitter with pride. It nods its head slowly, as if in admiration and respect, and tells me how skinny I'm becoming. How people will notice me and be eager to be my friend now that I'm beginning to look good, and that no one will ever bully me again. It tells me that my problems are vanishing before my eyes, that perhaps the world has found a little pocket for me after all, and that perhaps I am worth it and do deserve to live, assuming of course that my weight loss continues.

I'm dedicated to my illness, it has swallowed me whole. It's my life and my entire being; I am nothing without it. For once I don't feel cheated that it's taken away my personality and dreams for the future, it's given me a sense of identity that I've never had before. I want it more than I've ever wanted anything in my life. I want to be 'me'. The 'me' that's beginning to live through the illness, the 'me' that can refuse, even whilst hurting. The 'me' that's making my own decisions about my life and my body and is finally doing something that feels right for once.

But, of course, there's still a lot more work to do, as the monster won't let me forget. There's still weight to be lost before everything is truly alright again.

I raise my lips slightly and smile back at the monster. Am I afraid of being Sectioned? A little, but I know the monster wouldn't lie to me. They can't Section me; you have to be sick for that. If the team did come, they would take one look at me and laugh at my diagnosis. 'How can this child be anorexic?' they would snigger. 'Why, she looks obese to me! I've never seen a girl so fat in all my life!'

They can't Section me. I'm stronger than them.

I raise myself into a seated position and reach for my phone before slowly searching for a new exercise routine to try in the mornings. I'll keep the old one too, of course, but it's important to shake things up once in a while.

Truth no.5 – If you do the same exercise too many times, you stop burning calories because they get used to it and build up their resistance. It's important to change the routine every so often to catch them off guard and burn them faster.

My thumb hovers over a particularly tempting one involving squats, push-ups and mountain-climbers as I being to plan exactly what I'll have to do in order to trick the staff and get away with it. Just as I'm putting the final touches to my formulated plan, my allocated nurse for the day marches swiftly towards my bed, I hold out my wrist automatically for her to take my pulse. "Can you come with me for a minute please, Beth, you're needed in the treatment room," she asks gently.

"Ok," I reply, setting my phone back on my bedside table. They must want to do another blood test; it's not the first time that something has happened to my morning bloods so that another sample is requested by the doctor.

I follow her slowly down the hall and into the treatment room, repressing a slight shudder at the memory of having the tube inserted. There is another doctor in the room, one that I haven't seen before, and I can hear the movement of another in the medication room readying the needle and vials. I assume that she's here to observe for training or something. The nurse who brought me shuts the door quietly behind her and I hear her shoes squeak as she marches away. I feel uneasy with being in a room with a stranger; I can feel her eyes burning into my back as

~ Let Me Go ~

I sit on the table and roll my sleeve up to expose my arm for the needle.

The other doctor enters the room. The first thing I notice is the fact that she's a consultant, not a doctor, the second is that she's holding a large syringe full of a sickly yellow liquid in her gloved hand and the third is that she's wearing scrubs. Something clicks and falls into place in my brain at the realisation of what is to come. The other doctor isn't here to observe, she's here to hold me down. I make for the door, but my way is blocked by the consultant with her syringe, which up close I now recognise as containing a concentrated substance of pure calories. She's going to pump it into my tube.

"Now, let's get this done quickly and then you can pop on back to your bed and read some more of your books," she suggests kindly. "Can you sit up on the table again for me?"

My mouth gapes with shock and pure fear as I search my muddled brain for the words to tell her to stay away from me with that syringe. She approaches me, holding out her arm to guide me to the table. I shirk from her touch as if she is going to hit me and back like a caged animal into the table. I can feel the cool metal and crinkle of paper against my thighs. I am trapped. The other doctor comes up behind me; she leans over the table and lifts me onto it before I have a chance to react as if I weigh no more than a doll. At first I beg; I plead, tears and mucus running down my face as I scan hurriedly around the room for anything that can help me, anything that can get me away from this enclosed space with my living nightmares.

The consultant lunges for my tube like a wild animal stalking its prey. My body reacts instinctively; I curl my hand around my tube and shriek, using my other arm as a shield to ward her off with that syringe of poison. I lose control of my mouth, and I begin to shout and scream at the top of my lungs, with no thought of my actions. "Stay away from me!" I shriek, my voice echoing sharply around the small, tiled room. A sound like a dying fox, a scream to chill the blood and a noise full of such energy I didn't realise I still possess. It takes them off their guard,

making them stand stock-still as if I have physically attacked
them. They have never dealt with a patient who has so forcibly
rejected their treatment and haven't been trained to properly
restrain. They recover quickly.

"Don't you dare! Don't you touch me!" I yell. I scream for help,
but no one comes.

Grasping the syringe in one hand, the consultant grabs at my
enclosed fist and attempts to pry my fingers away from the tube.
I grip harder until I can feel the imprint of the clip burrowing
into my flesh. I can tell that she's afraid of pulling too hard.
Pulling too hard could pull out my tube and then, not only will
they be faced with the struggle of force-feeding me, they will
have to re-insert it as well. Adrenaline races through my system
and I know that despite the fact there are two of them and
they're much bigger and stronger than me (especially
considering the many days I have gone without some form of
sustenance), nothing in this world will make me let go. The
other doctor wraps her arms more firmly around me and pins
my arms tightly to my sides, and I shake myself back and forth
in an attempt to make her let go. The consultant pulls at my
fingers again and I feel them begin to slide with perspiration.

"Get off me! Fuck off, I don't want it!" I scream, tears racing
down my face as my body shakes with the effort of keeping them
away. "I don't want it! You can't do this! No! No! NO!" Barely
discernible as words, a tide, a flood of emotions pours out in a
state of pure desperation. I swat at them and scream obscenities
to the heavens, my words like paper aeroplanes, brushed aside,
barely making an impact and having no effect.

I pull backwards until I am flat against the table, hanging on by
my legs which I've wrapped underneath. That catches them off
their guard. "Bethany, please! You need to have this feed, your
body is shutting down!" Now they are the ones pleading with
me. The other doctor releases her grip in surprise before trying to
support my body, believing that I'm weakening and will fall.
My vision blackens and my strength begins to seep out of my
pores, impossible to catch like trying to hold water in your bare

hands. I have to remain conscious, I have drastically overexerted myself and it's beginning to show. If I pass out then they could push that poison in me and I wouldn't be any the wiser until I wake up and find another inch of fat hiding beneath my skin. I shriek once more and pull my tube further out of the consultant's grip.

The consultant shakes her head at the doctor over my shoulder and they simultaneously draw away. I jerk desperately away from the table and barely catch myself before hitting the floor. I swing out of the room and scurry shakily down the corridor towards my bed in the corner, the wide eyes of various patients and parents meeting me as I pass - the treatment room must not be sound-proofed.

I collapse in a heap on the floor beside my bed. My legs giving out beneath me, and curl tightly into a foetal position, wishing for all the world that I could wake up from the nightmare that has rapidly become my reality.

Chapter Four

A hand gently shakes my shoulder and I hear a soft, soothing voice begin to try and calm me down. I can feel the coolness of the linoleum floor along my side and the dampness of tears against my cheek. "Come on, love, you can't stay down here," says a nurse gently. "Can you stand up for me?" She pushes her arm under me and pulls me upright until I am sitting, my hair is matted to the side of my face and I can barely see out of my eyes after my prolonged session of crying. "Did you fall? Can you remember what happened?" I shake my head numbly. The nurse looks at my arms and tries to hide her shock at the bloodied crescent moons from where I had dug my nails into my skin in an effort to hold the pieces together. "Come on. Let's get you back into bed."

She helps me to stand and get into bed before smoothing the blanket over my legs in an attempt to quench their shaking. "I thought you might have wanted some alone time after the doctors told me what happened in the treatment room. I didn't realise you were on the floor," she says softly, wrapping one of the blankets at the end of the bed around my shoulders. "Do you want to come and try snack with me? I can sit with you if that helps." I shake my head. I can't. I just can't.

She smiles sadly. "How about telling me about this book you're reading, then?" she asks, pointing towards the book I left on my cabinet. I look bemusedly from her to the book, unsure of what I'm supposed to do or say. It feels like things are being filtered through to me so that it takes me a bit longer to make the connections and understand. The nurse seems to comprehend that I'm in a state of shock after the trauma of an attempted force-feed. "Alright then, love, I'll leave you to get some rest. Give us a call if there's anything we can do for you, even if you just want someone to sit with you for a bit, we honestly don't mind."

She gives me a quick hug before walking from the room. I turn my head to look out of the window and over the town, trying to imagine what would have happened if I hadn't developed anorexia and the whole world remained open to me. I wonder what lesson I'd be in at school, what I'd buy from the cafeteria with my lunch money and what plans I'd already have made for the following weekend. It's sad, but I can barely picture a life like that any more. Even before the illness came and turned my world upside down, things had been slipping beforehand. I'm so terrified of going out in public and I haven't had a friend over to stay for at least five years. I don't text, phone or use any means of social media, I am a recluse trapped inside the walls of my illness.

I want to cry, but I don't have any tears or the energy left inside me. My eyes begin to flutter closed as I drift into an uneasy sleep, an assortment of 'what-ifs' hovering on my tongue.

***

I'm sat in my chair again, aimlessly flicking through the puzzle book that Natalie bought for me from the gift shop downstairs. My parents are sat on my bed, looking at me concernedly, having just been pulled aside and told about the incident with the doctors this morning. Their eyes have black rings around them, and I can tell that they haven't had a decent night's sleep in a long time. I hate the way that my illness isn't satisfied with solely hurting me, but has to take its wrath out on those around me too.

"How was work?" I ask hesitantly.

Dad dismisses this question with a shake of his head. "You need to stop fighting against treatment, Beth," he says. I shake my head and turn slightly away from them. "I don't want to have this conversation," I reply uneasily.

"Well we're having it," interjects Mum. "If you continue to refuse treatment then they're going to Section you. If they do that, then we won't have any say about which Unit you're sent to and how your treatment plan will work. You won't have any say or any choice either. If you think that your eating disorder has taken your freedom, I promise things will seem so much worse if they do Section you."

"They're not going to Section me, it's all just talk, and they can't send me to a Unit because I'm not thin enough. You're only admitted there when you're skeletal and practically dying," I reply.

"You are skeletal, and you are dying," emphasises Dad slowly. "We had a phone call last night from your CAMHS psychiatrist, Dr Tate. They're actively searching for a bed for you which you will be assessed for as soon as one becomes available. There's a discharge in Birmingham in a fortnight, and they've already put your name down to be considered."

I try to arrange my face to make it look like this isn't news to me and doesn't bother me in the slightest. "There'll be others going for it, it's not like they'll even consider me," I say confidently.

"Well, we'll just have to agree to disagree on that one," says Mum. "We want so desperately to take you home with us, to be able to do fun things with you on the weekends, but you can't have your life back until you are more stable, and if that requires Inpatient treatment then that's what will happen."

"Our dinners are in the oven, so we need to think about making a move," says Dad as he stretches and smoothes the creases from his shirt after having his arms crossed in frustration for such a prolonged period. "Please can you try to have night snack for us?" I nod my head slowly. I'll try, but I'm not making any promises.

***

One of the night nurses sets a plate with two biscuits and a beaker of warm milk in front of me. She sits down beside me and pats my hand where it's shaking on my lap. "You can do it, Beth, I believe in you," she encourages. "Just take it one little bite at a time; I have the next half an hour to be with you before I've got to do the observations. I nod my head and look down at the milk and biscuits before me, my hands remaining firmly twisted in my lap. The biscuits begin to swell and expand before my eyes, growing until I don't know how they're managing to stay upon the plate. I look with shock to the nurse to see if she's seeing what I am. I know this doesn't happen to other people, they never believe me when I say it's always too much, but since she's so close maybe she saw it as well. She looks back at me and gives me a warm smile. "It's just two little biscuits," she says reassuringly. "It's not going to make you gain any weight, if that's what you're concerned about. As soon as you're finished you can go back to your bed and read some more of your book to take your mind off things."

I nod my head to show that I've understood, but continue to stare dejectedly at the food before me. I can practically see the calories dancing on the biscuits and swimming lazily around in the milk, pointing up at me and laughing at what a fat failure I am. I shake my head suddenly to try and make the thoughts go away. I don't want them to Section me, and I don't want to go to a Unit, at least if I try they might take pity on me and let me go back home. I pick up a biscuit uncertainly in my hand, feeling its gritty texture and the way it crumbles slightly between my fingers. I can do this. I raise it shakily to my lips and take a tiny bite, wincing as I feel the calories inside my mouth, preparing to jump down my throat and wrap themselves around my bones as fat. My legs begin to shake as I chew, and my thoughts become shouts and cries, telling me to spit it out before I can do any more damage. I try to swallow, but my throat isn't working properly, as if it's aware of the harm I'm about to do to myself. I react instinctively and spit the lump of chewed biscuit back onto the plate, before rushing back to my room and swilling out my mouth with water from the sink in case any of it remains inside me.

What's wrong with me? Why can't I manage what the vast majority of people do on a daily basis, and sometimes even look forward to doing? I grip clumps of my hair between my fists and look up into the mirror, staring past the gaunt outline of my face to the monster lurking in its depths.

"What did I tell you about eating?" growls the monster angrily. *"Do you even know the number of calories you were close to consuming then? At least you spat it out."*

"I know," I reply quietly. "But I didn't eat it. I think they're going to try and Section me, I just want to go home now."

"They won't Section you because you're too fat and not worth the help or the bother. You have to stay strong and never forget the importance of that number on the scale. It has to keep going down, no matter what," replies the monster, as it turns and slinks away through the mirror once more.

"Wait!" I cry desperately. "Help me! I don't know what to do!" I raise my hands as if I want to smash through the mirror and pull the monster back out, demanding for it to tell me exactly what it wants me to do and how I can make this all stop.

"Are you alright, Beth?" asks the nurse worriedly. "Who are you talking to?"

"No one," I reply. "I'm fine."

"Ok, well, do you want to come and try the supplement?" she asks.

I shake my head.

"That's your choice then," she replies. "I'll make a note in your folder, but I'll pass it on to day-shift that you did try this time."

***

The following day during the doctor's rounds, a different senior doctor and nurse enter the room and come straight towards my bed. I gulp. They're probably here to give me the 'you're dying' lecture to try and get me to try and eat something again, since I refused to even try breakfast this morning. The doctor is tall and broad-shouldered and has the distinct tone of someone who drinks a large quantity of protein shakes and has spent copious hours body-building. I get the impression immediately that this is not someone to get on the wrong side of and feel a nervous tingle of fear as she approaches.

The nurse remains behind her as she steadily draws the curtains around my bed, and I wonder if she feels intimidated in the presence of this woman as well.

"Good afternoon, Bethany," she says in a deep, Spanish accent. "Dr Mulane has told me that they were unable to give you your feed yesterday because you were uncooperative and that you refused your entire dinner and snack again last night. This has to stop, now, and we are going to act against your will in order to save your life. If you could just remain still and compliant then this will all be over quickly." The nurse comes out from behind the doctor and I see a large jug of sickly-yellow fluid and a large syringe clasped firmly in her gloved hands.

I shoot up from my chair as the book on my lap falls and skids across the floor, my eyes wide as I understand exactly what she's implying. They're going to try and force-feed me again, and this time I have a nasty feeling that they won't stop until they succeed. I dart left and right in search of an escape from the curtain cage, but am blocked each time by one or the other standing in my way. I climb across my bed and back into the corner where the wall meets the cabinet, my hands raising automatically in defence, my eyes tearing and pleading to be left alone. Please, please don't get me. My heart hammers like a piston against my rips and my breath comes in short painful gasps.

"We've called the Mental Health Team, Beth, they'll be here to assess you later this afternoon, it will look much better in your notes if you complied with us rather than having to be restrained. What do you think?"

I suggest that they do something anatomically impossible to themselves and back further into the corner, wedging myself into the gap until I can feel the sharp ache of being tightly restricted.

"Stay away from me. I'm warning you to stay away!" I try to speak calmly, but with each word I utter my voice rises in pitch and volume until I am shrieking.

I hear the resonating squeal of hinges as another nurse closes the door and encases me with my nightmares. The doctor crosses towards me with three strides of her muscled legs and wraps her hand around my tube. "Get off! Get off! I don't want it!"

She prises my fingers away from my tube with one hand as if it's no more an effort than removing a cap from a stubborn bottle and twists the first syringe of liquid onto the end. "NO! Stop it! Get off me! I don't want it!" I scream at the top of my lungs, my mouth and my brain no longer connected so that I am screaming profanities and clawing at her unresisting hand to get my tube back.

As she pushes down the plunger, I feel the coolness of the liquid as it runs through the tube into my nose, down the back of my throat and into my waiting stomach.

I shriek again and shrink further into the corner as I feel the calories rejoice within me, they begin to multiply and grow and I feel them begin to wrap around my bones and encase me in their fat.

"It's alright, it's alright," soothes the nurse as the doctor presses plunger after plunger of the foul poison inside of me. I can barely hear her over the sounds of my screeching.

When my torture is finished the doctor and nurse leave, taking the empty jug with them and leaving me broken and sobbing on the floor. I shake and feel the tears barely make contact with my face as they drip into a puddle on the cool, hard linoleum. I claw at my face and rip the tube from my nose, gasping as the acid stings my throat before throwing it under my bed.

The 'urge' comes, overpowering and all-consuming, searing unrestrainedly through my mind like the trajectory of a bullet. I've managed to resist for so long, the dieting and exercising taking control of it for once, pushing it aside with the knowledge that my eating behaviours (or lack thereof) is causing much more physical damage than the 'urge' ever would.

But now I relent.

I stand and reach for my wash bag, pulling out the razor blade that I had concealed for 'just in case' and draw it across my skin, gasping as the blood wells and drips over my arm. I sigh with the pain as I cut again and again, desperate to get rid of the poison that they pumped into me and to reduce the intense hatred for myself. They find me that way, on the floor again, lying in a mixture of my own tears and blood with my hands over my ears and screaming at the top of my lungs to drown out the sounds of the monster's anger in the mirror.

Chapter Five

"Miss Thomas is a sixteen-year-old female patient who was admitted through A&E on the 22nd of May following a period of distress at home in which her parents feared for the collapse of her weakened heart," states Dr Ybarra. "Miss Thomas has been diagnosed with Anorexia Nervosa and has consistently refused full compliance with her treatment plan upon arrival. Pending four days of no intake, either liquid or solid, doctors feared for her life and attempted to initiate a forced-feed … something which doctors were unable to carry out due to Miss Thomas's … err… methods of avoidance. With aid from the nursing team I then successfully passed five-hundred calories of Fortisip through Miss Thomas' feeding tube as she cornered herself against the wall and was restrained by both myself and the head nurse. We, as a team, believe strongly that Miss Thomas requires specialist treatment which we are not at liberty to provide on this ward and spoke with her psychiatrist a

few days ago to begin the search for a bed in an Inpatient Unit.
Due to her lack of compliance with treatment and our inability to
make life-saving interventions against her will, we feel that she
needs to be detained under the Mental Health Act so that her
treatment can be fully received."

I mentally suggest to the doctor where she could stick her
Fortisip rather than down my tube and glare at her out of the
corner of my eye. My intense fear of her has been replaced with a
simmering hatred; she put five-hundred calories down my tube.
I'll have to try and get away with doubling my exercise routine
tonight to burn that off, and they've probably already made
themselves at home around my bones.

I'm sitting on the leather sofa in the 'Sunshine Room', a space
used for private patients, formal meetings between patients and
staff and where children are moved to when they're about to
pass away. It's a calm and pleasantly bright place, with large
windows on the left which look over the town. There is a large
flat-screen television on the wall and a shelf crammed with
various toys and books. A large bed sits in the middle,
accompanied with numerous sealed packets of medical
equipment so that, despite trying to replicate the comfort of the
stereotypical home environment, you are still forcibly reminded
of the situation that has brought you here.

Three suited men sit before me, briefcases tucked in between
their shined shoes and various photocopies of paperwork and
clipboards on their laps. A bronze, ornate mirror hangs above
their heads. "Thank you, Dr Ybarra," says the man in the middle,
scanning through the copious documents.

"I think we'll speak to Miss Thomas now if you could please
excuse us." Dr Ybarra shakes their hands firmly, her own broad
palm swallowing their own before leaving the room and shutting

the door behind her.

I smile pleasantly at the doctors and fluff out my jumper. I've deliberately chosen one of my larger pieces of clothing to conceal my bones, hoping that they will assume there is flesh where there is nothing but air.

This is my one chance, and everything rests upon it. I have done my research. They can only Section me if the majority of the party agrees that it's appropriate, and they can only agree if I a) pose a risk to myself or b) pose a risk to others. Yes, you could argue that I am a risk to myself, but that's me for goodness sake, quite frankly who cares? I've never deliberately hurt anyone, although I did suppose that my latest suggestion of what the nursing team could do with my snack can be deemed offensive, so really they have no ground to stand on.

All three look up from their paperwork and look me directly in the eyes. I fight the urge to break eye contact and clasp my hands firmly in front of me to hide their shaking and straying to fiddle anxiously with the hem of my jumper.

"Good afternoon, Miss Thomas, my name is Robert, and this is Samuel and Jackson," he says, indicating the people on either side of him. "How are you feeling?"

I swallow down the tempting 'how do you think I'm feeling? I'm stuck in hospital and am about to be potentially Sectioned you bunch of stuck-up bastards,' and instead respond with a cheerful "I'm very well thank you!"

"I- I'm glad to hear it," says Robert, clearly shocked by my positive presentation. "Are you aware of why we've been called here today?"

"Oh, yes," I reply smoothly. "I'm afraid there's been a bit of a misunderstanding. I'm terribly sorry for you all to be called out of your way to come and see me. You see, I was admitted here two weeks ago as a mistake, there's nothing wrong with me whatsoever. I'm completely healthy!" I stop suddenly, worrying that my growing anxiety has got the best of me and I've been a little over-enthusiastic with my fabricated story.

They blink rapidly for a minute at me, trying to comprehend and make a link between the girl before them and the girl whose name is on the notes clasped firmly in their hands.

"I see," replies Robert. "If you're not unwell, Miss Thomas, would you mind telling me why you've refused any nutritional intake over the past four days? Your notes clearly say that your heart is failing from malnutrition, despite your age you're the healthy weight of a nine-year-old and that you are being monitored around the clock by nurses and doctors who feel that your body will inevitably shut down within the next few hours."

I grind my teeth together. Stupid doctors. How am I supposed to talk my way out of this? I consider my words carefully; one wrong utterance and I will be Sectioned, potentially sent to some sort of Psychiatric Hospital and worst of all made to put on weight.

"I have been misdiagnosed," I respond.

"Oh?"

"I have been falsely labelled 'anorexic' and as you can see that's obviously not the case." As I speak I watch as my body blows up like a balloon. My thighs expand at an alarming rate until I fear they'll bulge and run over the sides of the sofa like some toxic waste. My face swells unexplainably until I can feel my chin multiplying and growing down until it rests firmly on my chest. My stomach begins to balloon and I feel as layers of fat begin to wrap themselves around my bones as my jumper stretches painfully around my torso.

I look up into the mirror and see the monster staring back, baring its fangs and glaring menacingly down into the room. *"Trying to Section you, are they fatty?"* leers the monster. *"Don't you dare give in to them. They're liars, the lot of them. They don't want to help you; they want to fatten you up like a pig for slaughter. You don't deserve to eat; you're a disgusting piece of work who deserves nothing more than a slow and painful death. You're lucky I came to help you feel better. You have to remain an informal patient; otherwise, I swear I'll make your life an even greater misery than it already is. Tell them fatty; tell them why they can't Section you."* It leans against the side of the frame and rubs its clawed paws together in malicious contempt.

"Y-you can't Section me," I say nervously. The monster's presence has shaken me, knowing that my every move and utterance is being observed by it. I don't want to let it down, I want to live up to my illness and be left alone to do as I please. "To Section me I have to be a risk to either myself or others and I'm neither!"

Robert removes his glasses and looks up at me with sad, pained eyes. "Oh but Miss Thomas, doesn't starving yourself and cutting your wrists count as harm? You're not in a position to help yourself, so let us help you. I'm sorry, but we've made our decision."

He looks to Samuel and Jackson on either side of him who nod their heads sadly in agreement. I shake my head rapidly from side to side, making the world tilt and spin before me.

"As of today, you are detained under Section 2 of the Mental Health Act 1983 for a twenty-eight day assessment period. If you are not compliant with your treatment plan and medication then it will be given forcibly and against your will."

I clasp my hands over my ears and shut my eyes tight, convinced that this is all some horrific nightmare. They don't Section people in real life. This is just some joke; some stupid joke the doctor is pulling on me to scare me into eating. I can hear the three men

~ Let Me Go ~

talking to me and repeating my name as if speaking from down a long, dark tunnel, before pressing the emergency call buttons around their necks.

The next thing I know I'm being pulled upright from the sofa, two nurses on either side of me, one arm gripping my hand firmly and the other wrapping like a vice around my waist, pulling me upright and half-carrying me back down the corridor towards my bed. "Come on, sweetheart," they murmur soothingly. "It's ok; everything's going to be ok."

They sit me down in my chair, ensure I haven't dislodged the monitor attached to my chest and tuck a blanket over me to try and reduce the tremors which are shaking through my body in waves. "We'll give you some space, love, but we're just over at the nurses' station if you need anything." They each give me a hug and withdraw from my bed, looking concernedly over their shoulders as they leave. I stare at the empty bed in front of me, my eyes wide and unseeing, too shocked to produce any tears.

Chapter Six

I slouch moodily in my chair and glare at my psychiatrist across the room. I try to suppress my anger and hatred which has been simmering inside me ever since he called the ward and said he was going to pay me a visit, if I shout at him I'm even more unlikely to go home anytime soon. In regards to intake, I'm now expected to eat a total of three meals and three snacks a day; on top of which I have five NG feeds a day, amounting to a shocking five-thousand calories. I try not to even think about it, the mere mention of it sends me jittering and panicking until I become so overwhelmed that I have a full-blown panic attack. On the bright side, however, considering my body has been profusely starved for so long, any sign of nourishment has been rapidly "spent", as the doctor coined it and I've only gained three pounds rather than the kilos I was expecting. If I'm "uncompliant" with my meals (aka: throw them in the bin or on the floor, hide them and say I've eaten it, drop it out the window or just point blank refuse) then it's made up in Fortisip and pumped down my tube regardless of my inevitable pleading and

tears. Whether I am compliant with that or not doesn't matter, if
it's going down then it's going down.
I shriek, scream, beg and plead with the staff on a daily basis
until they've become so used to it by now that they barely bat an
eyelid and have almost come to expect it of me. I've scratched,
cut and clawed at my arms until they've been wrapped in
bandages to prevent me from getting at them and I've been
forbidden from having my curtain drawn around my bed – a feat
that means I can no longer exercise without being threatened
with some extra Fortisip or self-harm without someone
immediately noticing.
I feel as if the whole world is against me, hell-bent on causing me
as much physical and psychological pain as is humanly possible
– but then again, as the monster frequently tells me, it's no less
than what I deserve for having the audacity to be alive.
Dr Tate shuffles his papers nosily, bringing my attention
unwillingly back into the room. I stare at a spot directly above
his left shoulder, determined to not even look him in the eye.
Despite the fact I know it's impossible, a part of me is still half-
hoping rather childishly that Dr Tate will just take me off my
Section, say they've made some terrible mistake and send me
back home to my family.
As my consultant psychiatrist, it's his say over everyone else's
what happens to me in regards to treatment.
"So, you're Sectioned," states Dr Tate. I remain silent. Of course
I'm Sectioned, I wouldn't be here after what the nurses and
doctors have done to me if I hadn't. He pulls my notes out of the
large folder on the desk and riffles through them, one ankle
propped upon his knee as if he hadn't a care in the world.
It's alright for some.
"Your bloods have stabilised, which is good," he mumbles,
peering down through his square glasses at the abundance of
charts before him. "Your pulse is still weak and your heart trace
shows a prolonged QTC complex which is rather concerning.
Have you felt anything?"
"Yes," I reply slowly. "It flutters and I can feel it skip beats and

sometimes stop suddenly for a few seconds."
"Do you know why that is?" he asks.
"I'm dying?"
"If you weren't Sectioned and had continued as you were then yes, most certainly you would be dying, but at the present moment, Miss Thomas, no." He removes his glasses and pinches the bridge of his nose between his thumb and forefinger. "You're still physically compromised, fragile and mentally unstable, but with the nutritional intake that you have, umm, unwillingly received, I am pleased to confirm that you are no longer at risk of death. Your weight is beginning to steadily increase, a sign that your body is beginning to physically recover and repair the damage caused by starvation and your vital signs are beginning to look more stable. I understand that this probably scares you and I can only imagine what things must feel like from your perspective."
I remain silent.
I want to shout at him and tell him that he doesn't understand; no one does unless they've witnessed it first-hand. Whilst the news of an improvement in health should be positive and celebratory for most people, the very mention of it makes me feel even more of a failure than I already am. I don't know who I am without anorexia, it has been my only way of life for so long that I struggle to remember how things were before it and the monster entered my life. It irritates me when people speak and act like they know the ins and outs of everything - including the way that I'm supposed to be feeling when I don't even know that myself. He can say that weight gain 'scares' me, but he doesn't really have any idea of the vast range of emotions I feel when it's so much as suggested.

Truth no.6 - I would rather die than gain weight.

I understand that he's a trained doctor and has probably had loads of experience with cases like mine, but I am more than just a case and an eating disorder affects each individual uniquely.

~ Let Me Go ~

He can't even begin to comprehend what it's like to hate yourself with such an all-consuming intensity that you're willing to put yourself on the brink of death in order to be able to, ok so maybe not like yourself, but to just accept the fact that you're alive. No one can understand the crippling pain it causes when your vital organs begin to shut down as you literally consume yourself, or when your parents beg and shout and cry for you to stop something you no longer have any control of.

All previous thoughts of controlling my anger evaporates. I glare at him furiously.

"I see you're angry, Beth, is anything upsetting you at the moment?"

I suggest the same as I did to the doctor and nurse who force-fed me, that he go and do something anatomically impossible to himself and leave me alone if he's not going to help me.

He chuckles quietly. "I must say, you do make me laugh. I should tell you off for using that sort of language, but I don't think you're aware or in that much control considering your current condition."

I repeat my recommendations.

He chuckles once more before wiping his eyes and sliding my notes back into the folder. "I must leave in a minute; I have an appointment with another patient in half an hour at the clinic. I have two more things I need to tell you though, things which you may find hard to hear. I've already phoned your parents this morning to update them on the situation and have told the staff you might need some additional support after our meeting," he says. He places his foot back on the floor and leans forward to look me in the eyes.

I gulp and try to look confident. What could they possibly have in store for me now?

"Firstly is that I will be making a note in your folder before I leave that it's my medical advice as your psychiatrist that you won't be sitting your GCSE exams this year, quite frankly you're too weak and it's unfair to put that amount of stress on you considering the large amount of time you've been unable to attend school. And secondly, as you're aware, I have sent a request to numerous Psychiatric Inpatient Units in search of a bed for you. We have been lucky and have had a reply today that there's a possibility of a bed being available soon in Edinburgh which they're considering you for. I am aware that this isn't particularly local so my request will remain open, but if none other becomes available beforehand then that is where you will be going for an assessment prior to your admission."

"Edinburgh?" I repeat quietly. "You want to send me to Edinburgh?"

"Well, obviously it's not ideal, but -"

"Not ideal? It's hundreds of miles away and I'm not going!"

He leans further forwards and looks me sternly in the eyes. "I don't mean to sound harsh, Beth, but you're Sectioned. Whether you go willingly or unwillingly is up to you, but you will be going to a Unit, whether it's in Edinburgh or not and that's final."

I stand up suddenly from my chair and swipe my arm across the desk, scattering papers and documents everywhere before hurrying to the door. I swing it open and try to slam it as hard as I can behind me, forgetting that the doors are weighted by hospital regulations so that, despite my efforts, it continues to close slowly whilst omitting a soft whistle.

"And for your information, I was slamming that door!" I yell over my shoulder.

Dear Friend,

Looking back at what happened still makes me shiver with pure fear. Prior to my admission, I rarely left the house without my parents by my side, such was my anxiety that I failed to make it to the bottom of the street by myself. Admission to hospital wasn't easy either; I spent the vast majority of the day by myself and only had visitors in the evenings. Staff had warned my parents of my impending situation and that, in order to better prepare me for what I didn't believe would come, they had to gradually withdraw so that I could begin to come to terms with the fact that they couldn't be with me constantly.

At the time I failed to understand the reality of my situation, the fact that, if not by law than by moral rights, staff would not just leave me to die - no matter how hard I wished for it at the time. I failed to understand that the general hospital didn't have the specialist training or the means to treat me; I would be sent indefinitely to a Unit to receive the help that I needed. Even now, as I look back into the past, I still tremble at the thought of not knowing where I would be the following week, and whether I would have the means to contact my family or not. The fear of being alone, completely alone, and yet not being able to do anything about it overrides everything.

Chapter Seven

I rest my head on my over-bed table, my racing thoughts beginning to grow quiet and slow down with the gentle coolness of the plastic against my cheek. I need a plan, but after being told of the whole 'Unit situation' a mere hour ago the only thing I've come up with is to just slap the lot of them, an action that will undoubtedly end with me being sedated and stowed in the back of an ambulance to go anyway. My parents will be here in under two hours and I want to have the finer points sorted before they arrive.

There's no way in hell that I'm going to sit around here and wait for them to hand over my fate in a sealed envelope, no way that I am going to let them take what little control of my life I have left.

Truth no.7 – I am afraid. For the first time ever I am afraid of what the consequences of having an eating disorder might mean for me and my family.

~ Let Me Go ~

Despite being told about the active search for a bed, and the many discussions held with me and my parents regarding Inpatient treatment, it never seemed even remotely real. I perceived it as an empty threat, almost a scare-factor to make me eat properly again, not something that could actually happen to me. Those sorts of things only happen in the movies; surely it couldn't happen to someone like me in real life? But on the other hand, the side of me that tentatively listens to the doctors and their words believed that should the time come and a bed is made available for me, I'd simply refuse and that would be the end of it. I didn't even begin to consider the fact that I might be Sectioned and would have no choice in the matter. No choice and no voice at all.

Fuck them; fuck them all.

I feel the hot whisper of tears sliding down my face. It's frightening, being in a position where you have no say over what you can do or where you can go, and even more so when you don't know where you'll be next week. Next week I could be in an Inpatient Unit in Wales, in Exeter, in London or maybe even in Edinburgh if another doesn't become available soon.

As much as I hate it in here, I'm guessing it's no comparison to an actual Psychiatric Unit.

I sigh and glare reproachfully at the pump by the side of my bed, whizzing quietly away as it drips calories into my stomach. If I could do something to the pump then maybe, if it couldn't work properly, the nurses couldn't feed me and I'd deteriorate into an even more critical condition so that I'd have to stay in a general hospital. But even to me, that sounds irrational and unrealistic. Even if I could kid myself into believing for a mere second that this would work, the pump is indestructible.

The pump is called Neil. We seem to spend so much time together that it's necessitated in me naming it. The nurses thought it would be a good idea, believing that it might make me more comfortable and be accepting of it, but considering it pumps food into me it's needless to say that this plan worked to no avail. I've tried to 'de-wire' it, a process that resulted in three

split nails and a severe telling-off from the head nurse for
'damaging hospital property', 'accidentally' pushed it over and
stood on it and slammed it in the toilet door (where I go, Neil
goes – like I said we're practically inseparable.) The one thing
that Neil does not like, however, is when I squeeze the tube that
connects him to me. He wheezes and splutters, trying in vain to
pump against my unresisting pinched fingers, something which I
thought was genius at first as it meant nothing was going in, but
after a few brief seconds he admits a continuous bleeping that
can probably be heard in the ward below to alert the staff to my
plan. Using Neil to my advantage is clearly not an option.
Bastard.
I turn my head and look out of my window. From the Paediatric
Unit on the top floor, I can see across my entire town. I can sit
and watch for hours the people bustling into shops, queuing
along the roads in the morning rush-hour, babies being pushed
in prams or the occasional dog being led this way. They mock
me. They're free, they have the whole day in front of them to do
as they please, and they can live their lives without the presence
of anorexia in their heads, dictating their every move and
making them spend countless hours searching for diet tips and
exercise routines on the internet. They're not Sectioned and
about to be sent to a Unit potentially hundreds of miles from
home.
Lucky them.
I don't want them to take my life away from me, not before I've
had the chance to live it properly. But those hopes of a life
without the illness are just dreams, wild thoughts trapped in the
twilight zone between sleeping and waking.
I don't deserve a life – if I did then the monster in the mirror
would leave me be, my parents would not be scared witless
because they don't even know where their daughter will be next
week, and I would not have been bullied by almost everyone I
met at school.
The truth hits me with the force of a wrecking ball. I am not
meant to live. I know what I have to do to make the pain stop –

both for me and for those around me.

Suicide.

It's the only option left; all other cards have been played. I sit up straighter and pull my writing pad towards me. Half-formed ideas begin to rush to the forefront of my mind in an attempt to be acknowledged first. As far as suicide goes (at least for a non-Sectioned individual) the options are virtually limitless. There are a whole plethora of possibilities that the majority don't even consider until the cord is loosened and all that previously tethered you to the world becomes nothing more than a thought, a twist of smoke that's long separated from the flame. Even in the modern day world, freedom comes at a high price and, whilst very little of my own remains, I feel determined to retain that single ounce of power I have left over my being for myself. My thoughts deepen and I sit up straighter as things the monster has often repeated to me stream around my head with an intensity that almost makes me cry out, yearning to be acted upon. It was not my decision to be brought into this world and I pity my parents for the day I was born, the day when, as unsuspecting as they were, they gave life to something so unnatural and repulsive that it has no right to be here. It was not my decision to be born, but what is my decision is when and how I leave.

I am not going to be sent to a Unit hundreds of miles away from home for numerous nurses and doctors to try and save a life that isn't worth saving. I am not going to put my parents through the torture an Inpatient Unit is sure to bring them, having a child being treated so far away with no say over their treatment plan and unable to visit. Not without a fight first.

The ward lights are set to dim, my parents have long since left and I can hear the gentle murmurs of the night staff gossiping behind their desk when I finally come to a conclusive decision. Tucking my notebook safely beneath my pillow, I slip into an uneasy sleep of hospitals, screaming children and empty graves.

***

~ Let Me Go ~

The morning dawns bright and crisp, and I open my window the few inches it'll allow to welcome a fresh gust of wind inside and to hopefully carry the stench of disinfectant away with it. I sit in my chair, barely noticing the activity of the ward as I doodle absentmindedly on a paper towel and consider my options. It's needless to say that they're few and far between and anything I do try will most definitely need to be carefully planned down to the last second. I am nothing if not efficient. I hear the squeak of rubber shoes on the floor as a nurse comes towards me; I shove the book hurriedly beneath the sheets only just realising that my drawings had manifested into a skeleton and a noose.

"Alright, love," she asks warmly.

"Yes, thanks," I reply. "How are you?" I wonder what she wants, my next meal isn't for another hour at least and she took my blood pressure and temperature less than fifteen minutes ago.

"I'm good, thanks. Dr Tate wants a quick word with you in the 'Sunshine Room'. Your Mum's already waiting for you." She leads me down the hall and I knock nervously on the door, my pulse quickening and my palms sweating with nerves. Dr Tate only came to see me yesterday; this must mean he has something urgent to tell me that can't wait until our next appointment. Why is Mum here and not at work? Does this mean the bed in Edinburgh has become available sooner than they expected and they're sending me away today? My breath catches in my throat. They can't send me away today; I haven't had a chance to kill myself yet.

Mum smiles at me reassuringly as I go inside, but I can tell she's concerned from the drawn look on her face and the tired shadows beneath her eyes. Dr Tate looks up briefly before returning to the copious paperwork before him. Both feet are on the floor – something that further heightens my anxiety considering he usually maintains a relatively relaxed posture. The nurse closes the door firmly behind her and I sit down next to Mum on the sofa, looking at Dr Tate expectantly. He shuffles through the papers on his lap before pulling out a specific document. "Good morning, Beth," he says. "I've just had a quick talk with your Mum and updated her, but I just wanted to let you know to keep you in the loop." He clears his throat noisily before continuing briskly.

"Your Mum's told me that she mentioned to you about the possibility of a bed in Birmingham and that you're currently being considered, well, you've been called for an assessment today and –"

"Today?" I interject, trying to come to terms with what he's telling me. How have things escalated this quickly?

"I only found out myself late last night, and I didn't want to phone the ward and worry you unnecessarily. You're not going to be admitted today, and there will be others attending at different times throughout the day for the same thing. They'll just want to talk to you about your situation, hear it from your Mum's perspective and probably do some physical observations like a blood test, take your blood pressure, weight and height. I know it sounds daunting, but just see it as a day-trip."

I nod my head slowly to show that I understand, imagining it as a day-trip is definitely not going to happen – especially considering that, should they choose me, I could be there potentially for months or even years to come.

Dr Tate turns to Mum and gives her the postcode and a piece of paper on which he's written all the things she can be expected to be asked during the assessment. I look down at my hands although I've been told that I'm not being admitted today, there is still an irrational, underlying fear that they'll change their minds and not let me out. I don't want to go, but I can't refuse.

Dr Tate dismisses us and Mum leads me back towards my bed where I pick up a jacket and book for the journey, we've been advised to leave straight away because of the traffic and my assessment is in less than three hours. Mum's told me that two people need to come with me to the assessment, one to drive and one to give me support if I should need it, so we're going with my Aunt because Dad couldn't get the day off work. It's all happening so quickly that I'm moving robotically, barely considering my actions as I'm presented with this stream of information.

It's strange leaving the hospital, to walk on concrete and hear the roaring of traffic. It's even stranger to sit in a car and watch the world stream past my window, to drive past the places I've grown up around and yet know that I'm not allowed to stop. It feels like the town has undergone some drastic transformation and has become another place entirely, one in which I'm not accustomed to and not meant to be in, like a tinted screen has been placed over everything so it's not as it was before. But maybe I'm the one who's changed to coincide with the development of my illness, not the other way around. Mum and Ruth have been given strict instructions to not stop on the way there or the way back, my form has only been signed to visit the Unit and that's that, I'm not even allowed to stop at home on the way back and see Tia. I wonder if she'll even recognise me now - I don't know how long a cat's memory is.

The drive is relatively short, despite being around two hours away depending on traffic. But maybe that's just because I'm dreading our arrival. Ruth plays the latest pop music and they both share a packet of supermarket brand jelly-babies, with Ruth pausing every time she reaches a lemon one to unceremonious spit it forcibly out the window. The staff had packed all of the meals I'll require in a paper bag, and I was given the warning that, should anything come back, it will inevitably be replaced in Fortisip.

The hospital itself is a nondescript, semi-detached building made of a grey stone, identical to the others on the road. If it wasn't for the fact that the Sat-Nav directed us here, I wouldn't have believed this was the hospital. I feel very self-conscious getting out of the car, worrying that I look almost alien with the tube hanging from my nose. I can feel the eyes of those passing by burning into my back as I walk through the door, wondering what could be so wrong with that girl that she's like that out in public.

The assessment itself only lasts an hour, Mum and I sit around a large, wooden table whilst we answer questions about how my illness developed, my current situation and what could have been the potential cause of it. Ruth waits in the corridor outside. After that, I'm led into a medical room, which is so dark and gloomy due to the lack of windows that not even the small lamp in the corner can keep the darkness at bay. There are cabinets lining the walls and what looks like a dentist's chair in the centre of the room. I don't even need to ask to know what it's for. She motions for me to sit in the chair and she draws blood from my arm, before doing my blood pressure and taking my height and weight to calculate a BMI.

Once this ordeal is over, we are taken on a brief tour of the hospital where we see the dining room, living area and a patient's bedroom upstairs. I catch a few glimpses of some of the patients, but they avoid eye contact and move aside whenever we go past. Ruth and Mum make the occasional positive comment as we're lead from room to room, but I can see just by looking at their faces that they're saying them purely for my benefit. The whole building is dank, cold and inimical. The walls are bare and painted a dull cream and I can hear the frequent closing of weighted doors about the building which seem to reverberate through the walls and down in my bones.

When my assessment comes to an official close, I leave the hospital with my own personal cloud of depression and disappointment drooping unshakeably above my head. I don't know what I was expecting, but it certainly wasn't that. The whole place had an atmosphere of suppression and restriction, something that wasn't helped by the foreboding and unfriendly nature of the interior. Despite being told that it was definite I would be going to a Unit, I had never fully considered exactly what it would be like. What I experienced today makes me want to run away or hide like a small child because if I can't see the situation then it wouldn't be real.

There are some things that you just can't hide from, and unfortunately, this is one of them.

Chapter Eight

We arrive back at the general hospital just before I'm due to have dinner, thanks to the large quantity of traffic on the motorway and the Sat-Nav's confusing instructions when navigating Spaghetti Junction. Ruth and Mum sit with me for a few minutes to rest from the drive before heading home whilst I make an attempt at dinner. Dr Tate has advised my parents to not be with me during meal times any more, considering I am definitely going away for treatment and they won't be there. After I have the replacement put through my tube for the half I couldn't manage, I sit in my chair and try and come to terms with what happened today. I'd be kidding myself if I didn't admit that I'm more scared than I've ever been before. I want to go home. I blink my eyes rapidly to try and repress the tears, but they overwhelm me like a wave. I turn away from the nurses' desk and clasp my sleeve firmly over my mouth to silence my sobs. Tears run in streams down the plastic covering of the chair as the dam inside me bursts and I finally let go.

~ Let Me Go ~

***

The sun has hidden behind the horizon and the sky has changed from burnt auburn to the deep-blue dusk of the night before I've made the final adjustments to my plan. Visiting that Unit today has only made me more determined to end things on my own terms before it's all too late and, after wiping the tears from the back of the chair and washing the puffiness from my face, I had spent the entire evening developing it. I tear the remaining pages of crossed-out ideas into shreds and scatter them from the window into the night, a soft breeze carrying them away. Now the world knows I'll be leaving soon, but those within it will remain unaware.

A nurse squeaks towards me and unhooks Neil from my tube, before pressing a syringe-full of water through to prevent it from clogging. "You're looking a little pale, love, is everything alright?" she asks, reaching for the charts at the bottom of my bed.

No, things are not alright, but they will be soon.

"I'm fine, thank you," I reply quietly.

"You're charts look reasonable, but just to be sure I think it would be best for you to lie down and rest for a while. Try and do something nice to take your mind off things. Why don't you read one of your nice books?"

I shake my head in response and swing my feet onto the bed before obediently lying down. She looks at me concernedly, half expecting a tirade of torment about how just because I'm Sectioned I don't have to do everything they tell me to, but I remain silent. She presses her hand against my forehead. "You're a little cold; would you like me to fetch you another blanket?" she asks kindly. I shake my head again. I already have seven piled on top of me and I highly doubt that an eighth will make much of a difference.

Truth no.8 – The problem with anorexia is that you're always cold. No matter how many layers you wear or hot baths you take, nothing but a thick layer of concealer can hide the pale-blue tinge of your skin and nothing can prevent the aching shivers from rattling your body every hour of the day.

"I'll leave you to get some rest," says the nurse as she turns to leave, but she spins around almost instantly. "I don't suppose anyone's told you, have they, considering you've been out all day, about the lady coming tomorrow?" I shake my head and pull myself upright, instantly assuming the worst and that this stranger is coming to take me away to some unknown Unit. She motions for me to lie back down and only continues when I've done so. "Now that you're Sectioned you're meant to have twelve-hour constant supervision by law, something which we've only just been able to arrange." I groan and turn my face into the crinkly plastic of the pillow, pulling the covers up over my head to create an airless, warm cocoon of safety from her biting words.

"Oh come on now, love, it won't be that bad! The lady's name is Joëlle and she sounded really friendly when I spoke to her on the phone this morning. She'll be here from nine in the morning through to nine at night; if anything it'll be some company for you. You spend an awful amount of time sat in here on your own, don't you?" She pats me quietly on the head and I hear the soft squeak of her rubber shoes retreat.

My heart drops, that puts a spanner in the works for sure. I want to look into the mirror over the sink, but the nurse is seated once more behind her desk in order to make sure I don't exercise before going to sleep. I'll have to speak to it first thing in the morning before the lady arrives. The monster will know what to do.

***

"A clever idea," says the monster, grinning up mischievously at me from the mirror. I fold the paper tightly and tuck it safely into the waistline of my trousers. I have to hurry; Joëlle is due here at any moment. "It has to work," I reply quietly in a voice barely

audible through a mouthful of toothpaste. "I don't have time for a botched suicide. We have to do it, and we have to do it soon before they find a bed and cart me off to another hospital. I don't ever want to go to another place like that Unit in Birmingham again. You do realise that if they can't find a specialist bed, I'll be put in general psych?"

'Don't complain,' sneers the monster. *'At least you'll be locked away. If you manage to screw this up like you've done with everything else in your life then it'll be the next best thing. Locked on a ward, kept in isolation – the only person you could hurt would be yourself, and you don't matter, do you?"* I shake my head. *"They shouldn't let someone like you roam free, not when you consider the number of people you come into contact with that become infected by your poison on a daily basis. You are filth,"* the monster curls its lips in plaintive disgust. *"You hurt everyone; they're just too kind to say it. You would be doing everyone a favour by killing yourself. You have no place in this world and everyone would be a lot better off without you destroying their lives. But you must go carefully. You have one chance of doing this, one chance',* it repeats aggressively. *'If you screw this up then you'll ruin the lives of those you care about, even more so than you've managed to do already."* The monster flexes its claws and drags memories into my head, memories that I thought have been long since forgotten.

I remember back to the final few months of Year Eleven at secondary school, two months before my hospitalisation. Natalie trailed behind me at break times and lunch times, missing out on the opportunity to socialise with her friends to check if her big sister was eating. I would always see her, out of the corner of my vision, tailing me to my next lesson, even if hers was at the other end of the school and she'd be late as a consequence, to check that I didn't collapse from the exertion of walking. Mum cooked dinner with me stood watching in the corner, analysing every move she made and every ingredient she added to make sure nothing was added in excess or spontaneously. I listened on the stairs to Mum sobbing on Dad's shoulder as she'd come home after another long day at work to discover that her daughter's physical health had further declined, that her intake had reduced to a single small apple a day and that she'd had a missed call from the school saying that they weren't sure if she should be in any more.

Truth no.9 – The saying 'an apple a day keeps the doctor away', is not applicable when an apple is the only thing eaten in the day. In fact, it works to the opposite effect, a certain way of guaranteeing hospitalisation and direct contact with the doctor you were trying to avoid in the first place.

Mum went on a long-term absence after that to care for me, to offer me food and water every set amount of hours and to support my frail body as she led me to the bathroom when I could no longer walk upstairs without assistance. She became imprisoned in the house as much as I had become a prisoner to the monster in the mirror. My poison seeped into her and tainted her existence too. Dad used to peer into my bedroom last thing at night and first thing in the morning whilst he thought I was asleep, studying the gradual rise and fall of the duvet and to check I was still breathing and hadn't died in the night. There is no hope for me. The scientists are yet to discover a magical pill that can take this away and make it so that it was all just a bad dream. There is no hope in anything any more.

The monster pulls away, leering up at me from the mirror. *"Do you see what you've done?"* it says quietly. *"Do you see the number of people you've hurt… and that's just the start. Do you want me to go on? You've got sixteen years' worth of suffering you've inflicted on people to get through yet."*

I shake my head. I don't want to see any more. The monster's right, I don't deserve to live. People shouldn't have to put up with me; they only 'care' because they have grown so used to my poison that they're virtually resistant to it. That's what I am, a poison. I infect all those who get too close to me; I ruin their lives by causing them misery and suffering. I am toxic. And what is one of the best ways to destroy toxic waste? Incineration.

~ Let Me Go ~

People might hurt to begin with, the shock of death is enough to upset anyone, but once they experience life in a world that I'm not a part of, they'll see me for what I really am - an ugly, fat failure that should never have been born.

I swallow down my fear and spit out my toothpaste before returning to my corner and reaching determinedly for my writing pad. Soon, very soon it will all end, but there are things I need to do first. I can't leave this world without leaving a little something behind for my parents to remember me by.

Remember the baby they raised and taught to walk, the toddler that was so excited to receive an apple in her Christmas stocking and the child who would never hesitate in putting others first. That child will die when I destroy the evil that has taken over, the good that's long been lost to anorexia.

~ Let Me Go ~

Dear Mum,

I'm sorry that I'm writing a letter to you that no mother ever wants to receive, that I'm about to put you through a process of grief that I'm not sure you'll ever be truly ready for. I want you to know that it's not your fault; none of this has anything to do with you. I don't want you to see what I've done as suicide, more as passing on from one world to a place where I might belong. I'm sorry that you'll never have the chance to celebrate my next birthday or argue with me over a petty board game under the Christmas tree.

I'm sorry that you'll never hold my hand after a heartbreak, take me shopping for a wedding dress or meet my first child. I'm sorry that I let you get hurt. I know you'll grieve, but I need you to move on, to live your life happily and forget about me. I would much rather you be happy than spend a lifetime grieving for me when I can't come back. I wish I had told you more that I love you and that you're the best Mum anyone could ever have, that you're my best friend and I'd move heaven and earth to make you smile again.

I also want to thank you for everything you've done for me. Thank you for supporting me through things that no parent should ever have to even think about going through. Thank you for always being by my side and for fighting the demons away when I was too confused to recognise them. Thank you for being my Mum. I'll wait for you.

Love Beth xx

~ Let Me Go ~

Dear Dad,

You will always be my big, strong hero, and I'm sorry that you couldn't win this battle. I'm sorry to put you through what you're going through now; no parent should ever have to bury their baby. I wish that I could take all of your pain with me, that I could click my fingers and every wrong in your life would miraculously be righted. But I can't.

I want you to remember me as your little girl, and not as the monster I have become. Remember me for the times we spent playing ball games at the park, the family holidays we used to go on over summer and the times when we used to play pranks on Mum.

I'm sorry to have had to leave you in this way, but I don't feel that such a small word as 'sorry' can heal the amount of pain I have caused you over the years. I'm sorry I got sick, although I never intended for it to happen. I'm sorry for the nights you spent half-awake, expecting to need to drive me to the hospital at any minute. I'm sorry that you stopped going to work to support Mum who supported me, but most of all, I'm sorry for letting my illness take away your little girl.

I wish you a lifetime of happiness and for all your dreams to come true. Please look after them all for me.

Love Beth xxx

~ Let Me Go ~

Dear Natalie,

I'm sorry little sis, I'm sorry that I let it hurt you. As your big sister, it was me that was always meant to look after and protect you, but it seems that the role has been reversed for a while now. I wish I could turn back the clocks and change so that you didn't have to care for me at school. I wish that I hadn't got so wrapped up in what was happening inside my head that I didn't see that it was hurting you too.
I wish that I had told you how much you mean to me, we always believed that it was far too affectionate to say things like that between siblings, but I wish I had told you sooner. I wish I had told you how special, important and talented you are, and that you're going to have an amazing future because you're the most honest and hardworking person I've ever met.
I wish I had told you that you've been a better friend to me than anyone and how I wish things could have turned out differently.
I'll never truly be gone, little sis. Death can't change the fact that I'll always be your big sister. I just want you to know that, although you may not be able to physically see me, I am always here and will always be watching over you throughout your life.

Love Beth xxx

~ Let Me Go ~

Dear Friend,

Do you remember the amount of letters I wrote that night? I wrote one for every occasion that I'd miss; Natalie's wedding, Mum's fiftieth birthday and Dad's retirement, convinced that a simple note from my sixteen-year-old self could stench the hole that would have been permanently agape in their hearts. It gets no easier. I wrote many more after that and on more than one occasion throughout my journey, each time wholeheartedly believing that this would truly be the end.

I believe, dear Friend, that we as a society have a habit of taking things for granted every single day; from the water in our taps, the family in our houses or the lack of voices in our heads. People take for granted the fact that they can walk down the street without having to be followed or have tabs kept on them. They take for granted that they can go to school and receive an education, all because it's so normalised that there's no other option to consider. Or, if they think about it, they use the standard phrase 'there's always someone worse off', but they probably never take into context what that means and how that person may live as a consequence.

Indeed, I have also fallen prey to this common societal problem.

I took my freedom and my dignity for granted, naively assuming that I would always have the final say over what happens to my body, that I would have the freedom to walk down a street rather than being incarcerated on a ward. It's almost funny now to look back at that version of 'me'. Almost. Even though I may have thought I was aware at the time, I didn't fully comprehend the impact my suicide would have had on my family. It was only after my second year of therapy that it began to dawn on me just how close I had been to throwing my life away, and those I care about too. It was only after putting myself in the shoes of a parent and looking at the world from another perspective that I began to understand. Cradling your baby one day, and placing them in a coffin the next. I can't even comprehend it, having to let go of your child

and let them be embraced by the hard, cold earth rather than
wrapping them in your arms that will always be calling them
home.

Chapter Nine

"You 'ave never done zat before?" asks Joëlle in surprise, holding up her perfectly finished origami flower. "No," I say, as I shake my head. "Can you show me again?"

Joëlle had come at dead on nine o'clock; firstly signing in at the nurse's desk and then heading straight my way. I had woken up an extra hour earlier to tidy around my area and ensure there isn't a single crease on my bed sheets – if she writes in my notes then I want her to be able to put something positive that may help towards my discharge.

"Come now Beth, zis must be ze fifth time I've 'ad to show you!" she laughs and quickly unfolds her work of art and I begin to replicate her actions clumsily again. As much as I thought she would be a pain, what with watching over me all day and being within arms reach of me at all times, I am actually enjoying her company.

I finish my third attempt and hold it up for her approval. "Ha!" she laughs. "Zat looks more like an 'ippo zan a flower!" I crumple up my hippo/flower and pull another sheet towards me. "Again?"

A nurse squeaks over to us and places a plate with two biscuits an apple and a strawberry milkshake on. "Snack time, please Beth," she says smiling down supportively at me. "Once you've finished, Dr Tate would like to see you in the 'Sunshine Room', he's reading your notes now so don't hurry."

I grimace and look dejectedly at the food in front of me, automatically calculating the number of calories in each item and the amount of exercise I would need to do to burn it off. I've pretty much forgotten most of the content of my lessons at school, but I can easily recall a list of at least one hundred items and tell you the exact calorie content in them. It's quite impressive really.

I can see the monster out of the corner of my eye in the mirror, looking down in disgust at the food before me. *"You're not seriously thinking about eating that, are you fatty?"* it asks, sharpening its claws against the frame. *"73 calories in each biscuit, 53 calories per 100g of apple and 135 calories in the milkshake... do you know how much weight you'll gain if you eat all that?"* I glare at it and mentally tell it to shut up and leave me alone, that I don't have a choice because if I refuse then it'll be made up for in Fortisip and pumped down my tube anyway.

Joëlle looks at me seriously. "Pick up ze apple, Beth," she encourages. "Each bite is closer to finished."

I look back down at the plate and the apple grows before my eyes. It looks like someone or something is pumping air into it like a balloon – is the monster doing this? Am I really meant to eat the whole apple? I look at the two biscuits and can practically see the calories dancing upon them, laughing at me as they plan what bones to conceal next.

"Do I have to eat all of it?" I ask hesitantly.

"Of course you do. Zis is virtually nothing; you're on a beginning meal plan in regards to weight restoration. An apple and some biscuits aren't going to make you look any different. You must eat it," she states matter-of-factly.

"What if I –"

"Non," she interrupts quickly. "It's non-negotiable. You 'ave to 'ave it, you're detained."
I pick up the apple and blow on it.

Truth no.10 – You can blow some of the calories off of food. If you do it suddenly you can catch them by surprise and they fall off. You can't get rid of them all though because some hide inside the food and won't budge.

"Non," says Joëlle, "we don't blow on food when it's not hot. Zat's an unnatural eating behaviour and you mustn't do it again. If I see you do it, zen I shall remove you snack and it'll be replaced down ze tube instead."
I glare at her. I pick up the apple uncertainly and bite into it, feeling the calories rush in glee down my throat as I swallow. It catches on my tube and tugs it uncomfortably. We sit there like that, for the entire thirty minutes that it takes me to eat. Joëlle making the occasional supportive comment about how 'brave I am' and me slowly eating, giving up on wiping away the tears that won't stop flowing.

***

Dr Tate closes my folder and looks across at Neil whizzing away by my side. It's so unfair that snack time coincides with feed time – I'll gain weight for sure! He looks tired and miserable, his shirt is slightly ruffled and untucked at the front and his hair is standing on end as if he's dragged his fingers through it in frustration on more than one occasion.
"I've just been reading through your notes," he begins quietly. "Your bloods are now stable, and I think it's about time we got that monitor off your chest."
I nod my head rapidly in agreement. This is the best thing he's ever told me. The monitor is a pain, as it consists of six different cables which are stuck to my chest, and the monitor itself clips onto the front of my shirt.
"I understand that you probably don't want me to discuss your

weight with you, I know the nursing team haven't been telling you what the number is and that's probably making you quite anxious. Do you want to know how much you weigh?"
I nod my head nervously and I subtly cross my fingers automatically; the monster peers down in anticipation from the mirror above his head. The number will tell me exactly what I'm worth. If I've lost then the monster will be proud and I'll be able to sleep tonight, if I've gained then I'll have to punish myself and try harder to hide the food when Joëlle isn't looking.
"You've gained 2kg this past week," he says softly.
My mouth falls wide open in pure shock.
Two whole kilos…
"Unfortunately that's not all," he continues slowly. "I know you're going to be devastated by the news I'm about to give you, but we're all really pleased and positive about this. We've found you a bed in a specialist Inpatient Unit, Beth. Do you understand? We've been successful in securing you a bed at 'Birchmoor Unit for Eating Disorders' in Reading. You are going there to be assessed in two days' time and will be admitted there until you are either discharged or transferred. I think you'll –"
I didn't hear any more. I ran out of the room and towards the main doors at the end of the corridor. I have to get out of here now before they can catch me and send me away. If I put enough distance between myself and Dr Tate's words maybe it'll all go away. This is all a horrible, horrible nightmare. There's no way this can even be remotely real. I pump my arms and run faster, my body aching in protest after spending so long on bed-rest. I skid forwards suddenly and land spread-eagle on the floor. My legs have given out beneath me, lacking the strength to help me escape from this place.
I claw my way up the wall in desperation, shaking and gasping from fear and exhaustion. Two nurses move quickly to stand in front of the doors, blocking my way.
Shit.
I am trapped.
I claw my way forwards and turn sharply into the shower room,

sliding the door shut hurriedly behind me and clicking the lock into place. I can hear the rapid squeaks of their shoes as they run towards me, calling for security and asking for me to please unlock the door. I'm gasping for breath, my face hot and sweaty so that my hair is sticking to my skin.

"Beth, honey, you need to open the door!" calls a nurse. "We know you're scared, but we want to help you. We can't help you if you're locked in there, can we?" Her knocks become more frantic against the door, they don't want me in here on my own in case I collapse. I almost wish I would collapse, to be taken away from all of this for just a moment for me to get my head straight and form a logical and cohesive plan.

I look into the mirror next to the shower and see the monster. *"What have you done?"* it growls. *"You're a failure. You're going to go to this Unit unless you stop them. Kill yourself. You're worthless. You're ugly. You're unwanted. You're fat. Fat. Fat. FAT!"* The monster screams at me, chanting an endless stream of insults. I lose control of myself and rip at my hair, tearing chunks from my scalp and raking my fingernails down my cheeks, leaving enflamed red trails that travel with my tears. The tables have turned, I want to get out of here and away from the monster's anger, but out there is no better.

"Beth, it's Mum! Come out please, we need a hug. We need you to come out!" I strain to hear her words as the monster's anger doubles in velocity and volume. "It's going to happen, Beth. We have two days left to get ready before you go, will you spend it with me?"

The realisation hits me with the force of a train, these are the last two days I have with my family, my final days of being alive. In two days' time I will be dead and, rather than coming to the hospital to take me to Birchmoor, they'll be coming for a meeting to be told the news of my suicide. My heart beats faster, as if to try and fit in its remaining pulses before it's forced to stop completely.

I search with shaking fingers for the catch and flip the lock open, wrenching the door wide and falling into my parents'

~ Let Me Go ~

outstretched arms. I feel like a coward for allowing myself to be with them, my death will only hurt them harder, but I don't think I have neither the bravery nor the courage to let go just yet.
"Please, please make it stop, make it stop!" I cry. They hold me tightly in their arms, my face pressing into the middle, right where I can hear both of their hearts beating as one.
"Make it stop, make it stop, make… it… sto -"

~ Let Me Go ~

Dear Friend,

I don't know about you, but I know that I'll never forget that day. Despite telling myself it would only make things harder for them when my end came, I clung to them and the belief that it would all just blow away in the wind, my fears no more substantial than smoke. It took my parents two hours, numerous hugs and uncountable reassurances to placate me, only for me to call them later that night to cry over the phone again. I begged and bargained with them to take me home, all rationality gone as I forgot the Section hanging over my head like a death sentence.

I promised that I would try harder to eat, that I would gain some weight back, that I would improve my grades at school for my impending GCSE's and would do more jobs around the house. When that failed, as it was undoubtedly ordained to, I shouted at them and told them things which I will never be able to take back. Words have the potency to inflict far greater damage than physical force can ever attain.

They were dispersed from my mouth like poison, inexorable once they had started. So that, whilst one half of me was scrabbling wildly to take them back, consciously aware of their damage, the other let them flow free and with little thought of their intention and how they'd be received.

You know as well as I do, dear Friend, that once you've started it's almost impossible to stop. Like trying to hold water in your bare hands, each trickle lost causing more to follow. No matter how many times I apologise, or even when I'm told that I'm not to blame as it's my illness and not me, I can never take it back. I wish I could tell you that this was my one moment of pure anger, but I'd be lying to you. Recovery, whether it's put upon the individual or undertaken willingly, is a long and arduous process in which it's commonplace for almost every emotion possible to be presented. Human nature itself makes it so.

Arguably, the sole intention of parenting is to protect and nurture and I don't think I'll understand or even begin to be

able to appreciate the situation my parents were put through on that night. Their child begged them to make the pain go away and to be taken back home and be cared for, and yet they were powerless and instead had to refuse and place them in the care of a second party. A second party consisting of trained and experienced individuals who stood a better chance of fighting the demons away, so that the very fundamentality of parenting is questioned.
Unimaginable.
Absolutely unimaginable.

Chapter Ten

Two days pass within the blink of an eye, so that it feels like I'm waking up with the whole day to contend with and only an hour later my head is touching the pillow again at night. I see my therapist numerous times each day, rushing hurriedly onto the ward and then leaving less than five minutes later in the same manner with bundles of my medical notes clutched in her arms. Everyone is preparing for my impending departure. My parents are at my bedside all day, playing games with me and generally keeping me company in between answering questions from the various doctors that visit for last minute check-ups and reassuring me that everything is going to be ok. When they're not by my side they're packing my bag at home and putting together a folder of all my letters from health professionals and discharge notes from my previous hospital admissions. They've already been sent a list from Birchmoor of all the contraband items that I'm forbidden to take (such as deodorant, shoelaces, headphones and technological devices) and every item has to be clearly named, which has made an upsetting situation both long and tedious.

Joëlle has taken up residence outside my room in order to give me some privacy for the little time I have left to be with my family. She sits there with her arms crossed and a stern expression on her face like a prison guard; following me every time I leave to go to the bathroom or speak with one of the nurses, and only resumes her position when I'm within arm's reach of my parents once more.

I know that any hope of committing suicide during the day is spurious, what with the number of staff who have been told by Dr Tate to watch over me, especially with my parents by my side each day. The only time the staff relent is at night, and even then they've called in another agency nurse for support in case I cause trouble. I have finalised my plan, choosing to opt for a more natural and profound method. I am going to leave the hospital and my past behind and die of exposure to the elements. I understand that it's still likely to be prolonged and painful, as the nature of forced death generally is, but I want to do what is right and go on my own terms.

Time is running out.

It will happen tonight, I will not be attending my admission at Birchmoor tomorrow. There will be no one left to admit, and someone with a life worth saving will get the bed instead. At least I'm safe with the knowledge that I'm saving a life when destroying another, almost as if this counteracts the crime and makes me repented.

Mum reaches across my over-bed table and encloses her warm hand around mine. My actions tonight are going to destroy them, but I have no other choice left available to me. The monster says it's the only way. It told me that, although it'll indisputably hurt them, they'll get their lives back. I don't mind that my illness is killing me, but it's hurting those I love too.

I look away from our hands and out of the window, towards the dark patch of woodland in the distance that I'll be travelling to tonight. I don't want to die in a clinical, unnatural way. I want to die on the grass, trees reaching up above me and sheltering me from the winds with a scattering of stars watching over me as I come to them. I want to be away from the mechanisation of our society, somewhere the traffic can't be heard and smoke can't be smelt, to be at one with nature before I'm ripped away from it. I won't last long out there. I highly doubt I'll survive the storm forecast for tonight and the exertion it will take to get there. I glance at my bed and see in my mind's eye the rucksack that is stowed beneath it, ready packed with the handful of items I have with me that might be of some use in getting away. The letters are tucked safely beneath my pillow.

Mum sighs quietly and lifts her handbag up onto my bed. "I need to go now," she says quietly. "Natalie will need her dinner soon and I want to make sure everything's ready for tomorrow. I'll see you in the morning, please make the right decision." She's referring to me being compliant so that the doctors won't need to sedate me and transfer me via ambulance. I look at the floor, focusing all of my efforts on not letting the tears loose. She won't be seeing me tomorrow. Once I start I won't stop, my plans will spill out like an unyielding tide, extra staff will be called in for the night shift and I'll have someone who's trained in restraint with me around the clock. I'll never get away. My family will never get their lives back. She wants me to promise to be safe so that Dr Tate can call them in the morning and say I'm safe to travel with them.

My parents want to take me to Birchmoor, they say that if we go in as a team, it won't be long before we're back out again and ready to face the world. I can't make any promises, if my plan succeeds then the only place I'll be going tomorrow is the morgue.

Dad stands and wraps his arms delicately around me, squeezing me gently as if I might crack. "See you tomorrow, kiddo," he says thickly, trying to remain my dependable, resilient hero and not let the tears flow. "Natalie's picked out some CDs you might like for the car, and she found your old favourite teddy to pack in your bag." I nod slowly against his shoulder; they're trying so hard to make an impossible situation easier.

~ Let Me Go ~

Dad releases me and I'm encircled within Mum's arms. I breathe in deeply and inhale the warm, homely smell. I voraciously inhale her scent that never fails to make me feel safe; the smell that comforts me from a nightmare and calms me during illness. A tear slips out of my eye and drips softly onto her shoulder, a part of me that will symbolically remain with her forever.
I walk them to the end of the ward, one of their hands clutched firmly in each of mine. Their hands slip out of my own at the door and I watch as they look back to smile at me before walking away. I stay that way, looking in the direction they've gone, long after the door swings back and clicks shut behind them.
Goodbye, Mum.
Goodbye, Dad.

***

I crouch down by my bed, the strategically angled chair blocking me from view. The rucksack rests heavily against my back, my pyjamas are stuffed into a sleeping position beneath the layers of blankets and the letters are stacked neatly upon my pillow. I peer out from under my bed and watch the nurse's shoes gently squeak down the hall, another pair remaining seated under the desk. I've been awake for the past six hours, alternating between crouching by my bed and waiting for the area to clear, and hurriedly scrambling back under the covers when they come by to do my general observations.
There's always a nurse at the desk, sitting right in front of my room. Someone must have informed them of my plan, but I know I haven't breathed a word to anyone about it. Maybe it was Dr Tate, he was always fairly accurate at guessing my emotions, perhaps he suspected I would try something and told them to stay alert at all times. I don't stand a chance in reaching the end of the corridor before one of them comes running after me. Can I outrun a nurse?
Maybe.
Can I outrun the police officers that will undoubtedly be called

when a Sectioned patient escapes?

No.

I'll be caught within half an hour and sent back here with heightened security. There's no way I'll be able to get out then. I just have to be patient. They'll get tired eventually, or they'll make a mistake and leave my room unguarded for just a minute. One minute is all I need.

The clock ticks despotically, each second passing another less I'll have to escape and the narrower my chances of success. The monster paces agitatedly in the mirror, twisting its head sharply at me with each change of direction and pinning me with its questioning stare. *'What are you still doing here?'* it asks frantically. *'Do you want to let them fatten you up and take even more of your freedom? Don't you want your family to have a decent future?'* All in good time, monster, we must be patient. I check my watch, almost three in the morning, and shift my weight silently to my other foot, gritting my teeth at the numbing pain caused from being in the same stationary position for an extended period of time. If I can't get out soon, then my legs may become so numb that I won't be able to run anyway.

I peer out from my vantage point and scour the floor for rubber shoes. I can still count one pair behind the desk, that means one must be on break and the other two must be tending to patients. A hushed bleeping sounds from above the desk and a dull, red light begins to flash repeatedly to alert staff that there's a patient in need of assistance. I flex my fingers nervously against the floor, this might be it. The nurse rises from her chair and I watch as the shoes squeak out from behind the desk, before pausing hesitantly. "Jackie… Jackie!" she calls softly, "can either you or Rosa tend to Room Six? He'll probably want some more pain relief." There's no reply, they must be tending to someone in the room furthest from the desk. The bleeping sounds again and the red light resumes its flashing. The nurse begins to shift from foot to foot in agitation and I can practically hear the cogs turning in her mind as she processes her internal conflict. The monster stands still, peering out at the nurse in preparation to give me the

~ Let Me Go ~

all clear to run. I clench the muscles in my legs and raise myself into starting position, every second will count. I silently begin to beg and plead in desperation with whoever may be listening to me. 'Go on, go and see to the patient. Leave your desk for just a minute, go on!' The nurse hesitates once more before squeaking hurriedly in the direction of Room Six.

I look across the darkened room towards the mirror; the monster nods once in confirmation and I dart out from my bed. I run softly towards the door, my heart thumping painfully against my ribs and my eyes dart from left to right so rapidly that it makes me feel dizzy. Before I even make it ten metres from the nurse's station I hear a soft squeak to my left and my breath catches in my throat.

Shit.

Why hadn't I thought about the rooms down this end? I scan hurriedly for something to hide behind but the corridor is empty. Before I have a chance to run back to my bed and try again, a nurse walks out of Room Two, peeling off the blue gloves that cover her hands and stops dead in front of me in shock. She recovers quickly. "What are you doing?" she asks gently. "It's early morning, you should be in bed."

"I-I-I" I stutter, fear clawing up my throat.

"Come on, let's get you back in bed. Why aren't you in your pyjamas?" she asks, eyeing my coat and rucksack suspiciously. "Don't tell me you've been up all night." She takes me firmly by the arm and begins to lead me back up the corridor, away from the door at the end. What am I doing? Why am I going with her? I shake my head to clear it from the undulating fog of exhaustion and shock.

"I don't want to go," I say suddenly, pulling my arm out of her grasp. I motion towards the door. "Please, let me go." All strength drains out of me, and the dread of going to the Unit tomorrow makes my legs being to tremble and threaten to collapse beneath me.

It looms over me like some grotesque demon, horrifying and yet ultimately unavoidable, and makes me shiver with pure fear. My

~ Let Me Go ~

plan has failed. There's no way I can outrun this nurse whilst she's so close to me, she'll catch me before I take three steps. Why am I so stupid? Why hadn't I waited to make absolutely sure it was clear? Why hadn't I kept tabs on where all the nurses were and not just if someone was behind the desk? I see the nurse who tended to Room Six squeak back towards her desk and place her hand on top of the ward phone.

"Do I need to call security, Jackie?" she asks quietly.

"No, I don't think that'll be necessary," the nurse replies quietly. "We're just going to have a little chat."

She takes me gently by the arm once more and leads me into one of the empty rooms behind the desk. She shuts the door quietly behind her and tucks her short, black hair behind her ears. I look out of the window at the dark street beyond, faintly illuminated by the dim amber glow of a streetlight. I'd been so close to my freedom ... so close. She watches me looking down at the world outside, so despairing close and yet at the same time so excruciatingly far. "It won't be too bad," she murmurs reassuringly. "I can't even begin to imagine how scared you must be feeling right now, but things will get better with time."

"I want to go home now, please," I beg quietly. "I don't want to go to the Unit; I just want to go home. I didn't ask for any of this!"

"I know, love, I know," she soothes, reaching towards me and placing her hand reassuringly on my shoulder. "You know we can't let you out there, it's not safe for a young girl like you to be out alone when it's dark. We wouldn't be doing our duty if we let you go home now, would we? You'll go home when you're ready. I know you will."

"But it's just me, it doesn't matter. If you let me out right now no one will notice, and I won't tell anyone. I promise!" I cry desperately.

"It's not 'just' you at all and you *do* matter. You're a human being, Beth, and whether you can see it or not there are so many people that care about you and would be devastated if something happened. I really don't want to have to phone for

~ 88 ~

security to come up here, not on your last night with us. They can be terribly moody in the mornings so it would be best for the both of us if we let them be. If I have to call for help then Dr Tate will be phoned in the morning and you'll be travelling to the Unit in an ambulance with security staff. I know your parents want to take you themselves tomorrow. You can do this for them... can't you?" I open my mouth to reply but no words come out. She wraps her arm gently around me and leads me back to bed, before placing my rucksack on the floor and tenderly tucking the blankets around me.

"I'm not going to be here in the morning, my shift ends earlier than the others, so this is goodbye. You'll be fine. I know you will. You're a strong and talented young lady and I know there's more for you in this world than this illness." Despite my efforts to stay awake, I feel my eyes begin to droop as her words wash over me, soothing and calming like a cool breeze on a hot summer's day.

I hear her turn and move quietly away. I'm not sure whether it's the squeaking of rubber or my extreme fatigue, but I think I hear a whispered "good luck."

~ Let Me Go ~

Dear Friend,

Do you remember that night? At the time I believed so wholeheartedly that I was going to die, that I was going to run from the hospital and perish in the woodland. I never fully considered the possibility that I'd be caught, or that my admission to Birchmoor was definite and that there was nothing either I or anyone else could have done about it. I thought that, if I couldn't physically break out myself then the staff would aid me in leaving. That I would win them over with my pleas for help and they'd press the button for the doors to open and let me out into the night, all trace of me wiped away before day shift started so that I was nothing more than a bad dream. I was so terrified of stepping into the unknown that I was willing to take my footprint from the world entirely, to become no more than a memory to all those who held me dear.

To this day I'll never forget the words of the nurse that night, spoken to me in that little room on the top floor of a hospital at 3 a.m. It was the first time that words had begun to sink in, for me to understand what people were trying to tell me and could actually begin to understand where they were coming from. It was the first time in the hospital that someone had seen me as a person with a future and a family, rather than a name on a file, a number on a list of tasks and a diagnosis. It awakened a part of me that I thought had long since been destroyed by my eating disorder and the monster in the mirror, an instinctual element that yearned for life, and in particular a life with meaning and quality.

Many a time I have thought back to that moment, wondering what would have happened if I hadn't been caught, if I'd made it outside and whether or not it would have killed me. Many a time I questioned why I listened to the nurse, why I let her lead me away from the door that, at that particular moment in time, had become my metaphorical representation of freedom. To this day I still do not know, and perhaps a small part of me doesn't want to, but what I do know now is that no matter how hard I tried to leave the hospital that night, I didn't stand even the slightest of chances of getting out. Little did I realise that the doors were firmly locked so that not even pressing the release button on the side would open them. Little did I know that, even if by some miracle I'd made it out of the ward unnoticed, there was security waiting in reception that had been told to keep an eye out for a severely underweight teenage girl. What chance did I stand against that?

I can't remember what I did with all those letters; I may have simply lost them or thrown them into the bin. I like to think I did the same as I did with my suicide plans, tore them into tiny, illegible pieces and gave them to the night so that despite never being read by anyone but myself and the monster, there are hundreds of little pieces of me out there somewhere.

Chapter Eleven

The sky is crying. Tears streak down my window, barely making contact with the glass before glancing off the side and being added to the collection on the road. I look out my window, at the blurred outlines racing past. All traces of my hometown have long past and been replaced with the monotonous grey of the motorway. We'll be there in fifteen minutes. In one respect I'm glad it's raining, it's almost like the world is crying for my impending incarceration. I don't think I could bear it if it had been a pleasant, sunny day.

I tuck my tube nervously behind my ear and try to form a mental barrier between my conscious mind and the panicked thoughts. As usual, the thoughts bombard my metaphorical barrier and the avalanche of fears and questions I'd been so desperately trying to suppress become cemented into the forefront of my mind until I can focus on nothing else. Will I be allowed to see my parents? Will the staff be kind to me? Will my roommate be really skinny? As egoist and cowardly it makes me feel to admit, it's the last one that's bothering me the most. I can't imagine what it'd be

like to be admitted onto the ward for anorexia and have your
roommate be thinner than you, especially as they're there first
and have already had some treatment.

Another thought enters my mind, more prominent and
dangerous than the first. What if I'm the fattest one there? I look
down at my clothing, leggings and a hoodie, the only clean
clothes I had left on the ward to wear. Should I have worn
something tighter like my elasticated top that you can count my
ribs through? Do these leggings make my thighs look big? What
if I get there and the whole ward is filled with stick-thin girls and
boys in wheelchairs and they laugh at me for being admitted for
anorexia when I look practically obese?

I look back out of the window at the traffic racing past, wishing
that I'm going to Reading for the same reasons as some of the
other drivers undoubtedly are, going to visit family, going
sightseeing or to see a show rather than to be admitted to a
mental hospital. None of this seems even remotely fair. I didn't
choose anorexia; anorexia chose me.

I look at my phone again, as I've been doing every few minutes
since we left the hospital, nervously counting down the time left
before I'll be inside. I have five minutes left.

I swallow my fear and choke back the tears. I'm not going onto
the ward crying, I don't want them to think that I'm weak and
pathetic because they might trick me into consuming more
calories than is necessary. I don't know how these places work.
I'm going in strong, with my head held high, they'll all see soon
enough that my case is hopeless and that there's no point in
saving someone like me. I bet they'll discharge me within a
month and I reckon I could lose all the weight I gained in the
paediatric ward with two weeks of fasting.

*Truth no.11 – If you fast for a certain amount of time then the calories
already in you will get tired and will give up on making you fat because
they have no energy. They'll die and drain out of your pores and
evaporate into the air. You have to be careful to cover yourself*

completely so they soak into your clothes, otherwise you could breathe them straight back in again.

We leave the motorway and the tedious grey landscape is replaced with rows upon rows of houses, each with an expensive looking car parked outside. We pass parks, schools, shops and the occasional religious building, each metre passed another one closer we'll be to the hospital. Dad takes a sharp right and we wind up a long, steep driveway, dotted with trees and various plants alongside. A large, sand-stone building looms above us, hidden behind a thick, metal fence. I look up at the sign: 'Birchmoor Unit for Eating Disorders'.

I press myself against the back of the seat, praying for it to swallow me whole so I don't have to do this. Dad climbs out of the car and presses the button next to the mouthpiece. After a few seconds of static crackling a voice answers.

"Hello, we're bringing Bethany Thomas for her admission at 2 p.m."

There's a loud click and pause before the reply. "I'll open the gates, come on into the reception."

On cue, there's a loud buzzing in the metal posts and the gates begin to creak as they swing open. Dad gets back in and drives us slowly inside. We park quickly before hurrying under the porch out of the rain, Dad pulling my case behind him. The few seconds of exposure are enough to soak me to the skin and make me shiver with a combination of both the cold and fear. A lady in impossibly high-heeled shoes marches out of an office and touches her work ID card hanging from the lanyard around her neck to the door. She holds it open for us and welcomes us inside into a well-lit reception area complete with matching chairs, a coffee table, water machine and a collection of leaflets. Despite the fact the interior looks aesthetically pleasing and relatively comfortable; I'm not letting my guard down as this is obviously a trick. There's no way a hospital is meant to look inviting. The door closes swiftly behind us and I hear the resounding click of a lock sliding home. From what I can tell from the way the

receptionist opened the door, they only open by having a fob card. There's no getting out.
She greets my parents warmly and offers them a drink, which they politely refuse, before asking for us to sign in on the small visitor book. I read Dad's scrawl upside down.

Name: *Bethany Thomas and parents*
Date: *22/06/16*
Time of arrival: *13:25*
Reason for visit: *Admission*

We sit in the group of chairs in reception, watching the various doctors, receptionists and ward staff hurrying past, each one smiling at me warmly and welcoming me to the hospital. Each time I attempt a courteous smile in return, but it comes out as more of a painful grimace. My parents pretend to read the various information leaflets about symptoms and treatment of eating disorders and the brochures detailing the setup of the hospital, but I know they're just as nervous as I am. I jiggle my legs rapidly up and down in an attempt to release some of my pent-up anxiety.
We aren't kept waiting for long. The door adjacent to the main reception clicks and swings opens and a lady in a smart business suit, black heeled boots and long brown hair tied back into a bun smiles widely at me. "Hello," she says, in a distinctly foreign accent. "Welcome to Birchmoor Unit," she shakes my parents' hands firmly. "Hello, Bethany, it's nice to meet you. I'm Dr Ilona and I'm going to be your speciality doctor throughout your stay with us." I try to smile to show that I understand, but the muscles in my face are frozen in fright and I can't raise my lips or open them to speak. "If you'd like to follow me through to the visitors' lounge we can begin the admission, I'm sure you'll feel much more settled when you're up on the ward with the other girls and boys, they're all very excited to meet you."
No, I would not like to follow her; I would not like that at all. Instead, I want to walk in the other direction, out of the main

door and back into the safety of the car so I can go back home with my parents and pretend that none of this ever happened. What did she mean that the others are 'excited' to meet me? No one has ever been happy to see me before, let alone 'excited'. I feel a shiver of fear at the prospect of meeting the boys.

Truth no.12 - Despite knowing it's irrational, I've come to fear men and I don't know why.

I'm the sort of person who people try and avoid, the person who's always the punchline of the majority of jokes and people only look pleased to see me when they're about to trip me up or push me down at school. Is she lying to try and entice me into being compliant and working with them?

If she is then her efforts will be wasted, I'm catching on and learning all of their tricks faster than they must be expecting. I know what the main purpose of treatment is here, to make me fat again.

She beckons us through the door and leads us into a comfortable lounge, complete with a large sofa, a glass-fronted cupboard containing various board games and activities, extra chairs to accommodate everyone and an oval coffee table on which stand numerous steaming mugs. The people already seated stand and shake my parents' hands, each introducing themselves with a name and title that I immediately forget.

"We're just waiting for Dr Sergei, he's just had to phone a parent quickly," says Dr Ilona, motioning for us to take the sofa and pulling up a spare chair opposite us. The staff begin to make small talk with my parents. I study each one nervously, trying to see behind their 'nice person' masks to the people within who are going to keep me locked away from my family. After a few minutes of awkward conversation in which they discuss things like the weather and fuel prices to keep our minds off of what's to happen, there's a steady knock on the door and a broad-shouldered man enters the room. He shuts the door swiftly behind him and smoothes back his greying hair with one hand, an expensive looking notebook and fountain pen clasped in the other. He shakes my parents' hands, nods warmly at me and introduces himself as Dr Sergei, my new consultant psychiatrist. I sit nervously on the leather sofa, glancing fearfully around the room at the collection of adults sitting around me, all staring intently at me as if I know something they don't. I look up at the ceiling and notice a CCTV camera in the corner. They're watching us too.

Dr Ilona reaches into the bag at her feet and pulls out a stack of paperwork, before handing pages out to the staff in the room. In the next thirty minutes, we cover the possible reasons for my diagnosis, the development of my eating disorder, the various attempts to treat me in the general hospital, my lifestyle at home and my current physical and mental health. I feel like I'm being ripped open from the inside out, exposing my inner self to this room of strangers, all listening intently and making notes on their paperwork. I shut my eyes tight.

This isn't happening.

This isn't happening.

This isn't happening.

Mum touches my arm concernedly. "Are you alright?" she asks. I open my eyes and nod slowly, I don't want her to see how much I'm hurting, not on top of what I've put her through already. There's another knock on the door and a short lady with jet black hair tied back into a ponytail and wearing a burgundy jumper enters the room, more paperwork clutched in her hand. My parents shake her hand as well and she pulls out a chair to sit down and lays her paperwork on the table.

"Hello," she says smoothly to me. "I'm Karen and I'm one of the nurses on the Intensive Treatment Ward that you'll be going to. The ward is mixed with two boy bedrooms and two girl bedrooms and also two separate bathrooms for the two genders. I'm going to be your key nurse which means that, on the ward, you are under my care, so if you have any worries or problems you can come straight to me. Is that ok?"

I open my mouth to speak but no words come out.

~ Let Me Go ~

"I know this is all very daunting for you," she continues, "but we'll all make you feel welcome. There're four boys and four girls including you on Intensive. When things settle down for you, you'll be able to go to school and join in with the activities with them. I'm sorry it's just a quick introduction but I need to go back up now, it's almost snack time, so I'll see you in a while." She turns to my parents. "If you have any questions, please don't hesitate to ask, I can come back down once the others are finished to answer any queries and give you a tour of the ward. I just need you to sign some paperwork, which I'll leave for you here," she taps her hand lightly onto the sheets of paper on the table. "I know Beth's Sectioned, but that will be running out in a week's time and we hope that she'll consent to treatment as a voluntary patient. I think it's best to get all of the admin done on the first day so we can move forward into recovery." She smiles at me once more and then leaves, shutting the door quietly behind her.

"Can you come with me, Beth?" asks Dr Ilona. "I just need to examine you before we go on up to the ward, we can use the little treatment room outside my office. It'll give your parents time to sign the documents with Dr Sergei and ask any questions."

I don't want to go with her; I want to stay with my parents. She sees my hesitation and smiles sadly at me. "You'll be fine, I promise." Mum and Dad nod at me in encouragement and I follow her out of the room, looking back at my parents before the door closes the gap between us. What if they're made to go without saying goodbye? Are they about to lock me up for good now? "They'll be here when we come back," says Dr Ilona reassuringly, seeming to read my mind. "We won't be long." I nod and follow her back through reception and down another long corridor. She wraps her arm around my shoulders protectively and leads me into a little box room at the end of the corridor. "Can you take off your jumper please, and also your bra if it's under-wired. We'll have some fun with this ECG machine; I haven't used it in ages!" She speaks jokingly, trying to make light of a strange and scary situation. She draws a curtain around the bed and pulls the machine towards me. I remove my jumper and silently thank Mum for having the initiative to buy me unwired bras when it was known I'd be going into hospital soon. I lie on the bed and my ribs stretch tightly against my skin, my stomach becoming painfully concave and lying flat against my spine, the sudden jar of my pelvis pulling it back up again. She unhooks the cables and attaches them to my chest, as well as one on each wrist and ankle. She doesn't make a comment at the array of bruises, cuts and bandages snaking up my arms.

After the ECG she feels my hands and feet, and tells me that my extremities are very cold. She then weighs me and measures my height before taking my blood pressure lying down and standing to compare later. I look the other way and clamp my teeth shut against the bite of the needle as she takes my blood. Five vials are drawn. Once she's done every test she can think of, she puts her arm back around me and leads me back down the corridors. Despite having walked down them less than fifteen minutes ago, I have no recognition of it, as if the whole place is some winding rabbit's warren. I feel more trapped than ever.

She leads me back to the visitors' lounge, but it's empty. I look around hurriedly in fright. Where are they? They didn't leave without saying goodbye, did they? Noticing my shock and fright, Dr Ilona holds out her hand. I take it, completely forgetting my age and allow myself to be led like a small child. "They've probably gone upstairs to see your room," she says. "Come on, let's go and find them." She holds my hand tightly and takes me back through the corridors until we stop at a lift. She presses the button with her free hand to go up. We stand in awkward silence and I cling onto her hand like it's a life-line. After a journey full of unexpected lurches and trembles, the doors open and we turn to the right as she unlocks the door to the Intensive Treatment Ward. I hesitate briefly before passing over the threshold. This is my last moment of freedom. How long until I'm allowed outside again? Will I ever get out? With a deep breath, I step from the linoleum landing onto the faded purple carpet of the ward. Never once did Dr Ilona let go of my hand. She shuts the door firmly behind her not a moment after I've cleared the doorway.

I'm standing at the top of a long, narrow corridor, with a white door at the far end. To the right of me is a large display board protected by a sheet of plastic containing an array of artwork, information sheets and a large colourful banner produced in many different handwritings which dictates 'Welcome to Birchmoor Unit!' The faint imprint of erased pencil underneath it suggests that it'd previously read 'Welcome to the Loony Bin!' Dr Ilona squeezes my hand gently and begins to lead me slowly down the empty corridor, seeming to take her time to give me a chance to acclimatise to my new surrounding and to read the plaques on the doors as we pass.

"I know it must all seem a bit scary at first, but you'll get used to things on the ward and the people on them. Honestly, we've got everything you could need!" says Dr Ilona reassuringly as we walk. "The door to your right is the school room. We've got specialist teachers who come here during the week to give you lessons and opposite that are some therapy rooms for the patients who can't leave the ward. The other patients are all in the Education Room at the moment, but they'll be out soon." We pass another set of doors and she continues the tour in a well-practised voice. "In here is the lounge, and opposite that's the dining room. And then all that's left is the two bathrooms, four patient bedrooms and the Nurse's Office and treatment room at the end. All the therapy rooms and such are away from your rooms to try and give you all a more homely atmosphere, as you can see some of our patients have been quite inventive with the decoration." As we walk past the door labelled 'Dining Room' there's a sudden change of colour as if we've entered a different place entirely. There are pieces of artwork on the walls, pictures from magazines and posters of artists and movie casts. On either side of me is a small row of bedrooms, and directly in front is the white door with the label 'Nurses Office' upon it, staring directly up the corridor so that you're in sight at all times.

~ Let Me Go ~

I look around me rapidly, trying to commit the exact layout of the ward to memory, looking for any weak points in case there's even the slightest chance I can escape. Dr Ilona smiles broadly and pulls me gently to a halt in front of one of the closed doors, a plaque saying 'Bedroom 3' hanging on the wood. "This will be your room; you'll be sharing with a young lady called Rachel." She issues three sharp raps onto the door before tapping her fob card to the box and swinging it wide. I drop Dr Ilona's hand, my breath expelling out of me in surprise as I gasp "Mum" and run into her waiting arms. I burst into tears and sob on her shoulder, letting my tears fall freely and soak into her scarf.

Truth no.13 – I am more scared than I have ever been in my life, the realisation of being in a hospital hundreds of miles from home scares me more effectively than any threat of weight gain.

Mum holds me tightly against her, stroking my head softly just as she did when I was little and would come crying to her after a fall at the playground or a nightmare. "It's ok," she reassures me, her voice muffled by the sound of suppressed tears. "We're going to make everything alright again for you. Karen has just been showing us around the ward, and it looks so lovely here Beth! Honestly, I think this place will really do some good for you. All the staff I've met here are so supportive and kind and Karen has told me all about your roommate. I'm sure you'll get along just fine!"

I pull back slightly from her so that I can get my words out properly. "Take me home, please," I cry, an irrefutable tone of desperation in my voice. "I'll be better, I promise I will! Please, please give me another chance. I don't want to stay here, I want to go home!"

"Oh, baby," says Mum, and I can hear that she's given up all pretence of not crying, that she's crying onto me just as much as I'm sobbing onto her. "I want to take you home, we all want to so much! I promise you'll come back home, just as soon as you've got yourself sorted out a bit."

"No…. no…." I plead, unable to find the words to express what I want to say.

"You're very ill, Beth, you need some proper help. We've tried to help you as much as we can at home, but you need specialist treatment now," she says.

I feel the warm pressure of Dad resting his hand on top of my head. "We wouldn't be doing our duty as your parents if we took you home now," says Dad. "And even if we wanted to we can't because you're Sectioned. I love you so much darling, but this really is for the best."

Karen clears her throat noisily. "I don't mean to be insensitive, but I don't think this is helpful for Bethany now. I think it would be easier for you to both go home; it'll give her a chance to settle down before dinner. She can call you in the evening when you're at home." I feel Mum nod as Dad embraces the both of us, enveloping us in the warm cocoon of his aftershave. They both tell me they love me, and then they're pulling away before I have time to protest, moving swiftly out of the room with Dr Ilona, who shuts it firmly behind her.

"It'll all be ok," says Karen softly, sitting down on the bed. "You're on 1:1 for now, that means that somebody will be within arm's reach of you at all times. I'll be with you for the next hour until you've calmed down and then one of the HCA's will take over, alright?"

I try to muster the strength to swear at her, to tell her that no, I'm not alright. Do I look alright? You've just told my parents to go away and leave me here. Instead, I collapse onto the floor, wrapping my arms around myself to hold the pieces together and cry for my parents and the life I've had to leave behind, as I hear them driving back out of the gate. Karen sits there and watches me quietly, a silent witness as the walls I've maintained for so long crumble away to nothing more substantial than dust.

Chapter Twelve

Rachel looks across at me with a slight smile playing about her lips, her eyes burning with curiosity as to who this strange new-girl is occupying her room.

"What's your name?" asks Rachel curiously.

"Beth Thomas," I reply quietly.

"How old are you?"

"Sixteen."

"What's your BMI?"

"Rachel! What have the nurses told you about asking questions like that? I'll have to report this you know," warns the HCA on my 1:1 for the next hour. After I'd cried myself out, Karen had given me another talk about what to expect of life here on the Unit, before handing me a small guide full of information about Birchmoor and introducing me to the first HCA on the rota to watch me. "Beth's only just arrived here and the last thing she's going to want to be asked is about that. Please have some respect for her privacy and remember how you felt on your first day."

Rachel tuts at the HCA and rolls her eyes in obvious discontent before reaching for the magazine stashed underneath her pillow. My 1:1 turns to me. "Just so that you're aware: questions, conversations and general comments about eating disorders are not tolerated here. Those sorts of thoughts and ideas are to be voiced in your therapy sessions or with a member of staff in private." I nod my head rapidly in response, eager to show that I understand so that they'll see I don't need to be so closely monitored.

I'm sitting on my bed, with my 1:1 sat within arm's reach on a chair to my side. She won't stop staring at me. The room is split roughly down the middle, with a bed on either side as well as a narrow wardrobe, bin and shelf. Rachel has covered her walls with pictures of her family and various members of boy bands, each one scantily dressed and flexing their muscles. My side is bare. Upon my wardrobe is a mini-whiteboard complete with erasable pen, the only thing I've used to personalise my area so far. Whilst prisoners may scratch in each day they're kept inside, I wipe one away in my five-day countdown until I can next see my family.

My 1:1 stands up and pulls my suitcase out from the corner which the receptionist had only delivered a moment earlier. "I have to search you and your bag; you can't leave this room until it's done. I'm afraid it's something everyone needs to go through, it's just to make sure that no one brings any contraband or anything dangerous on the ward so we can keep you all safe." She asks me to empty my pockets. I remove the crumpled tissue and put it slowly and deliberately onto the bed, pulling my pockets inside out as I do so to reiterate my point. She then asks me to remove and shake out each shoe which I do, hanging them upside down before her. The laces are swiftly removed. "Unclasp your bra and jump."

I stop dead. "I'm sorry?"

"Unclasp your bra and jump, a lot of young people here try and conceal contraband in their bras and it's a routine check every time a female patient comes onto the ward." I open my mouth to protest that this isn't fair, that I've just been admitted to a hospital far from home, have no idea when I'll see my family and haven't the slightest notion of when I'll be allowed back outside. She cuts me off before I can utter the first syllable.

"Do I need to call for Karen?"

I shake my head in defeat, blinking rapidly to stop the tears from falling. I will not cry in front of this lady. I unclasp my bra and jump once with clenched teeth, my face a vivid red from humiliation. I knew things were going to be bad in here, but I didn't realise how bad. Why did I let those bastards Section me? Once that ordeal is over she lifts my suitcase onto my bed; I move towards it automatically to unpack but she motions me back sternly with her hand as if I am up to something and am deliberately trying to cause trouble. She unzips it and pulls back the canvas top. "Is there anything in here that you would like to tell me about beforehand that's dangerous or sharp?" she asks. I'm too shocked to reply.

"Is there anything in this bag that could cause me harm when I search your case?" she reiterates sternly. "If you have anything to hide it would be better for both you and me if you tell me about it before I go searching."

"There isn't anything, I promise," I say quietly. I have never deliberately hurt anyone before, and nor will I ever in the future. I'd so much rather me be in pain than anyone else. I deserve it, they don't. Is this what they all think of me here? That I'm some selfish, demonic teenager hell-bent on inflicting as much pain on those around me as the world has bestowed on me?

My 1:1 begins to unload each item in my case, a long and tedious process as she first inspects every inch of it as if I've disguised some contraband in the seams or in the spines of my books before making a detailed log on a chart.

"Five t-shirts," she reads, handing them to me so I can put them in my wardrobe. "Three pairs of jeans, one skirt, two jumpers, and four hoodies." I collect each item, habitually squeaking a silent "thank you" as I did so. She digs deeper and withdraws handfuls of my underwear and socks. She unfolds each of my socks, turning them inside out to check for any items hidden within. Once they pass inspection I refold them and put them in my wardrobe too. "You don't have to do that, please," I say desperately, blushing a deep crimson as the HCA digs through my pile of underwear for contraband. Rachel looks up from her magazine and smirks at me and my underwear being so openly displayed. "I do. I understand that this probably isn't the best kind of 'welcome' you could receive, but it's protocol. I don't like having to go through this as much as you don't." I highly doubt that, she's not the one with her underwear being exhibited. She hands me my underwear and I stuff them embarrassedly around the back of my jumpers. She makes a note on her chart.

I hear the soft tap and squeak of a door opening at the end of the corridor and Karen's voice floats up the hall. "Five minutes until dinner, people. It might be a good idea to use the bathroom before we go in!" Karen's head pops around the door. "That includes you too newbie! Patients aren't allowed to use the bathroom for half an hour after snacks and an hour after main meals so I recommend you go beforehand. Your 1:1 will show you which one the girls' bathroom is." She turns to Rachel. "Your Mum's just called. She's caught in traffic on the motorway, but should be here around eight."

"Thanks," replies Rachel sarcastically. I get the impression immediately that she doesn't like this particular nurse very much, and I wonder why that may be. Rachel stuffs her magazine back under her pillow and struts out of the room. "Feeding time at the zoo, folks! Nuthouse chow all round!" Karen storms after her and I hear her reprimand her curtly as she rouses the others from their rooms. I suppress a slight smile; at least I'm not the only one who evidently hates it here.

"Toilet?" asks my 1:1.

I nod my head quietly; I haven't been since I left the general hospital this morning. She leads me out into the corridor and we pass a few patient rooms towards the communal bathroom. I glance quickly into each room as I pass, and see two of the boys in the room next door reading books and listening to music. My 1:1 taps her fob card to the door marked with the outline of a stereotypical female and holds it open for me. I step inside and inhale a mix of various fruity shampoos and soaps which barely manage to disguise the underlying 'public toilet' smell that pervades the air.

To the right of me is a partitioned cube of shower stalls, and as I walk further into the room I can see three toilet cubicles, a sink with a plain mirror above it and the outline of a bath concealed behind a plastic curtain in the corner. I stand in front of the mirror and look into its depths. The monster looks back. It seems I can rely on it being in the closest mirror, no matter where I am in the country. I want to tell it that I'm scared and that I don't want to be here, but my 1:1 will think I've truly gone mad because she can't see what I'm talking to.

The monster steps forwards until its face is in line with my own, blocking out my own reflection until the mirror can barely contain it. *"You're being watched now, you stupid girl,"* it whispers angrily. *"How am I supposed to help you lose more weight and protect you from the calories if you're being watched?"* I want to reply back that I don't know how, and for goodness sake please help me. I look away from the mirror in despair. My 1:1 pulls open the door of the first cubicle and motions me inside, there's a sliding lock accessible on both sides. I step inside and hurriedly close the door behind me and click the lock in place, grateful for the brief moment of privacy after being obsessively watched and monitored for so long.

My 1:1 unlocks the door and pulls it open, standing directly in the doorway and watches me once more.

"I haven't finished," I say obviously.

"You haven't earned your privacy. All patients with no bathroom privacy must be watched at all times. Your observation level is Level Four: Arms Reach' a member of staff need to be within arm's reach of you at all times, whether you're using the bathroom, having your meds or reading a book. Don't worry though, obviously, only female staff can supervise the girls and only male staff can supervise the boys. I'm sorry, but you'll get used to it," she states matter-of-factly, not sounding the least bit sorry at all.

"I'm not going to do anything, I promise!" I plead in desperation. "If you're going to stand there and watch me then I just won't go!"

"I'm glad that you're not going to do anything, it will undoubtedly make your stay here a lot easier. But unfortunately the rules remain the same. Don't worry I've seen it all."

"I don't care whether you've 'seen it all' or not, I haven't and I don't want to have the experience. It's not right to watch someone use the bathroom. Privacy shouldn't be earned it's a human right!" I protest angrily.

"You are more than welcome to discuss this with your consultant but I highly doubt that things will change... every patient I've seen come through this ward takes at least three or four months to earn their privacy back and I've been working here for eight years. If you continue refusing to use it then you can be restrained, believe me, that's not a pleasant experience for either staff or patients."

"That's sick."

"That's necessary for treatment. We're not monsters here Beth, we want what's best for you, but we've also got rules to follow as well and whether you like it or not they apply to you too. Now, are you going to use the toilet or not?"

At the prospect of either being restrained or having an accident, I use the toilet in silence. My eyes burn and blur with humiliation as this lady, whom I've only met fifteen minutes ago, watches me. My dignity disintegrates alongside my privacy. I no longer have any say over my rights or my own body.

***

"Pick up the sandwich please, Beth," says Karen encouragingly. I'm sat in the dining room for dinner. Mealtimes are reversed here and we have a hot dinner at lunch and a sandwich or soup or something at dinner. The dining room is painted the gentle blue of early morning horizon, with scattered pictures of palm

trees and beaches around the room. There are two tables of
medium size, each one seating four patients and two staff
members to supervise. I was expecting the tables to be
segregated, not by choice but by habit as they were at school, so
I'm surprised when I see that there's a mixture of both sexes on
each table.

I look across at Karen, in the seat adjacent to me. She nods at me
encouragingly. "It's what your body needs, and if you can't
manage it then we'll put it down your tube." I catch the boy
sitting opposite from me staring at me out of the corner of my
eye. "Alex," says the other member of staff tasked with meal
support on my table. "Focus on your own meal, please." Alex
evidently returns to his own meal because I don't hear another
comment.

"Rachel!" calls a male member of staff from the other table. "Stop
smearing your butter, this is the second time I've had to ask you
this meal time. If you do it again then you'll get another strike
and I'll have to send you out."

Karen touches me softly on the shoulder. "Come on, let's get
started. The quicker you start the sooner you can leave and go
into the lounge. Look, I'm having mine too." She nods pointedly
towards her own sandwich and picks up a quarter before taking
a large bite as if to reiterate a point. How can some people have
such easy relationships with food? Why isn't everyone terrified
of the calories that lurk within? Don't they know that if you
swallow them they'll make you fat?

I look down at my sandwich and watch as the calories multiply
before my eyes. Are these sandwiches bought or handmade?
How am I going to calculate the precise amount of calories in
them without any internet? The calories begin to run around and
dance on top of the bread, laughing at me as they know that
they're coming to get me no matter what I say. If I don't eat it
then it'll go down my tube, and there's no guarantee that the
number pumped in will be less than what I'm eating.

~ Let Me Go ~

Truth no.14 - The calories inside those bottles of Fortisip must be so much more than what it says on the label and what we're served in the dining room. In the bottle they must breed and multiply and, as they have nowhere else to go, they wait in there for the next poor person who swallows them.

I pick up a sandwich quarter and blow on it, hoping that at least a few of the calories will fall off. "Beth" warns Karen quietly. "I don't know why you're doing that but that's not a normal eating behaviour. I'm going to give you a strike, if you get three strikes then you will have to leave the dining room and the entire meal will be made up in Fortisip regardless of what you've managed."
Shit.
I raise the sandwich once more to my lips and take a small, hesitant bite, cringing as I feel the bread and tuna mayonnaise enter my mouth. I can feel the calories on my tongue, balancing on the edge as if taunting me before they jump down my throat. I chew, mashing the calories into tiny pieces. Oh God! Does chewing them make them multiply rather than kill them? I fight the overwhelming urge to spit it back onto my plate, to put my hand in my mouth and scrape out every last bit of the pulp, before making myself sick in the toilet in case any have snuck into my stomach.
Karen sees the look of pure fear and self-disgust on my face. "Come on, Beth," she encourages. "You need to eat everything on your plate. You're one bite closer to the end, let's finish this up and then go into the lounge to watch some TV." I nod and raise the sandwich to my lips once more because there really is no other option.
"Rachel, that's enough," says the member of staff once more. "I've given you three warnings, please put your plate on the trolley and leave the dining room. I'll call you in afterwards for your replacement." I jump in my seat and drop my sandwich in surprise as there's a sudden, harsh squeal as Rachel throws back her chair in anger. "What the fuck?" she shouts. "That's not fair! I haven't even done anything!"

~ Let Me Go ~

Karen turns in her seat and stares at Rachel coolly. "We do not tolerate that sort of language in here; you'll see me afterwards in the Nurse's Office. You need to put away your plate and leave the dining room, you're distressing the others and it's not fair." Rachel storms across the room and tosses her plate on the tray as she leaves so that it makes a loud clatter and her half-eaten sandwich falls to the ground.

"Pick that up, please," says Karen.

Rachel walks out as if she hasn't heard a thing. I hear her distinctively mutter 'fucking joke' under her breath. I turn back to my meal, my legs shaking uncontrollably under the table. I clutch my hands in my lap to hide their trembling; I don't want them to see that I'm afraid. I look back at my sandwich as the others pick up their own sandwiches and make painful attempts to continue eating. I feel sick to my stomach with fear. I have to stay here, with these people for the next however many months - maybe even a year.

I think of Mum and Dad, they're probably almost half-way home now and my little sister who has taken the day off school as she was too upset at the thought of me going away to learn anything today. I close my eyes and think of Tia, she'll cry for me in the evenings when I don't come and play with her. I see my room; my door shut tightly to prevent my family from the flashes of pain every time they walk past and see it empty, the air growing stale and the furniture gathering its quiet coating of dust.

"Beth?" asks Karen concernedly.

"I don't feel well, can I go now please?" I say in a voice barely above a whisper.

"Ok, but you'll be called back to have a full replacement once the others have finished," says Karen.

"Ok," I reply as I stand up and tuck my chair beneath the table quietly. I avoid the looks of curiosity from the others as I cross to the trolley and put my discarded sandwich on the trolley. My 1:1 is ready and waiting for me in the corridor outside.

"Alright?" she asks. "Shall we go into the lounge, then? We could play a game of cards until it's time for your replacement."

~ Let Me Go ~

I shake my head slowly, my eyes dazed, dreamy and not really seeing. "I don't feel well," I mumble.

"That's ok," she says, rubbing my arm soothingly. "Most of our new patients don't feel like themselves on admission day. I promise you that with each day things will get easier." My stomach clenches painfully and I throw out an arm and gip the wall for support. "I need the bathroom," I say suddenly.

"You've just been," states my 1:1. "Come on, let's go and-"

"I'm going to be sick," I gasp.

I walk quickly to the girls' bathroom door and my 1:1 taps her fob quickly on the box to let us in. I rush to the toilet and vomit into the bowl, tears streaming down my face as I retch painfully again and again as my stomach fights to empty itself when there's nothing in there to remove.

"Karen!" calls my 1:1 hurriedly.

I hear the sudden running of footsteps up the corridor before a fob is tapped to the box and Karen bursts in.

"Beth's being sick," my 1:1 explains. "It's not intentional."

"Alright," says Karen as I retch bile into the toilet bowl. "It's alright, Beth, you're not in any trouble," Karen reassures, rubbing my back supportively. "When you've finished in here your 1:1 will take you back to your room so you can lie down. I think its best if you go on bed-rest at the moment, today must have been too much of a physical and mental strain on you. I'll come by once I've sorted replacements out with some medicine to settle your stomach, we'll do some blood tests as well to see if there's an infection and you need to be quarantined. "

I nod as I retch again, my stomach feeling like it's trying to turn itself inside-out. Karen leaves and my 1:1 remains stood in the doorway to the cubicle, watching me as I crouch hesitantly over the toilet.

"Are you done?" she asks, unable to restrain the clear note of disgust in her voice.

I gingerly stand up and flush it away, rinsing my mouth and washing my hands in the sink outside. I look up into the mirror above the sink and see the monster looking back.

~ Let Me Go ~

"I told you," it says menacingly. *"I told you that you were a disgusting piece of filth and that you should have tried harder to kill yourself last night, even the staff here are repulsed by you. You make me sick. You just ate something. Do you know how many calories were in that? Loads. You're going to get fatter and more disgusting the longer they keep you here. Some anorexic you are."* The monster tuts and shakes its head in obvious displeasure. I turn from the mirror and my 1:1 leads me quietly back to my room. I curl up in my new bed and pull the duvet over my head to block out the world. Whatever I've done that's so profoundly wrong, I'm sorry. Please, please make this stop now. I never asked for this illness, please let me go home. A silent tear escapes from beneath my clenched eyes, clinging to my eyelashes in a bid to hold on, before letting go and soaking into the pillow.

~ Let Me Go ~

Dear Friend,

It's probably no surprise to you at all, but I just want to reiterate that my first week in the Unit was literal hell. It felt like my whole world had been flipped, or as if I was peering at it all through a kaleidoscope; everything I once knew no more than a scramble of patterns that I could no longer make sense of. Even now, I can still remember the sleepless nights whilst staff watched my every move; of the countless hours I spent curled up in a corner of the living room crying to go home. I wish I could write to you and tell you that I've managed to convince myself that it was nothing more than a particularly bad dream, but the memories of it all continue to play inside my head like a continuous loop, making me wonder whether I ever got out of the ward at all.

I feel like I have more of a point to this letter than my usual reminiscing, I want to get something off my chest and, although I know you won't agree with me, at least it's being read by someone who listens. There is one thing that I hate about this illness more than anything else – even more so than the death rates or being Sectioned and sent to a specialist hospital, and that's the views of society. Don't get me wrong, my Friend, there are many wonderful people out there who have dedicated themselves to raising awareness for those affected and challenging the stereotypes that are seen daily in the media, but there are far more who cause great damage to lives without even realising it. It irritates me more than words can describe when people call anything they deem "smaller than average" anorexic or state that, whenever a diet is undertaken, the person is automatically suffering from the disorder. Anorexia is not a physical illness; it's a mental illness with the potential of physical consequences. It's a silent illness that can develop unnoticed for years and can only begin to show when you're under stress, suffer a trauma or some other circumstance. Anorexia is not a choice, and it's not "just a diet". What many people don't know is that Anorexia Nervosa has the highest mortality rate of any psychiatric disorder, with roughly 20% of those suffering dying prematurely from complications. It is not a joke.

There are many people I have met throughout my journey who have adopted the label 'anorexic' as a means of describing their whole being, and if truth be told it's still sometimes the way I feel and relate to myself. People hold onto the label like it's a lifeline, throwing away personality, childhood and anything else that stands in the way of what society deems appropriate for the said label to remain. Some raise it like a flag so that, despite how their lives may be so drastically changing, they can still use it as a means of self-identification regardless of the fact that it's an illness and not a characteristic.

I think I've gone on a bit of a rant, haven't I? You're always complaining at me for doing that when I've told you my thoughts on the matter many a time before. I'm sorry, but I feel it's something I have to say, to release these tiny bubbles of truth into a world that's becoming overridden with stereotypes and assumptions that have become more "fact" to the average person than truth itself. I know you don't perhaps have the same views as me, Friend, but I think we'll have to agree to disagree on this one.

I have anorexia, but I am not an anorexic.

Chapter Thirteen

I sleep badly that night. At first, I have a panic attack at the thought of having to sleep in a different bed hundreds of miles from home that isn't my own, and then I cry and beg for my 1:1 to give me some privacy. It's needless to say that this is refuted. I can't stop worrying about what the others will think of me when I formally meet them tomorrow and when I'll be able to see my family again.

Each time I roll over to get into a more comfortable position I heard the whispered warning, "Beth, you need to stay still now and go to sleep!" and every time I tuck my hands under the duvet I am told "Beth, put your hands where I can see them!" because they think I'll self-harm under the covers. It also doesn't help that I have my general observations monitored precisely every two hours so that, even when I do manage to fall into a light dose, I am woken to have my blood pressure, temperature, blood oxygen and blood glucose levels taken. My finger is sore and bruised from the numerous pinpricks it's sustained, and it hasn't even been twenty-four hours yet.

~ Let Me Go ~

I rise early and wait uncomfortably on my bed for the rest of the others to get ready for the meeting. They're gathering in the lounge to meet me before we all go in for breakfast. I still haven't worked out what I'm going to say to them. First impressions matter, I don't want them to treat me the same way as my peers treated me at school, at least I could go home to get away from the bullying at the end of the day, here there will be no escape. The living room is full by the time me and my new 1:1 for the hour enter the room.

The walls are painted a soft cream, with bright, inspirational artwork framed along the walls with quotes on such as 'Nourish to Flourish' and 'Eat it to Beat it'. There are two plastic-covered sofas and numerous soft chairs grouped around the TV and a large table at the back which is covered in a collection of school books, board games and crafts. However, the most interesting and captivating element of the room is the wall around the activity table. Painted a slightly different shade to the rest of the room, the wall is dotted with handprints of every colour, each with a printed name underneath and two sets of dates, which I presume to be the dates of admission and discharge. I look at all the names, Anna, Carl, Phoebe, Robert and many more each with a beginning date and an end. A monument for all that have suffered but survived, I wonder if mine will ever be displayed among them.

Every seat in the room is taken, apart from a beanbag in the very centre of the room, with some of the girls draped over the arms and moaning slightly about the time they had to get up. Two boys are sat on the floor playing some kind of card game. I stand hesitantly in the doorway, unsure of where my place is in this room of so many. I think I should leave; they don't want someone like me in here with them.

"Are you coming in?" my 1:1 asks kindly. I shake my head reluctantly. She must see some of my hesitancy and unease as she puts her arm around my shoulder and leads me over to the far corner so that I can observe the room better before joining in. A couple of the others look up with clear curiosity written upon their faces; I avoid their gazes and keep my eyes trained on the floor.

"Hi everyone, can I just get you to listen up for a minute," she calls, my heart stops still. I didn't realise I'd have to introduce myself right now! They grumble half-heartedly before turning with interest towards my 1:1, towards me. I can feel my heart begin to pick up speed again, until the very tips of my fingers are pulsing with trepidation and anxiety. "I don't know whether you've all had a chance to meet our new patient, Beth, but I think she's feeling a little lonely having just moved into a very new and difficult situation." My 1:1 turns towards me, and I can feel the gazes of the others burrowing into me, analysing me and judging me on who I am and what went wrong to bring me here. "Beth, do you want to introduce yourself? Maybe you could tell them some of the things you like to do in your spare time?" I shake my head reluctantly and flush a deep crimson. She's referring to the 'About Me' worksheet I had to fill out last night which consisted of questions about my home life, things I enjoy and personality traits to help the staff and others get to know me. A painful reminder of everything I've left behind. I don't think I want them to know. I imagine the worst scenario possible in my head. I tell them about myself and hold nothing back, and they laugh at me and tell me that I shouldn't be here, that I'm not worth the time, effort and money it takes to be treated here. I pray that the floor will swallow me whole or that I suddenly develop the characteristics of a chameleon and blend indistinguishably with the paint-work behind me. My 1:1 turns back to the group as if nothing has happened. "This is Beth," she says as she introduces me to the room at large. "She is sixteen years old and she enjoys creative activities like writing, craft, music and caring for her cat at home. Beth is a quiet, kind and sensible young lady who always goes out of her way to do things for others. In the past she has had a few difficulties with making friends, as I know many of you have, which means that she's very nervous and anxious about being around you all. She's sharing a room with Rachel and is an avid Harry Potter fan! Is that all?" she says turning back to me for confirmation. I nod slowly and hold my breath; waiting for the antagonism and mocking that will surely follow.

They sit in silence for a moment, absorbing the influx of information.

"It gets better," says one boy boldly. He's wearing a tropical shirt decorated with birds of paradise and has slicked his hair back and away from his forehead. He shrugs as if being in an Inpatient Unit with a group of strangers is really no big deal, and I instantly wonder whether this is his first admission or not. "We're not too bad here, apart from Courtney in the mornings." The person whom I assume to be Courtney raises her head from beneath her blanket before throwing a pillow across the room at him, but he dodges it easily as if he's had many months of practice. "We don't bite," he finishes.

"Alex!" reprimands my 1:1 sternly. "Making jokes about the illness is not appropriate on the ward." She is barely heard over the cacophony of giggling and snorts that fills the room. I suppress a smile in the back of my hand.

"How about you all go around the room and introduce yourselves and say something about you that might help Beth get to know you all a bit easier," she suggests brightly, seeming to completely forget her previously firm tone. There is a collective groan, as if this is an activity that's been done numerous times before.

"Alex, do you want to start?" asks the HCA encouraging. "You usually have a lot to say."

"Hello, I'm Alex. I'm fourteen and love collecting records which I'm obviously not allowed to keep here due because they're contraband." He scowls comically at my 1:1 before elbowing Rachel who continues. "I'm Rachel, but you know that already, I like reading magazines and drawing nudes of my boyfriend – I'm joking!" she states hurriedly, as my 1:1 opens her mouth to angrily intervene. "Jesus, can't anyone have a joke in this place?

"I'm Simon," says the next boy nervously. He looks at me uneasily, as if he doesn't really want to be giving me this information about himself. "I'm seventeen and want to be an astrophysicist after university." The girl sitting across from him pokes her dishevelled head back out from under her blanket, and I notice the NG tube protruding from her nose. "Hi, I'm Courtney. I'm from Leeds. This is stupid."

The boy next to her sighs dramatically, in response to Courtney's reply before introducing himself. "Hello, I'm Jacob. I'm sixteen and play rugby for my school team, or I used to at least. And this is my roommate Ethan," he says, pointing at his motionless form on the sofa. "Ethan is fifteen and has an impressive collection of fantasy books in his wardrobe, in fact so many that there's barely any room for his clothes!" He ruffles Ethan's hair, but he barely looks up or even acknowledges he's heard.

My 1:1 says thank you and they return to their activities. I look across the room at them all, wishing I could find the words to say thank you for speaking to me, something which I can't quite get my head around considering the only interactions I'd had with people my own age normally ended with them shouting or swearing at me.

I look around curiously at the others; now that they're not staring at me any more I compare myself to them. There're a couple of patients who look painfully skinny, their collar bones visible through the necklines of their tops, with gaunt faces and a lack of spark in their eyes. There're ones who look near weight-restored too, some more confident about it and others shying away, trying to shrink into a shell that the doctors have made them outgrow.

Am I the fattest one here?

I catch the eye of another boy, I think it's Simon, he looks me up and down with an indistinguishable look of frustration in his eyes, before walking out of the room towards the Nurse's Office. Why would he look at me like that? I look back at my lap, my face burning. I must have done something wrong. My 1:1 leans towards me, and I can feel the soft tickling of her hair against my ear as she whispers "don't worry. Lots of people here find it difficult when a new admission comes, most of the others have been here a while, and it's hard when someone comes in because of their low weight. Don't worry about it; it's not your fault." She rubs my arm reassuringly and I raise my head slowly to check if anyone noticed.

My 1:1 checks her watch before getting up and addressing the room at large once more. "It's breakfast time in three minutes so you might want to think about using the toilet, you don't want to be late for school again." There's another loud groan, as they pick themselves up and begin to line-up outside the dining room opposite. A few of them refuse, and instead cocoon themselves within the safety of their blankets or stare morosely at the walls in silence. Karen comes in and starts speaking to them individually in an attempt to coax them into complying.

I press my back into the corner, wincing as the prominent bones of my spine protest. I wish the walls could hide me, or that the ground could form a gaping hole and I'll fall back down to the main floor, back to where the opening door is so that I can get out of here.

"Come on, Beth," says my 1:1, motioning me towards the door where I can hear a loud bell ringing from the room opposite. I shake my head. No, I am not going into that room; I am not going to eat breakfast. I just can't do it. I don't want to eat, especially not in front of all of the others and staff. What if they think I'm too fat to eat? What if they watch me eating and think I'm greedy? What if the boys start making fun of me like they all used to do at school?

"Beth," begins my 1:1 warningly. "If you aren't sat in the dining room in five minutes then you won't be allowed in at all and will have to have the whole thing replaced. At least come in and give it a try, it's much better if you can manage food and drink rather than supplement."

"I don't feel very well," I protest quietly.

"I know," she says. I don't think she understands what I mean. I begrudgingly stand and follow the line into the room, their shoulders hunched forwards and their heads bowed close to their chests, each one looking for all the world like they'd rather be doing anything but this. How is it possible to feel like this about something that's supposed to be so natural? I step up to my allocated place and look down at the bowl of cereal and juice. I flinch as if they've physically slapped me, turn and walk away. I can't. I can't. I can't.

I can feel the disapproving stares of the others on my back as I leave, burrowing into my skin as if trying to telepathically communicate with me and tell me that I have no choice, that this is the only way out. I turn at the door and look back at them, each sipping at their drinks and making a start on their food, some of them with tears streaming down their faces and hands gripping the table painfully. Their feet tap a rhythm on the floor, every other second punctuated with a staff's request to please stop jiggling, that this behaviour is not allowed. They're brave to be doing what they're doing, each one picking and nibbling at their food, but eating it none the less.

Without even consciously making the decision, I walk back through the door and move slowly towards my meal, meeting the eyes of Rachel and Alex who look up at me in surprise as I sit down. If they can all do it, then so can I.

***

The lounge is silent whilst the others are in the Education Room. I sit petulantly in the corner of the living room and look up longingly at the sliver of blue sky above me through the window, my eyes following the occasional aeroplane that travels past, the passengers oblivious to the fact that there is a locked ward below them in which eight patients are being held for treatment.

I asked Dr Ilona when she came to see me this morning when she thinks I'll be off 1:1, but she says not for quite a while yet – at least until my Section runs out. They want me to sign the papers and become informal when the Section goes in two weeks' time, otherwise, they say they'll call in the team again and this time I'll go straight to Section 3 which is a six-month detention. It's strange to think that. Throughout my whole time in secondary education, I've only received two detentions before, and they were whole class ones that usually only lasted about fifteen minutes. It's outlandish and oddly amusing to compare that to the twenty-eight-day detention I've been given, and even more concerning to think I have the potential of being upgraded to a six month one. What did I ever do to deserve this? I can practically hear the monster's reply: I was born.

In the rational part of my brain, disregarding however slight that partition may be, I know that if I refuse they'll only Section me again. However, I also know that there's no way in hell that I'm ever going to sign those documents. No matter the intensity of my inner self-loathing, nothing can ever condone that. How can they possibly expect me to sign myself away and actually stay here? The truth is, however difficult it is to even admit to myself, let alone anyone else, I'm not entirely sure that I want to get better.

I asked to go to the Education Room with the others this morning; I would jump at the chance of some aspect of normality again. When this was refused, I asked to go to my room, an attempt to surround myself with the familiarity of my own possessions so that I may feel, at least metaphorically, that much closer to home. The answer was no. The bedrooms are only unlocked after dinner and are closed the minute the breakfast bell sounds in the morning. They say that it's not 'therapeutic' to isolate yourself. I told Karen that was a load of bollocks, but she told me off for swearing.

What's worse is that I have literally nothing to do apart from divulging within my own thoughts, a place that's not particularly pleasant to be considering the circumstances that led to my admission here. All I can think about is my family back at home and what they're doing now, so much so that it's an effort to keep from letting the tears fall freely down my cheeks. I try to distract myself with the usual thoughts of diet and exercise, but I can't even summon the sense of pride I could usually sustain because of my low weight. I will be gaining from now on and my exercise will undoubtedly be scarce, a fact that scares me almost as much as being so far away from home does. I sit in a corner of the living room, half-beneath the table at the back, and look out of the window behind its plastic shield to prevent people from absconding.

It only opens a half-inch.

Looking out the window only makes me think of home again, and wondering whether the same piece of blue sky is looking down on my home. This leads me to think of school and wilfully hoping that they'll change their minds and let me go to the Education Room so that I can at least check my emails to see if my teachers have emailed me any work. There is no internet access on Intensive, apart from in the Nurse's Station and Education Room. Rachel told me last night that the teachers there don't make you do work unless you want to so most of them spend their time shopping online or playing board games. I don't know why though, some of them are the same age as me... don't they realise it's exam season soon? Despite hating having to go to school with a passion, a feat purely derived from the extent of the bullying that happened whenever a staff's back was turned, I wonder what lessons I would be having today. I wonder whether the students have already forgotten my name as if I'm no more than a bad memory and whether my seat has been filled by another student, replaced without a thought.

I turn away from the window and try to brush the thoughts from my mind, I must stay alert here. I look across the lounge towards the blank television screen and my 1:1 who is texting secretly on her phone. I look around the room in an effort to entertain myself to some degree to make the time pass faster; I just want to phone my parents tonight. Maybe, once the Section's been lifted, my parents will agree to take me home.

I'm not the only patient in the lounge. Despite not being on 1:1, I don't think Courtney's allowed to go to the Education Room either. She's curled beneath her blanket on the sofa like a cat and I think she's asleep. Ethan is sitting on the other sofa with his 1:1, so far I haven't seen him in the dining room, nor have I seen him walk, talk or make any movement without help. He slumps in his seat, his hair matted and clothing dishevelled; he's drooped so low in his chair that his chin rests upon his chest. I don't think he's even here, if that makes any kind of sense, as if he's living in another world entirely separate from our own.

There's a gentle knock on the door and Dr Ilona walks in, smiling broadly around at me and Ethan and giving a dirty look to the HCA more interested in their phone than the job they're paid to be doing.

"Good afternoon," she says brightly. I manage a small smile back in acknowledgement, Courtney remains asleep and Ethan doesn't raise his head but continues to stare unblinkingly at his lap – I'm not sure he's even aware that there's anyone there at all. "I'd just like to speak with Ethan quickly, and then I'd like to have a catch-up with you, Beth, we need to take some more blood I'm afraid." The HCA with Ethan unfolds a wheelchair in the corner and lifts him into it, before pushing him down the corridor after the muffled clicks of Dr Ilona's heeled shoes on the carpet. At the sound of the doctor walking away with Ethan, Courtney raises the blanket from her head and peers out uncertainly, her long blonde hair a matted mess on top of her head from spending so long under the cover.

She looks across at me and, seeing that I've noticed that she's 'awake' pulls the blanket back over her head and feigns sleep once more.

After a few minutes, Ethan's 1:1 wheels him back into the room and lifts him back onto the sofa before sitting down next to him and trying to interest him in a book. He barely raises an eyebrow or so much as glances at what she's showing him. I feel an intense feeling of pity for him. He looks so weak and vulnerable sitting there in that state, I want to help but I don't know how.

"Come on then, Beth!" says Dr Ilona cheerfully, juggling her pile of folders into one arm as she wraps the other around my shoulders protectively once more. She leads me pass the row of bedrooms and unlocks the Nurse's Office at the end of the corridor with a tap of her fob. Karen barely looks up from her computer screen where she's reading some long-winded document as Dr Ilona leads me into the adjacent treatment room. I sit on the table and automatically roll back my sleeve, looking away as I feel the sharp prick of the needle whilst she draws two vials from my vein.

The cuts on my arms that I inflicted back on the general ward would have started to heal by now if it wasn't for the fact that I reopened them each night under the duvet once staff thought I was asleep. As hard as I have been trying (considering it's a battle having been fought relentlessly for over three years) I can't seem to quit the habit or quench the urge in order to refrain from carrying it out.

Truth no.15 – There is poison in my blood (that is why everyone bullied me at school because they knew how toxic I am to those around me.) By making myself bleed, I release a little bit of the poison so that the people around me have less of a chance of getting hurt.

Dr Ilona carefully labels up the vials before taking my arm in her hand. "These are taking an awful time to heal, Beth," she puzzles. "I think I'm going to prescribe you some cream so we can make these heal a bit faster, I don't want you getting any infections." I roll back my sleeve and bite my lip, somehow highly doubting that the cream will make even the slightest amount of difference.

She leads me out of the treatment and unlocks my room before sitting on my 1:1's chair across from me. She gets straight down to business.

"Dr Sergei and I have decided that, should you feel up to it, you should be allowed to sit your GCSE examinations this year."

I open my mouth and close it repeatedly like a fish that's been suddenly removed from water. I wasn't expecting that.

"I know this will probably make you panic, but we thought that it's only fair that you be given the chance to try," she continues slowly, more than aware of the conflicting thoughts that are whizzing through my brain. Of course I want to take my exams! But how on earth will I ever pass them considering I haven't been at school or been allowed to study for the past two months? "The leading teacher, Mr McPherson, who organises examinations, will be coming to see you next Monday to tell you about the Education Room and what the set-up will be for the exams themselves. You don't have to say yes, I know that you'll want to do your best, but honestly, anything you can do in your condition will be marvellous."

I nod my head slowly. "Can I revise?"

"You can for two hours a day outside of lesson time, once you're allowed to go to the Education Room. I think we'll give you the rest of the week to settle in, it's only two days until the weekend, and then after the teacher has seen you on Monday you can go to school. You're not physically stable enough to deal with the stress of school work yet, so you must use the school hours to rest. Ok?"

I nod slowly again and feel as my mind slips naturally back into the old mind-frame that has been gradually diminishing since I'd left school.

As the monster has told me many a time before, these exams will show me exactly how much I'm worth. If I fail, then I really am a waste of air and should have killed myself whilst I had the chance in the general hospital. I know my chances of passing aren't particularly great anyway. My shoulders slump forwards despairingly. I want to sit my exams to make my teachers and family proud, but I can already feel the incessant hammering of doubt in the back of my mind. I'm a let-down, they all know I'm going to fail anyway, they're only letting me take them so that I'll be mentally weaker and easier to fatten up.

Chapter Fourteen

I call my parents later that night, we're not allowed anything with a camera or internet access on the ward which means that, unless we purchase an unadorned version ourselves, we have to use to use the one in the Nurse's Office.

"I miss you, Mum," I say thickly as I try to repress a sob. I don't want to end up crying on the phone again like I did last night, it's not fair to upset my parents when I can't even begin to imagine the inner turmoil that they're already subjected to.

"I miss you too, Beth," she replies quietly. "How are things in Reading? What have you done today?"

"Things are ok," I lie. "I saw Dr Ilona today; she says I can sit my GCSE's if I want to."

"Do you think you're going to try?" she asks.

"I guess," I reply. "I don't think I could not try considering the years of work it's taken to get to this point. Everyone else is sitting them, so I should too."

Mum pauses for a moment as she considers her words. "Yes, everyone is taking them, but not everyone is in your situation.

~ Let Me Go ~

What you've got to remember, Beth, is that you've been very poorly recently and you haven't had the time or the energy to put in as much work as the others. You've had a lot more to deal with than most of them can even begin to comprehend."

"I still want to do well."

"You'll do whatever you can do, and that will be enough for me and for everyone else," she reassures softly. "I received a phone call from your head of year at school this morning, she just wanted to say that they're all thinking of you and wishing you the best of luck in the Unit. They also told me that, considering the circumstances, you've been granted special consideration and will be given extra time in your exams due to your brain not being able to work at the same speed as everyone else's."

"What's that?" I ask.

"Special consideration means that, should you not be able to complete an exam, they'll take your previous marks into consideration and give you a grade based on your class work and your mock exam results. I know this isn't brilliant, because you were still learning the content when you took your mocks, but it should mean that you'll at least get a grade and it takes the pressure off of you should you not feel in the right place to sit them."

"I haven't even covered all of the content!" I say, panicking at the thought of sitting an exam, a stressful enough concept, without the means of being adequately prepared. "I was hospitalised when the final topics were started!"

"Try not to worry, whatever happens will be. No one's going to be disappointed or think any less of you, I'm just so proud that you're even considering giving it a go!"

She pauses again and I can hear the loud closing of a door behind her. "Dad's just got in," she announces. "Do you want to speak to him quickly; I know you haven't got long on the nurse's phone."

"Yes please," I say quietly. "I love you, Mum."

"I love you too, sweetheart, stay strong." She blows me a kiss down the phone and I hear the rustle of it being handed over to

~ Let Me Go ~

Dad.

"Hey, Beth," says Dad, "how are you?"

"I'm fine," I reply. "How are things at home? Is Natalie alright?"

"It's weird without you if I'm to be honest, the house is reasonably quiet and it's strange only taking one of you to school in the mornings," he sighs quietly, deep in thought. "Other than that, work was fine though, I made a good deal with Tom, so hopefully they'll be a bonus in the post at the end of the month." Tom is the man Dad has the main trade relationship with between the two companies, if he makes enough deals, then he gets a percentage of the profit as a bonus. "Natalie's fine," he continues. "She's at a netball match with the school team at the moment, and I think she's planning on calling you tomorrow."

"Ok," I reply. I hope Natalie's really ok, I feel so guilty about the amount of stress I have caused her. "What time are you coming at the weekend? I think most of the others have Leave on Saturday so it should be really quiet."

Dad hesitates, and I can practically hear the inner turmoil playing inside his head. Something is wrong.

"Beth," Dad begins slowly, a note of obvious strain in his voice. "Mum and I have decided that we're not going to be coming up this weekend."

"Why?" I interject angrily.

"We just think its best so that you can have some time to settle in."

"Settle in? How am I ever supposed to settle in? It's a Psychiatric Hospital! So that's it, you're giving up on me in the first week." I try to quieten my voice; if I become too loud and distressed then the Karen will take my phone privilege away.

"We're not giving up on you, don't you dare say that! We just think you need more time to settle in, it's a big change for all of us, and it'll only make you even more upset if you see us so soon after your admission."

I shake my head silently, wishing I could find the words to express how I'm feeling. I want to tell him that I need him to come, that I'm not just asking on a whim. I want to explain that I don't think I can wait until the weekend after, it seems a lifetime away, and I don't think I can go on for that long by myself.

"I'm sorry. You're not on your own," he says, seeming to telepathically read my mind. "You need some space to settle, and we can call you during the morning anyway. We'll be up early the weekend after, I promise."

"Please," I cry, unable to hold back the tears that have been threatening ever since I dialled their number.

"It's non-negotiable," he replies solemnly. "I think it's best if I go now, I don't want to cause you any more upset. I just want you to know that we're all very proud of you, and that we think of you every moment of every day. We all want what's best for you, and right now we think that you need some time alone to come to terms with what's happened."

I try to object, but he cuts me off with a goodbye before I can even form the words. He tells me that he loves me, and I send my love back, wishing I could see them in person rather than depending solely on technology. I hand the phone back to the nurse on duty wishing, despite the fact it's impossible, that I could somehow cut its cord and keep hold of it so that I could hear their voices whenever I needed to.

I wipe the tears from my face and go back into the lounge, where I sit down miserably in my little corner under the table. I want to give Rachel some privacy whilst she uses the phone. I make a mental note to add on the additional days to my white-board countdown.

Courtney, Alex and Simon are grouped around the TV watching a game show. They try and involve me as soon as I enter, but when I say 'no thank you' and they see the look of crumbing despair on my face, they leave me be. After a few minutes, in which Simon is reprimanded by my 1:1 for swearing colourfully at the contestants three consecutive times, there are loud shouts and whoops of delight from up the corridor. "Imo's back!" calls Courtney, her attention immediately withdrawn from the TV. I can hear movement from the bedrooms next door as the others come out to see. A tall, pretty girl with long, brown hair enters the room, carrying a large duffel bag over her shoulder. "Hi guys," she says happily. "How are things on the ward?" "Pretty much the same as when you left," replies Simon. "We've got a new admission though." The girl drops her bag with a loud thud onto the carpet and scans the faces, stopping when her eyes rest upon mine. "Hi," she says warmly. "I'm Imogen, I room with Courtney."

"I'm Beth, I room with Rachel," I say nervously. The others come into the room and take it in turns to either hug Imogen or awkwardly high-five, asking for stories about what she did on her Leave. After enlightening the room of her activities which involve a heavy hint at partying and getting reasonably drunk, which she subtly tones down considering there's staff in the room, she comes over to me and sweeps me into a hug too as if I am the same as everyone else.

I hug her back uncertainly, confused at why this girl, who has never met me before, should be so kind to me when at school no one ever was.

"I'm not going to be here for much longer, I turn eighteen in a month's time and I'm being discharged just before my birthday." "That's great!" I say enthusiastically. "How long have you been here?"

"Just over ten months. Honestly, I can't wait to get out of here, not to be ironic or anything, but I can practically taste the freedom!"

"Imogen!" comes a loud call from the Nurse's Office. "I thought I told you to bring your bag straight here, it needs to be searched before it can go in the lounge, you know this." Imogen sighs and rolls her eyes before lifting her bag back onto her shoulder. "I'll see you later, I've brought a cool DVD we can watch later if you want."

I turn towards Alex, who is packing away a board game on the table above me. "Aren't disks contraband?" I ask.

"Yes, little newbie" he replies. I repress a smile; he has to be younger than me by at least a year. "But they're allowed to be kept in the Nurse's Office and brought out for use, just not for us to keep in our rooms."

"Why?" I ask curiously.

He looks at me with exasperation, as if this is something I am clearly meant to know by instinct. When he sees I'm not joking, he replies "they might 'accidentally' break." Realisation dawns, of course.

That night, I'm successfully persuaded by Courtney to squeeze onto the sofa amid the others, and for once I find that I'm not worrying about food, calories, or what the scales say when we're routinely weighed on Monday morning. Instead, I watch the film that Imo brought, which has to be muted in a few places when the language gets particularly strong, and for a moment forget that I'm in a hospital at all. I can feel the warmth of Alex and Courtney on either side of me, Rachel's back pressing into my knees as she leans against me in the beanbag. I feel like I'm accepted, a cog in this machine that seems to hold everyone together, something I haven't felt in a long time. Even when the nurse comes in dragging the vital observation machine after her, they all make jokes about needing to be monitored and laugh at each other having their BP taken and temperature read. I find myself smiling, the muscles in my face aching slightly after doing a movement that has been alien for so long. Maybe, just maybe, things will be alright.

***

The dining room is empty apart from me, Dr Ilona, Dr Sergei and Karen. Whilst the others are in the Education Room for their final lesson, I have been summoned to be given an overview of what my care-plan looks like. Now," begins Dr Sergei as he reads from the sheaf of papers in front of him. "I understand that you don't want to be here, nobody particularly does, but you must at least understand that you're very sick and need specialist treatment. It's time you took your recovery into your own hands now, I'm not saying any of this is going to be easy, but it will most certainly be worth it all in the end." He clears his throat and squints down through his large, square glasses at his untidy scrawl. "We've had a meeting this morning regarding your progress and subsequent care-plan, something which we've comprised to give you an outline of what you're treatment will look like whilst you're with us. This can, of course, change depending on your health and any situations that may arise, but at the moment it's a basis to work on. We all think you've made lots of progress this week. Your blood results came back with no signs of infection. We think that the reason why you vomited on your first night was due to stress and homesickness more than anything else." I clench my jaw tightly until I feel a dull ache of pain. Homesickness - seriously?

"What's also good," he continues smoothly, "is that you've managed all of your meals and had the NG tube removed this morning." I nod slowly to show that I'm listening. Karen asked me if I'd like to have the tube removed after breakfast, and I agreed purely because it's irritating and slightly painful whenever I move my head or neck. How is it progress that I'm managing all my meals? I am Sectioned for fuck's sake, given the choice I wouldn't even hesitate before refusing the lot entirely. I only eat my meals because the consequences are much worse.

Dr Sergei moves on to his final point, either unaware of my simmering anger or ignoring it in hope of it diminishing. "We all know you want to go home, Beth, most of our patients here will tell you that they don't want to be here either. It is, however, crucial that you remain. If you were left to your own devices, you'd most certainly become weaker and likely die from starvation or heart failure." I open my mouth to respond, but am cut off abruptly before I can even manage the first syllable.

"We all know that Dr Sergei's right," says Karen bluntly. "If you hadn't been picked up by your community team or Sectioned in your general hospital then you'd probably have died. As medical professionals, and as human beings with morals, we can't just sit back and let that happen again. Not to you or any of the others in this hospital."

Dr Sergei clears his throat noisily and turns to the next sheet of paper on the table. "Would you like to hear an overview of your care-plan?" he asks.

"Yes, please. Can I come off 1:1 and have my privacy back yet?" I ask hopefully. I can't believe I'm asking for my privacy, I thought that was something that was an irrefutable right, not something to be earned.

"No, definitely not yet. You've only just arrived and we want to make sure you're properly settled and have been assessed first so that you're safe to be on your own. As Dr Ilona told you yesterday, though, it would be a good idea if you could start attending the Education Room for an hour each day, starting on Monday, hopefully, we'll be able to increase this steadily to ease you back into the school routine if you manage it well."

I nod. The Education Room sounds more enjoyable than spending hours after hours sitting in the lounge and looking out the window, surrounded by the handprints of those who've managed to make it back into the world again.

"The dietician has also decided to increase your diet plan by an extra two hundred calories. The dietician has decided that the easiest way to do that is to add in two biscuits with your evening meal. You have a lot of weight to restore, Beth, and unfortunately, you can't be discharged until you're a healthy weight for height."

"How much?" I ask quietly, feeling sick to my stomach at the idea of putting on weight. Can't they see how fat I am already? I'm practically obese, if anything they should be telling me to lose weight, certainly not to gain it.

"We don't like to be too specific with numbers here, it's not very helpful for you to focus on and also because the numbers change depending on whether you grow taller or another physical factor changes." He sighs, removes his glasses and pinches the bridge of his nose as if in preparation of the onset of a headache. "To give you a rough estimation… we're thinking of at least 10kg. That will put you on the cusp of the healthy weight for height bracket, although it would be best if we can manage to get you up to a bit more, that way if something should happen like a

sickness bug or a period of starvation, you will have something
to fall back on." I gape, my mouth hanging wide like a fish out of
water. They're going to make me gain 10kg … 10kg!
Shit.
"We've also decided to continue monitoring your physical health
every two hours, and your bloods will be taken daily as usual,"
he says.
Dr Sergei pushes his glasses back into place before laying the
documents down in front of me. "I know you're aware that your
Section is coming to an end next week. It would be much easier
for you in regards to your treatment here if you would consent to
being voluntary and to comply with your care-plan. I know this
must be horrifically scary for you, I don't doubt that all, but we
really do have your best interests at heart. If you can't manage
then we will call in the team to assess you and potentially put
you on Section 3, but this is much more different than the one
you're on now." He pauses briefly to let the words sink in.
"Section 3 is for a maximum of a six month period, although it
can be renewed at the end if that's deemed necessary. You can
also be taken off of it if your mental help improves and it seems
unnecessary because you're compliant. However, it will affect
things for you in the future. For example, this Section will always
be on your records, it may be seen by employers and may cause
some difficulty when travelling to certain places abroad. Do you
understand?"
I nod again. I understand. I do not want one of those.
Dr Sergei points to the documents in front of me, clears his throat
and continues. "This does, however, leave us with some
difficulties. We're all hoping that, once the Section ends next
week, you'll agree to sign the document to say that you'll be
voluntary rather than committed. This means that you will stay
with us until you're discharged and will abide by all rules laid
out by staff and conditions in your care-plan."
"No," I say automatically.
"I'm sorry?" He asks. Dr Ilona and Karen look at me quizzically.
"I'm not signing anything. I just can't. I'm not going to sign that

document so that you can take what little of my dignity I have left, fatten me up and keep me on a locked ward. No," I say with finality to reiterate and emphasise my point, hoping desperately that they'll understand where I'm coming from.

"Beth…" says Dr Ilona. "You don't have to decide this now. Once the Section ends I'll come up and we can sign those documents together. If not, then I can give you until the end of the week to change your mind. If you don't sign them, then we'll have to call the team to Section you."

I lean back in my chair and close my eyes tight. It's the same scenario as previously on the general ward, and it feels like a nightmare playing on a loop, only much worse considering this is real life and it's can't just be paused and walked away from. There is no choice at all.

A half-formed plan begins to form in the back of my mind, as is common when I'm looking to find a loophole within the system. Maybe this could be an opportunity for me to lose some more weight. After all, if I'm not Sectioned, how can they make me eat and drink?

"Ok," I reply. "I'll think about it."

"Good girl," says Dr Ilona, smiling across at me once more. "Keep on going with your meal plan and try and spend some more time with the others, I'm sure you'll find things a little bit easier with a distraction. I'll come back to see you when your Section ends with those papers, we can sign them together and then you're one step closer to going home again."

I smile slightly and tuck my chair under as I leave, shadowed by my 1:1 once more as I go back into the lounge opposite and sit down in the corner. There's no way I'm going to eat, no way at all. How can I eat voluntarily? Who does that? But losing weight isn't my main objective at the moment, despite how incredibly strange it is to admit it, I want to die. I think back to the numerous plans I made in the general hospital. Severe dehydration can kill you in a matter of days or weeks depending on the circumstances. I know deep down that I am physically weak and that I'm not stable. So, in reality, I'm hoping that it'll kill me pretty quickly. They can't make me drink; all I can do is stay strong and hope like hell that it kills me within three or four days. I am fairly certain that it will… and there's nothing anyone can do about it because I will soon be set free.

Chapter Fifteen

The ward is eerily quiet over the weekend. There's only five of us even here, me, Simon, Jacob, Ethan and Courtney. The rest are either on Home-Leave, in which they spend a certain number of nights at home or on Day-Leave where their families take them out of the hospital for a certain amount of time.

I found it excruciatingly difficult watching Rachel pack her weekend Leave bag, especially considering I'd only unpacked my own two days previously. From what the staff and others say here, I'm unlikely to be awarded Leave for at least a few months. I'm trying not to think about it.

We're allowed to sleep in an extra half-hour later on weekends, and lights-off is put back an hour to compensate too, but the day seems to drag out much longer, with countless hours spent looking out of the windows or listening to the music channel. Whilst the others organise trips to the Games Room to do activities such as clay-sculpting and challenging each other to tournaments on the games console, I spend my time doodling in my notepad and finalising my suicide plans for the following week. I have not been granted the privilege to leave the ward yet, meaning that all of my meetings are either held in one of the therapy rooms on the ward, or in the dining room – a place I like to avoid at all costs. I'm due to start Cognitive Analytical Therapy on Monday after the teacher has come to see me, and I should be starting Psychotherapy on Wednesday. But that's not all. We, as a ward, have Group Therapy after afternoon snack on Thursday's too, an event that Alex has told me is reasonably painful and is usually sparse in terms of attendance, considering that many of the others attempt to hide in order to get out of it. In regards to my suicide plan, I have decided that, as soon as my Section gets lifted on Tuesday, I will refuse all of my fluids and meals. That way the results should be immediate and, according to my calculations at least, I should be dying after the second day due to dehydration and a weakening heart. Dr Ilona said she'd give me until the end of the week in order to sign those papers, which means I have four days maximum in order to die. I may potentially have the weekend too depending on how things work out. I am fully aware though that this might fail, as did my previous attempt at running from the general hospital and dying of exposure.

That being said, I'm hoping that they'll decide treatment would be better for me if I was moved back to the general hospital, considering I would have deteriorated since going to Inpatient. I'll be much closer to my family and they're bound to discharge me sooner than this place will.

I look down at my doodling; only now becoming aware of what I've been sketching. The page is full of skeletons strung from nooses around their necks again. Their heads are drooped with the impact, and their stick bodies are at odd angles as if caught in an imaginary breeze only present within the confines of the paper. There is a fleet of hung skeletons, some hanging from the same rope in order for more to fit on the page. I want to screw it up and throw it away in disgust; this preoccupation with death is evidently getting into my subconscious.

Jacob comes over and sits next to me, attempting to look over my

shoulder at my drawing. I quickly rip it out and stuff it into the pages, leaving a blank piece on top for my next stint of creativity. Jacob is reasonably tall, with an abundance of dark curls on his head. From what I've seen so far, he's seemed to have made it his personal mission to irritate the staff as much as possible.
For example, if you're struggling in the dining room, Jacob will whisper sarcastic encouragements, not in a mean way, but in a way that usually gets the patients eating again and the staff whom he's mimicking to glare at him reproachfully. If someone has had a particularly bad therapy session, Jacob will make jokes and do the most inappropriate dancing in the middle of the lounge or in the corridor directly in front of the CCTV camera, only stopping when he's been shouted at by at least three different members of staff and threatened with supplement. He doesn't hesitate before taking your side, even if you're obviously in the wrong.

Truth no.16 - I've always wanted a big brother. To me, Jacob was the brother that I never had, and I loved him for it.

"What're you drawing?" he asks with interest.
"Nothing," I reply. "Just doodling, really."
He stretches like an indolent cat that has spent the entirety of the day dozing in the sun. He looks at his watch, "almost snack-time," he comments. I remain silent, I feel so awkward with a boy sat next to me and I simply don't know what to do. Throughout my life, disregarding that single year in primary school in which I had a 'boyfriend', I've never really known boys which I would consider as friends. I feel my muscles contract and I try my best to not let the anxiety show on my face.
How can it be snack-time already? I'm so bloated that I look like I'm in the early stages of pregnancy and I still feel full from lunch. I'm already panicking at the prospect of being weighed on Monday morning. I'm bound to have gained weight, especially with all of this food I've had to eat and having to sit around motionlessly all day. He sees the look of discontent on my face

and twists until he is directly facing me. "I know it sucks being here, but you'll get through it," he says reassuringly. "Just take whatever the doctors throw at you, that way you'll be home before you know it."

"How long have you been here?" I ask curiously.

"Six months," he replies sadly. "I got too addicted to the gym, but that's the nature of anorexia." He laughs without humour. "God it was so embarrassing being admitted for it, everyone only seems to think the illness effects girls, so all my mates would take the piss." My 1:1 tells him off for his choice of language.

Truth no.17 – Anorexia doesn't just affect girls. The number of boys being affected by the illness is steadily increasing.

"What about you?" he asks. "You don't have to say if you don't want to, I know I'm nosy."

"I was bullied pretty badly at school, although I'm only beginning to see that now once I'm away from the situation. I'm a perfectionist and the stress of exams caused me a lot of distress, it sort of developed from there really."

He nods sadly. I hear the musical chime of the lift, and the chattering and laughing from the others as they come back from the Games Room. They come straight into the lounge and, after depositing their things on the sofas, head towards the bathrooms to get ready for snack. I look after them longingly. Things would be so much easier if I could go with them and do something to take my mind off things rather than sitting aimlessly in the lounge with staff. Jacob sees me looking after them. "I'm sure can go with them soon," he reassures softly. "You just need to wait until the doctors say you're stable enough first, and then you can go into the Games Room too." I nod sullenly.

"I hate being on 1:1," I mutter angrily.

He laughs suddenly. "You've only been here for less than a week; it took me three months to get off mine!"

The nurse on duty rings the bell and I watch as they form a line outside the dining room. I take a deep breath. As of yet, I have no choice, with the Section hanging over my head like my own allegorical noose I can only comply – unless I'd rather have a tube inserted and force-fed again. But my actions this week will be amended after I'm freed next week. Any weight I've gained will be easily lost after a few days of fasting, and hopefully, I will have died by then anyway.

I let Jacob pull me to my feet and follow him into the dining room towards my waiting snack where I sit next to Courtney and let her complain to me about how Simon had beat her on the games machine. I look at her NG tube covetously, despite how I hated having my own. The nature of the illness makes me worry that I don't look 'sick' considering I don't have one any more too. I shake my head in an attempt to dislodge the uncomfortable thoughts and turn back towards my own plate. I've got to keep going, only then will the monster be proud of me again.

***

On Monday morning, as promised, the teacher comes to see me. He stands in front of me and reaches out a broad hand as he introduces himself as Mr McPherson, the lead teacher who oversees the running of the Education Room. He sits on the adjacent sofa, the others are all in the Education Room for their second lesson so we have the room to ourselves, and asks me about my subjects are my home-school.

"Apart from English, Maths and Triple Science," I begin nervously; "I was also taking Music, History, Geography and Spanish."

Mr McPherson nods as I speak, writing down my subjects in his notebook. "We can do all of those here," he says. "I understand that you'll be coming over to us for an hour a day over the next week and then hopefully for longer the following week, am I right?"

I nod. Panic beginning to settle in at the prospect of re-immersing myself in the preparations necessary before exams. Despite missing learning, I have managed to push school and exams to one side, to brush it under the rug and focus on more omnipresent matters such as my health and subsequent treatment. He looks up at me before I can hide my worries behind the mask of a forced smile. "I was told by Dr Ilona that you were bullied badly back at your home-school, how long was this going on for?"

"The whole time I was there, from year seven to the middle of year eleven when I left. They started leaving me alone more when I became sick."

He nods sadly. "A lot of the young people I've had come through our Education Room have had similar experiences, so coming to the Education Room, or indeed any school again is often a daunting experience. I just want to let you know, though, that such behaviour is not tolerated within the room, and never once have I had to remind anyone of it."

I smile meekly. I want to believe him, but he hasn't had someone like me in the Education Room before, someone in which there's such a vast array of things to mock that people usually can't help themselves. "Your first exam is your Maths paper in just under two weeks, so how about we do some gentle revision tasks to start you off? If, of course, you think this is too much, then we can tone it down."

I nod slowly and defectively. That's less than two weeks away. "Have I missed any already?"

"You've missed about a third," he replies, consulting his notebook once more. "You've got special consideration so you'll still get a grade, so just try to not worry about those." He hands me a sheet of paper upon which is a printing of my exam timetable, he has crossed-off in red ink the ones I've missed. "You're lucky you've got a bit of a lapse now with the exams, it'll give you a chance to settle in more on the ward and get used to things in the Education Room."

"Ok," I reply.

"I know you've missed a large proportion of the content, not just through hospital admission, but I highly expect you weren't feeling the best beforehand either, were you?" he asks.

~ Let Me Go ~

"No," I say, remembering back to those early dark days when no one knew I was ill. I would throw away my lunch and move restlessly beneath the desks. I couldn't concentrate on the classwork and my grades began to slide. When I used to come home from school in the evenings, tired and so cold that I couldn't feel my feet, I would fall into a restless doze, unable to open a book and start my requisitioned homework tasks.

"If on the day you don't want to sit them, please don't feel like you have to. You will get a grade automatically through your special consideration anyway. If you want to have rest-breaks or only sit half the paper, then that will be alright as well. Anything you do will be brilliant, you don't need to get top grades, and your best will always be good enough, no matter what path you chose to take in life."

He leaves the exam timetable with me as he heads back towards the Education Room at the end of the corridor. I look down at it and feel lost within the dates and times, so many papers that I was meant to sit but haven't even had the chance to try. I was predicted the highest grades for all of my subjects, the teachers never doubted my ability considering I consistently handed in homework and studied hard at home. Even during the final grips of my illness when things were at their worse, I would always attempt to learn.

The exam timetable in my hands only heightens my beliefs that my proposed plan for next week is essential. I don't want to fail my exams. Despite my family and staff saying they wouldn't be disappointed but would be proud of my effort instead, I will always be dissatisfied, knowing I had the ability to achieve more. This has to end before I can become an even bigger failure than I am at present.

For once in my life, I think I might hate anorexia for what it has taken away from me.

Chapter Sixteen

I pull myself into a more upright position as Karen enters my room, asks my 1:1 and Rachel to step outside for a while and shuts the door firmly behind her. My Section was removed on Tuesday. Dr Ilona came straight up to the Intensive Treatment Ward that morning in order to try and persuade me into signing the consent forms; she says they can't treat me without them. I had tears streaming from my face as she held my hand with the papers in front of me, a pen clutched shakily in my other. Despite knowing internally that it would be in my best interests to ensign my scrawl within the space provided, I couldn't bring myself to do it. The space seemed to gape in front of me, tucking relentlessly at the tip of the pen, so much so that I was afraid a drop of ink would fall and it would be classed as consent for them to do what they liked with my body.

I'd spoken to the monster earlier that morning whilst using the shower. At first, I was shocked when my 1:1 told me they had to watch me shower. As disgusting as it undoubtedly sounds, I'd been refusing to wash because I was so afraid that one of the girls might come in and see my naked body and call me fat. It was an effort to protect myself from the impending further depletion of my dignity. Eventually, however, I had given in as I became overly self-conscious of my own personal hygiene, especially considering that summer is arriving and the temperatures are steadily increasing. They reassured me that the glass is frosted in certain areas, so that all that can be seen is your head and feet with the rest of your anatomy being an insubstantial blur.

Rachel told me to both undress and dress in the shower cubicle rather than outside where it's dry, that way I get to retain at least a little of my diminished privacy. I could see the monster through the misted plastic of the stall in the mirror. Staff are relatively considerate whilst you wash, despite having to be in the room and looking in your general direction, I was able to communicate with the monster without them getting overly suspicious. It had warned me not to give in, to not place my name at the bottom of those documents that I would be undoubtedly faced with today. It told me that I must follow through with my plan, that this is the only way to stop my illness from hurting anyone else who has the misfortune of getting too close to me.

Refusing any form of consumption is no longer a conscious choice, although I'll freely admit it was at the beginning, now it's such an ingrained and natural process that I barely think before the refusal comes out of my mouth. The only thing that comes out of my mouth are refusals, and the only thing that goes in is air. They've offered to feed me via NG tube if I find the concept of eating myself to daunting and great a challenge, but how can I agree to something that I think is wrong? It would be selfish to oblige with their offers, doing so would only prolong my life, and that's not something that's beneficial to anyone.

She sits on the bed across from me and looks me in the eyes. "I don't know what you're trying to achieve, but it needs to stop." I look down at my lap as she continues. "I can see quite clearly that your body is weakening rapidly, you can barely support yourself." She motions at the pile of pillows behind me that I had methodically placed to support me without it being entirely obvious. I haven't had anything to eat or drink for three days, a feat that has left me barely able to lift my head and all speech is a momentous effort.

My throat feels like a chainsaw has been let loose inside it, my lips are cracked and my mouth is continuously bone dry, no matter how many times I lick my lips or swallow. Whenever I move my head too fast or try and stand up the walls begin to tilt nauseatingly. I keep falling asleep without meaning to and I'm struggling to decipher between what I dream and what is real. I've been trying to keep it as subtle as possible, despite the fact that I've been put on bed-rest again and I can't leave my room even if I want to. I can no longer use the bathroom; whenever I try to stand my legs shake violently and I don't want to risk staff finding out how bad I am. If they realise how weak I've become, they'll call in the team to Section me and they'll save my life.

"Beth," starts Karen sternly. "You know what will happen if you continue to do this. Dr Ilona has come to see you twice each day since your Section was lifted, everyone here wants to support you but we can't if you don't listen and accept the help that's on offer."

She sighs and braces her elbows on her knees to lean further towards me. I decided to take a more subtle approach to my planned suicide. If I starved myself and refused all fluids straight away, they wouldn't hesitate in calling back the team, and so I've complied with roughly a third of what I'm meant to be doing. As a result, I haven't gained anything over the past three weeks, but it has slowly been weakening me so that the final push of complete refusal is much more likely to be successful.

"You're dying. You know that, don't you?" says Karen bluntly. "You're critically underweight, haven't eaten or drunk anything in the past seventy-two hours and we can't even properly monitor you." Karen had to try seven times to draw blood from me this morning, and in the end, when she had finally found a compliant vein in my wrist, had only managed to draw half a vial which isn't enough for the test to be run. "Your vital signs have plummeted back into the unstable category, you're hypoglycaemic and your latest ECG trace shows your heart is beginning to struggle again. You're not in a position to tamper with your health, Beth."

She stands up to leave. "I hope my words have had an effect on you, I'll leave you back with your 1:1 for now so you can think over what's been said and the consequences of your actions. I expect to see you in the dining room for afternoon snack, if not then you can be expecting a visit from the Mental Health Team, they are already aware of your situation and can be here within the hour." Karen leaves, and my 1:1 resumes her position by my bed. I raise my knees and rest my chin on them. It's just under an hour until snack, which means I have barely two hours for my body to hopefully fail. This is going to work, I know it will. Karen is scared, the doctors are too. They know this is serious, but they must be giving me the benefit of the doubt – no one wants to have a Section on their records for the rest of their lives so that, even when trying to move on and forget about the circumstances, it still hangs over you like an unrelenting rain cloud. Is it really worth the risk? Yes, absolutely. Judging by the way I'm feeling at the present moment, I don't have long left. It doesn't even scare me, not really. I fully accepted my impending death that night in the general hospital that seems like years ago. We are all dying; it's just that some of us do it quicker than others.

***

The visiting room is crowded with doctors, nurses and three representatives from the Mental Health Team, all gathered here to incarcerate me once more. I can't stop shaking. Karen keeps putting her hand on my knee to repress the shudders, thinking that I'm doing it for some calorie burning purpose, when in fact it's an automated response to concentrated fear.

I grip my hands firmly in my lap and repress the overwhelming urge to scratch at my skin, to claw at my eyes or rip out a chunk of my hair as punishment for my stupidity. Why hadn't I hidden my symptoms better? If I had paid better attention to masking my true feelings and physical health, then maybe the team wouldn't have been called until tomorrow – and I could be dead by then. The lady in the centre of the trio looks up from her copies of my medical notes and observations. "Miss Thomas, please could you tell us in your own words why we have been called in to review this case today?" I gulp, and flush a brilliant red as the eyes of the room's occupants burn into my own. I can feel the weight of their stares burying into my skin, searching beneath the surface for the fragments of truth that I have kept hidden for so long.

I know what the monster will want me to do, it'll tell me to lie through my teeth, tell them any rubbish that would sway them to let me remain voluntary, which might buy me a little more time in order for my systems to fail. But that didn't work last time, so why should it work now? I take a deep breath and look down at my twisted hands in my lap, the knuckles white and prominent through the skin so that, if I clenched them any harder, they might burst through.

If I can just make them understand why I deserve to die, why my life isn't worth the bother saving, maybe they will let me go. Maybe they will let me slip through the net. Karen will tell my 1:1 to give me some privacy and they will shut my door and let me slip away quietly without a fuss. Dr Ilona will phone my parents in a day or two's time saying how sorry she is that treatment has failed, that my body is being transferred back to the local morgue for my cremation.

If I can make them understand just how worthless and disgusting I am, make them hate me with the same intensity as what I do, then maybe I stand a chance. Or, if not, perhaps they might at least sympathise with me and have pity for my drawn-out, incurable pain and let me have my own say about how I die – that I want to retain what little of my dignity remains and go on my own terms.

~ Let Me Go ~

Truth no.18 – There is no direct cure for anorexia. Sixty percent of suffers will make a full recovery or manage their symptoms in the community, the other forty percent do not improve and are frequently seen in hospitals and treatment programmes until they die. There are therapies, treatment programs, observations and interventions, but there is no magic medicine that can make the thoughts and beliefs go away. Nothing but time itself, and that's something I don't have a lot of at the minute.

The truth it is then. "There are some things in this world that shouldn't be here, things that cause more harm than good," I begin, ignoring the prickly feeling I get whenever I look someone in the eyes. "I am one of them. I am a poison, I seep the love and the life out of those who get too close to me. It would be better off for everyone if I was no longer here to cause pain to those I love. My family could move on and have their lives back again. I know you're probably just thinking that this is my illness talking, but it's not. I want to die… I'm ready. I have nothing in this world worth living for; I have no future apart from a long and painful death at the hands of anorexia. I cannot fight against it, because I don't know how, and even if I did I wouldn't because I don't deserve to live. I want to die on my own terms, not at the hands of my illness. This is not suicide, its letting go of a life that I never really had."

I stop and take a deep breath, blinking rapidly to prevent the tears from falling at the pure and honest truth that I am laying bare onto this chipped coffee table before me. The lady looks at me closely, as she analyses whether I am making this all up or whether this is truly how I feel. I stare back unflinchingly as if we're the only two people in the room.

She nods and smiles sadly; I let go of the breath that I didn't realise I was holding. She believes me. I glance to the left and right and see the other two representatives nod slowly too. They all believe me.

"It's incredibly sad to hear that you feel this way, but

unfortunately we can't just let you die," says the woman quietly. Wait, what?

"There is no doubt that what you're saying is the truth, I can see that in your eyes and with the intensity that you told us, and I thank you for being so brave and honest today. But, we can't let you die." I clench my teeth and fight back the urge to swear and throw something at her, sitting there with her sad little smile as if she understands exactly where I'm coming from. She's going to make me suffer.

Bitch.

"Since coming off of Section, you haven't had anything to eat or drink, and you've even been refusing your medication. Your medical observations of your physical health, not even to mention the effects on your mental health, have drastically deteriorated to within a region that's life-threatening. It's a good thing we came today; I'd say it would be incredibly unlikely that you'd even make it through the night from what your charts are saying." I grit my teeth, what is she rubbing it in for? I am so ridiculously close to it all ending, so close, and now they're going to take that too.

"I'm really sorry, Beth," she begins, and I know what she's going to say as the other two representatives begin to nod in unison like those stupid nodding dogs which can be stuck to the dashboard. "You are detained under Section 3 of the Mental Health Act 1983 for a six month period, unless your psychiatrist takes you off of it sooner. You can, and will, be treated against your will if necessary and will be unable to leave the grounds of this hospital without a signed Section leave form from your doctors. Do you understand?"

I try to open my mouth to swear at the lady and tell her exactly what I think of this idea that, Section or no Section, they couldn't make me live if I didn't want to, and that in the meantime they couldn't make me gain any weight either, but I have no words. I search in my empty, numb brain for the words I need, but they are hiding from me. I look around the room for a mirror, but there isn't one, so I don't know what the monster would like to tell them either.

I stand up and walk out of the room without being dismissed to find my 1:1 waiting for me in the corridor. She tries to wrap her arm around my shoulders supportively, but I shake her off. They're all in this together. They're all out to get me. I can't trust anyone.

I hurriedly wipe away the tear that's escaping down my cheek as I go back into the lounge. I don't want the others to see me in this moment of weakness, and especially not the staff, they might start thinking I'm weak and try and hide extra calories into my food. The lounge is empty and silent, a pack of cards and a book lay in the middle of the floor, as if whoever had left them had gone in a hurry. I blink rapidly and clear my throat to get rid of the thickness of tears. "Do you know where they are?" I ask, aware of how loud my voice sounds in this empty room.

"They're all in the Games Room organising Imogen's leaving party," she replies. "I would take you down but Dr Sergei says you're not to leave the ward yet."

I nod and sit back down in my corner, pulling my knees up to my chest and resting my chin upon them, a Section hanging over my head like some bad omen once more. It's strange to think that, whilst my admission to Birchmoor is only just beginning, someone else's is finally coming to a close. I can't wait to get out of here, but I can't even begin to imagine having a leaving party for myself. The only way I think I'll get out of here is in a coffin.

Chapter Seventeen

My new psychotherapist, a middle-aged lady who introduced herself as Carmen, sits in the office chair opposite me, twiddling a pen absentmindedly between her ringed fingers. I missed what was planned to be my first session last Wednesday due to refusing treatment, meaning Dr Sergei told me I was unable to attend any therapies because I didn't have the energy to positively respond. I look at the clock subtly above her head, I've been in here for almost five minutes, and yet already I can feel the uncomfortable, nauseous sweat coming that has accompanied all therapy sessions to date.

Karen told me that it's highly recommended I stick with the therapy sessions and give them another go, considering I spent the vast majority of my allocated time at CAMHS sitting in silence for the entirety of the sessions.

"How are you finding things at Birchmoor?" she asks thoughtfully. "Are you settling in alright?"

I nod my head in response. She continues to look at me in that interested, analytical way like I am a particularly fascinating specimen under a microscope. I quickly realise that a simple head movement will not quantify as a substantial response.

"Things are ok," I say honestly, sifting through everything that's happened in the two weeks since my admission. "The others are all really nice to me; they always try and include me in whatever they're doing. I want to say that I've settled in, but I don't think anyone ever does in places like these, and I don't want to 'settle in' when I should be at home."

Carmen nods thoughtfully, mulling over what I've said and forming a new question from my response.

"How are you feeling about being on a mixed ward? I know some of our patients have found that difficult to deal with at first," she asks interestedly.

"I was nervous to begin with, the majority of the bullying at school was done by the boys, so I've always assumed they'd all be the same. I feel a bit better about it now, though, they're all friendly and we respect each other's privacy." Apart from having separate bathrooms, there is also a clear rule that no girls are allowed in a boys' room and no boys are allowed in a girls' room unless a member of staff is present.

"How do you think you're finding things eating wise? I understand you had quite a challenging time last week."

I think back to my refusal to eat and drink after coming off of Section, a feat that lasted no longer than three days as my health rapidly deteriorated causing the team to be called in to Section me in order to save my life, again.

"Difficult," I say quietly. "I was taken off of my Section 2 last week and I refused all forms of treatment, after three days the team was called back and I was detained under Section 3."

"How have things been since then?" she asks gently.

"Still difficult," I reply. "I manage about half of my meal plan, the other I have to drink as supplement in the treatment room afterwards."

"What do your parents think of this?"

"I saw them at the weekend; they came into one of the therapy rooms on the ward for a few hours. Mum said that, despite it obviously not being ideal, it will probably help me in regards to treatment. Dad said that it should take some of the guilt and blame off of me eating, considering that I'm not choosing to because if I don't they can restrain me and force-feed me through a tube again."

"And how do you feel about that?" she asks interestedly.

"I don't want it," I reply angrily. "I hate having the NG tube put in, and I hate it that people then have access to my stomach, they could pump in whatever they wanted into me." I glance up towards the clock again, another five minutes has passed. How am I supposed to sit here and engage with this for an hour?

She notices my eyes flash towards the clock. "You keep looking at the time, Beth," she comments, not sounding the least bit perturbed by my palpable insolence.

"It's just... Imo is discharged today and I think the Education Room is ending early so we can go to her leaving party."

Carmen considers this for a moment. "I understand that she's leaving, and I'm guessing that you'll probably want to say goodbye?"

I nod fervently.

"I really want to wish her luck for the future, she's such a lovely person and she always makes me smile. I don't know what time the party is being held though?"

"I don't think it's due to start for another ten minutes, shall we finish up our session early today so that you can attend?" she asks.

"Yes please," I say gratefully.

I adjust my position on the chair; I can manage another ten minutes of this.

"How are you feeling about your exams?" she asks.

"Alright, I guess," I reply. "A bit stressful considering I haven't finished all of the content and am only allowed to do a limited amount of revision." My parents had brought my revision guides and class notes with them when they visited on Saturday, along with some spare toiletries and my piano music. Mr McPherson said they have a special music teacher that comes in twice a week to tutor piano, guitar and singing and that I could start going through my Grade 6 prep again if I felt ready.

"I can imagine," she sympathises kindly. "GCSE's are tough exams, especially considering the amount of content you're supposed to learn beforehand. I'm really impressed that you're giving it a go, though. Some of the people I've worked with in the past used hospitalisation as a sort of excuse, if you like, as a means of boycotting the exam period entirely. But, no matter what grades you receive, the most important thing is that you're trying – and that's something no one can ever take away from you."

I nod, deep in thought. Everyone keeps telling me about how inspirational it is that I'm choosing to sit my exams, especially considering I've missed so much of the work and have special consideration already.

"I think my Maths exam went ok," I say reflectively. "There were a couple questions on algebra and binomial probability that I couldn't complete, but on the whole I was surprised at how much I remembered, especially considering I've missed so much school and never really liked Maths in the first place."

"Indeed," she says. "What exam have you got next, do you know?"

"I've got a Geography paper tomorrow and then English the day after. In two weeks, though, I'll be done." I look towards the clock once more and am surprised that our agreed ten minutes is almost up. She sees me looking and turns her chair to consult it too.

"Would you like to end here?" she asks. "You have another thirty-five minutes if you would like?"

"Can I go now, please," I reply earnestly, already planning what I'm going to say to Imogen at her party.

"Of course," she says. "I'll see you the same time next week. I hope things improve for you and your exams go well!"

"Thanks," I say. She leads me back outside and hands me over to my 1:1 who is waiting for me in the corridor outside. She heads towards the Nurse's Office at the end of the corridor to write up

my notes as, despite the fact that the rules of confidentiality
prevent her from telling others of what's been discussed (unless,
of course, it could be harmful to myself or others) she has to
make a note that she's seen me and I've responded
appropriately.

The ward is strangely quiet. I thought they were finishing up
early?

"So," says my 1:1 casually, "how was the therapy?"

"Brilliant," I say sarcastically. "How was waiting in the
corridor?"

"Thrilling."

"I bet," I reply. "Where is everyone, are they still in the
Education Room?"

She looks at me dejectedly as she leads me into the deserted
lounge, bags and books left strewn over the chairs and floor as if
they'd left in a hurry.

"Imo's parents arrived earlier than we expected. They said the
traffic was reported to be particularly bad going west and they
wanted to get home before it started getting dark."

"Oh," I reply disappointedly. "They were going to wait, but they
needed the Games Room later for a training session so they had
to do it early anyway."

"Have we missed it completely?" I ask.

I'm afraid so, pet," she says, flopping down into one of the only
spare chairs that don't have some possession upon it. "The others
will be back up in a minute; I think Imo's already gone." I nod
quietly and sit down in my little corner under the table. I wanted
to say goodbye to her, but I understand sometimes these things
can't be helped. I squeeze my eyes shut tightly wondering in a
childish manner that, if I can think hard enough, she might know
I'm thinking of her and wishing her luck. 'Be safe, Imo,' I pray
silently. 'I hope everything goes well for you in the future and
you can get your life back from your eating disorder. Stay
strong!' I look up and find her handprint, its fresh blue paint
only just beginning to dry. It's a permanent reminder of the time
she spent here and the difference she made.

~ Let Me Go ~

***

I'm sitting in my room when I first hear the screaming. I've just had my dinner supplement, and have the urge to hurt myself as a punishment for drinking it. Rachel is in the lounge watching some reality TV show with the others so it's only me and my 1:1 in the room. She sits on the chair, absentmindedly flicking through a magazine she found and confiscated in the lounge. I think it has diet tips inside. I'm trying to read my book, but because of the strength of my feelings and thoughts after eating, I find myself reading the same line over and over and yet taking in nothing more than the first word.

It starts as a low wail, so slight that I may have been able to convince myself that it's nothing but the wind. But then it increases in both intensity and velocity, from a howl to a shriek to a scream of concentrated terror and pain. What are they doing to them for them to produce that sound?

My 1:1 looks up at me as I jump as the noise starts up again. I stare fearfully in the direction of the treatment room. It sounds like someone is being tortured.

"It's ok," she reassures me. "It's just a feed. I know it's distressing at first, you'll get used to it."

I remain silent as I face the room and the horror within it, as if my eyes are burning through the bricks and plaster and witnessing the monstrosity of the scene it's concealing. It sounds almost alien, a sound that shouldn't be made, let alone by a child.

"Haven't you heard it before now, it happens twice a day?" she asks.

I shake my head. No, no I haven't and I never want to again.

"Unfortunately, one of our patients here needs restraint to follow their plan. I know it's not ideal and hard to hear but it's done for their own good and they're in no physical pain. I guess you wouldn't have heard the feeds because you're mostly in the lounge; the others always turn the TV up or put music on at that time," she flicks through her magazine absentmindedly, and I wonder how people can carry on with their activities whilst something as profound as this is happening.

"Who is it?" I ask quietly.

"We're not supposed to talk about patients' care-plans," she says calmly. "If it upsets you, we can go to the lounge now. It won't take more than fifteen minutes," she suggests.

Of course it upsets me; it would upset anyone to hear someone in such internal agony and despair. I shake my head and sit there with my book in my lap throughout the person's entire feed. I'm unsure of whether it's one of the boys or one of the girls. They want help, but there's nothing I can do but acknowledge it. I never read a word, and instead, bear silent witness to the suffering and screams for help on the other side of the walls.

Chapter Eighteen

There is a new nurse on Intensive today. Well, new as in I've never met her at least. She introduces herself first thing in the morning to me as Steph and says that Karen has been covering her shifts whilst she was on a family holiday in Portugal. She is overly bubbly and very enthusiastic, with a short pixie cut that bounces merrily upon her shoulders whenever she walks.

After breakfast and morning medication is given, of which I'm only required to take potassium, calcium and magnesium supplements, she calls us all into the lounge for a brief meeting before we are needed in the Education Room. Once each seat is taken with the others mumbling quietly amongst themselves as they theorise over what has happened, Steph enters and addresses us at large.

"Right," she begins perkily. "I know you're all aware that Imogen was discharged two days ago."

She is abruptly cut-off by a collective moan as if they've already guessed what is to come.

"Oh, come on!" she says jokingly. "There's going to be a new admission this afternoon on the ward, her name is Poppy and she'll be rooming with Courtney." A few heads turn towards Courtney with mixtures of pity on their faces. Jacob punches her playfully on the shoulder which I assume is his way of showing support. All their faces are drawn and grim as if they've been given the news of the death of a pet rather than an admission. Is this how they reacted when they were told I was coming?

"How old is she?" asks Alex.

"She's sixteen, we don't know anything else about her yet, only that she's coming mid-afternoon."

Steph leaves in order to check that the teachers have arrived in the Education Room and that they're ready for us to come down. I can feel a knot of panic growing inside of me like a beast, gnawing away at my insides as it increases in strength. I know I haven't gained weight since being admitted, thanks to the period of starvation last week, but I'm bound to have gained when I step onto those scales come Monday morning. What if the new admission is skinnier than me? What if she's so thin and frail that I'm not good enough any more? What if she's done better than me and makes the weight I've lost look like a joke?

My head pulses with these thoughts and unanswered questions, and I can hear the worry of the others in the room as they contemplate the same thing. "Do you reckon she'll be, you know…" asks Courtney nervously, wrapping her blanket more tightly around herself to obscure her tiny frame.

"I expect so," says Simon sadly. "They all are, aren't they?"

Jacob stands from his seat next to Ethan on the sofa. "Come on, guys, I'm sure it'll be alright, you never know she might come in and be really compliant."

"Speak for yourself," mutters Courtney miserably.

"Just remember how you were feeling when you were admitted, it's not her fault and we just need to try and accept that what's on the outside does not necessarily represent what's on the inside."

"Oh, puke!" says Alex, throwing one of the discarded cushions at him. Jacob catches it deftly with one hand and throws it back where it hits him straight in the face.

"Come on, people, education time!" says Steph as she re-enters the room. They grumble as they file out of the room, a few attempt to hide beneath piles of blankets and cushions, or else duck behind the sofa in order to remain unnoticed and skip the lesson. It's needless to say that this works to no avail, Steph knows all of their tricks, and in the end everyone makes it to the Education Room on time. The only two people who don't come are Rachel, who has therapy and Ethan.

The Education Room consists of a single classroom, with various displays of work from different subjects around the room. There are pieces of artwork hanging from the ceiling, giant cut-out flowers, intricate drawings of animals and indistinguishable artistic interpretations. There is one large table in the middle, upon which stand pots of pencils, reams of papers and various are other pieces of stationary. There are no scissors or pencil sharpeners out, these are kept in a locked box inside Mr McPherson's desk.

Each 'student' (as we're referred to upon entering the Education Room as if by just crossing the threshold we become a different, and more normalised person entirely) sits around the desk and, should they need tutoring, a teacher sits next to them.

There are three teachers within the Education Room, an English teacher, a Maths teacher and a Science teacher, each one capable of teaching from Key Stage Two to college level depending on what's required. I take my seat and Jacob slouches down moodily next to me. I suppress a sly smile.

"Ready to learn, Jacob?" I tease sarcastically.

He notices my tone and gives me a scathing look. He presses his finger subtly to his lips before twisting the phone in his hands to show me he's playing *Candy Crush* under the table. I raise an eyebrow questioningly, the formation of 'how?' upon my lips. He nods pointedly towards Courtney across the room who appears to have her head buried in her book, but one subtle glance under the table tells me she's doing exactly the same. "If you don't tell, you can have a go as soon as you get off 1:1," he bargains. I nod my head and smile to show that I won't tell and pull my revision guide and a piece of paper towards me, smiling slightly despite the fact I have my Biology paper tomorrow morning.

***

My eyes scan frantically and nervously around the dining room, like a bird wary of a lurking predator, as I search for the unknown face we're all been expecting, but there is no one other than the usual seven of us, one nurse and three HCA's in the room. I release the breath I didn't realise I'd been holding. She's not here yet.

I can see the others doing the same, the identical manic look in their eyes and the anxious crinkling of their brows as they scan for the new admission too, both curious and afraid of what they'll see looking back.

"Come on Beth," says Steph, who is supervising our table, as she pushes some mashed potato onto her fork. "You need to make a start," she encourages. "You have three minutes and then I'll have to ask you to leave the dining room." It's not just me who's slow to start today, there's a greater quantity of encouragements and more warnings for us to stop smearing our food and jiggling our legs under the table. We're all on edge, perturbed by the looming prospect of meeting the new admission. The microcosmic ward like a symbolical snow-globe, tipped upside down and roughly shaken so that our vision is clouded once more.

"Simon," calls a HCA on the other table, "I saw you drop that food, that will have to be replaced you know." I hear him grumble darkly in response. "If you use language like that then I'll send you out," she warns.

"Fine then," he shouts angrily. "Why would I want to eat all these fucking calories anyway?" He shoves his chair back with a harsh squeal before slamming his uneaten lunch down on the tray with such force that the plate cracks clean down the centre. I hear him shouting and punching the walls in the corridor as another member of staff tries to placate him.

Steph sighs. "Carry on with your meals please," she says calmly. "I'll be speaking to Simon afterwards." Rachel looks across at her, and I can see the glint of a tear in her eye. "I don't find it helpful eating with Simon when he behaves like that," she says quietly. "It's hard enough already without him talking about calories and everything." We nod our heads in honest agreement.

"I agree that it would be easier for both Simon and the rest of you if you eat separately, that way you'll be excused from his behaviour and he can have more support. I'll speak to the doctors and this will be put in place by afternoon snack, so try not to worry. If you want to talk about this after lunchtime then I'm more than happy to, but you need to keep going because I don't want to be handing out supplements."

I look down at my plate, at the pile of mashed potato, the mound of peas and the breaded chicken, wishing desperately that I had some sort of power that could burn the calories away by look alone. I hold the knife and fork shakily in my perspiring hands, the very notion of even holding cutlery feeling like an alien concept after all those months of eating the bare minimum to survive and continue losing weight. The mashed potato is heaped and I look at Alex's portion next to me. His is much smaller than mine. I check mine again, to make sure that my eyes aren't playing tricks on me but, if anything, the volume of potato has seemingly increased in the short space of time I turned my gaze. How are they doing this? I look across at Alex's once more, but find that his portion has significantly shrunk, despite the fact I know he hasn't touched it yet because he's eating his peas. I think the size of his chicken breast is considerably smaller than mine too.

"Beth," warns Steph. "Don't look at anyone else's; focus on your own please. That's your second warning, if I have to give you another then you'll be asked to leave and will have it replaced later." I look down at my plate despairingly, irrational thoughts beginning to swirl around my head as I panic. What if, by mashing the potato, the calories are dispersed and multiply? Did the cook use any cream when she made this, if so how much fat does it contain?

Steph leans towards me and whispers into my ear. "You can do it," she murmurs encouragingly. "I know you can do it."

I turn towards her and mouth silently, "Alex's portion is smaller than mine." Steph looks subtly across at Alex where he is meticulously spearing one pea onto his fork at a time. "No it isn't," she whispers back. "Everyone's portions are exactly the same; you know the cook measures everything out exactly."

I look back at my plate and see that the pile of mashed potato has grown again. Are they trying to trick me? I can practically see the calories dancing across my plate, laughing and mocking me in their thousands. I can't do this. I'm being weighed on Monday, if I eat this then I'm bound to gain weight, especially considering my helping is so much bigger than everyone else's.

The prospect of eating the food in front of me makes me what to throw the plate against the wall, watch as it smashes and smears before falling into a heap on the floor. I want to look the other way so that I don't even have to acknowledge what's before me. Without even consciously making the choice, as if I knew to some degree that I wouldn't complete the meal upon entering the dining room, I push my chair under and walk away. My 1:1 is waiting for me in the corridor outside. She leads me back into the lounge and, after she attempts to get me to play a game with her, I sit beneath the table in my little corner. Did I do the right thing? I'm not sure. Simon sits on the sofa once more, his hand wrapped in an ice pack.

The HCA next to him nudges him meaningfully and he turns begrudgingly towards me.

"I'm sorry," he mutters.

I shrug as if it's no big deal, but in reality it really is. Rachel's right, the last thing I want to hear in the dining room is someone

talking about the calories that's in what I'm about to try and eat.
At the prospect of supplement, which I know is a necessity that's
lurking around the corner, my thoughts change to fears of
Fortisip. What if Steph measures out too much? A couple
millilitres extra are a significant amount of calories. Would it
have been better if I'd eaten the meal? At least that way my body
would have had to work, to some extent at least, to break down
the sudden bombardment of calories.

I'm called back into the dining room once more as soon as the
thirty minutes for the main meal is up and the room has been
vacated. I am the only one needing supplement for lunch today
as Simon will have his later with his feed. I sit down next to
Steph and look at the two full cups for supplement before me. I
squint and see that the calories are swimming around in their
containers, laughing at me because they knew they'd get me
anyway, whether I had my meal or not.

I look at Steph uncertainly. "Have you measured it?" I ask
nervously.

She sighs. "Of course I have, I've been doing this for many years.
This is the correct amount of replacement that you require for
missing your meal. You have ten minutes to drink it, if you
refuse this then we will feed you via NG."

I nod, I've heard all of this many a time before. My shoulders
shake with suppressed sobs and my face is streaked with tears as
I sip fearfully at my replacement, hating myself for swallowing it
and letting it wrap around my bones. I am the only one to blame.

***

We are not allowed to see the new admission and we know
immediately, as if by some sixth sense, that something is terribly,
terribly wrong. From the lounge, we can hear the stuttering beat
of her heart monitor, stalling from time to time so that we
collectively hold our breaths and wait despairingly for the next
beep. We sit rather closer together than we would normally have
done, cramped onto the sofas, half in each other's laps as we

wait. I'm not sure exactly what we're waiting for, but waiting seems the only appropriate thing to do at this moment in time. They had to call in an extra Agency nurse. Steph is closely monitoring the new admission, there is a HCA in the corridor outside in order to quickly pass messages and another nurse is in the Nurse's Office, poised to phone for the doctors at any moment. We saw oxygen tanks and the defibrillator brought across from the treatment room outside the doctors' offices. Something is terribly, terribly wrong. Her parents are in the room with her, that much we do know, something which I didn't realise was even allowed.

Parents are only able to glimpse their child's bedroom on admission day, and any visitors from then until discharge are only able to go into the therapy rooms on the ward if you're not permitted to go to the ground floor. Her parents have been with her for hours, long after we returned from the education and heard the first hesitant beeps from the monitor. As I lean against Rachel beside me and wrap my arm reassuringly around Courtney it dawns on me, they don't think she's going to live for much longer.

Chapter Nineteen

The bathroom is lit by the dim orange glow emitted from the ceiling light. I stand before the mirror, my face so close that my breath fogs the glass as I search its depths desperately for the monster. My current 1:1 has her earphones in and is sitting on a chair in the corner looking down at her phone. She doesn't pay much attention to you when you're in the bathroom, and so she has become the favourite to ask for supervision for those girls who haven't earnt their privacy back yet.

I can see the monster lurking in the back, in the space just beyond what my eyes can firmly see, so that it's nothing more than an indistinguishable black, pacing mass.

I think it's angry with me, and it doesn't take a genius to work out what for.

It gradually comes closer, clawing itself up out of the depths until my reflection is replaced with its own. Its eyes are no more than mean slits, and it rubs its claws deftly as it considers me. I don't know what I'm wanting it to say to me, perhaps reassurance that I've tried my best, or perhaps to shout at me

and give a voice to the feelings inside which I can't express. It
looks me up and down with a mixture of discontent and disgust
written plainly across its face. Its eyes seem to burn painfully
into my skin as I struggle to retain eye contact.
I saw the new admission, Poppy, earlier today when I was
walking past her room to the lounge. I hadn't meant to look in,
but my eyes had seemingly turned of their own accord to the
frail form supported by the mound of pillows on her bed. Even
after the brief glimpse I had of her, I can tell that this is serious.
She doesn't even look alive, she looks like a skeleton. The
monster's revulsion of my body mirrors my own.
Why don't I look like that?
"I thought I told you to be skinny," says the monster quietly. *"You
make me sick. You've been admitted to a Unit with Anorexia Nervosa
and yet you barely even look underweight. You saw Poppy today, that's
dedication. You should look like that, and yet you obviously don't. Why
is that, I wonder?"* The monster pauses to let its words sink in, and
I feel as my legs start to tremble as the force of what it's saying
hits me. *"You should have tried harder whilst you had the chance,"* it
continues, its voice full of irrefutable displeasure. *"But you
wouldn't listen; you were always too greedy for your own good. You
only restricted to an apple a day within the final weeks before
admission, why didn't you do this sooner? Why did you even eat the
apple? It was all purely out of greed, you couldn't even fast properly."*
I wish it would shout and scream profanities at me, anything
would be better than this calculated, malignant disappointment.
"I tried," I whisper back. "I tried."
"Where's your heart monitor then, fatty?" asks the monster. *"Why
can't I hear your stuttering heartbeat?"*
I shake my head and repeat what Karen told me on my
admission day. "They said I didn't need one because of how long
I spent being monitored in the general hospital. They said that
considering I'd been detained for a while under the Section
beforehand, I was more stable than if I'd bypassed the general
hospital and come straight to Inpatient. We don't know her
circumstances," I add, an edge of pleading to my tone that I can't

seem to shake away.

"*They're lying,*" it returns smoothly. "*They're all lying in order to fatten you up even more than what you are already. You had so better not have gained weight when they weigh you on Monday, if you have I don't know what I'm going to do to you. You're a failure, you always were and you always will be.*"

The monster's threat hangs like a stagnant poison in the air before me, as I watch as it slinks away and merges with the shadows once more. I look back at my reflection, at the fat I can see bubbling beneath the surface of my skin. I want to smash the mirror so that I never have to see myself looking like this again, and then use the shards to punish myself for having the audacity to live like this.

I jump as the bathroom door suddenly swings open as Rachel and Courtney come in with a member of staff to supervise them using the toilet.

I turn hastily and try to remove the look of horror and disgust from my face. No one can know that I talk to the monster; I know instinctively things will become an awful lot worse for me if people ever find out.

I follow the line into the dining room as the bell rings announcing snack time with my shoulders slumped inwards in an attempt to shield myself from further pain. My head is slumped so low that I can barely see where I'm going due to the weight of the monster's anger and accusations, something which is highly ironic and seems to represent my life as a whole in itself. As the monster told me, and I have no reason to doubt it, I am not good enough, and perhaps I've been kidding myself into believing that I ever will be.

Truth no.19 – Anorexia Nervosa is a highly competitive illness.

***

The questions leap at me and slap me like fish before diving back into the depths of the pages, a whole collection of imperatives telling me to do things that I don't think I can at the moment. *Describe. Explain. Define. Analyse. Suggest.* Line after line waiting to be filled with answers that I'm not sure I know. Despite my efforts, I can't get into the right mind-frame to concentrate on the Biology paper before me.

Thoughts swirl nauseatingly around the confines of my head, pulling against their restraints as they strain to be released. I want to hurt myself for having eaten snack after what the monster said to me. I want to go to the bathroom and stick my fingers down my throat and flush the calories down the toilet before they have a chance to do any more damage. I can practically feel the fat wrapping itself gleefully around my bones, stretching my clothes and making my skin feel unnaturally tight. I want to get up and run for an extended period of time in an effort to burn them all away before they get too comfortable. I shake my head to try and forcibly clear away the thoughts. I have to concentrate, otherwise I don't stand a chance of passing and then, not only will I be fat, but I'll be a fat failure too.

I press my pen into the paper, willing my brain to acknowledge the question and form a relevant answer, there's nothing I can do about snack now. I try to ignore my 1:1 staring at me from across the desk, endeavouring to block out the whole world and focus entirely on the task before me. At least they're no mirrors in here. I bend over my paper as I begin to steadily write, whether it's correct or not I don't know but, as said by both staff and my parents, I'm sitting them, and that's got to be something at least.

***

I wait outside the Nurse's Office with the others, my perspiring hands tapping repeatedly in agitation against my thighs. Everyone is silent, as if there's some unspoken rule that prevents anyone from even breathing too loudly. Alex is sitting on the floor, his head buried in his hands, Simon looks distractedly at the ceiling and Courtney is hiding beneath the safety of her blanket. The others are still in the bathroom being supervised as they use the toilet. No one has privacy the night before or the morning of weigh-day. The only patient not present is Poppy, she's going to be wheeled in whilst the rest of us go back to our beds where we'll attempt to 'sleep' but in reality will stew over whatever number we've been given.

Please, please don't let me have gained.

The nurse calls us in one by one, a judge announcing a death sentence to an innocent defendant. I would rather die than gain any weight. Alex shuffles through the door and into the treatment room as his name is called and Rachel comes out, tears beginning to fall as she brushes angrily pass us and heads back towards our room. Jacob comes out of the boys' bathroom and joins the line at the back and begins clicking his fingers hurriedly in apprehension of what's to come. The line gets shorter and I get closer to the front, each person coming out in varying states of distress of what they've seen on the scales.

Please, please don't let me have gained.

I am next. Simon comes out of the room, his head folded forwards in defeat and my name is called. Without even telling my legs to move, my feet carry me through the Nurse's Office and into the treatment room. The night nurse holds a large, red folder in her hands with records of all patients' heights and weights. The scales stand before her. I can feel my heart beating in my throat, pulsing in the tips of my fingers and toes. I feel sick. What if I get on the scale and it breaks because I'm too heavy? What if my number is too high and the nurse laughs at me? What if I'm heavier than everyone else? I lick my lips nervously.

Please, please don't let me have gained.

"Bethany Thomas?" asks the nurse.

I nod. I seem to have left my voice in the line outside with the others. "Can you take off your bra, trousers and shoes please?" she asks, although I know it's not a question. I don't have a choice in the matter and nor do any of the others.

I stand by the scales in my long-sleeved top so that the nurse can't see the reopened wounds snaking up my arms. "When you're ready," she says in a bored manner, leaning over me and waiting for the number below. I'm not ready; I don't think I ever will be. When I was restricting, I use to find pleasure in weighing myself, in watching as the number crept further and further away from where I'd begun. I don't know what I'll do if I see it creep back up again. She clears her throat noisily.

I close my eyes and step onto the scales, hearing the scratching of her pen on paper as she makes a record of it. I glance down and gasp. I am 2kg heavier. I step off hurriedly and fumble with my clothes as I re-dress myself. I am 2kg heavier.

My 1:1 is waiting for me outside, she leads me back to my room and I get clumsily back into bed. I am two kilograms heavier. I lie there stunned, and suddenly I can feel exactly where that additional 2kg have gone. I can feel that my pyjamas are hanging off of me that little bit less, that the mattress is compressed slightly more beneath me. I am 2kg heavier. I look across at Rachel, but see no more than a vague form shielded by her duvet; a safety cocoon in which you could kid yourself that weight doesn't matter. But it does, weight will always matter, at least to us anyway.

I roll up my sleeves beneath the covers. "Hands where I can see them please," says my 1:1 sternly. I grip the top of the duvet with my hands, exposing my arms beneath the sheets. I push my head under the covers and bite down hard, feeling as my teeth break the skin and as the iron taste of blood seeps onto my tongue.

I am 2kg heavier, 2 fucking kg heavier.

Chapter Twenty

There seems to be a monotonous, predictable ritual to the moods of the inhabitants on Intensive. Sunday nights and Monday mornings are undoubtedly the worst. On Monday, the lounge is practically silent as we sit huddled beneath blankets and either worry that because we haven't gained weight there'll be a diet increase or coming to terms with what the scales have told us and our subsequent alteration in BMI. Even Jacob becomes sullen and drawn as the evening draws to a close in anticipation of the morning. Things get better as the week progresses until the ward reaches a peak on Friday, the night before the majority of its inhabitants go on some form of Leave or have a visit from their family.

Without fail, my parents and Natalie have been up to see me every week, excluding the week after my admission. I'm allowed to go off of the ward now in order to use the visitor's lounges downstairs. My 1:1, for once, gives me some privacy and waits on a chair outside of the room whilst I see my family. They always come with smiles on their faces and stories to tell me about their weeks, despite the fact I've heard them all before as I call them every night too, but it's just nice to hear their voices. A familiarity that reminds me of home and the life I've had to leave behind. I found the last time they came to see me more difficult than usual, although it was of no fault of their own, so my own mood wasn't particularly buoyant that weekend either. My school had their final leaving photo taken in front of the sports field a mere two weeks after I was hospitalised. My parents brought me my copy of the photo to decorate my room, but so far it's only succeeded in decorating the underside of my bed. My face is not amongst the sea of my peers, and my name is not listed within the year group, it's as if I never existed at all and those four and a half years I spent there were all for nothing. The overall mood dips suddenly again on Sunday evening, as people come to terms with the fact that they have to go through the process of the week again before they can see their loved ones and procrastinating about the impending weigh-in the following morning. It's an incessant loop with no off-switch available.

On Tuesday morning, Karen calls me into the dining room to have a catch-up with me and to discuss the changes to my care-plan that have been decided on in the most recent meeting with the doctors. She leans her elbows casually on the table and observes me quietly as I fidget, instantly assuming the worst and that she'll tell me I have to stay here for at least year, double my target weight and increase my meal plan by another two hundred calories. I remain silent and wait for her to start.

"It was handed over that you've gained two kilos," she states matter-of-factly. "How are you after knowing this?" She goes straight in with probably the most significant and difficult to answer question possible considering the circumstances that have brought me here. I want to shrug and pretend that it doesn't matter, but I can't because it does. It really does.

"Not good," I reply quietly.

She seems to sense that I don't want to enlighten upon this any more than what I have done so already. "I know it must have been difficult for you, but it's an essential aspect of recovery. You're still critically underweight and have quite a way to go until you reach your target weight, and even then you'll be on the cusp of being healthy." I nod, still not feeling overly reassured. "You must be feeling good, though, that you're exams are almost over!" she says, trying to change the subject and prevent my mood from diminishing further in response to my weight. "You can't have many left now, is it three?"

"One more tomorrow," I reply, as my lips raise a fraction of an inch into a slight smile. Things should be easier once exam season is over. I'm not expecting a drastic change, but at least it's one thing less to worry about.

"That's great!" she says happily. "Now, let's move on to your feedback so you can go back to the Education Room to do some last minute revision. Dr Sergei has decided to give you five minutes of toilet privacy which means that, should you be in the bathroom for longer than five minutes, a staff member will come in and supervise you. You haven't earnt back your bathroom privacy yet, so you'll still need someone to supervise you when you shower." I nod. I still don't understand how privacy has to be 'earnt' back in this place, what did I ever do wrong to lose it in the first place, I thought it was a basic human right?

He's also decided to change your 1:1 Level overnight. During the day, you will still be 1:1 Level Four: Arm's reach, but during the night you'll be Level Two: Fifteen minutes. Someone will come and check on you every fifteen minutes, as the name suggests, but if this goes well then you're likely to gradually come off of 1:1 during the day shift as well. It's also been suggested, although please note that this is a suggestion and nothing definite yet, that you might be given some Leave with your family over the summer holidays."

"I can go home?" I ask, shocked at my sudden change of fortune. "No, not for a while yet," she replies. My frown returns with full force. "We'll start you off with fifteen minutes Leave outside of the Unit, and then build you up to managing snacks and meals outside of the hospital." I shake my head, there's no way in a million years that I can ever do that. How can they expect me to eat outside the hospital when it's so ridiculously easy to refuse? Karen ignores this and continues. "We'll trial you outside of the hospital first, though, with a walk with a member of staff as I understand you haven't been outside in quite a long time." I nod once more, the only part of the 'real world' I have seen in a while is the small slither of sky visible through the windows. She taps her hands lightly on the table, a clear sign that this meeting is drawing to a close. "Do you have any questions?" she asks pleasantly.

"No, thank you," I reply.

"I think you're doing really well, Beth, just stay strong and keep doing what you're doing." I thank her again as I leave before she leads me back out to the corridor where my 1:1 is waiting. As soon as the door shuts and I become acclimatised to the change of scenery, I notice that something's wrong. I can hear the same wailing and screaming as what I had done previously. I look at Karen nervously. "Don't worry," she says reassuringly. "The doctors are just starting the feed whilst I talked to you; I'm going there now to take over." She smiles at me and motions for my 1:1 to take me into the Education Room. I allow myself to be lead inside, automatically breathing a sigh of relief once the door swings shut behind us and those horrific sounds are silenced. I look around the room and scan the faces to see who's not here. Ethan isn't but that's usual, he's mute so I highly doubt he's even capable of making those noises. The only other person missing is, "Simon," I whisper.

***

It's strange not having someone watching over me, although it felt distinctively unnatural at first having some stranger watch me sleep. I'm not accustomed to this sudden freedom that's available to me – although, of course, I'm still checked on every fifteen minutes, so my freedom isn't that great. I expect Rachel to be pleased when she comes into the room after using the bathroom, considering that her privacy has been reduced too as an effect for my 1:1 always being in the room, but when she comes in I can tell immediately that something is wrong. I ask her what the matter is and if there's anything I can do to help, but she ignores me and continues to forcibly put away her toiletries. I sigh quietly to myself and roll over to face the wall and give her some privacy; she evidently wants to be left alone. I hear the gentle murmur of the springs as she settles down into bed. After a minute of silence, in which I contemplate saying something encouraging and supportive, Rachel begins to talk. "I hate it here," she says quietly. I don't answer, and instead just listen as she talks openly. "I don't want to be here any more. I'm sick of being trapped on this fucking ward." There's a pause as she composes herself before continuing. "I'm sorry to bother you."

"You're not," I reply. "If you need to talk then talk, I can listen for as long as you want."

"No, I'm just being stupid," she replies sadly and I hear the gentle creak of springs as she moves into a more comfortable position. "I've just had a pretty bad therapy session with Carmen today, it brought up a lot of things I've been avoiding."

"You're not stupid; you just need help like everyone else does here. I would say that therapy's helpful and good for you, but I hate it myself too," I reply.

"I know right," she says. "All that 'how does this make you feel?' nonsense.'

I attempt to mimic Carmen's high-pitched, slow and deeply thoughtful voice. "I see you've been admitted to a psychiatric hospital, how does that make you feel?"

Rachel laughs. "I hear staff watch you go to the toilet, how does that make you feel?"

I giggle quietly.

Rachel sighs heavily. "Thanks for cheering me up, roomie. The 'loony bin' is really getting to me; it's nice to have someone who's finally off 1:1 to talk to."

"Gee," I reply sarcastically. "This is the only time available in my

diary to fit not being stared at it in!"
"Good night," chuckles Rachel.
"Night," I reply as I smile into my pillow.

***

I'm awoken in the early hours of the morning, and at first I'm not
sure what for, whether I heard the footsteps of staff or had a
particularly bad dream that I can no longer remember. I roll over
and punch my pillow into a more comfortable position,
burrowing beneath the duvet in search of sleep. I hear a dull
thud coming down the corridor and at first I don't move,
thinking it's just the staff doing observations. When I hear it for
the second time I sit upright, convinced there is something
wrong. I consider waking Rachel, but she looks so peaceful in
sleep and it's probably my mind playing tricks on me, as minds
generally do within the cloaking of night.
I slip out of bed and pad softly down the corridor, seeing nothing
out of place other than a discarded book on the floor. I look
towards the light from Nurse's Office at the end, but the door is
firmly shut and I can't hear anything unusual coming from there
apart from the gentle tapping on keyboards and murmur of
chatter. I hear the thump again. I turn, my heart quickening in
my chest as I make my way towards the lounge, scared of what I
might find within.
The room is dark, and I can scarcely make out the hulks of
furniture within the room. I feel my way around nervously and
switch on the lamp in the corner, enough to see by but not
enough to wake the others or make the staff suspicious. I hear
sudden movement behind me and I turn to see Alex curled
tightly on the floor, his hair dishevelled and his face turned away
from me. "Alex?" I ask quietly. "What on earth are you doing,
it's the middle of the night." He doesn't reply, but instead seems
to twitch and move slightly.
I move towards him and, as I do so, he rolls over and I see
exactly what he's doing. He has a zip-tag around his throat. I

begin to panic. Can you actually strangle yourself? You have to move your arms to strangle yourself, don't you? My breath begins to come in panic gasps. Oh god.

I am frozen with fear. Ice runs through my veins and solidifies my limbs, so that I find I can neither move or talk even if my brain could catch up and process what is happening before me. I have no idea how I remain standing.

"Alex… Alex…" I murmur despairingly, my lips numb and my tongue uncooperative. Why won't my fucking voice work? I'm screaming inside my head, an ear-splitting crescendo that I can't flip the switch to release. He twists himself to get a better grip on the cord. I know in an instant that he's serious. I try to move towards him, but the ice is so thick in my limbs that I'm entirely paralysed with fright. I open my mouth to try and shout and scream for help, but all that is coming out is a silent gasp. I'm screaming inside my head, pleading for him to stop this, to stop tightening the zip-tag and say that it's all some sick joke, but he doesn't. The night nurse pops her head around the door, confusion etched clearly on her face at why a patient is in the lounge at this hour. She notices me first and starts when she sees the mixture of raw shock and fright upon my face.

"Beth," she begins cautiously, "what's…" she stops suddenly as she sees what I'm seeing. "Lisa! Rosaline! Come here now!" she shrieks as lurches to the floor beside Alex. I back into the corner of the room and put my hands over my ears, but nothing can block out her desperate calls for help. The other HCA's run into the room and help the nurse as she peels Alex's fingers away from his throat. I see the white strip of the cord digging into his throat as the nurse gives up on trying to loosen it, each tug tightening it even more. "Get some scissors!" screeches the nurse as a HCA sprints back towards the Nurse's Office. Alex's face is slowly beginning to turn purple and his eyes look so swollen I think they'll explode. I try to scream, but I can't do anything. I rip at my hair, trying to cause a sharp shock of pain to wake me up so that I can help. What can I do? What can I do? What can I do?

~ Let Me Go ~

The HCA returns and cuts the cord. Alex gasps as colour begins to return to his face. In shock, he begins to claw at his throat and is immediately held down. "No, no!" he cries hoarsely. "I don't want to be here!" He strains to pull away. "Let me go!" he shouts. They pull him upright and take him towards the treatment room, saying that they're going to give him some medication to help him sleep. Even when the Nurse's Office door closes behind them, I can still hear him shouting and screaming at the staff who have taken his chance away. I'm shaking so much that my muscles are beginning to ache. The HCA who cut the cord returns, shock and anger clearly printed across her face. "Why didn't you call for us?" she says heatedly. "You should have got help!" Her accusatory stare and angry comments bury themselves into me like knives. What have I done?

The HCA leads me back to my room and helps me into bed. I'm still in shock when I see Alex carried past to his room a moment later, his limbs limp and his head lolling with the movement. It's a long time until I fall back to sleep. I sleep restlessly, my dreams full of corpses with bloated, purple faces and the knowledge that it's all my fault.

~ Let Me Go ~

Dear Friend,

That night was, with a shadow of a doubt, the most frightening and anxiety-provoking night of my life. To this day both my conscious and sub-conscious are still plagued with a plethora of 'what if's' that I'm yet to find an answer to. I still worry and wonder in anguish what would have happened if he had succeeded. What would have happened if the nurse hadn't seen the light and come to check at that exact moment? What if the HCA couldn't cut the cord loose from around his neck? What if there weren't any scissors in the Nurse's Office? The fact that I could neither shout nor move to get help is no excuse; his death would have been my fault.

Would adrenaline have kicked in so that I'd have been able to do something? I don't know, and in some respects I don't think I'll ever want to know. I can't seem to figure out who I hate more, Alex, for putting me in that position, or myself for not acting upon it.

Dr Ilona came to see me the morning after. She held my trembling hand and told me how brave I had been and how terribly sorry she was that something like that happened in front of me. She told me it may have been more of a cry for help than an actual suicide attempt, considering he was aware I was in the room when he continued to tighten it. But whether it was a plea or not doesn't matter, I didn't answer it. She repeated multiple times that it wasn't my fault, that I mustn't ever blame myself for what happened that night, that it was Alex's choice and nothing I could have said or done would have changed that. She reassured me that Alex had never been in any actual danger, but these were just words to calm me, he had been and I'd done nothing about it.

Chapter Twenty-One

The days begin to lengthen and the temperature peaks to an uncomfortable average of 28 °C as we steadily creep into the summer months. The ward has become a furnace, with the blinds doing nothing to prevent the sun rays from infiltrating the room and effectively cooking all those inside –something that is heightened considering the windows will only open a fraction. We are trapped like flies in a glass in this prison of heat that not even a shower can refresh and remove. All running water in the bathroom is warm, we're not allowed to have the temperatures searing hot or shivering cold for obvious reasons.

The Education Room closed during the middle of July meaning that, unless you're lucky enough to have been awarded Leave, you're trapped in the ward with very little to do in regards to entertainment. As we now know, there are only so many re-runs of *Friends* and hours of the music channel you can watch before you find yourself going stir-crazy and, thanks to the influences of the lack of fresh air and heat, arguments seem to be the common way to pass the time.

~ Let Me Go ~

I stare up at the small slither of sky visible through the window above my corner, shutting my eyes each time the wind blows through and washes over my face. It's strange both seeing and feeling the outside world and yet knowing that you're not allowed to be a part of it. The others are grouped around Monopoly which has been set out in a last-ditch attempt of entertainment. I was offered to join in too but I declined, it sounds silly but Alex is having a good time and it'll only spoil it if I play too. Alex has barely spoken to me since that night with the zip-tag, he acknowledges me with a grunt or the odd vacant response when I ask an open question and that is all. He blames me for the nurse coming into the lounge at that precise moment in time.

If it wasn't for the fact I turned the lamp on, he may not have been found. I still shudder at the memory of being frozen and unable to act, despite the fact I wanted so desperately to shout for help. As a consequence of my fear that he'll try again and self-hatred for doing nothing the first time, I've got into the habit of waiting until I think they're all asleep before I eventually close my eyes and give in to rest. I'm afraid that he won't wake up the next morning. I'll go into his room and shake him and he'll be stiff and cold, his face a bloated purple with another zip-tag cutting into his throat.

Alex's and Simon's room was stripped the morning after the incident, and nothing else was found, but I don't find this overly reassuring. What if they missed something? I'm not complaining that Alex blames me; it was my fault after all. If he had died that night, and thank God he hadn't, it would have been all my fault for not doing anything about it. Karen spoke to me two days after the incident, the first time she'd been in and heard of what happened and talked to me at length about it, asking me question after question that I wasn't at liberty to answer.

"Did he say anything during the day about his plan?"

"No, he seemed happy and made fun of me in a joking way. He wanted to watch a film with me and some of the others who didn't have Leave over the weekend."

"Did you know he had the cord?"

"No, if I had I would have done something." I hope.

"Do you know where he got the cord from?"

"I don't know."

She said the same as Dr Ilona, that it wasn't my fault and that she's proud of me for the way I coped afterwards, but I think I saw a slight glimmer of doubt in her eyes. Alex was put back onto 1:1 for a few weeks after that, and he lost all of his bathroom privacy too – something which ultimately gave him that little bit more fuel to hate me with.

It's my fault.

Even now, after seemingly being in a more stable mood and no longer being followed by his 1:1, he still ignores me. I find myself mentally counting down the days until the weekend because I'll get to see my family and get to pretend, to some extent at least, that everything's ok. They haven't said any more about the possibility of me getting Leave yet, and I don't want to say anything in case I jeopardise any chances I might have.

I look down at my stomach and pinch the slight layer of fat that is forming beneath the surface, thanks to my diet plan and lack of exercise, I am steadily beginning to regain the weight I'd lost. My clothes are starting to fit again now, and I can only just count my ribs through my skin. My self-harm has now reached its worst as a consequence as I scratch the skin off of my arm for each meal that I eat. There are more reasons for me to engage in these behaviours, despite the fact I know they're counterproductive, than to repress them. My arms are covered with scabs, open wounds and in some cases infection. They're covered at all times, despite the heat, as I refuse to wear nothing but full-length clothing, something which has led to the doctors getting suspicious of my behaviour. The only thing I'm even slightly worried about is the infection, if it starts to smell then I'm more likely to get caught, the only way I can clean them is in the shower, but the sharp sting of the water means that I can't stay in there for long.

I don't want to go back onto Level Four 1:1 arms reach, but what else can I do? If they want me to eat, then this is what I have to do in order to manage that. I don't care about the scarring, my weight gain is ruining my body anyway and I know that, thanks to the numerous comments I received at school, that I am unattractive anyway.

Karen gets up from where she's spent the entirety of the morning slumped on the sofa, occasionally getting up to do my two-hourly observations or to toss a pillow at one of the others when they get too loud. Jacob seems to be having a pillow thrown at him every ten minutes. She comes over to my corner and squats down next to me, a layer of sheen glistening on her forehead and dark patches of sweat beneath her arms. "When I trade 1:1 in a minute, I'm going to take the others down to the Games Room to play balloon volleyball, do you want to come?"

I nod my head rapidly. I'm not thinking about the change of scenery or the option of doing something different other than sitting in my corner, I'm thinking about how many calories I might be able to burn, and whether I could melt away the layer of fat around my stomach before the end of the day.

"You know you have to compensate though, right?" she asks, noticing the adamant look of glee on my face and guessing exactly what it's for.

"Compensate?" I ask.

"If you play with us then you'll need to have an extra biscuit with your next meal," she replies.

The smile disappears from my face as rapidly as it arrived. Of course there'd be some sort of consequence, why am I always stupid enough to get my hopes up?

"I'm sorry," she sighs, "but that's what the doctors have said. As your key nurse, I'd be really pleased if you joined us and complied with the snack afterwards." She leaves me alone to think it over for a while before they all go downstairs. I desperately want to go, to be able to actually do something after spending so long sitting in a corner by myself, and to finally stretch my legs. Apart from the visitor's lounges, which I use when my family comes to see me, I have yet to see the Games

~ Let Me Go ~

Room. I don't want to be the person who always says 'no' and refuses to interact and have fun with everyone else. I know we're not here to make friends, we're here to learn the tools that will help us beat our illnesses and ultimately survive, but I don't want to be an outsider again.

It's all a risk. Do I chance it and play volleyball and hope that the amount I burn totals or exceeds the amount of the biscuit? Should I just play it safe and not take the risk, considering that Karen didn't specify what biscuit we're expected to have? I choose the latter; my weight is not worth risking, not even for the temptation of doing something fun. I don't even have to go to the bathroom mirror to know what the monster will say; it'll tell me it's all just a ploy to make me gain weight faster. A sick and twisted trick, but a trick none the less.

I shake my head sadly as Karen herds the rest of the others towards the lift, her look quite clearly saying 'it's your choice, I did offer.' After one final shout from Simon that I'd better not mess with the Monopoly pieces, I hear as the lift doors clang shut with finality and as their excited voices drifts to the floor below. Apart from my 1:1 watching me beadily from across the room, I am alone. Ethan is with one of the doctors in the dining room and Poppy is still on bed rest. I sit back and look at the sky, imagining what it would be like to look up and see the endless, rolling blue and know that there's nothing to hold you back.

**

Karen isn't impressed with my decision to remain on the ward rather than interact with the others. "You have to start making an effort to include yourself," she says. "I know I told you that you're not here to make friends, but I know how much you struggle with social skills, and practice is the only way you're going to overcome it." I sigh quietly. Karen leans forwards on the edge of Rachel's bed and rests her elbows on her knees. "Dr Ilona has suggested that you might benefit from taking a form of antidepressant, potentially beginning on a starting dose of 20mg of Fluoxetine to help stabilise your mood and decrease your anxiety – something which should help with interaction as well. What do you think of this?"

I answer without even processing my words, as if subconsciously I'd already considered the notion of medication and formed an answer, despite it never being voiced before. "I'm not taking it," I say decisively.

Karen raises a questioning eyebrow.

"I don't want to have 'fake happiness', I want to be happy naturally and by myself. But, then again, I'm Sectioned so I guess you'll do it anyway."

Karen frowns. It's not that we'll 'do it anyway' but that we'll act for your own good and to the benefit of your health and psychological well-being. Dr Ilona suggested it because she seems to think you're managing to self-harm, despite being on 1:1." My bloods runs cold and I clench my hands firmly in my lap to prevent them from visibly trembling. "Can I see please?" she asks.

I shake my head, no. Karen sighs. "If you don't show me then I can do it forcibly and without your consent. I scowl and slowly roll back my sleeves, wincing as straying strands catch on my wounds. She turns my arms over gently, examining the array of bruises, cuts and scratches that snake up them. "I'm going to tell Dr Ilona who'll probably prescribe you some more cream to help them heal. I'll also be warning the staff to keep a greater eye on you. I don't want to have to prolong your time on 1:1, I feel that'll be detrimental to moving forwards."

Karen releases my arms and I roll my sleeves back into place. With their covering of fabric, you'd never know about the mess hiding beneath.

"That's not the only reason why I wanted to see you, and I'll be speaking to some of the others when they get back too." I gulp, this doesn't sound particularly promising and I wonder what new form of horror they have install for us – surely nothing can be worse than watching someone use the bathroom or force-feeding them, can it?

"Dr Ilona didn't want me to tell you sooner because she thought it would only worry you unnecessarily, but you're going with some of the others for two appointments tomorrow at Great Ormond Street Hospital." I look at her in surprise; this is not at all what I was expecting.

"You're booked in for a bone scan and for a pelvic ultrasound. As you know, developing anorexia during childhood and adolescence can be very damaging for your health in later life. Your bones will only strengthen through growth and calcium intake until your early twenties, in which they steadily start to deteriorate as you age. Now, normally this wouldn't be a problem, but obviously with a reduced intake, and subsequent lack of calcium, you are more prone to developing osteoporosis. This test is done to all patients within the first three months of admission purely to check your bone density and whether any damage has already been done. If damage has been done, then we may be able to rectify it before it's too late."

I nod to show that I understand.

"The pelvic scan is purely to check that your ovaries are still working. I know that you're yet to have your period return –" I blush a deep crimson, I don't think I'll ever get used to my bodily functions being discussed so openly, and to be honest I don't think I ever want to. Karen either doesn't notice my sudden change in colour or ignores it. "Basically, it's just to check that things are still working. The boys are obviously excluded from having that one," she concludes.

"It's nothing to worry about, nothing painful or anything like that, just make sure you wear leggings or something that hasn't got metal on it."

I nod once more and thank her as she leaves and my 1:1 comes back into the room. In spite of myself, I can't help from being relatively excited at the prospect of getting out of the hospital for a few hours, even if the only time I'm actually allowed out is to visit another one.

Chapter Twenty-Two

The ride to the hospital is never-ending and painful, considering the fact that I've been told to sit in the back with Jacob and he insists on spending the entire journey alternating between jiggling his legs rapidly up and down as if doing a one-hundred-metre sprint and making inappropriate jokes. It's not fair that he manages to get away with it; if any of the others try we'd be instantly given a supplement.

We stop and start so frequently that I begin to feel sick within a few miles of the Unit. I feel like I want to ask the driver to pull over so that I can be ill, but I've left my voice back in the Unit. I haven't been outside properly in so long; and I'm reminded of how ironic it is that the only time I'm let into the outside world, albeit in a taxi and with trained restraint staff, is to receive medical treatment in another hospital.

I knew travelling into central London would be hell, what with pedestrians cutting across the road and vehicles swinging from one lane to the next like a pendulum, but I'd never considered just how bad it would be. The further we get into the heart of the city, one car length at a time, the worse the driving becomes. There is no use for indication or turn-taking and people rely purely on the use of the horn which is slammed on with untrammelled frequency, both by our taxi driver and those we pass. The horns create a discordant symphony, and I swear a minute ago I saw one man leaning out of his sun-roof conducting the array of honks like they were some kind of royal orchestra. Thank the Lord my parents never decided to settle down in a city. We pass shop after shop, apartment after apartment, brakes squealing and pedestrians darting before the cars with little thought of the consequences. People shake fists out of the windows and cigarettes are thrown onto the road, where they smoke and spark until they're crushed beneath a wheel and carried on through the city.

The others have fallen silent. Courtney and Simon began the journey singing loudly and boisterously to the latest songs on the radio, singing them with such vigour and gusto that the driver had gritted his teeth in frustration and slammed onto the brakes with a little too much enthusiasm so that we flung against our seatbelts. I can see them gaze unseeingly out of the window, probably doing the same as me and worrying about the tests we're going to have, and the memories that being in a general hospital will undoubtedly bring back.

I don't want to go.

The HCA and Steph have evidently noticed our abrupt change of mood, which spirals further the nearer we get to the hospital because they keep trying to engage us in little games like eye-spy and name-the-song. I don't want to play. It's not the fact that I'm going for x-rays and scans it's that I'm so close to freedom, the outside world literally rolling slowly past my window in an attempt to mock and tease me. I am not free. I wonder what Steph would do if I smashed my fist through the glass and climbed out onto the street, it probably won't even surprise them – I bet someone's tried it before. When you're Sectioned and you go outside of the hospital, the person you're with needs to carry a Section 17 Leave form signed by the Responsible Clinician (in my case Dr Sergei). That way should staff need to restrain me or forcibly bring me back; they can show the form to the Police to prove I'm detained. I have the urge to run into the streets when we reach the hospital, run towards the nearest person I see and tell them what these people have been doing to me. The others all need to be here, they're sick, but I'm not.

Truth no. 20 - If I actually did this, I highly expect they'd agree with the staff anyway. They'd take one look at the glimpse of bandages beneath my sleeves and the small bald patches on my head from where I pull at my hair and push me straight back into their waiting arms.

We screech to a sudden stop and slide effortlessly in between two parked taxis. The nurses get out and let us out of the doors – they're all locked for 'patient safety'. Once we're all out the driver speeds off towards the traffic at the other end of the road, before being enveloped within the mass of vehicles and swallowed by the fumes. The hospital stands before us, the entrance nestled between two large buildings, with a grand, sheltered archway leading the way.

The doors open onto a large, open reception area with various corridors leading off in all directions. The walls are painted a periwinkle blue and have a scattering of multi-coloured fish dotted around them. There are collections of bright chairs in groups around the room and even the desk itself is shaped to look like the hull of a boat. There's a section of interactive floor with fish swimming around lazily and, when you step on it, the fish disperse and ripples fan out from where you stand. The receptionist welcomes us warmly and motions for us to follow the signs towards the x-ray department where our tests will be carried out. I can feel my heart beating painfully in my chest as memories of my time in the general hospital comes back. The last time I was walking into a hospital I was admitted for six weeks and then sent to an Inpatient for an indefinite amount of time. I remember that evening, sitting in the A&E waiting room on those cold, metallic chairs, shivering as the doors continuously swum open and admitted new potential patients to be treated. My mind was numb as I waited for my name to be called, not really believing that this was happening and I was facing admission yet again. I had been admitted twice before due to heart problems and electrolyte imbalances, but those had only been for two or three days. They let me out after speaking to my psychiatrist and receiving my word that I'd continue to eat in the community. I broke my promise into a thousand pieces and crushed it to powder beneath the toe of my shoe.

I lean back into the soft, worn plastic of the chairs, all laid in rows with various toys and interactive games available for the patients in a separate area before them. A Disney film is being projected onto the wall opposite. Nothing bad can happen to me here, I'm not at GOSH to be admitted, I'm here for some tests and then I'll go back again. The only problem is that I don't want to go back either.

We're called in by a nurse one by one, first for the bone scan and then me and Courtney for the pelvic ultrasound. Steph sits in the waiting room and watches the others whilst my 1:1 sits beside me. By law, there needs to be one member of staff for every three patients, both inside and outside of the hospital. Courtney is led back to the waiting area, where she joins Jacob where he's playing on the games machine in the corner.

"Bethany Thomas, please," announces the nurse. Although it sounds childish, I hope Steph will come in with me so that I don't have to be alone with this stranger. I look at her fervently as I get up, asking with my eyes for her to accompany me, but she nods towards the waiting nurse and smiles gently. I have no option but to turn and follow the nurse further into the labyrinth of the hospital. She asks me to first remove any metal, of which I have none, and lie down on the bed as she presses buttons on the side of the machine. I can feel my breath catch in my throat and my limbs begin to shake uncontrollably. She tells me not to worry, that the machine will pass over my abdomen and then stop, I'm not to move even a muscle until the light at the top goes off. I nod to show I've understood.

~ Let Me Go ~

I close my eyes as the machine groans into action above me. My thoughts are torn, the very nature of my illness wants there to be a problem, a reassurance that I've at least done something right, and yet at the same time I'm afraid of what they'll find, that I'll have to spend even longer in Inpatient treatment and away from my family. My mind begins to spin and I clutch desperately at thoughts which, should I have been calm and able to think logically, I would have recognised instantly as irrational. What if my bone density is so low that they can't treat me at Birchmoor any more and they send me to some other Unit even further away? My parents wouldn't be able to visit me as frequently, and I might end up being there for years. What if my results are -

"You're all done, dear," says the nurse. I jump and notice that the light has gone. She shows me the black and white x-ray image of my spine on the screen of her computer, and tells me that she doesn't know what to look for, only how to run the machine. I thank her and she leads me further down the corridor to a room with the sign 'Ultrasound' printed in bold above it.

There's already a doctor inside, a middle-aged lady with horn-rimmed glasses and a large mole in the centre of her cheek. She smiles at me warmly before motioning for me to climb up onto the bed. I lie there in silence, watching as she presses buttons on the machine. The nurse is waiting for me in the corner.

The lady rolls up my top and pulls down my leggings slightly to expose my stomach before squirting a large proportion of an icy gel onto my stomach. She doesn't comment at my ribs which leap out or the jarring of my hips that's visible whenever I lie down. She must have been doing these tests on girls from Birchmoor for a while and has grown accustomed to it. She slides the transducer across my skin and I watch as an indistinguishable, grainy image forms on the screen. She speaks aloud, and the nurse begins to make notes onto a clipboard. It's over in less than five minutes.

I wipe the gel hurriedly from my stomach and pull my top back into place before thanking the doctor and allowing myself to be led back to the waiting room. They're all waiting for me; I was

the last one to go in. My 1:1 wraps her arm around me
reassuringly as Steph leads the others back out of the hospital
and into the waiting taxi. We spend less than a minute in the
fresh air outside. The ride back is much the same as our journey
here, the jarring stops and sudden starts making me feel queasy
once more as we blend with the hectic traffic of London.
Courtney and Simon begin singing once more to the radio. Jacob
joins in with his interpretation of beat-boxing which only half of
the time is in sync and I clap my hands and hum to the melody,
all thoughts of hospitals and tests forgotten for that brief in
moment in time which we share together.

The driver grits his teeth once more and glares at us angrily
through the rear-view mirror and the HCA and Steph laugh at us
from where they're wedged in next to the driver and
humorously tell us that our racket will shatter glass if we're not
careful. They place their hands over their ears and moan
comically, which only succeeds in making our noise louder and
more energetic. We stay that way, singing song after song until
our voices are hoarse and my hands are numb from all of the
clapping until the gates of Birchmoor open wide and swallow us
whole once more.

Chapter Twenty-Three

I am waiting with the others outside the Nurse's Office to be called through to take my medication. I'm lucky that I only have to take electrolyte supplements, some of the others have to take a whole array of brightly coloured pills, some of which leave them in a state of unconsciousness for the vast majority of the day. After this, the HCA's are planning to take us all down to the Games Room to experiment with some of the craft activities someone found gathering dust at the back of one of the cupboards. I'm looking forward to going. Just the prospect of a change of scenery is enough to persuade me to join, even if we just end up finger-painting like toddlers at a playgroup, it also helps that we don't require an extra biscuit for partaking. Unlike the line for weigh-day, this one is full of people making jokes with each other, arguing about which film should be watched that evening and contemplating new ways in which they could smuggle their phones onto the ward. We're called through one by one, where we swallow the pills handed to us and drink the sludge that is the electrolyte supplement before making a joke about having to take 'crazy-people meds' (a term coined by Simon and frowned upon by staff) before the next person is called through.

I look sideways subtly at Ethan who is being supported by two agency HCA's. Ethan refuses to take any medication as well as sustenance so it's passed through his tube during his feed. I want to ask him if he'll come down with us too, I can remember only too clearly what it was like at school to never be a part of anything and always feeling like I wasn't good enough to be asked. He probably won't reply to me, but I understand that's not because he's being rude, he just physically can't at the moment.

I shuffle up the line as Rachel is called through.

It's not that people don't make an effort to talk to Ethan, those who go on weekend Leave with their parents always tell him stories about what they got up to, and we always ensure to put the TV programme about the animal shelter on during the late afternoon because he smiles slightly as if he seems to enjoy it. I know that Ethan has Pervasive Refusal Syndrome which causes eating difficulties rather than an eating disorder itself, it's obvious considering that it's not just food he refuses, but everything else needed to function on a daily basis too. I want to help him, but I don't know how and I'm afraid I'll just make things worse. I sometimes see one of the nurses teasing a comb through his hair in the morning or reading a book to him. Maybe I should offer to read to him; I always used to read to Natalie when she was younger.

"Beth!" calls Karen, interrupting my thoughts as Rachel shuffles out through the door. I go through to the treatment room and she shuts the door swiftly behind me. I make a conscious effort to ignore the scales hidden under a plastic cover in the corner; it doesn't help to stew over the unknown. I knock back my three cups of supplement like shots at a bar, although I've never actually participated in this activity, say thank you and turn to leave. Karen puts her arm out to stop me. "Do you remember what we were talking about in regards to your medication the other day?"

"Yes…" I say slowly, not sure what she's getting at considering I made it quite clear what I thought of that idea at the time.

"Dr Ilona has written you up for a dose of Fluoxetine to be started today," she says.

"I'm not taking it," I say adamantly. Karen holds the paper cup with the single pill inside it towards me. I shake my head; there's no way I'm swallowing that.

"Why not?" she asks.

"I don't want it," I reply incessantly. "I don't want 'fake happiness' I want to do it for myself." That and the fact that the monster told me last night that it might interfere with our connection, I add internally. It told me that, should the medication cause me to no longer be able to communicate with it, how can it help me? What if the medication changes who I am and makes me willing to gain weight? I shudder at the thought of it potentially taking my eating disorder away. As much as I wish it'd never happened to me, I know that I'm nothing without it.

"You have to take it," says Karen with finality, shaking the paper cup so that the pill shakes from side to side. "I know you don't think you need it, but you evidently do otherwise it wouldn't have been prescribed for you. There're no calories in it, it's not going to make you gain weight, all it's going to potentially do is help stabilise your mood and decrease your anxiety. Can you take the pill please," she asks. "There're others waiting for their meds and you're holding them up."

It feels like there's some barrier in my mind. It's not the calories that I'm worried about, I know they're not hiding in the pill, it's the fact that I don't want it. The very stubbornness and finality of my decision makes me hold my ground and I know that nothing either she or anyone else can say will make me swallow that tablet.

"No," I say with a quiet assertiveness. "I am not taking that medication because I don't need it and I don't want it."

"Fine," she says sternly, "that's your choice. Don't go down to the Games Room, I'll need to phone the doctors so you'll have to stay on the ward."

Bitch.

She opens the treatment room door and motions me outside, calling in Simon as I leave. I go back into the lounge and sit down in my little corner, my 1:1 following behind me as usual.

"Are you alright?" asks my 1:1 concernedly. "Did something happen in the treatment room?"

I pull my knees up to my chest and rest my chin upon them, only now does it dawn upon me that there might be consequences for my actions. What if they change their minds about letting me try Leave? Will they increase my diet plan in punishment?

"Dr Ilona put me on Fluoxetine, but I don't want to take it," I reply morosely.

"You're on Section though, aren't you?"

I nod.

"I don't think you really have a choice then." She pulls up a chair and sits down next to me. She places her hand on top of my shoulder and together we sit in silence.

***

It's an hour after the others have gone to the Games Room that Karen calls for me. At first, I consider ignoring her, but I think that will only escalate the situation. My 1:1 leads me towards the Nurse's Office where Karen is sat at one of the computers, reading a document on the screen. She turns away as I stand and wait in the doorway.

"I've just spoken to Dr Ilona," begins Karen matter-of-factly, "she's said that you have to take the medication."

"I'm not taking anything," I reply quietly. "I don't want it and I don't need it."

Karen sighs in frustration. "Beth, how many times have you been told this?" she says with an undertone of anger in her voice. "If you didn't need it then it wouldn't have been prescribed. Dr Ilona has been working here for the past ten years; do you really

think she'd give you a medication that wasn't necessary?"
I remain silent. She's made a mistake this time. I don't want 'false
happiness' and I don't want to be dependent on a pill the size of
a thumbnail. I want to do things naturally and by myself. "As a
human being, I have rights," I begin boldly, "and there are
certain things I agree with and certain things that I don't. I don't
have an issue with other patients taking whatever medication
they're given, that's their choice to take it, but I do have a
problem with taking it myself. I don't like things that are
unnatural, you know that. I don't wear makeup, use damaging
hair-products or take pain-killers unnecessarily and I'm not just
going to take this medication that I don't need. This is obviously
the way things are meant to be, and I'm choosing to respect
that."
"Beth" warns Karen, "this medication is going to help stabilise
your mood, and nothing else. It's not going to make you gain any
weight, it's not going to change who you are or have any of the
other kinds of effect that you're probably worrying about. If it
was going to do you more harm than good, then it wouldn't be
given to you. You're not thinking rationally at the minute, I can
tell that both by what you're saying to me now and the fact that
you're not weight restored."
"My weight has nothing to do with it!" I say angrily. Why can't
they just understand and let me be?
"I'm not having an argument. Come with me please." She
unlocks the door to the treatment room and motions me inside. I
plant my feet firmly on the ground and shake my head. I don't
know where this rude and stubborn girl has come from, but now
that she's out and in the open I can't seem to quieten her down.
"Do you want to be restrained?" I shake my head, who in a
million years would ever want that? I've had enough experiences
with that to last me a lifetime. "Come inside."
I hesitate before following Karen into the room, knowing
instinctively what's about to happen without even needing to be
told.
She motions for me to sit on the table and I oblige without a

comment, staying silent in rebellion as she prepares the tube. I stare at her unblinking, even maintaining firm eye contact when she instructs me to tilt my head back so that she can insert the tube. I wince slightly despite myself as it slides down inside me and settles in my stomach. After checking the tube is in the right place and hasn't been inserted into my lung by accident, she screws the syringe into the end and presses down firmly on the plunger. I stare at her all the while, my eyes burning into her own and questioning how she could ever do this to someone who said no. What goes in your body ought to be your own choice, not to be dictated and controlled by someone else to such an extent that you can no longer recognise it as your own. She removes the tube and I shudder slightly as the acid scalds my throat and nasal cavity, not once do I say a word or show any sign of emotion.

It's only once I've left the treatment room and Karen has shut the door firmly behind me that I can feel the mask start to slip and my barriers beginning to crumble. I wrap an arm tightly around myself to hold the pieces together and trail aimlessly down the corridor. When it becomes too much to stand any more I slide to the floor.

Only then, as I'm curled tightly into a foetal position with my hands over my head, do I let myself go and let the emotion I'd been holding inside flow out of me like a burst dam. Tears flood my face and I gasp for my breath as I sob into the carpet, I don't even have the strength to pull myself upright and off of the floor.

Truth no.21 - When emotional pain is so great, it can be felt physically too.

Poppy looks at me concernedly when I eventually return to the lounge with my 1:1 after my breakdown in the corridor. I blush slightly, I didn't realise she was in here, I bet she heard everything. She's lying down on the sofa, lost in the mound of pillows that are used to support her tiny frame, her 1:1 by her side. "Alright, Beth?" she asks, "didn't you want to go to the

Games Room?" She pats the chair next opposite her and I obligingly sit down. As much as I like talking to Poppy, it can be difficult at times. Dr Sergei, who is Poppy's consultant too, came onto the ward to talk to us collectively the day Poppy first came into the lounge. He told us that, due to her condition, Poppy's mood fluctuates quite extremely and that how he was pre-warning us, not to break patient confidentiality as it would become blatantly obvious to us sooner or later, to not be alarmed should she start hysterically crying or laughing. He ended with the well-used phrase "everyone's circumstances are different" before leaving us to mull over what he'd said.

"I'm fine, thanks," I reply automatically, although we both know that's not the case. "How are you finding things at Birchmoor?" I ask her tentatively; afraid of saying anything that might cause her upset. As bad as it is for me to even admit, I try to avert my eyes whenever I talk to her, looking at her makes me feel so self-conscious and a failure for not looking the same.

"It's ok, a bit scary to begin with!" she laughs. "Much better now, though, since I've had that monitor taken away – that incessant beeping was starting to drive me crazy!"

I perch anxiously on the edge of the chair nearest to her. It's strange sitting in the centre of the room when I'm so used to hiding in my corner, but something about Poppy makes me want to be with her and talk openly. She seems to emit a vibe that draws you closer and makes you want to smile and embrace life. From the moment she was first wheeled out of her room into the lounge, a mere six days ago, she has paid countless compliments to both patients and staff and has reflected such a positive attitude about the prospect of recovery. Just listening to her makes me half-believe that it's true, that maybe there is a better life out there waiting for all of us, and that maybe I can achieve it too. "I can't wait to get out of here," she sighs.

I nod my head fervently in agreement, neither can I. "We're all so lucky to be here and receiving this treatment, honestly it's going to completely turn my life around!" I smile at her warmly. I wish I felt that way. I wish I was able to embrace treatment here so openly and with such trust, as she has done. As much as she dedicated her life to maintaining her illness before admission, it seems that the tables have turned and flipped that mound of dedication the other way. So that, rather than being content with destroying her life, she's eager to live it. She seems to instinctively know what I'm thinking. She reaches out her bony hand and places it on my knee reassuringly. "You're going to be fine, and I know it."

"What do you have, the sixth sense?" I tease jokingly.

"I wish!" she laughs. "If I did I'd already be living in my mansion with my walk-in wardrobe full of dresses of every colour under the sun – and the ones above too!"

I smile at her. She reaches for my hand, the sudden smile and glimmer in her eyes wiped entirely away without a trace. "We have to stay strong," she says, squeezing my hand gently to emphasise her point. "I've wasted too many years to this illness, and I'm sure you have too. Don't let it take you, Beth, don't let it take you!" Tears pool in her eyes and begin to slide down her face.

"It's ok, I won't let it take me," I assure her, passing her a tissue from the box on the table.

"Don't let it take you!" she sobs, clutching my hand in her vice-like grip. "Don't, don't d- " The nurse on Poppy's 1:1 lifts her gently into her wheelchair and prises her hand away from mine. "Come on, love," she says gently. "I think you need a little lie-down."

"I want to help Beth," she sobs as her 1:1 wheels her way.

"I know you do. Let's go and have a lie-down, shall we?" I hear as her 1:1 tabs her card to the box on the side of her bedroom door and the receiving click as it opens. On the spur of the moment, I stand and rush from the room, ignoring the sudden shout of my 1:1 as I dart out of her sight.

I knock on Poppy's door and go inside, where she's being helped onto her bed, tears still streaming silently down her face.

"Thank you for helping me," I say warmly, forcing a smile onto my face.

~ Let Me Go ~

"I helped?" she asks, the tears beginning to slow as she looks up at me in surprise.

"Yes," I say empathetically. "You've helped me so much. Have a nice rest and I'll probably see you later on, maybe you can sit with us tonight when we watch a movie?" Poppy nods her head enthusiastically, all traces of tears vanishing as a smile lights up her face once more. "I'd like that!" she says happily.

I smile once more as my 1:1 leads me away. "That was a very kind thing you just did," she murmurs into my ear as she leads me back into the lounge.

"I know," I reply simply.

***

Dr Ilona comes on to the ward that afternoon to see me in light of the incident that morning. I can tell immediately that she's not impressed by my actions by the way she greets me slightly less enthusiastically than usual and negates to look my way for too long. I follow her into the dining room and she shuts the door silently behind her. We sit at the least messy table and she shuffles the papers nosily in her lap before finding the one she's looking for and laying it on the table before me. "You know already what I think of your actions this morning."

I look down at my lap and feel my face flush a deep red. Now, once away from the situation and looking back upon it with a more rational mind-frame, I can see that what I did was not the most sensible of ideas. No, I still don't want to take it, but I forgot for that single moment in time what being Sectioned means for me. I was being stubborn and irrefutable, something that led to extreme actions being taken. Despite not feeling I need nor want the pill, I have no choice but to take it.

"I know," I reply solemnly.

"I won't be hearing about this again during handover, will I?"

I shake my head. I may as well comply with my treatment plan, even if I don't agree with it. The longer I spend refusing help, the further away my discharge day gets. Dr Ilona nods in approval and becomes her usual, bubbly self once more. "I came to give you some feedback in regards to your care-plan," she says, "and I'm very pleased you've just made the right decision otherwise my news would be very different! I've decided that it's time to reduce your 1:1 level during the day. You'll be on Level Two: Fifteen minutes the same as what you are during the night." I nod happily; I can barely even remember what it's like to walk around without my own permanent shadow.

"I've also decided to reduce your general observations to every four hours, and…" she says slowly, obviously aware that what she's about to say means a lot to me, "I've decided to give you an hour local Leave with your parents this weekend!" I smile broadly at what I'm hearing. If truth be told I honestly believed I had lost all hope of Leave after my refusal this morning.

"Thank you! Please, can you not tell my parents, though," I say, excitement brimming in my voice. I jiggle my legs under the table, but not for any other reason apart from the fact that I'm excited – something which I haven't felt in a long time.

"Why not?" she asks with adamant confusion.

"I want to tell them myself."

She smiles at me. "You can call them now if you want to, I'll let Karen know that I've given you special permission." My smile becomes so large that the muscles in my jaw begin to ache in response to being held in a position which has been considered 'unnatural' for so long.

There are always some positives to be found in each day, no matter how deep you have to dig to find them

~ Let Me Go ~

Dear Friend,

I wish you could have seen me the first time I went back outside, you'd probably have laughed at my seemingly unnecessary anxiety and my childish wonder at the world I was slowly beginning to re-discover. I remember stepping out of those gates for the first time, Karen by my side, and how I'd looked back as they slowly slid into place behind me, marvelling at the fact that, this time at least, I was on the other side. We walked slowly down the road, passing shops, a primary school and a small park; my eyes darted from side to side as if I was following a rapid tennis match. I was so eager to absorb it all.

I remember that my senses felt bombarded with the sheer volume of smells, sight and sounds, rushing towards me. I must admit it was strange to smell something that wasn't stale with disinfectant and see the sky through my own eyes rather than through a digital screen or window.

You probably think I'm being trivial, reminiscing on something that shouldn't have been as significant as it was as, of course, walking outside isn't exactly an unusual experience to the average individual, but it was for me after spending three months in some form of hospital and not being allowed outside. I jumped at the slightest of things; the back-firing of a car, the excited squeals of children in the playground, the sudden barking of a dog intent on chasing a pigeon. To me, it was all new, something that I felt I had to take in and appreciate immediately, lest they change their minds and keep me inside for another three months. I felt the strong urge to run, to put as much distance as was humanly possible between myself and the Intensive Treatment Ward but I knew, rationally at least, that I would inevitably be caught and returned, and then who knew how long it would take to earn back the rights to the outdoors? Karen walked on the outside of the pavement in silence, a physical barrier between me and the streaming traffic, in case I should have decided to step into the road and let the cars take me away.

~ Let Me Go ~

I remember that I trailed my hand along everything that we walked past, the rough scraping of a stone wall, the grimy smoothness of a wheelie bin outside someone's house, the cool hardness of the peeling railing. I felt it all to make sure it was real and not some other trick of my mind. As you well know, my mind can be a cruel place sometimes, my Friend.

When I returned to the Unit, some thirty minutes after first leaving the gates behind, I refused to wash away the dark stain of dirt upon my hands. It was only at the threat of not being allowed into the dining room, something in itself that neglected to give me the incentive to comply but rather the thought of the consequential tube, which made me wash the grime away. As I washed the proof of the outside world's existence down the sink, I vowed that never again would I be separated from the world for so long.

I remember the first Leave I took with my parents, that single hour that I was given way from the ward, staff and everything it had come to represent. Now off 1:1 I revelled in the idea of having more freedom, even though my parents had been warned to watch me and I wasn't allowed to go further than a few miles away. Natalie's face beamed up at me as Karen led me to the front door where my parents were waiting. She practically skipped the whole way there and back because she was so excited and overwhelmed at seeing her sister walk outside of hospital after she was told she was dying three months earlier.

The weather had been pleasantly warm with a slight breeze only strong enough to gently ruffle the loose strands of your hair. We spread our old blanket beneath the boughs of an old oak tree and simply enjoyed each other's company without being watched by staff and without the imprisonment of four walls around us.

Chapter Twenty-Four

I wish I could say that things improved drastically after that first outing with my parents, that I suddenly 'saw the light', so to speak, and stopped listening to my illness and reformed my ways. But that's not the case. I can feel my mind beginning to 'slip' the night after my trip to the park, something which I pray with every ounce of being that I possess will go away and leave me be. Seeing the outside world makes me want more of it, much the same way as when adrenaline-junkies seek their latest thrills. The knowledge of having to spend another week, or potentially longer depending on my feedback, imprisoned within these four walls makes me lose hope now that I can fully embrace the tantalising freedom that's being dangled just beyond my reach. I hold off and place what I believe to be impenetrable barriers around the cracks so that not even a thin whistle of air can creep through, but the cracks grow wider until they're yawning and my barriers disintegrate into little more than dust. The thoughts begin to slide through and I feel as my mind-frame begins to coincide with the cognitions of my illness, much the same way as it had all those months ago in the general hospital. On Monday morning, almost directly after I've climbed back into bed to feign sleep after being weighed and shown that I've gained another two kilos, it all becomes too much and I fall.

I can't do this any more, I absolutely can't.

To me, recovery feels much the same way as I imagine climbing a mountain would be, exhausting and unrelenting. The only difference being that, rather than climbing with appropriate footwear, I am climbing in flip-flops and have fallen so many times that my legs are a patchy blue of bruises and my feet are bleeding with the open wounds of blisters.

Impossible.

The prospect of there even being a summit to this mountain, a definitive goal to achieve, seems more farfetched the further I travel. And who knows what could be waiting on the other side anyway? For all I know, the other side might contain a feat even more distressing and life-consuming than the one I find myself faced with at the moment. So instead I find myself holding up my hands in surrender, a white flag billowing in the frosty gusts behind me as I give in to the illness that has plagued me for so long.

***

The Games Room is a reasonably large, rectangular room with soft carpet, a large flat-screen TV with an accompanying game console and cupboards full of craft sets, board games, books and DVD's. Some of them have locks on; I suspect that's where they keep the scissors and more dangerous activities like sewing kits. I'm sifting aimlessly through one of the boxes, searching for something that isn't broken and that peaks my interest. I come across a slightly squashed box with a sticker with a picture of a key upon it. Why is this here if it's meant to be kept safe? I open it inquisitively, firstly checking that no one is looking my way, it's full of various threads, cords and an instruction sheet for making friendship bracelets. I don't know what makes me do it, but I take one of the cords and stuff it deep inside my pocket, before replacing the lid and putting it back obviously in the cupboard. I want one of the HCA's supervising us to notice the box on display so that he'll lock it away to prevent anyone from getting hurt. I don't care about myself.

Karen comes for me at ten. I was expecting her but thought that, by hiding away in the Games Room rather than waiting on the ward like a sitting duck, she might forget about me. Evidently, that is not the case. I haven't eaten in three days, and have instead been force-fed through an NG tube that is both inserted and removed three times a day. I ignore her and continue hugging one of the cushions from the sofa to my chest, as much as I'm aware of the childish connotations it invokes, I need something to hold onto at the moment. "Come with me please," she asks. "It's time for your morning feed."

I shake my head. I don't want it and I'm not coming. Karen sighs loudly; she's been losing her patience with me more frequently now that I've stopped eating again. I understand where she's coming from, though, I'm frustrated with me too. I've tried to explain it to her and Dr Ilona multiple times before, I never chose this illness and I never signed up for treatment here. It's not my choice any more whether I eat or not, it's become a physical thing rather than purely mental. I literally can't do it, much the same as a person who's suffered a stroke can't walk, despite however much they wish they could.

"Right," she replies briskly, "I'll call the doctors then." She turns to leave. "No!" I cry,

"Come with me now then," she says, spinning to face me once more with her hands placed firmly on her hips. She lowers her tone to prevent the others from hearing, not that they're even aware of our conversation anyway considering Jacob is organising another game. "If you can't manage the supplement then that's fine, I'll just put it through the tube. But you have to come with me now and not fight me in the treatment room, because I won't hesitate to call them."

I stand slowly and drop the cushion back onto the sofa, dragging my feet slightly as she leads me into the lift and then into the treatment room when we're back on Intensive. I feel as if there're invisible strings tied around my arms and legs, forcing me to go places and do things that I don't want to. She motions for me to sit up on the table and my heart begins to beat so hard that I worry for a moment that my shirt is pulsing alongside it too. I know exactly what's coming, but that doesn't make me any less scared or make it not hurt as much.

I'm reasonably compliant whilst she inserts the tube into my left nostril, tilting my head back as asked and swallowing when instructed. I wince violently as it reaches the back of my throat and slides down inside me. If anything, it seems to be getting more painful the more feeds I have, I suspect that's due to my nasal cavities becoming damaged by the sudden stress and burn of acid upon removal. I don't know how Simon has managed to keep this up for all these months, perhaps he can see a monster as well.

I become much less compliant once the tube has been taped to the side of my face. I swallow awkwardly and my hands begin to perspire. I mutter to myself under my breath in an effort to soothe my anxiety and stay calm. I know I have to remain still so that Karen can do my feed successfully, but remaining still whilst something like this is happening to me is not something I'm very good at. She approaches me with a jug brimming with watered-down Fortisip, six-hundred calories of it in total. She places the jug on the side and uses a large syringe to draw the poison before approaching me and my tube. I lose all sense of rationality, my previous thoughts of remaining still and complaint vanish as swiftly as smoke in the breeze so that I question whether it was ever there in the first place. My hand wraps instinctively around my tube, a ploy that was successful within the general hospital. I don't want those calories anywhere near me, I'm fat enough already.

"Give me the tube Beth," says Karen sternly. "We're not going down that route, remember?"

I shake my head rapidly from side to side in distress. My grip on the tube becomes painfully tight until I can feel the bite of the clip burrowing into my palm. Tears begin to stream relentlessly down my face, and no matter how much I blink they won't seem to stop. She takes another step towards me and I lean back, feeling the coolness of the wall through the thin cotton of my shirt. I continue to shake my head and my body begins to shake with pure, undiluted fear. Karen opens a door and calls for a HCA to assist. The HCA comes swiftly into the room and peels my hands away from the tube as effortlessly as removing a piece of paper from a notebook.

Karen secures the clip of my tube to the syringe and begins to slowly press down the plunger. I moan and sob as I feel the coldness of the Fortisip, firstly along my face and then down the back of my throat and into my waiting stomach. I want to pull my tube out, but my hands are being tightly bound by the HCA, who is gripping them so hard that I can barely even move my pinkie. I pull my head back suddenly and it smacks with a dull thud onto the wall behind me. The syringe comes away and a stream of the liquid spurts onto the floor where it remains in a sickly yellow puddle. I'm crying harder now, both afraid of the situation and afraid of myself. I'm no longer in control of my actions, as if a switch has been flicked and someone else is occupying my brain and commanding me. Karen opens the door and calls loudly for a second HCA. I cry harder.

The other HCA shuts the door firmly behind her and grabs at my head painfully, they both use their bodies to pin me to the table. I can't move at all, no matter how hard I strain against them All the while, Karen presses plunger after plunger of that foul mixture inside of me.

Whenever I attempt to twist my head away, both to dislodge my tube and to avert my eyes, her grip on me tightens until she's

painfully compressing against my skull. I understand now why
Simon makes the noises that he does now. I want to shout and
scream at what's being done to me, but I'm in such shock at how
rapidly things have escalated that I can't do any more than sob.
I've had enough of living like this, enough of being afraid of
myself and the future. I've had enough of hospitals and being
Sectioned and not having any dignity or say over my life. I want
this all to stop and to go away so that it's nothing more than a
bad dream.
I wish.

***

Courtney enters the lounge, a large grin plastered upon her face
and with a slight lilting swagger in her step that can only be
caused by one thing – good news. She has everyone's attention
immediately.
"What's up bitches?" she says jokingly and is immediately
reprimanded for swearing.
"What's up with you?" asks Poppy from her place on the sofa.
"You look like you've swallowed a coat hanger!"
Courtney's grin elongates until you can count each of her teeth.
She strolls casually over to the sofa and takes a seat next to
Poppy, stretching her arms up and above her head and sighing
dramatically.
"Well?" asks Alex eagerly.
Courtney yawns, a playful glint in her eyes. "I might have just
received some news," she says, toying with her words. Jacob
groans and throws a pillow at her.
"And?" asks Alex.
"I might be being discharged in a few days!" she says excitedly,
unable to hold it in much longer.
"What do you mean?" asks Simon doubtfully. "You've only been
here a few months, there's no way they'd discharge you so
soon."
"Well, they are," she concludes happily. "I'm self-discharging." I

roll my eyes; I've heard this from so many people countless times before. A professional makes one comment and then it's taken out of context and exaggerated to mean virtually anything.

"No offence," I say, "but I'm fairly sure they'll Section you if you try and leave."

"A fair point," muses Courtney, not sounding the least bit phased by my logic. "They agreed though. They said that as long as I'm compliant over the next few days and agree to work with my community team then I can go home. I've already met my team and I work well with them, and I'm weight-restored so not in any physical danger. I'm good to go, man."

We're all taken aback by this, not completely convinced that she's telling the truth. However, there are no interjections from staff, so her claims must be legitimate. Rachel looks at her concernedly. "Will you stay safe and keep fighting?" she asks quietly, voicing our one collective fear that she'll return to her old ways and potentially kill herself this time.

Courtney looks her straight in the eyes before she replies. "I never want to be in a hospital again, I want to live and not be controlled by some stupid illness. I'm not going to fuck up again." No one tells her off for swearing that time, not even the staff can argue with that.

Chapter Twenty-Five

I go to bed early that night, hoping that a good night's rest will make things seem easier in the morning – at least that's how it used to be when I was little, everything would always seem better in the mornings, only now it seems things get worse with each new day. I toss and turn, unable to get to sleep thanks to the surfeit of thoughts racing around my mind and stinging with the potency of bees whenever I dwell on one for too long. Rachel is yet to come to bed, she's in the lounge watching a chick-flick with Poppy; the others (in particular the boys) said they couldn't stomach all of the kissing.

I think back to when Courtney told us her news. How is it fair that she gets to just walk out of here and I don't? She's been here almost a month longer than me, Simon's been here the longest, even though he has restraint feeds, surely he should go next? I sigh and punch my pillow angrily into a more comfortable position, trying to block out the music of the film coming from the TV. I don't want to be here any more, I don't want to live in this hospital and be looked after by staff rather than my parents,

~ Let Me Go ~

I don't want to sleep in this bed that's not my own. I don't want to be here. This isn't living; this is existing in a world of torment that won't end. I fight back the tears. No one understands; no ever does.

Truth no.22 - No matter how hard you hope and fight for it all to go away, there is no off-switch. It only begins to relent after time and dedication to recovery rather than self-destruction. It's incredible how time can heal almost anything.

Anorexia, namely diet and exercise is the first thing I think about every morning and the last thing I think about every night. I worry constantly about my size and panic that I've gained weight from doing even the slightest of things, such as manage a meal or sit down to study. I feel constantly guilty for eating, drinking and taking my meds, despite the fact that, should I refuse, I'll be restrained and have it pumped inside me anyway. This is not living. Anorexia 'got me' when I was eleven years old so that, rather than worrying about what to spend my pocket money on or thinking about what I was doing at the weekend, I was worrying about the way I looked and planning diets to make everything better. Only it didn't make things better, it made things a whole lot worse until it was off the scale entirely and in a different league of its own.

It took my life before I'd even had a chance to live it. But it wasn't just the anorexia that took me away, it was the anxiety, depression and obsessive-compulsive disorder that plagued me too so that, rather than collecting cards or some other form of gimmick, I found myself unwillingly collecting diagnoses and labels. I remember how I became so anxious that I refused to go out with my friends, even though I would receive invitations, I never accepted, and eventually they stopped asking. I remember how I had to cut my arms open every morning before school just to be able to get through the day, wrapping myself in bandages and refusing to wear anything short-sleeved, even in P.E. I would exercise late into the night until I could barely stand. The sly comments and bullying from my peers only made things worse, but not even they could hate me as much as I hated myself. The weight fell off of me, and as I disappeared, their comments did too.

I wipe away the tears that have crept unnoticed down my face. I don't want to be here any more. A sudden wave of calmness washes over me, obliterating and neutralising every negative thought beforehand.

I breathe in and out deeply, feeling the way the air moves in and out of my lungs in a rhythmic motion. I feel in control, and yet out of it at the same time. I reach behind me and pull lose the cord I'd taken from the Games Room and run it through my fingers, caressing it as if it's some delicate prized possession rather than a lone strand from a child's friendship bracelet set. I place the cord around my neck, loosely at first and then I gradually tighten it. I test its strength, I think it will work. I take one last, deep breath before pulling the covers up and over my head, I don't want to make the same mistake as Alex and get caught.

I'm not killing myself, anorexia already did that a long time ago, I'm simply removing the shell that has encompassed it and kept the illness going so that it could hurt those around me too. I don't want to live like this, in a state where I have no hope and no future worth fighting for. I am tired. I am so very tired of fighting this battle which seemingly cannot be won. I am fed up with feeling the way I do, of hating myself and being trapped in this non-relenting cycle of misery and pain. I don't want to have to hurt myself just so that I can get through a day that I don't want to be present for. I accepted a long time ago that, whether I like them or not, this is the way things are, the way things were meant to be. Only now I don't think I want to comply with what fate has planned for me, I want to go on my own terms before it's all too late and I hurt anyone else.

I pull the cord tighter around my neck until I can feel as my face begins to swell and pulse with my heartbeat. I'm never going to have any friends, I'm never going to go to Sixth Form, and I'll never make it up to my family for the years of pain I have caused them. Enough is enough.

I pull it tighter still until I feel the slight sting of it burning against my skin, my eyes begin to pop and I worry that they'll burst due to the pressure. I can't breathe. I begin to shake, my face burning and my throat working furiously in an effort to allow air to pass through against the unyielding string. Things begin to dim slightly around the edges of my vision so that I can no longer make out the darkened pattern of my duvet cover, and little white pinpricks of light dance a slow waltz before my eyes. I know I should secure it like Alex did with the zip-tag, but a small part of me is aware of what those actions could mean and, as much as I don't want to admit it to myself, I'm scared to die. I feel lightheaded, and I find myself beginning to slip so that I'm not sure whether I'm awake or dreaming.

There's a sudden thump from the other side of the room and I jump, the cord loosening around my neck as I automatically suck in a breath. Rachel is back, and I'm suddenly very much afraid that she's caught me and that my behaviour will affect her and she'll attempt suicide too.

"Sorry," she squeaks. "Did I wake you?" She moves around the room a bit more, replacing items she must have used in the bathroom before climbing into bed. I struggle to make my breathing slow and steady to feign drowsiness.

As much as I want to try again, I know that I'd never forgive myself if I failed and she found out. I'll never forgive Alex for the position he put me in that night when he almost killed himself in front of me, never in a million years would I even consider doing that myself and putting someone else in that situation, no matter how desperate I may feel. I stuff the cord silently into my pillowcase and lie awake until I hear the deep and even breathing of Rachel's sleep until I stop listening and the sounds mingle with my own.

***

~ Let Me Go ~

The following day it's slightly drizzling outside and the good weather we had been blessed with over the past few weeks seems to have been blown away during the night. I wear a polo-neck jumper to hide the bruising of the cord, and nobody even raises an eyelid. I walk around the ward like nothing happened and, as far as the staff are concerned at least, nothing ever did.

**

Courtney is discharged two days later, much to our surprise. She leaves without a party, insisting that the sooner she's shot of this place the better. I can't say I blame her.

I attend therapy as usual on Wednesday and give an honest answer to everything that's asked of me, whether it's right or not I don't know, but it's an answer none the less. The only thing I do lie about is when she asks me about how I'm finding my medication. "It's ok," I tell her as I fiddle absentmindedly with the hem of my jumper.

"How does it make you feel now that you're taking it yourself?" she asks. "I understand it was given against your will the first time."

"It's alright, I just don't think about it and get on with it," I lie.

She commends me on my positive attitude before concluding the meeting by saying that I must tell someone should my feelings change, they're all here to help me after all.

Dr Ilona comes to see me on Thursday to update me on my care-plan, despite the fact that nothing's changed and to have a general catch-up with me about how I'm finding things on Intensive at the moment. I try my hardest to be honest and tell her that I'm finding things a bit more difficult at the moment, although I negate to explain how much because I'm afraid of losing what little Leave I have as a consequence. It's not until she draws the conversation to a close after stating that she has to phone someone else's parent that the urge to tell her something overwhelms me.

Dr Ilona leans against the table to stand up. "Wait!" I say

suddenly. She sits back down obligingly and waits for me to speak with patience. "I don't want to live like this any more," I admit quietly. I'm glad that I've got that out and in the open. I feel like I've made some form of promise to try harder, despite the fact the very notion of it scares me.

"I'm glad you've said that," she replies with a slight smile. "The only way that you can live without this is to fight back. I can't imagine how difficult it must be, love, but it won't get any better until you stand up against it and fight back."

I nod. I think I already knew that deep down. I have the sudden urge to pull down the neck of my jumper and show her the band of fresh purple bruises beneath, but I relent, instinctively knowing that this is a secret for my eyes alone.

"Ok."

Chapter Twenty-Six

Much to the discontent of the others, the rest of the summer passes surprisingly quickly. My parents book a hotel in Reading for a weekend in order to spend more time with me, and I graduate from thirty minutes Leave to two hours providing I manage snack out. The first day back in the Education Room is met with a collection of responses, adamant groans and complaints from some saying they'd rather watch the music channel or play games, and yet something gleefully received by others purely for the prospect of having a change of scenery and something productive to fill their time with.

I am firmly within the latter, as much as it was nice to have a break, this hasn't been the most positive of summer holidays for me and I'm more than willing to put it behind me and start with a fresh slate. That and the fact that I'm curious about the Sixth Form in the school called Wellbrook Academy I would have been attending if I wasn't an inpatient.

It had been organised at the end of the last academic year that my home teachers would set me work and email reflection activities and my marks to my teachers in the Education Room. Everything's being coordinated between Mr McPherson and Mrs Hooch who is Head of Year Twelve in the Sixth Form. Despite not having met any of my home teachers before or barely even seeing the school itself, I'm excited at the chance of learning something new that's not on the GCSE syllabus and starting my A-Levels. I wonder if I'll ever go to the Sixth Form in person. I highly doubt it; I can't even begin to explain the whole plethora of problems that will undoubtedly bring.

As is expected, Kate is not allowed to go to the Education Room yet. She was admitted on Friday last week to occupy Courtney's old bed, and she came onto the ward in a wheelchair and in floods of tears, her suitcase being dragged by her Dad behind her. From what I've seen of her, she's skeletal, much the same as when Poppy first came, although her emotions have begun to stabilise now that she's putting on weight (something which she tells me she's happy about). I try to do as Karen suggested and look past the illness to the person within, Kate is not anorexia and neither am I, but it's difficult when you look at someone and see there's no light in their eyes.

But as bad as it makes me feel to admit it, being with Kate only increases the strength and frequency of my thoughts and makes me hate myself even more, despite the fact I know she wouldn't ever mean to. It's something experienced by everyone, whether they let on or not, whenever someone new is admitted to the ward.

We eat breakfast at the normal time and I try to refrain from thinking about the half kilo I'd seen in addition on the scales that morning before lining up outside the Nurse's Office to wait to be called in for our medication. I try not to think about Kate as well as I walk into the Education Room for my first lesson, but I can't help it. Seeing her like that, lying so weak and frail on that bed, only makes me hate myself more and feel disgusted that I'm not like her. I can't help myself from feeling guilty that I'm almost weight-restored and she's no way near, such is the nature of the illness, it makes me want to give in and let the staff tube-feed me again. At least that way it's entirely their doing and I'm in no way accountable for the consequences. I feel as my cognitions begin to slide back into the rebellious nature of my illness, but fighting it is, in itself, a rebellion too. As is quoted on one of those pictures in the lounge, 'If you have the strength to sustain an eating disorder, then you have the strength to beat it too.' The door swings shut behind me and the incessant beeping of her heart monitor disappears. I shake my head in an attempt to forcibly remove the thoughts and tell myself once more that if I want to go home I have to comply with my treatment plan and, if I never want to come to a place like this again, I must be able to stay strong in the community too. I sit down in between Alex and Rachel and wait for the teachers to finish organising their lessons and greet us. Once everyone's seated, they smile around at us all and welcome us back to the Education Room and that they hope we're ready to do some learning. I nod and agree alongside the rest. It's good to be a 'student' again rather than a patient, even if it's only for a few set hours a day.

After checking in with some of the others and handing out timetables to those taking actual classes, Mr McPherson pulls up a chair next to me. "Hello Beth," he says warmly. "How was your summer?"

"Alright," I lie effortlessly. "How was yours?"

"All good, all good," he replies, shuffling through his papers before laying my timetable down in front of me. "Are you still thinking of taking A Levels in English Literature, Biology and Music?" I nod. "Well, we can teach you the English and Biology, that's not a problem, but if you want to take Music then you'll only be able to have that lesson on Thursday when our music teacher's here. Have you met him yet?"

I shake my head. "He's called Luke and he's very nice. He often gives quick lessons in piano and guitar for anyone wanting to keep up with their grades or just take up an instrument as something to do. He hasn't taught an A-level course before, but we're in correspondence with Mrs Hooch at Wellbrook Academy and she'll be emailing us the work so that you'll be roughly on

~ Let Me Go ~

the same page as your peers back at home."

For the rest of the three and a half hours we spend in the Education Room a day (in between snack times and lunch) I look interestedly through my new books, both marvelling at all this new content to learn after countless months of revision and feeling the budding growth of panic at how much is being expected of me. Although, as both staff and my parents have reminded me on multiple occasions, the same process of thinking applies to this challenge too - it's enough that I'm trying. I begin by making some notes on the first chapter of Biology and read the opening chapter of Jane Eyre, the book we're required to read for the literature course. It's strange not having your lessons dictated to you, if you don't want to work, then quite simply you don't have to. You set your own goals and own agenda for the lesson and, despite having a lesson with a teacher a few times a week, I know that the vast majority of the course will be self-taught.

When the door to the ward opens once more and we stream into the corridors, Jacob and Alex playing the 'bogey' game and seeing who can shout it the loudest without getting told off by Steph, the beeping of the heart monitor reaches me once more. I am immediately swarmed with intense feelings of guilt for not being the one attached to the end of that machine, and I begin to feel my thoughts slip into the mind-frame of the illness. Why am I not on 1:1? Am I not sick enough any more? Why am I not on prescribed bed-rest? Does that mean I'm too fat? Why have I just been sitting down and studying? Don't I want to lose more weight? I place my head in my hands as the intensity increases ten-fold. What am I doing? Why am I here? How did this happen? "Are you alright, Beth?" asks Alex, turning as he notices that I'm no longer with them.

I shake my head to disperse the thoughts. I don't know whether or not this actually helps, but it's the only thing I can do and it feels good to be doing something.

"I'm fine," I reply with an attempt of a smile.

They look at me dubiously. I feel an instant flash of guilt for

causing them inundated worry. I might not be able to stop
myself from feeling guilty about Kate, but I can fix this one.
"In fact, I feel so fine that I'm going to be beat the lot of you," I
say, a legitimate smile replacing the fake. Their looks of doubt
turn to obdurate confusion. "BOGIES!" I yell at the top of my
lungs as Steph storms out of the Nurse's Office and begins
shouting at us for 'disrupting the ward with inappropriate
behaviour'.

***

Dr Ilona comes to see me that evening and at first I'm concerned
that she's here to reprimand me for disturbing the peace on the
ward, especially considering those moments are relatively few
and far between. She smiles at me broadly as she shuts the door
firmly behind us and leads me over to the table. Her smile is
contagious, and I can't help but reciprocate with my own as I sit
down opposite her. Either she approves of my screaming of
'bogies' or she's come to deliver some very good news. As it
turns out, the latter is the case.
"We've decided to give you your first Home-Leave this
weekend. How does that sound to you?"
I am flabbergasted. For a minute I'm lost for words, my mind
reeling at what I've been told. I was expecting to have Leave, yes,
but I thought she'd give me an extra hour within the vicinity of
the hospital, not a whole night!
"A whole night, for real?" I ask uncertainly, half-expecting her to
point her finger at me and laugh, saying that it was all some
tasteless joke.
"For real," she says, unable to refrain from laughing at my
reaction. "I've already spoken with your Dad, and he's coming
up to get you early on Saturday morning, and then Mum's going
to drive you back after breakfast on Sunday. We're also giving
you back your bathroom privacy as well since you're going to be
beginning to manage things in the community."
I seem to have lost my voice. My heart beats thick and fast in my

chest, although for once not out of fear and dread, but pure, undiluted joy and excitement for what is to come. I am going to go home. I'm going to see my family again and see Tia. Will she remember me? I'm going to sleep in my own bed and wake up to my own room not one that, no matter how much body mist you spray, you can't seem to shake the tang of disinfectant that comes hand in hand with hospital.

My internal exultation at receiving my first overnight is instantly diminished as I realise exactly what a Home-Leave will comprise of. I will have to manage three meals and three snacks, and the last time I was at home I wouldn't touch food with a barge pole. It's almost like I can see a ghost of myself in my mind's eye, going through all the actions of starvation until admission as my advancing death loomed above me. I shake my head; I must try not to think like that any more. In the words of Courtney, if I fuck this up then I won't be looking at the prospect of Leave again for at least another month. Things are beginning to change and, as much as that's undoubtedly a daunting and arduous process, I think I'm ready. Whether I embrace it wholeheartedly or take things one step at a time, I'm ready to try, to release my sails and see where the wind takes me, because anything must surely be better than the prevalent storm I am stuck in at present.

Chapter Twenty-Seven

I don't need to set an alarm for my first day of Home-Leave, despite how the night nurse recommended that I do so. I wake at seven and use the toilet under supervision before being weighed (each patient is required to be weighed both before and after they go on Home-Leave so that the doctors can ensure they haven't done anything untoward and their meal plan is adequate for their change in activity level.) I then get dressed and pack any last minute items before having breakfast early with the support of a HCA.

Dad is waiting for me in reception, slightly bleary-eyed and dishevelled-looking, but here and smiling at me nonetheless. The night nurse hands him my Section 17 Leave Form and my bag of medication. "Don't take it all at once!" she jokes as he thanks her. She presses her fob card to the door and I step out into the crisp, serenity of the early morning. I can hear a pair of birds begin their morning chorus in a tree nearby and the steady rumble of traffic gliding past on the other side of the gate in an effort to beat the impending rush-hour. I slip into the worn leather of the car, inhaling the familiarity and safeness of it. The last time I was in this car I was being driven to the Unit, scared witless and sick. Whilst I am still sick now, I am going home, something that I never thought I would have the ability to do again.

Truth no.23 - Weight gain does not diminish anorexia nor make you any less 'anorexic', it is purely an element of recovery. Being classified as 'underweight' does not class you as sicker or more 'anorexic' than a person who is of a healthy weight. Anorexia in itself is a mental illness with the potential of causing physical side effects.

Despite telling myself that I would stay awake for the entirety of the journey home and talk to Dad, considering he set his alarm for five in the morning to come and get me, I end up dozing the whole way back. When I eventually reopen my eyes, it's to a landscape of rolling fields and towns alongside the dual carriageway. Each signpost we pass sends a shiver of recognition through me as if I am greeting old friends after an extended period of self-isolation. "Almost home," says Dad. I know, even after all these prolonged months of separation, I can still recognise and plot the map of my home on the back of my hand. It's something you never forget.

The closer we get to home, the more excited and nervous I feel. I can't believe I'll be spending time with my family without being incarcerated in hospital or with a staff member watching over me and analysing every move I make. If it wasn't for the fact Dad had my Section form in his pocket, I would have believed I was free. When we eventually park on our driveway some fifteen minutes later, I get out of the car and look up at my home in wonder, inhaling the rich perfumes of the flowers that have seemingly burst into bloom for my arrival, having been bedraggled and forgotten when I'd left them all those months ago. I place my hand upon the doorknob, hesitating as the cool metal seems to embrace me after so long apart before opening the door and stepping inside.

I am instantly enveloped by the scent of home, a soothing mixture of washing powder, safety and rest. I hear as Natalie squeals and races down the stairs and Mum comes out of the kitchen from where I can smell lunch cooking. At the thought of eating lunch, my stomach tightens and I feel my mind falter, instantaneously panicking about the calories and macros I will be expected to consume. I mentally shake myself, if I spend the entirety of my Leave worrying, then I won't enjoy myself or remember it as anything other than what my illness wants me to. I hug Mum and inhale her scent and shampoo. "Where's Tia?" I ask excitedly.

"Typical!" laughs Dad, carrying my night bag over the threshold and shutting the door firmly behind him. "It's her first Home-Leave and the first thing she asks about is the cat!"

I laugh as I pull away. "I miss her! Do you think she'll remember me?"

"Come and see," says Natalie, leading the way into the lounge. "I've had to feed her so many treats to keep her in so she'd be here when you came home!"

I kneel down by the basket and hold my hand towards Tia cautiously. She sniffs me, giving me a disgruntled look as if to say 'Human, why do you smell like this?" She sniffs me once more before deeming me worthy enough to scratch her head. "Do you recognise me, Tia?" I ask.

She meows before stretching and nuzzling up against me.

"I'll take that as yes then," I say. I scoop her up into my arms and bury my face into her fur as I make a silent vow to whoever may be listening, that never again will I spend so long apart from the people I love.

Never.

***

It's strange using the bathroom by myself that night, to be able to shower with complete privacy and brush my teeth without someone staring at me, regarding me with suspicion as if half expecting me to attempt suicide with a toothbrush. It's even stranger to sleep in my own bed, to pull the covers up and slip my hands beneath the duvet, no one waiting to tell me off for hiding them. Don't staff realise how cold it is when you to have your hands on display all the time?

My usual worries about the food I'd eaten during the day, and whether my activity levels were high enough to prevent any more weight gain are less than normal, and instead I find myself reminiscing of the things I did. I'd sat in the garden and played with Tia, I'd gone for a short walk around the neighbourhood for some fresh air and I'd cuddled up close to Mum on the sofa and watched TV with my family, each person looking at me every so often to check that this was real, that I was truly home. I only briefly felt the nagging dread of it all coming to an end when the sun rose in the morning. But no, I reminded myself, this isn't the end. If I keep this up then my Leave will only increase, it's when I don't comply that they take all of my privileges away.

Truth no.24 – Being at home with your family is worth eating for.

That night is the first in a long time that I sleep straight through without the plaguing of nightmares that have haunted me ever since my restraint feeds and the zip-tag incident with Alex. I wake to the sound of birdsong in the trees outside my window and the sound of Tia scratching at my door to remind me that she requires breakfast at this exact moment in time. For a brief moment, fear chokes me as I forget that I'm at home, and I think that the very mention of Leave was all a dream before I come to my senses and recognise the familiarity of my bedroom once more. I groan as I get up to feed her. It will take some getting used to being at home, but I much prefer it to the atmosphere of Intensive, no matter how friendly and inclusive the others are,

~ Let Me Go ~

nothing beats family. It's when you start getting used to the hospital that things start becoming an issue.

~ Let Me Go ~

Dear Friend,

We are reaching a stagnant plateau in the story now and, as much as I could continue writing the day-by-day occurrences, I fear you will find them repetitive and onerous. I continued to perceive the dining room as a battlefield, with people occasionally smearing their food, hiding it or throwing it at the walls which only made things even more intense and upsetting for me. I inflicted battle wounds on myself afterwards, it's the only way that I could make my feelings seem physical and substantial, but it was also a punishment for what I was being made to do to myself. It became a ritual, I would injure myself once for every meal I consumed, and it peaked to the extent to which my room was searched and my fragments of the shattered pen I was using were confiscated. After that, I scratched the skin off with my nails, bit myself until I bled, punched walls and tore out a section of my hair so that the only style I can get away with now is a side plait to hide the bald patch. My body became more open wounds, scabs and scars than flesh. I don't think they'll ever truly fade.
I continued to steadily gain weight, something that both terrified me and caused my thoughts to increase to such a degree that at times I felt so out of control that I didn't know what to do with myself. Yet I kept going, feeling blindly forwards on the journey of recovery, partially because of the Section which took some of the guilt away, but also because I was starting to 'see the light'. I began to glimpse the light at the end of the tunnel, flickering and wavering but there all the same. I began to change, not to heal but to mend. Like the little fragments of my mind that had been so ruthlessly and malignantly destroyed by anorexia began to, not rebuild, but to organise into a more succinct pattern. I was eventually caught spitting out my medication, something that caused me to lose my toilet privacy once more for a few weeks. The staff checked my mouth more thoroughly after that and I took them as I was supposed to. Due to my weight gain, medication and subsequent improvements to physical health; I began to start

~ 233 ~

perceiving things rationally and realistically. This might come as a surprise to you, my Friend, but brain matter actually shrinks as a result of anorexia and is often still not fully rebuilt after six months of recovery. Although my cognitions, beliefs and internal hatred for myself raged on, I began to hope that things could change, rather than my previous certainty and stubbornness that this was inevitably it for me.

The seasons steadily changed, with the leaves turning varying shades of auburn and clinging stubbornly to their bows, shrivelling and decaying as the summer slunk away like an alley cat. They struggled to maintain their grip before the frost settled and they were pulled to the ground and crystallised by jewels of ice into skeletal fragments. With the change of season came the prosperity of Christmas, another thing that brought plenty of challenges for all of us on Intensive. Although I could count on receiving some form of Leave over the period, I was uncertain whether I would be able to take it. At the time, I had only managed to be away from the Unit for a maximum of twenty-four hours, and it wasn't fair for me to expect my parents to spend the entirety of the holiday travelling to Reading and back, especially considering the upsurge in traffic. Whilst it was nearly certain for some, it was not so definite for others that they'd see their families. Not so definite at all.

Chapter Twenty-Eight

The doctors are on the ward, giving us our feedback one by one. The others in the lounge are giggling nervously and making attempts to wind each other up, only half engaging in games and watching the film on TV. Every time one of the doctors enters, the room seems to collectively hold its breath as the next person is called through, each one hoping that they'll be next and yet at the same time dreading their name being called and finding out whether they've got their wishes. This feedback is extra important. Today we'll be finding out whether we have been granted Leave for the Christmas period, whether we'll be allowed to go home and celebrate with our family or spend the day on the ward. It's more definite for some than others. For people like Jacob, Alex, Poppy and Rachel who already have weekly Leave, it's fairly certain that they'll be given they're desired Leave (the maximum amount of time you can leave the ward for is five days), but for some of the others, and even me to some extent, it wasn't quite so certain.

I hope desperately to be given leave, preferably Leave I can actually take. So far, I've only managed a single overnight, despite having these given to me almost every weekend, and I don't think it's fair to ask my parents to come and get me on Christmas Eve only to have to take me back on Christmas Day. I cross my fingers, not caring if anyone is looking, and pray to whoever may be listening that they give me more than a single night so that I can go home. But then again, why would they do it now when they haven't before? Especially considering that there are less staff available over the Christmas period. Surely they'd want to keep any patients they had doubts about on the ward for monitoring? I take deep, measured breaths in an attempt to slow the panicked flutter of my racing heart.

We all look up suddenly as we hear the dining room open as Rachel walks into the room, grinning from ear to ear. "Guess who's got five nights?" she says to the room at large. "I knew I was going to get it! I can't imagine having to spend Christmas locked in the loony bin!"

Her utterance is perceived with mixed reactions. Some of the others, in particular Poppy and Alex are pleased for her and congratulate her on this achievement because they're fairly certain of their own, whilst others appear more bitter and make no comment believing her to be tactless considering they're aware their own chances are microscopic.

Simon stands and tuts at Rachel before leaving the room. "What's your problem?" asks Rachel.

"We all knew you'd get five nights, there's no need to rub it in," he says coldly.

Rachel stifles a laugh as I hear Simon slide to the floor in the corridor, more contempt with waiting his turn alone than with the rest of us. I feel a rush of sympathy for him, as much as I find his behaviour unhelpful, I can't help empathising with him for getting his hopes up for Leave he can't have. There's no way the staff will let him go when he has restraint feeds twice a day. The only other person with a hundred percent guarantee of not obtaining some form of Leave is Ethan, but as usual his head is drooped on his chest and his eyes are wide and unseeing. As sad as it is to say, I think it might be better for him at this time of year in this way. He's not aware of what he's missing out on. I don't even think he knows it's nearing Christmas, despite the gaudy handmade decorations littering every surface available.

"As if he stands a chance," scoffs Rachel.

"That's unkind," I say, speaking out before I have a chance to stop myself.

She looks at me with shock, as if only realising what she'd just said. Jacob clears his throat noisily. "I think you're lucky Simon wasn't in the room then," he says slowly. "Please don't ever tell him what you said."

Poppy nods in agreement. "We're not 'ganging up on you' or anything like that, but we have to stick up for each other and lend out our strength to those who might need it," she says thoughtfully.

Rachel hangs her head ashamedly. "You're right," she says quietly. "I shouldn't have said anything. I'm just so happy with my news that I spoke without thinking."

"Said what?" I ask from my corner.

Jacob catches on and so do the rest who look around at each other in mock confusion. "What did you say?" asks Alex.

"Rachel, have you taken some extra 'crazy people meds' this morning?" asks Jacob seriously.

Rachel laughs before swinging onto the sofa and wrapping her arms around Poppy and Alex. Dr Ilona leans through the doorway and calls my name. I look up anxiously. "Can you follow me please; I need to update you on your care-plan."

"Good luck," they murmur quietly as I leave. I follow Dr Ilona into the dining room and sit down opposite her, twisting my fingers together anxiously as she takes her seat and flips through the document on her lap. Updates are something you both dread and look forward to; it's the only time that things can change, although they rarely ever do. This one, however, is way off the importance scale and on a different one entirely.

She glances through my notes and I can see her lips moving over the words, skimming through what I should be told and what might upset me. "You've gained a half kilo this week, which is good, you're now 89% weight restored, so hopefully we can be reaching full restoration within the next month," she smiles at me reassuringly as I grit my teeth and stare at my shoes. Hearing my weight gain progress only makes me want to hurt myself even more, but if I react to it then I'm even less likely to get the Leave I desire.

"Your education is going fine and you still have your toilet privacy." She looks up at me and I nod slowly to show that I understand. We're just going through the basics here, I can pretty much guess what she's going to say first – it's the Leave that I'm interested in. "You will be remaining on Level 2: fifteen minute observations and your diet plan will stay the same. Now," she continues briskly, as if only just becoming aware of the anxiety and tension radiating off of me in waves, "on to Leave." Leave? Does this mean I have substantial Leave, or is she just going to say that I've got a single night I'll be unlikely to take?

"Now, I know that Christmas is a big deal for you, as it is for all of our patients here." My heart drops into my stomach and I suddenly feel sick, this doesn't sound promising. Please, please, please don't make me spend Christmas on the ward. "After much discussion, the team have decided to give you five nights of Leave over the Christmas period."

My mouth hangs wide in shock and I stare at her unseeingly, half expecting there to be some kind of punch-line. Some, 'Ha! Just kidding, you'll actually be spending the entire period on the ward and won't be allowed to see your parents on the big day!' But it doesn't come.

"I-I-I can go home?" I stutter quietly, "for real?" She smiles warmly and nods at me; I think I can see a glint of a tear in her eye. "Your parents will be coming to get you on the morning of Christmas Eve, and then they're going to take you home for the holiday and bring you back after five nights. Do you think you can manage that, Beth?" she asks.

I don't know what to say, hell yes I can manage it, but the words

won't come. I stand up suddenly and tuck my chair back.
"Beth?" she asks concernedly, believing that I'm upset. I walk
around to her and, without thinking, give her a hug. "Thank
you," I say quietly into her scarf. "Thank you for giving me
Christmas."

I feel her hug me back. "That's ok, my lovely, I know you've
found things difficult here, but you are trying so hard and we do
recognise that. Have a lovely Christmas, and don't let me down!"
"I won't!" I promise. The magic of what Dr Ilona has done for me
is as thrilling as when children wait for Father Christmas. I let go
of her and she walks back into the lounge opposite. I grin at the
others to show that I've been successful as I walk past and go
straight to the Nurse's Office at the end. It's propped open
slightly so that Karen can overhear what's happening in the
lounge. I don't bother knocking and go straight in.

"Hey!" she says indignantly, "you're meant to knock."
I ignore this.

"Can you step out of the Nurse's Office please," she scolds. "You
know patients aren't allowed in here unless using the treatment
room."

I ignore this too.

"Guess what?" I ask happily.

"What," she says in defeat. "There'd better be a really good
reason for this."

"I've got five nights Leave!" I squeal excitedly.

"That's great!" she says. "I'm so proud of you!"

I rush forwards and wrap my arms around her neck.

"Alright, alright!" she says, attempting to dislodge me. "Get off, I
don't do hugs!" I squeeze her harder.

"I'm so glad you're going away for five nights," says Karen,
finally managing to pull me off as she leads me back to the door
and points adamantly towards the threshold as if to say 'here is
the line, don't cross it!'. "It gives me a break, having five nights
off from you is a luxury – Dr Ilona's granted two Christmas
wishes!" I laugh along with her, glad that things have finally
begun to look my way.

~ Let Me Go ~

From then on until Dad comes to collect me early morning on Christmas Eve, I find I'm able to appreciate and enjoy the homemade decorations we'd covered the ward with (no string or tinsel, of course) and participate in bellowing carols loudly up the corridor. Although I'm aware it will undoubtedly be difficult for me in places, a Christmas with my family is the best gift anyone could ever give me.

***

The house is bedecked with decorations and colours of rich red, luxurious golds and dazzling greens. Festive garlands adorn the bannisters and gas fireplace, with a large tree in the corner, bedecked with the ornaments we'd hung on the tree since we first understood the meaning of Christmas. Candles smoke gently along the mantelpiece, trails of smoke dancing in the air and doing a slow waltz with the scents of roasting turkey. I forget about the meal later on, procrastinating over it won't make it any less difficult or my portion size any smaller. Mum and Dad have been sent diagrams of the quantities I am supposed to have with each meal, and have received an email of the snacks I'm supposed to have in between.

It's just me, Mum, Dad, Natalie and Tia this year. We haven't got wider family coming around for the big day and are instead going to visit them over the next few days. My parents thought it would be easier for me to manage the Christmas meal and period without other people around, and I'm definitely glad they decided so. I find it hard enough to eat at home with my close family, let alone with grandparents and aunts.

Despite receiving countless presents from my family, nothing can compare to the gift before me. Dad has his arm around Mum on the sofa and in his other hand the porcelain collectable beer mug from my Grandma and Grandpa. Natalie is curled into a chair, engrossed in one of her new books and Tia is adamant that she can 'kill' her new toy in a single night. For the first time in what feels like forever, I feel at peace with the world. Despite the

~ Let Me Go ~

hardships and challenges I've faced on a daily basis to get me here, is it worth it? Most definitely. I am still ill, weight gain doesn't change that, but I am beginning to see what's worth fighting for, what's been here all along but my illness made me too blind to see. It scares me to think it, much more to admit it, but I think I might want to get better now. I know that saying those magic words aren't going to make some drastic difference, that I won't wake up in the morning and find the urge to lose weight has all but disappeared and I am satisfied with the way I am, purely as a body and not as an image. But at least now I have something to work with, something to clutch in my hands and hold fast in my mind whenever I conquer a particularly challenging meal. I think recovery might just be worth it.

~ Let Me Go ~

Dear Friend,

I wish that I could say that after admitting to myself that
recovery may be a viable option for my future it came within
months, but that was not the case. Recovery is not a saying or a
wish, it is a journey that is different in both difficulty and
length for each individual – no eating disorder is ever the
same, despite their similarities. I wish that I could say that,
currently, I am recovered and no longer feel the effects of the
illness upon my mind, but that would be lying. As much as I
hope and pray that one day I will get better, I still make the
conscious decision to fight every day, but even then I
sometimes make the wrong decision and choose the latter. The
truth is, if I don't fight then I may as well lie down and give
up.

In regards to Christmas, my Friend, I know that you're aware
of the complications it raises for me considering that I have
told you in detail many a time before. I don't think many
people realise this but, despite all of its festivities, Christmas is
one of the most difficult and challenging times of the year for
people suffering from eating disorders. Prior to the day, TV
adverts are bombarded with food commercials, each one
attempting to persuade you to purchase their products and
indulge yourself. What's even harder though is what comes
after, when the very next day the adverts change to advertise
gym memberships and diets, the famous 'New Year, New You!'
slogan appearing almost everywhere you go. Statistically, it's
been suggested that the average person exceeds their daily
requirements on Christmas Day by up to three times. This used
to terrify me and I'd be lying, my Friend, if I said it didn't have
some effect on me now, as if the very notion of the day could
make you consume more and gain weight, despite the fact I'm
on a controlled diet plan.

The adverts would increase my feelings of guilt and self-
loathing to such an extent that my urge to diet, exercise and
lose weight would increase ten-fold. The encouragements to
eat less and move more fed into my eating-disordered

thoughts, enthralling me and enchanting me with their power, until I felt it was something I had to do considering the rest of the nation was supposedly on this big diet together.

It also didn't help that I reached weight maintenance within two weeks of returning back to the Unit, something which made receiving all the encouragements and persuasions to diet even more painful to observe. There was no shutting off from it. Everywhere I went the shop windows would be replaced with diet adverts rather than the toys, gifts and food they had only recently advertised. Tell me, how is that fair? I wish I could write to you and tell you that it's no longer such a problem for me, that I am able to observe the change in adverts from another perspective and understand that they're not directed towards me and are of none of my concern, but I would be lying. If the truth must be told, and I think you're already aware, only last Christmas the New Year's adverts had such a detrimental effect on my physical and mental health that I unknowingly risked everything I had been working for, to throw it all away as I slipped down the slope that was relapse.

I managed to come to my senses eventually and see what it was doing to me, but not until it had wrought some of its effects on both myself and those I hold dear. Anorexia has many a mask to hide behind. Things grew easier as the winter months began to steadily recede, becoming replaced once more with the harmonies of birdsong, dew that clung to the grass like children to their mothers and a fresh crispness to the air that can only be brought about by new growth and life. This did come with challenges of its own, of course, namely that of maintaining my new-found healthy weight, something made all the more difficult with the pre-emption of exams lurking around the corner.

Chapter Twenty-Nine

My detainment under Section 3 of the Mental Health Act will be drawing to a close within the next few days. The detention itself is a six month period unless your clinical physician takes you off sooner. I honestly can't believe I've been detained for so long, and even before that I had a month on Section 2. I'm sitting in the lounge once more, watching as Poppy and Alex bicker half-heartedly over which Disney film is the best. "It has to be 'The Little Mermaid', says Poppy, "she has a fish friend called Flounder for goodness sake!"

"Nah, it's got to be 'Mulan' it's a classic!" rivals Alex before launching into a highly in-depth analysis as to why his favourite is the best. I'm not particularly interested, partly because of the fact I'm worrying over my Section and secondly because, despite the fact I love Disney, I have a feeling where this conversation is going to end up.

~ Let Me Go ~

Truth no.25 – The media often portray very unrealistic body images of women, bodies that are both unattainable and quite frankly unnatural.

Rachel joins in with her favourite and argues against the others. I turn to the window and sigh, looking up at the tiny piece of blue sky visible through the blinds. A few months ago, I would have given almost anything to come off of my Section, but now that the time has finally come, I'm not too sure what I want any more. My mind has once more split into two, and I can feel the consistent uncertainty of what lies before me no matter what I do to occupy myself.

I stand and leave the room just as Simon interrupts and tells Poppy that the only reason she like Ariel is because of her virtually non-existent waistline, of which he is immediately reprimanded by the HCA supervising.

I knock on the Nurse's Office door and wait until someone answers. "Can you unlock the bathroom please?" I ask.

The HCA agrees before leaving the desk to tap her fob card to the black box beside the toilet door.

"Thanks," I return.

I shut the door firmly behind me and walk past the cubicles until I am directly in front of the mirror above the sink. I look into its depths and search for the monster, yearning for it to come forward so that I can ask it what it wants me to do.

"Come on, come on," I murmur quietly as my eyes scan within. I think I can see it lurking at the back, bent over as if it's skulking or hunting something. It straightens and seems to face my way as if considering whether I am worth its time or not. I look anxiously at the door, praying that no one has the sudden urge to use the bathroom whilst I'm in here. I don't have long anyway as the nurse will almost definitely come and check on me in five minutes. The monster begins to steadily come closer, its shape becoming more recognisable and distinct with each lurching step it takes. It aligns its face with my own so that I can no longer see my reflection but am rather looking into the bottomless pits of the monster's red eyes. *"I hear you're coming off Section soon, fatty,"*

~ 245 ~

it purrs malignantly. I automatically feel as my body balloons out in response to its name for me, and I puff my shirt out anxiously to hide my shape.

"What are you going to do?" it asks, picking at its teeth with one of its yellowing claws.

"I don't know," I reply quietly, my breath fogging up the glass as I hurry to communicate before someone comes in. "On one hand I can feel myself slipping into the old mind-frame that I could lose more weight. If I come off Section then I can self-discharge and go home, that means no one will be able to control my intake or exercise regimes. I reckon I could lose everything I've gained within two months maximum." The monster nods its approval. I address my hands as I make my next suggestion, knowing full well what its reaction will be.

"I was also thinking," I whisper hesitantly, "that maybe I don't want to come off Section." I falter as I look up and am met with the angry, steel glint in its eyes. It begins to shake its head in disappointment and curl its lips with adamant disgust. "If I come off Section then I know I won't eat. If I self-discharge myself then I'm only going to go home and put both my family and myself through all of this again. Is it really worth it?"

I cringe as the monster struggles to retain its anger. It seethes out of the mirror in waves, and I can feel the power and heat of it pulsing against the exposed skin of my face. *"I thought you were better than this,"* it says with plaintive vehemence. *"I thought you wanted this. Why else do you think I've bothered to stick around for so long to help you? I knew I should never have bothered, you worthless piece of scum. I knew you'd never be good enough to maintain your diet. Did the temptation of all those calories get the better of you, fatty? Did you plan on putting on all this excess weight? They're lying about you being healthy, you're obese. You're a disgusting, fat mess and you've ruined yourself."*

I shake my head from side to side and blink my eyes rapidly to prevent the tears from falling. Surely it knows how difficult I find things in the dining room? I make a conscious decision to fight each time I enter it.

~ Let Me Go ~

"If you want to stay incarcerated and fat in this pathetic excuse of a loony bin then on your own head be it. I wish that I could hurt you to make you see just how stupid you're being; evidently what you're doing to yourself is not good enough. Punish yourself some more tonight. Make it bleed." I find myself automatically nodding. I'm so used to agreeing and complying with whatever it says that I barely even consider what it's telling me to do.

***

It bled a lot that night, so much so that I still have gauze taped securely to my arm from where I'd scratched each layer of skin away. It stings like a red-hot poker is being applied to my flesh every time I accidentally knock it or it gets wet in the spray of the shower, but as the monster rightly said it's no less than what I deserve.

I jiggle my leg up and down rapidly as I wait outside the meeting room on the ground floor. Karen places her hand firmly on my knee and warns me to stop otherwise I'll be having supplement when I get back onto Intensive. Dr Ilona appears and sits down next to me, wrapping her hand gently around my own. I don't need to say anything; she's dealt with this so many times she probably knows how I'm feeling better than what I do myself.

After another five minutes, the door to the meeting room opens and Dr Sergei welcomes us inside.

He's been reading over my notes closely for the past hour and is going to give me his final decision as to whether I shall be remaining under Section or not. As is protocol, he did make his initial analysis some two months before it's due to expire, but he said he wanted to revisit it the day before to ensure the correct decision has been made. I can appeal, of course, if he chooses to renew it but for now the decision rests with him.

The room is reasonably large, with an impressive oak table in the centre of which is surrounded by a surplus of chairs. The walls are a pale yellow and the large windows open up to the carpark outside, a slight breeze easing through and ruffling the papers discarded at the head of the table. I'm instantly relieved at the lack of reflective surfaces, the monster's presence would only undoubtedly complicate matters. Dr Sergei motions for us to sit down, Karen on my right and Dr Ilona on my left with my hand still firmly encased within her own. She must surely be able to feel the tremors running through my fingers and the perspiration forming on my palm, but she neither comments nor pulls away. Dr Sergei takes his seat at the head of the table and reorders his paperwork painstakingly slowly before leaning his elbows upon the polished oak and beginning the meeting. After greeting us all in turn, he focuses his attention on me. I squirm uncomfortably in my seat.

"Is there anything that you'd like to say?" he asks me.

I hesitate only briefly before shaking my head. After much consideration I've decided to not say anything at all, that way the decision will be based entirely upon Dr Sergei's words rather than my own. I want to jiggle my leg to release some of my pent-up anxiety, but if I'm detained again I don't want to have the additional supplement that comes hand in hand with being caught.

He pauses for a moment and scrutinises me in confusion, considering that I'm normally very open about the fact that a part of me wants to be free to diet again.

"Are you sure?" he asks.

I nod. If I don't say anything then it won't be my fault if I'm detained or discharged. The monster can't be angry with me then.

Dr Sergei takes a deep breath, and I know what he's about to say even before his tongue has formed the sounds.

"I'm sorry Beth," he says slowly, "but I've decided that it's within your best interests to remain detained under Section 3 of the Mental Health Act 1983 and I will not be discharging you from your Section tomorrow. You are of course more than welcome to challenge this with a Tribunal and either I or Dr Ilona can give you a list of Solicitors that can represent you. You don't need to worry about the funding for this; all will be

~ Let Me Go ~

covered due to your Section."

I sit there and stare unseeingly. I feel as Dr Ilona squeezes my hand in reassurance.

"Do you have any questions?" he asks.

I shake my head. No, no I don't have any questions. I don't know what I want and I don't know what to do any more.

***

Carmen stares at me thoughtfully with her large, hazel eyes. I've only been in the session for less than ten minutes and so far nothing has been said other than the usual courteous greetings. I perch anxiously on the edge of my chair and scan the room for something to look at and focus my attention on. The glass-fronted cabinets running the length of the small room are filled with various toys, colouring pencils, paper and a sandbox. Carmen sees me looking and turns to analyse the cupboard too, as if she's only just recognised it and doesn't spend copious hours a day next to it. She follows my gaze to the sandbox. I'm wondering how on earth it came to be in a therapy room in a Unit, as she stands to remove it carefully from the cabinet before placing it on the table before us. She sifts her fingers gently through the sand, leaving trenches and peaks in her wake. "Sometimes people find it easier to talk about their past when we project our feeling and emotions onto other objects." She reaches for the cotton bag in the corner of the box and empties an array of plastic animals onto the sand. As well as animals, there are princes and princesses, knights, dragons and other fictional characters. "If I were to ask you to pick the animal that represented you before you started having difficulties, which would you choose?"

I remain silent, not because I'm ignoring her or being rude, but because I'm studying each individual model and searching for the one I'd pick to represent my childhood. I pick up the lion and run my fingers over the sharp points of its mane. "What've you chosen?" asks Carmen interestedly.

~ 249 ~

I hold it up to show her.

"Why did you choose that particular one?" she asks.

"When I was young, before I became ill, I was fearless. I wasn't worried about anything and I felt infinite. I was free. I could do what made me happy and see the joy in life rather than the negatives."

"How old were you then?"

"Ten."

"Can you describe to me how things were for you during that period of your life?"

"I had lots of friends at school and I was reasonably bright so was doing well in my classes," I explain. "I was well-behaved so I rarely got into trouble and I was always busy at the weekends, either doing something with my family, having a sleepover with my friends, or playing at the park with Natalie and my cousin."

"Can you choose the animal that represents you when stated becoming ill?" she asks after a moment of consideration. I place the lion back amongst the sand and reach automatically for the little brown mouse which is half-buried beneath the larger models.

"That's interesting," notes Carmen. "What made you change from a lion to a mouse?"

"Things started going downhill for me," I say quietly. "I was bullied at school because I was clever and never really fit in with the others." I stop suddenly.

"What are you thinking?" asks Carmen gently.

"I think I've just realised why I was such a target for the bullying," I admit. "I let them do it. I began to hate myself and, although I didn't welcome the comments, I knew they were true and didn't blame them for voicing them. I never stood up for myself or told anyone about it, I let them treat me like that because I thought I deserved it all." Carmen sits there in silence as she mulls over what I've said.

"Is that what led to your eating disorder, do you think?"

I nod. "It gave me something else to focus on. It made me feel good about myself, something which didn't happen often with the lead up to exams. It was easy as well, and I found that I could get away with it."

"What did you do?" encourages Carmen.

"I cut out anything I deemed unhealthy and began exercising after school. I used to throw away my lunch and lie about when I'd eaten and how much I'd consumed, people didn't really notice until they saw my weight loss. Our school uniform was always relatively loose as well, tighter fitting trousers and skirts were banned, so it hid my figure and it looked like I hadn't lost anything."

"What happened when you were diagnosed?" she asks.

"At first I didn't believe it, but then I felt proud at what I'd achieved, although now I look back I can see that was because my brain wasn't functioning properly and I was so wrapped up in my illness. I remember that I had to go back to school and I sat in my English class whilst the others ate cake that the teacher had made and I had to pretend nothing had happened."

"That must have been very upsetting for you," she sympathises.

I nod. "I think it was detrimental than useful though. Although we now knew what it was in order to begin treatment, it meant that I no longer had to hide it, so my eating became even more erratic and my exercise routines even more extreme. I cut carbohydrates and my weight plummeted so much I could no longer do P.E. at school. In the end, they told me my BMI was too low and I had to stay at home. I couldn't move from the sofa because I was too weak, and I stayed that way until I was taken to A&E."

"What animal would you chose to represent yourself now?" she asks gently.

I hardly hesitate before dropping the mouse back amongst the grains of sand and picking up what can only be described as some monstrous beast, I stoke my finger over the grooves in the plastic that represents its fur, and press my fingers against the spikes of its teeth. Its mean, glinting eyes remind me only too clearly of the monster in the mirror. I don't even need to wait to be asked before I begin to explain. "My illness made me selfish and egocentric. I didn't care about what it did to me, and I therefore didn't see the effect it was happening on my family, or I thought I did but I never really had a clue. They had to watch me nearly die because of what I was doing to myself."

"It wasn't your fault," says Carmen reassuringly. "You didn't choose to become ill."

"I know," I reply honestly, "but I think that's what makes it worse." I drop the monster back into the sand, wanting to get it out of my hand.

"Which animal do you think represents you in the future?" she asks. I think for a minute, my hand hovering in temptation over the princess with the tiny waistline. I move my hand away and pick up the bright hummingbird, its wings spread in mid-flight.

"I'm going to be free," I say with certainty.

~ Let Me Go ~

Dear Friend,

I feel like I want to address something fairly substantial in regards to eating disorder cognitions in this letter, and that's the way it's glamorised – not just in our heads, but sadly by the media too.

I know I've said this to you many a time before, my Friend, but it's something I feel I ought to re-establish purely because I often forget it myself. Anorexia Nervosa is a mental illness with the potential of causing physical consequences, not the other way around as it's frequently implied. The physical consequences of developing anorexia are numerous and unpleasant, despite how desirable they're portrayed to be or perceived to be by individuals. For example; sufferers can be frequently cold, due to a decrease in body tissues, and can develop lanugo (soft downy hair) as their body's last way of keeping warm.

Sufferers can be prone to heart failure, kidney failure and infections. Anorexia can take other things associated with beauty too, such as skin becoming wrinkled, developing acne or peeling off. Sufferers' lips can split and crack, their hair can fall out in clumps and their nails can split. If they're unfortunate enough to develop the illness during their childhood or teenage years, sufferers can have stunted growth, become infertile and are at a much greater risk of developing osteoporosis later in life.

With all of this in mind, my Friend, how can anorexia ever be considered glamorous or desirable?

Chapter Thirty

Mrs Barber, the lady who teaches biology, sits next to me and points down at the open textbook before me as she speaks. She's trying to teach me about bone formation despite the fact that she's reading from an old textbook and my course is OCR. I subtly open my own revision guide under the desk and scan through the index. There is no mention of bone formation in the specification. I look sideways at Jacob to see if he's being taught the wrong thing by his teacher too, but see that he's staring avidly at his phone in his lap. I sigh quietly.

I raise my hand tentatively, despite being a lesson comprising of only myself and the teacher, old habits die hard. After a moment longer in which she continues reading through the book, her head in her hand as if there are a dozen other places she'd rather be (the feeling is, of course, mutual) she looks up.

"Yes?" she says, unable to conceal the slight tone of irritation evident in her voice. "Is there something you don't understand?"

"Yes," I reply nervously. "Umm, it's just that this isn't in my specification."

~ Let Me Go ~

'Pardon?"

'I'm doing OCR Biology and I don't think that textbook is the right one. Bone formation isn't in the specification."

She considers me for a moment, as if analysing whether I'm trying to be smart and deliberately irritate her.

'It doesn't matter," she says, returning to the textbook once more. "It's all Biology." I open my mouth to complain that it's not 'all Biology' at all, quite frankly if it's not in the specification for things I need to know for the exam then I don't want to learn it! All this is doing is confusing me, something which isn't particularly helpful considering I've had to teach the vast majority of the course to myself and so don't fully understand the content anyway. I never considered just how hard A-Levels would be. I begin to panic, and I twist my fingers together painfully in my lap to try and lessen the intensity of my thoughts.

Exam season starts within the next few months.

It's not just the fact I've self-taught nearly all of my four courses, it's the fact that the Education Room only runs for three and a half hours each day and on top of that we're only allowed to revise for an extra two hours out of lesson time. That's virtually nothing in comparison to what the other people in my year group must be doing. What makes things even more difficult, however, is that I'm unable to do the required practicals (due to lack of equipment and safety) and there're no computers available to patients on the ward, meaning I can't do any research or watch videos of the experiments online.

I look down aimlessly at the diagram she's gesticulating towards. There's no point saying any more, she'll only think I'm being rude and it's evidently not going to achieve anything. I glance subtly towards the clock on the wall opposite, at least I only have fifteen minutes until the lesson ends, but then it's snack time, and I think I'd rather stay than go into the dining room.

I sigh quietly again and continue pretending to listen to what Mrs Barber's saying, although in reality I'm trying my hardest to block her out considering the fact she's only confusing me. I really don't need confusing any more. Exam season is looming ahead of me; a disjointed black cloud that I'm unable to shake away or turn my back on and convince myself is non-existent. The storm comes closer with each passing day, each monotonous tick of the clock. I am not ready; I have never felt so unprepared for anything in my entire life.

Despite how much my Biology is concerning me, nothing can compare to the anxiety I'm feeling over my Music. For the past school year, Luke has insisted that we do practical lessons, in which he helps me with the more difficult sections of my piano music. This is all very well and good, but practical skills only make up a fraction of the grade, so far we haven't learnt any of the actual content – and my first exam is exactly three weeks away. I glanced up at the clock once more, five minutes left. Mrs Barber turns the page and continues reading from the textbook. What on earth are they paying her for? She's not actually teaching me anything, she's only reading from the book, and the wrong one at that.

The remaining minutes are both painful and slow in equal proportions as I stare unseeingly at the page and drown out her voice to a dull droning in the background. I'm almost pleased when I hear Mr McPherson announce that it's time for us to leave as it's nearing snack time. Almost. We file out of the classroom and head towards the bathroom, those without privacy attempting to blend in with the crowd to refrain from being noticed. It's needless to say that this works to no avail considering a HCA is ready and waiting for us. "How was school?" she asks casually, motioning for the first three girls to enter the bathroom. No more than three patients are allowed within the bathroom at any one time, that way those who need to be supervised can be kept an eye on.

"Fine," I lie. I feel the uncomfortable weight of my textbooks in my arms, dragging me and my mood down with them.

"It must be nearly exam season soon, are you ready?" she asks interestedly.

I shake my head despairingly.

~ Let Me Go ~

"Just remember to try your best," she says reassuringly, "I'm
sure Wellbrook Academy will be proud of you whatever your
results are."
I nod; I haven't even begun to think about Wellbrook. My
teachers and parents have been in contact with a lady called Mrs
Hooch for the vast majority of the school year I've spent on
Intensive. Apart from coordinating my work between my home-
school and the Education Room here, she has been starting to put
things in place for when I'm eventually discharged and join
them. I repress a shudder of fear. The thought of going back into
a mainstream school terrifies me, especially considering this is a
new school and I've never met this teacher before. The thought
of walking through those corridors by myself, being surrounded
by hundreds of students and being in an environment that I no
longer feel a part of is not entirely a pleasant one.
I take my turn in the bathroom and join the line outside the
dining room, waiting for the snack bell to ring. As much as I
want to get out of here, I'm starting to think that the ward, with
its protected environment, is a much safer place than the wider
world. The bell is rung and we file silently into the dining room,
each one searching deep inside of them to find the strength to get
through the meal. I find my allocated seat in between Alex and
Kate and look down begrudgingly at my yoghurt and apple,
wishing irrationally that it would disappear if I stare at it for long
enough.
"Take a seat please," says a HCA as she takes her place in the
seat opposite me. I look around and notice that I'm not the only
one looking down at their plates like they've been told to take a
leap of faith from the highest spring-board, only with no water in
the pool below. I sit and pull the lid from my yoghurt cautiously,
taking care to not get any on my clothes. I quickly hide the lid
beneath the pot and pick up my spoon.
"Beth," warns one of the staff members supervising my table.
"You know you need to scrape that lid. That's your first
warning." I scowl as I pick the lid back up and scrape the
yoghurt from its surface. I glance surreptitiously at Rachel at the

~ 257 ~

table opposite, where I can see the HCA supervising their table reprimanding Jacob for crumbling his biscuit as Rachel hurriedly wipes her own yoghurt lid on the underside of the table. It's not fair, how come Rachel can get away with it? If anything she needs the extra calories, I'm by the far the biggest one here.

After the allocated fifteen minutes for snack is over, the mood of everyone on Intensive brightens considerably at the knowledge of not having to go into the room again for another two hours. We retrieve our books and head back to the Education Room, the rest are planning on doing some art with the new acrylic paints that Mr McPherson ordered whilst I gather my piano music from my room for my Music lesson.

Luke is already waiting for me at the back when I enter the classroom. "Alright?" he says cheerfully.

"Yes thanks," I reply as I set my sheets upon the stand.

"I thought we might do something a little different today," he says sheepishly. "Mrs Hooch from Wellbrook emailed me some work. You've got your exam in three weeks' time so I thought we could start learning some of the content."

He sets a large pile of paperwork, sheet music and documents onto the table before him. I grimace, he's going to try and teach me the entirety of my A level course within three weeks of my exam. What makes it even worse, if it could ever possibly be any worse, is that I only have one lesson with him a week, meaning I'll be expected to teach the majority of this to myself. I take a seat and pull paper and a pen towards me, as I try and brush aside the magnitude of panicked thoughts. I have to learn a course in three weeks. How on earth am I ever going to pass? The lesson passes much as I expect it to. Luke reads information off of the sheets sent to him from the school whilst I scribble frantically onto my paper, wondering how I'm ever going to be confident enough to apply this information when I sit the actual exam. I jiggle my leg anxiously beneath the table, and for once he doesn't make a comment at the discouraged behaviour. He seems to have realised that it's virtually impossible to start teaching the course this late in the year. I wonder if he'll change his teaching strategies if there's another new admission taking it next year. He did try to encourage me halfway through his analysis of Bach's 'Violin Concerto in A minor' by saying that at least I have my practical mark to fall back on should I not be able to complete the paper. I made no comment to this; if I only have my practical mark to go on then I may as well not bother with any of it. Due to the lack of equipment, I was unable to use a computer or practice my piece much beforehand, and I can swear you can hear the hoover on the ward and Alex's cry of 'Uno!' in the background.

I trail despondently behind the others as they meander back up the corridor and contemplate whether they could play a quick card game before the lunch bell rings. My forehead feels sticky with perspiration and my hands are shaking slightly, so that my books tremble in my arms. I stop suddenly as the others go into the lounge; thoughts begin to swirl nauseatingly around my head. I'm going to fail everything. If I fail these exams, will Mrs Hooch let me into Wellbrook or will I have to fall back a year and start everything again? I find that I can't breathe, panic claws up my throat and black spots begin to blossom around the edges of my vision. I gasp, feeling as my lungs contract painfully as I struggle to pull in enough oxygen. I can't feel my legs. I see Alex in my periphery as he comes back into the corridor.

"Hey Beth," he calls excitedly. "Do you want to pla–" He cuts off suddenly as he notices me. I'm bent double, my books fall to the floor as I wrap my arms around my torso to try and hold the pieces together. I am breaking.

"Karen!" calls Alex. "Beth's having a panic attack!" The door to the Nurse's Office opens and I hear the jangle of her lanyard as she comes running up the corridor towards me. "Take slow, deep breaths," she instructs me calmly. She motions for Alex to go back into the lounge and shut the door as she places her hands reassuringly on my shoulder.

"You're ok," she emphasises slowly. "Everything's going to be ok. You need to calm yourself down and then we can talk about it." I nod to show that I understand, my face is a mess of tears and mucus and my legs are trembling with the effort of holding me up. She wraps her arm around me and leads me into mine and Rachel's room. I sit down unsteadily on my bed and she kneels before me. "What's brought this on?" she asks concernedly.

"The exams," I manage to gasp.

"Luke's only just started to teach me the content; it's less than three weeks away!" I curl inwards and sob loudly. "I can't do this, it's too much!" My voice begins to rise in pitch. "I don't want to do this any more!" I turn and, without even consciously making the decision or thinking about the repercussions it might invoke, I punch the wall hard.

Chapter Thirty-One

D ue to the anger I inflicted on the wall, I'm put on 1:1 for two hours and prevented from going to school for the afternoon lesson and instead have to sit on the table in the treatment room and have copious amounts of ice applied to my hand. "What did the wall ever do to you?" Jacob asks jokingly as he sticks his head around the door with interest.

"It keeps me here," I reply.

The rest of the day passes painfully slowly considering I have to spend the rest of it with a 1:1 in the lounge, something that brings back uncomfortable memories of the time after my admission. But when evening comes and my observation level is reduced once more, things become a little more interesting. I'm trying not to think about the panic attack/wall incident at the moment, I and the others have concocted a brilliant plan to get out of here. I steal a sideways glance at Kate who grins back at me mischievously, after all the things the staff have put us through (we're conveniently forgetting that it's all for our own good), we believe it's about time we caused some trouble for them. This being said, the trouble we can cause is of course limited, but with eight teenagers on the ward, we're determined to make a substantial effort.

The hospital itself is owned by a wealthy, middle-aged man who lives somewhere in South London in what we presume to be a large mansion of some sort. Every few months, he ventures onto the ward to inspect it, speak to the patients and to generally ensure that things are running as smoothly as they should be. Despite the fact it's only wishful thinking that the hospital will be closed, we like to believe we stand some chance in order to motivate us for what we'll be doing tonight. Quite frankly, I can't wait to have some fun and take my mind off of all the exam stress and general unease the day has caused. Alex and Poppy are just looking forward to playing pranks, but I know that Kate is feeling the pressure of the season too. Kate is now weight-restored, as she confided in me two weeks ago and, although we all negate to discuss things like weight, diet and exercise with each other, we frequently give encouragements and support. In the few short months that I've known them, the people on Intensive have become better friends to me than anyone from my old secondary school. It's strange to admit that I have friends after being in a period of isolation for so long, but it makes the world a whole lot brighter. Alex peers out from behind the door and scans the corridor before sticking up his thumb to confirm it's empty. As a group, we scuttle hurriedly like insects into Poppy and Kate's room. Simon, who is the last one in, shuts the door quietly behind him. We're all in serious trouble if we're caught, first because no more than three patients are allowed in a bedroom at a time, and secondly because there're boys in the room too.

Poppy lifts the book from her bed and upon it lies a single tampon. Alex is struggling to maintain himself, at the tender age of fourteen he's missed some of the crucial sexual education lessons at school such as menstruation in science and has never seen a tampon. The very notion of its purpose sends him dangerously close to the brink of hysteria. "Why are boys so

immature?" asks Poppy, shaking her head in mock
disappointment. I hasten to agree.
"How did you get it?" asks Kate in awe.
Poppy shrugs and examines her fingernails in mock contempt "I
have my ways and contacts," she says darkly. Despite the fact I
am obviously aware that the presence of a tampon is not
something to speculate and wonder over, considering we're on a
locked ward and they're one of the top items on the list of
contraband, we can only wonder at how she managed to sneak it
in. Poppy removes the wrapper, and Alex begins to snort with
suppressed giggles. "Alex, for goodness sake," I murmur
urgently. "Be quiet or we'll get caught!" Simon passes him a
tissue to stifle the noise in, warning him that if he can't behave
himself then he'll be sent outside.
Jacob punches him playfully on the shoulder. "Control it, bro,"
he says quietly. "It's just a lady-thing."
"Alex, have you got the pen?" asks Poppy. Alex holds up a red
pen in response.
"Have you got the tape?" Poppy asks me. I raise my shirt and
peel back the cellotape I'd taken from Education Room. "I like
your method," approves Poppy as I hand her the tape and she
sticks it to the end of the string.
"Would anyone like to do the honours?" asks Alex.
Simon raises his hand instantaneously. "Me," he says, "I owe
those bastards one." I raise my eyebrow towards Poppy. We all
know Simon has more reason than most to be angry towards the
staff, considering he undergoes restraint feeds with them twice a
day – despite the fact it's arguably his choice considering he
won't comply in the dining room. Alex passes him the pen in
silence and Simon scribbles all over the tampon. At this point,
Alex lets loose an unnaturally high-pitched scream of mirth,
making us all jump and Simon falter with his artwork.
"That's it," says Jacob. "You're out." He pushes him towards the
door. Alex turns and makes an attempt to punch him light-
heartedly in the stomach, but Jacob dodges him deftly and he's
out the door a second later.

"Done," says Simon happily, hanging up his artwork for all to see.

I look down nervously at my watch. "The manager will be here within the next five minutes," I say. "Is it too soon to hang it up?"

"I say we do it now," says Poppy decisively. "I've known him to come early."

Simon opens the door silently and peers out into the corridor. "All clear," he whispers after a moment. As the second stage of the operation begins, Kate slips away to the bathroom and I hear the door creak open gently as Rachel opens it from the other side. Rachel goes to the lounge to ensure the member of staff on Ethan's 1:1 doesn't move. I stroll casually to the end of the corridor so that I'm right beside the door to the Nurse's Office and flatten myself against the wall.

I hold my breath and feel as my hands and feet dingle with a mixture of nerves and excitement. I know they're never going to close the hospital for a prank like this, but at least we'll be causing trouble which is more 'normalised' rather than the usual 'I'm not eating/drinking/complying trouble'. After a minute longer, I hear the shrieks of Kate from inside the bathroom. Despite the fact I'm expecting it, I still jump and almost give myself away as Steph hurries out of the Nurse's Office towards the racket without so much as a backwards glance in my direction. I slip out my foot and catch the door before it has time to close and watch as Alex scurries up the corridor to add to the stress. "There's a spider!" shrieks Kate and I hear the raised voice of Steph telling her to calm down and show her where it went as Alex begins to yell that he can see it too from his position in the doorway. The others slip out of the room and together we head into the Nurse's Office. Poppy pulls out one of the chairs and Simon balances upon it to smooth the cellotape to the ceiling, the inked tampon swinging like some abhorrent flag. We scurry back into the lounge just as Steph comes out of the bathroom, claiming that there's no spider there and they're just being silly. The bathroom door has barely swung shut before we hear the

metallic chime of the lift and the heavy footfalls of the hospital
manager entering the ward. We hold our breath and snicker
behind our hands. Even Ethan has recognised that something's
happening because he raises his eyebrows a half centimetre as if
to ask what we've done.
"Wait and see," I reply.
Steph and the manager stroll past and we follow them silently as
Steph taps her fob card to the black box beside the door to the
Nurse's Office and pushes it wide to reveal the tampon dangling
from its string and drifting merrily with the slight breeze
through the window. The manager opens his mouth wide, too
shocked for words as Steph begins to explain that this isn't her
fault, that she had no idea this was here.
Evidently, it seems that everything comes with a price. Once the
manager had left some ten minutes later with Steph's repetitive
apologies chasing him down the lift, we're summoned into the
lounge for a 'very serious discussion' in which we pretend to
look ashamed of ourselves, but in reality laugh vivaciously as
soon as she leaves the room.
The only person who doesn't join in is Simon who looks slightly
dejected and annoyed. He can't have honestly thought they'd
shut Birchmoor, did he?

***

That evening, after a heated discussion with Rachel over who the
best *Harry Potter* character is, I lie back on my bed and begin to
read the next chapter of my book. It doesn't take long before I'm
disrupted. "He's gone!" gasps Alex, skidding to a stop outside
mine and Rachel's room. I sigh and mark the page in my book.
He must still have not recovered from this afternoon's activities.
"What are you talking about?" I ask sceptically. "Come on Alex,
you saw Steph's face when she saw that tampon, it's too soon to
do anything again yet."
"We've got to let them think they're in a period of calm again,"
interjects Rachel knowledgeably, "that way it's much more

effective." This isn't the first time Alex's tried to wind us up. Last week, he had half the inhabitants on Intensive believing that Steph had said we could play jousting with the two chairs from the Nurse's Station and the tubes we found in the craft cupboard – a feat that firstly began with a severe talking to for going into their office, and secondly for playing an energetic game classed as 'exercise' rather than fun. As much as he means well, I don't want to risk my Home-Leave.

"He's gone!" he repeats, brandishing his hands before us in exasperation. "He was here and then he stole a fob card and then he -"

"Hold on," I interrupt, as I notice the burning intensity in his eyes. "Say it slowly. What's happened?"

"It's Simon," explains Alex. "He's absconded."

I look at Rachel with wide-eyes.

"Alex, you're not joking with us again, are you? You know how they reacted when we played jousting."

"I'm not joking," he says earnestly. "I'm deadly serious." Poppy leans around the doorframe and looks at us quizzically. "Did I hear right?" she asks. "I saw Simon a few minutes ago; he's with Ethan in the lounge."

"No he's not," argues Alex hotly.

"Have you found the key to the treatment room and taken any of the 'crazy people meds'?" asks Poppy in mock seriousness. Alex swears at us colourfully and sticks up his fingers in frustration. We jump suddenly as Steph runs up the ward and into the Nurse's Office, Dr Sergei wiping the sweat from his brow as he follows.

"Oh shit, you weren't kidding," I murmur as the air is knocked from my lungs and dread fills my heart, spreading itself around my body with each beat so that I feel cold and faintly nauseous. We rush into the lounge and take it in turns to stand on tip-toes and press our noses to the windows. We can't see any sign of him. The area around the gate is crowded with staff organising a search party.

"I hope he's ok," I murmur quietly. "I hope he doesn't do

anything … you know."

The others nod sadly as I voice what we're all thinking. My heart begins to beat thick and fast in my chest and my throat begins to constrict with fear as the thought I'd been repressing creeps into my head. What if he doesn't come back at all?

We continue to peer out the window long after the other staff drive off in their cars and the Police arrive to ask for details.

"Come on Simon," I murmur furtively against the glass. "Where are you?"

At eight thirty, some two hours after his disappearance, the night nurse comes into the lounge to announce snack time. We ignore her and continue to stare concernedly out the window, scanning the night desperately for any sign of Simon. He hasn't been outside in two years. How can he possibly be safe?

"Don't ignore me," reprimands the nurse. "If you don't come and have your snacks then I'll have to give you supplement. You don't want me to have to hand this over in the morning, do you?" Once more we remain silent; somehow I think they'll have more pressing matters to discuss in morning handover.

***

I don't sleep well that night and I assume, from the numerous sounds of tossing and turning from the rooms adjacent, none of the others do either. It's gone midnight when the lift chimes and I hear the footsteps of people coming onto the ward. I count at least three. I hear as one person stops, just outside of my room, and the muffled sound of clothes crumpling as someone falls to the floor. I strain my ears to listen, and judging from the abject silence from Rachel's bed, she's doing the same.

"Simon…Simon," whispers the night nurse. "Simon… have you taken anything?" I feel my heart constrict. There's no response. I raise myself slightly and peer towards the doorway which is framed with the soft amber light of the night staff's torches. Simon stares back, his mouth gaping wide and his eyes unseeing. He moves his head slightly from side to side as if he's in some kind of trance and a trail of drool falls from his mouth. Simon, what have you done to yourself?

Chapter Thirty-Two

We're called into the lounge for an emergency meeting as soon as the bell rings signalling the end of breakfast. I don't need to ask what it's in aid of. After last night's events, you'd be a fool to not have connected the two together. The only person absent from the group is Simon, and I briefly wonder whether he's in the treatment room or was rushed to a general hospital in the early hours of the morning to have his stomach pumped. I sit down in my corner and watch as the others come in and take their seats, each one with an obvious expression of anxiety written clearly across their faces. Alex taps his fingers against his thigh in a rhythmic pattern; he must have been disturbed more than any of us last night considering he rooms with Simon.

Steph is the last one inside, and she shuts the door firmly behind her to block out the rattle of the meal trolley being taken back into the lift to be cleaned in the kitchen. She sits down on the sofa opposite and clears her throat before beginning. "I know that you're all aware of what happened in regards to Simon last night, as it was passed on in morning handover." We nod collectively to show we're listening and understand.

"Unfortunately, due to the fact that Simon ran from the hospital and took an overdose last night, he will be on 1:1 for the remainder of today and will not be joining you in the Education Room. I ask that you're considerate of his privacy and give him some space to come to terms with what he has done."

She looks around at us all and we nod and make vague noises of agreement.

"Is he going to be transferred?" asks Alex quietly.

Steph considers this for a moment before shaking her head slowly, her short hair flicking from side to side. "No, not at the moment, although I must impress upon you all the severity of his actions. I'm going to leave you in a minute, I'm sure you'll probably want to use the bathrooms and gather your books before first lesson starts, but if you have any worries or want to talk to staff, there is always someone available."

We begin to talk amongst ourselves as soon as she leaves to start Ethan's feed, voicing our thanks that he's back in the hospital and safe whilst also questioning why we didn't see the signs sooner. I know it's not our fault, much the same as I'm now trying to understand that neither was Alex's attempt, but it definitely feels that way when someone you spend practically all day with takes such dire measures in an act of desperation.

***

It's mid-afternoon when Dr Ilona calls me into the dining room, I finished Paper 1 of English Literature a mere half hour ago and the others have organised a large game of Monopoly which has taken up a large proportion of the carpet. I can still hear the half-hearted bickering over who owes who what even when Dr Ilona shuts the door firmly behind her. I sit down opposite her and notice the vast array of paperwork scattered haphazardly across the table. I'm unsure what she wants to see me about, she gave me an update on my care-plan yesterday, and I'm fairly certain nothing could have drastically changed in the interim period.

~ Let Me Go ~

She flicks through the documents earnestly until she's found the one she's looking for. "Good afternoon Beth?" she asks pleasantly. "How are you?"
"I'm fine thank you," I reply nervously. I'm always anxious when I get called in for a catch-up, I automatically assume it's for the worse, and that she's come to tell me something terrible has happened to my family or that they're going to keep me here for another year.
"How was your exam? You had English today, didn't you?"
I nod. "It was really hard, I honestly don't think it went too well," I reply sadly.
"Try not to worry about it. The main thing is that you've tried, and I know your school are going to make allowances for you."
I sigh before nodding in agreement. I don't want allowances to be made for me; I want to fit in like everyone else. Is that really too much to ask?
"Anyway, exams aside, I wanted to come and talk to you today about potentially discharging you within the next month or two," says Dr Ilona.
My mouth gapes wide in shock. "You're going to discharge me?" I ask quietly.
"Not immediately, but in the near future, yes. We're in correspondence with your Head of Year, Mrs Hooch, and we've arranged for you to visit the school on you Home-Leave on Monday to have a meeting. Don't worry," she says, recognising the sheer look of panic on my face, "we're going to do this as slowly and gradually as you need it to be."
"Ok," I reply slowly, "but I'm Sectioned. How will that work?"
"You've been managing your meal plan now for quite a while, and the medication has definitely helped, so I think we're going to try and take you off within the next few weeks. How does that sound?"
I shrug my shoulders to feign nonchalance. I'm not sure what to feel.

~ Let Me Go ~

Truth no.26 - As much as I want to get out of here and start living again, I'm almost as afraid of leaving the hospital as I was entering it. I've been on a locked ward for so long; I'm not sure what the real world is like any more. I'm worried that I'll get out and find there's no place for me any more. That the only place I'm meant to be is incarcerated in a Unit.

"Please try not to worry," she reiterates kindly. "This isn't going to happen overnight, but we do need to start looking towards the future and putting things in place." I nod once more. I'm nearing my eighteenth birthday in three months' time, and I'm more than aware that, once I reach that magical date, I'll become an 'adult' overnight. If I'm still in Birchmoor then, they'll have no choice but to transfer me, which means an adult general Psychiatric Hospital – not exactly somewhere I ever plan on visiting.
"You've already met your new nurse in adult services back home, haven't you?" she asks, looking down at her papers to check if she's got it right.
"Yes," I reply. "I'm not too sure if I like it though, it's much different than CAMHS."
"It will be," she replies bluntly. "Unfortunately, when you reach eighteen you have to move services if you require them. They're not there to be liked; they're there to give you support and help you get through your difficulties."
After a few more questions about how I'm finding my meal plan and medication, in which I give the same answer that it's difficult but I'm still fighting, she dismisses me and I return to the lounge to attempt to revise amongst the arguments that will have undoubtedly sprung out over the game in my absence.

***

I twist and turn in my bed, my eyes itching with fatigue and yet I'm unable to rest due to the number of distressing thoughts circulating my brain. I'm worried about being discharged and how I'm going to cope with seeing this new nurse from adult

services on a weekly basis, and I'm even more concerned about
the prospect of going to Wellbrook in four days' time.

"What's up Beth?" asks Rachel concernedly.

"Can't sleep," I mumble back quietly. Lights are supposed to be
out and rooms are meant to be silent after ten o'clock.

"No shit," she whispers back. "Do you want to talk about
anything?"

"No, other than the fact I'm potentially being discharged in a few
months," I whisper back.

Rachel's silent for a moment. "I think they're going to discharge
me too soon. I must admit, it's scary the prospect of going back
into the community again. It's been so long, you know?"

I murmur agreement before feigning sleep as a HCA walks up
the corridor, stopping at our room to shine a torch in our faces to
check on us. I can see the glow through my closed eyelids. It's
strange to think that, at first, I found it strange to have a bright
light shone into my face as I tried to sleep – it even woke me up
at times – but now I've become so accustomed to it that I expect
it. It's weird on Home-Leaves when I sleep through the night
without some form of disturbance. It's the littlest of things that
affect you the most. The light flicks from my face and
presumably onto Rachel's before I hear the quiet footsteps of the
HCA leaving and continuing up the corridor to check on Simon
in the room next door. He is alone, considering that Alex left for
his Leave this afternoon. I open my mouth to ask Rachel a
question, but my breath catches in my throat as I hear a shriek
from Simon's room.

"Nurse! Nurse!" shouts the HCA. I hear the hurried heavy
footfalls of the night nurse running up the corridor and bursting
into Simon's room. "Get some towels!" I sit up suddenly and see
Rachel doing the same; we look with wide eyes at each other as
the HCA streaks past our room for the linen cupboard.

"Simon … Simon …" I hear the nurse mumble. I hear a faint
moaning in response. The HCA runs back up the corridor to
Simon's room, puffing like a steam train and with a pile of white
towels clutched in her arms. I hear the night nurse tell the HCA

to press the towels tightly to Simon's neck and I grimace as I realise what has happened. My heart seems to falter in my chest. Oh God, please don't let him die.

"Come on Simon, stand up," says the night nurse. "We need to get you to the treatment room." I hear the shuffle of footsteps and watch as the night nurse and HCA half-carry Simon towards the treatment room. He has a red line across his neck that's still leaking blood and in the HCA's hands are a pile of bloodied towels. The door to Nurse's Office is shut and I hear the anxious murmurs of the others in their rooms. I can hear Jacob breathing heavily and swearing from his room, and as Ethan's 1:1 tells him to calm down and that everything's under control. It's a long time after Simon is carried back into his room, a large surgical dressing around his neck and his eyes bleary with a sedative that I finally drift off into an uneasy sleep.

Chapter Thirty-Three

We're summoned into the lounge once more the following morning, and this time there's no doubting what the topic of this meeting is. We group together on the sofa; the only person not present is Simon whom I assume is still sleeping off the remnants of whatever it was they injected him with last night. Our faces are drawn and grey, with black bags beneath our eyes. I don't think anyone managed to get more than a few hours of sleep last night. Steph shuts the door swiftly behind her and takes her seat once more on the sofa opposite, the whole thing procuring de-ja-vu, a sickening loop that's on repeat. She sighs before addressing us at large, exactly as she had done the following morning.

"I think most of you are aware of the incidence regarding Simon on Intensive last night," she begins. We nod solemnly. I don't think I'll ever forget that glistening trail of blood across his throat. The only person who doesn't move is Alex, who's looking at Steph with wide eyes, evidently aware that something drastic has happened, and yet unsure of what considering he went to bed early that night. Steph notices this and addresses Alex firmly. "Simon tried to commit suicide last night," she says. She turns and addresses the room at large once more. "I'm not sure how much you know, but I think it's best if we're open and honest with each other, it's not going to be beneficial to either side if rumours begin to spread and obscure the truth." We nod in agreement.

"We held a meeting yesterday, as you well know, in which I told you about how Simon ran from the hospital and was brought back by the Police in the early hours of the morning. Despite searching him when he came back onto the ward, he had managed to conceal a small pen knife which he used last night to try and slit his throat." Even though I know of his suicide attempt, and guessed how he had done it, it still comes as a terrible shock to hear those words voiced aloud. They flood through the air like some toxic poison, silencing us so that all we can do is hold each other's hands and stare at Steph with wide eyes. Simon had almost died last night.

"We wanted to let you know that Simon is alive and recovering well from his ordeal. The cut he sustained was superficial and staff were on hand immediately, however, the severity of his actions will have their repercussions. In light of what happened last night, we've decided to search all of your rooms." This is met with a storm of complaints.

"How is that fair?" asks Alex angrily.

"Yeah," seconds Poppy. "We haven't done anything wrong!"

Steph raises her hand to silence the outbursts. "It's a measure of safety and hospital protocol, the fact that a knife was found on the Unit last night is a great concern to us all. There will be no arguments and no exceptions. You will not be allowed into your rooms until the search has been carried out. We will also be looking through the lounge, dining room and therapy rooms during your first lesson. During lunch break, the Education Room will undergo a thorough examination as well." The room is so silent that you could hear a pin drop; something which I'm aware is ironic considering sharps are top on the list of contraband.

"Unfortunately, Simon was transferred in the early hours of this morning after he came around from the medication he was given last night."

"What?" asks Jacob furiously.

"You all know Simon was nearing his eighteenth birthday, and so he would have needed to be transferred within the next few months anyway. The doctors were called last night and the decision was made that it would be kinder and more beneficial for him to be transferred to a more secure Unit last night, we don't have the resources or the staff to appropriately treat him here any more."

Rachel splutters in disbelief and shock. "But this is a loony bin, why does he have to go to another?"

Steph clears her throat angrily. "This is not a 'loony bin'. Birchmoor predominantly treats eating disorders, alongside other mental illnesses that may accompany it. Whilst Simon does evidently suffer from an eating disorder, it's believed that he may require treatment in an adult general Psychiatric Hospital to tackle some of the other issues first. I know you're aware that Simon wasn't exactly responding to treatment here."

"So that's it," says Kate quietly. "He's just gone?"

Steph nods sadly in resignation. "We thought it would be easier for him and all of you if he left before you were awake, that way he could leave without a fuss."

We sit in collective silence, enveloped in shock once more. "This does mean, however, that there's a bed available on Intensive and the-"

"Don't tell me you've already found a new admission!" interjects Rachel angrily. "His bed's barely gone cold!"

Steph sighs, as if she has been expecting this response all along. "This is a hospital," she states matter-of-factly. "I can understand how shocked you must all be feeling, believe me it wasn't an easy decision for any of us, but this is still a hospital and there will always be patients in need of our help." Rachel storms out of the room and slams the door violently behind her.

~ Let Me Go ~

"Just stick together and try and stay strong," Steph concludes. "These next few days are going to be difficult, that's perfectly understandable, but it's not as hard if we take things as a team. If you have any worries or need someone to talk to, then I and the rest of the team will be available throughout the day. The new admission will be arriving at two this afternoon. He's seventeen and called Ben. I'm sure you'll all make him feel welcome and help him to settle in." Steph smiles at us all warmly before heading into the treatment room to ready our medications before the Education Room opens for the first lesson. We sit in silence. I'm not sure how much more of this I can take.

**

I find it excruciatingly difficult to concentrate on my revision that day, and by the uneasy looks and frequent glances at the clock from the others, I presume the feeling is mutual. There is an unnatural silence to the ward at ten, as Simon's screams are no longer reverberating through the walls of the hospital, but it makes me feel his absence even more, despite the fact the newfound silence should aid me in my studying.

I know I need to concentrate on my work, my second English exam is tomorrow and I know I didn't do too well in the first one, but my mind is still reeling at the news of Simon's suicide attempt and subsequent transferal and going through the usual worries of what state the new admission is going to be in when he arrives. I pray that he's only slightly underweight, something which can be turned around in a few months of treatment. I'm not sure how I'm going to be able to cope if he comes in a state of emaciation. It makes me feel so much worse about myself when I see people like that, and the monster's anger at me increases ten-fold at the fact that I'm relatively compliant with treatment and no longer look like that any more.

Despite being a healthy weight now for at least four months, I'm still not used to the difference of my body, and somehow I don't think I ever will be. Also, I know it's selfish to admit, but I hope he's quiet and compliant. I'm struggling enough with my

revision, let alone without the shouting and screaming.
When the Education Room eventually closes for the day, we
pack up our books and belongings nervously, anticipating what
type of challenge we're going to be faced with upon re-entering
the corridor. I hear the new admission before I see him. As soon
as the sound-proofed doors of the Education Room swing
forwards to emit us the sound of a low, keening wail reaches our
ears and we know instantly that we're in for a rough night and
next few days. It's one of those patients.

Truth no.27 – As a group, we've collectively come to the conclusion
that there are two types of patients, the ones that come in and accept
their fate, and the ones who give staff and patients hell beforehand.
There's no doubt about it, you have to comply with treatment to get
discharged, whether it takes you a second to come to terms with it or a
year.

I follow the others into the lounge to dump my revision notes
before the bell calling us to snack rings. I can hear his cries
louder than ever now that we're further from the Education
Room. I sit down uneasily in my corner, pulling my legs up to
my chest. I notice from the sideways glances of the others that
they're apprehensive about the new arrival too. It's not that we
have a problem with the new admission, it's just the fact that
there's no getting away from it. If they're in a frame of mind to
scream and cry the whole night through, then you won't sleep. If
they're going to shout about the calorie content of certain food
items in the dining room, then you've got to sit there and hear it.
Thank goodness I still have my Leave, but even that awakens
some of the old thoughts that I shouldn't be going home, that I
should be the one crying in the room. "I'm not eating it!" I hear
him shriek. "Do you think I'm going to be stupid enough to eat
that?" We collectively wince, our thoughts turning
uncomfortably towards our own waiting snacks in the dining
room.

"Come on guys," says Jacob. "We've got to stick together." But even as he says it I can see the doubt in his eyes as he's drawn towards the temptation of refusal and weight loss. The others nod their heads in agreement.

"Jacob's right," I say from my position in the corner. "If we give up now then we'll be even further away from discharge. We've all come so far and it'd be stupid to throw it all away now." My speech is interrupted by the new admission who wails about how many calories there are in the glass of orange juice he's faced with.

"As much as this is making me cringe, they're both right," interjects Kate. "We've got to stick together and get through this. The new boy will be here for much longer than any of us; we'll hopefully be leaving soon." We nod collectively once more. "I don't know about you, but I'd rather be discharged and get a second chance at life than be transferred." We remain silent, the memory of Simon leaving the ward still fresh in everyone's mind. I stand up to use the bathroom, in search of a few precious moments of privacy to settle my own thoughts. Despite the positive statement I just uttered to the group, I feel like I'm about to crumble inside like some old, derelict castle. I ask a HCA to open the door for me and close my eyes to try and quieten my racing thoughts as I step gratefully into the cool, semi-dark interior.

I open my eyes.

The monster is looking back at me. At first, I consider turning around and walking back out the door, closing it behind me to put a physical barrier between me and it, but we all have to face our fears eventually. I walk forwards slowly until I'm standing directly in front of the mirror, its face lining up with my own. It growls at me menacingly and flexes its clawed paws in a threatening manner. "*You should be ashamed, fatty,*" it says angrily. "*You should look like Ben, he's done it right, but instead you're a fat mess. You're nothing but a fat failure that everyone wishes were dead!*" I blink my eyes rapidly to stop the tears from falling. I've promise myself to never cry in its presence again. "*Going to cry? You're so disgustingly overweight that I'm surprised you can even*

~ Let Me Go ~

see what with all those rolls of fat on your face," it leers at me, its scarlet eyes glinting malevolently. *"I knew you'd never be good enough. I knew you didn't have the strength to stick to your diet. What is it they have you eating now? Two thousand calories a day, is it?"*
I stare it in the eyes unblinkingly. "The dietician says that's a normal amount for the average human being. He says that my body is like a machine, if I don't give it fuel then it won't be able to run and function properly," I reply quietly, repeating the things I've been told on numerous occasions. The monster smirks at me like I'm some little child who can't possibly understand the greater picture. *"They're just saying that. Calories are bad for you, they're disgusting little creatures that make you fat and you know that."* It takes a great amount of effort, but I manage to shake my head.

Truth no.28 - Despite what I'd previously believed, they are not substantial organisms able to think for themselves. Calories are units of energy and nothing more.

"How much weight is it they've had you gain, 10kg? You have to lose it all as soon as they take you off that Section. Discharge yourself and lose it all, only make sure you do it better this time otherwise I'll make you regret it," it threatens.
I clench my fists and look at it angrily. "Shut up monster, I'm not listening to you any more?"
"What?"
Without meaning to, I find that my voice is rising in both volume and power. "I'm not listening to you any more. You've fed me nothing but lies, and as for making me regret it? You can't hurt me unless I let you, and I don't want to give you that control any more."
I jump as the HCA presses her fob to the black box and the door clicks open. "Who're you talking to?" she asks curiously. "I could swear I heard a voice."
"Nothing," I reply, "nothing at all." I turn from the mirror and don't look back.

~ Let Me Go ~

***

The rest of the week passes as much as we expect it to. None of us gets much sleep considering Ben shouts at the staff all night and is frequently carried forcibly into the treatment room for his feeds. It comes with great relief when the week draws to a close and I go on my Home-Leave, despite the fact I'm facing more challenges whilst I'm away.

***

I lean back into the worn seat of the car as Mum navigates through the town. We're on our way to Wellbrook Academy for a meeting with Mrs Hooch about planning my integration back into mainstream school. Now that my discharge is being consciously thought about and planned for, I'm going to be going to one of my lessons each week on Monday and travelling back up to Birchmoor in the afternoon.

My breath is shaky and I feel faintly nauseous at the prospect of going into a large school and meeting this lady who I've never met, it' strange that she knows so much already about me and my situation and yet I know nothing about her. Starting at Wellbrook is supposed to be a fresh start for me, it was inevitable considering my previous secondary school didn't have a Sixth Form attached, but I'm extra nervous considering the vast volume of students and sixth formers that will be there. There're only seven of us in the Education Room – and even that's on good days. We drive through the gates of the school and Mum backs carefully into the bus bay, considering that they won't be here for another four hours yet. I don't want to get out of the car. If this is how I'm feeling today, bearing in mind I'm not expected to go to lessons only to a meeting, how am I going to be feeling this time next week? I feel a sudden, hot flash of guilt at the thought of Ben having his feed on the Unit; I feel that should be me. Does coming to school mean I'm better?

~ 282 ~

~ Let Me Go ~

Truth no.29 – The nature of the illness means that you both fear getting better, as being better means you're no longer what society deems 'anorexic' and yet yearn for a life without it.

Nervously, I get out of the car and follow Mum into reception where we sign in and are allocated visitor badges to wear. I sit anxiously in reception looking up at all of the pictures and artwork on the wall, jiggling my leg rapidly in agitation and pre-emption for what is sure to come. How will I ever belong here? Can a school of this size really have space for me? I can hear the rumble of students above as they move around during their break time and flinch automatically at the sound of a younger student shrieking with glee outside. I can't help myself, a year in hospital has taught me that all screams are of pain and distress, and I look around automatically for the person being restrained. We aren't kept waiting long, before the door labelled 'Cafeteria' swings open and emits a tall lady wearing a grey hoodie and bright pink sports short who comes straight towards us, her long hair swishing from side to side as she moves. She holds out her hand to Mum and smiles warmly at me.

"Hello, I'm Mrs Hooch," she says happily in a distinctly Welsh accent. "I'm the current Head of Year Twelve, although I do teach P.E. too. It's great to finally meet you both!"

She smiles down at me once more and I attempt to give my own in return, I think it comes out more as a painful grimace. Mrs Hooch reaches to shake my hand, and I'm grateful that she doesn't immediately wipe it on her shorts after due to the fact I'm perspiring so much in anxiety. "I'm glad to finally be able to put a face to a name," says Mum. Mrs Hooch nods rapidly in agreement, her ponytail swinging back and forth like a pendulum. "Thank you so much for everything you've done for Beth so far, I'm very grateful for the amount of correspondence there's been between here and Birchmoor, it should hopefully make her integration here a lot easier."

"That's not a problem," replies Mrs Hooch. "We just want

whatever's going to be easiest for Beth, that's all. I thought we'd start by having a quick tour of the school once the students have gone back to their lessons and then maybe we could have a catch-up in the meeting room."

Mum nods in appreciation. "That sounds perfect."

As the last of the footsteps disappear and the students outside return indoors, Mrs Hooch leads us into the Cafeteria. I hesitate briefly over the threshold, my mind instantly flooding with fear at the thought of walking through a place where food is prepared and eaten. I take a deep breath and cover my mouth and nose with my sleeve. Despite the fact therapy has made me come to accept otherwise, being in such an anxiety-provoking situation has awakened some of my old fears, the integral being that I don't want to inhale any of the calories that might still be lurking in the air. She leads us down corridor after corridor, stopping at places such as the English Department, Science Block and the 'Calm Space', an area that's predominantly for students who find things difficult and a place it's estimated I'll be spending a lot of time in initially. Each corridor we go down looks much the same as the others, and I find myself looking around in interest, more comfortable now that the students are quietly tucked into their classrooms. After the tour she leads us through the Sixth Form Common room, an area she tells me is notoriously noisy considering some students are on their frees. I wrap my hands around my torso and dig my nails painfully into my back to prevent myself from giving in to the urge to run away and get back into the safety of the car. Mrs Hooch leads us into the adjacent meeting room, an oblong room with pale walls upon which is hung various pieces of artwork, before shutting the door behind her. I take a seat next to Mum.

"Do you know what you're thinking of studying when you come to us next year?" asks Mrs Hooch as she sits opposite in her own chair and pulls out paper and a pen from her pocket. I remain silent, I think I've left my voice in the car and I hope desperately that she doesn't think I'm being rude. "Beth's doing Biology, Music, English Literature and English Language at the moment, but she's thinking of potentially dropping the Music next year," says Mum. "Her tutoring hasn't been particularly brilliant and I think it's put her off." Mrs Hooch nods as she takes notes. "I did get the impression things weren't going too well on that side, I've had emails from the Education Room with an urgent request for work. What we thought though, is that perhaps it might be easier if Beth resits Year Twelve next year, due to the fact she hasn't had the best of starts. It does mean that I won't be your Head of Year any more," she says, turning to me once more, "but I can introduce you to a lovely lady called Mrs Brennan who'll be taking over."

I nod passively. I don't want to go back a year, I want to stay where I'm meant to be, even if I don't quite fit in yet. "I'll still be supporting you of course," continues Mrs Hooch with a smile, "I've taken you under my wing!"

The rest of the meeting passes with Mrs Hooch asking various questions to Mum about my previous education and the kind of support I'll be needing when I eventually start. She continues making notes on the paper before folding it and tucking it safely away.

I jump suddenly as the noise of siren rings through the school, stops and then starts again. I look around with wide eyes and begin to tremble. "It's ok," replies Mrs Hooch reassuringly, "that's just the school bell. I should have warned you about that earlier. Shall we call it a day and I'll see you the same time next week?"

I nod gratefully and she leads us back to reception to sign out. "Don't worry Beth, we'll sort everything out. I'll have a think and a chat with Mrs Brennan about how we can support you and then we can all meet and go through it next week. How does that sound?" I nod, despite the fact that the thought of returning makes me feel like I've swallowed a large can of worms.

"Thank you," I say as she shakes my hand once more.

"It's not a problem, my lovely," she replies with a smile. "Not a problem at all."

Chapter Thirty-Four

Things are pretty much the same on Intensive as when I left it. Ben is still causing trouble for the staff and keeping the others awake at night and, once back from his Home-Leave, Jacob organises another prank for the staff. The only thing that has changed, however, is that Rachel has been given a discharge date too. It's been planned that we're both to be discharged within a few weeks of each other, I'm going first and then she'll follow after. The others have already spoken to us with feigned disappointment and asked us how we could put them through two new admissions so close together. Jacob enhanced this by saying that the girls are more irritating and less complaint when they come, something that caused me to land a pillow squarely in his face in response.

Although I knew it would only be temporary, it still hurts at the prospect of saying goodbye to the others. When you're forced into a situation where you're away from your family and all sense of familiarity, you find yourself drawn to those around you. If truth be told, they've become almost like a second family to me. I know that the logical answer to all of this is to ask for their numbers and arrange to meet up, but we all know from experience with those who've been discharged before us that it simply won't happen. Despite having all the good intentions in the world, people want to put Birchmoor behind them when they get out, and unfortunately, that means the patients too.

My exams are finally drawing to a close, and I'm grateful to be able to put the entirety of my course behind me until results day, at least until next year when I either carry them on to the second year or resit. I know which one I'd prefer, the last thing I want to do is go back a year and have to start all over again. Mrs Hooch has done so much for me already, most of it without me even realising it, and I don't want to have to meet someone else and relieve the pains of my story again. I'm trying to leave all of this behind me, despite the fact I can still feel the monster's claws within my mind, threatening to pull me under and choke me with the poison that is the illness. I don't listen to the monster any more.

***

It's Monday morning, and we're called from the Education Room at noon, only fifteen minutes into our lessons. The door to the Nurse's Office is shut tight, and I can tell instantly as soon as we enter the corridor that something is wrong. Never before has it been so ominously quiet. I shiver and notice that the others are all looking concernedly around the ward in the same manner, each one assuming the worst scenario possible. Have we done something wrong? Has someone been transferred? I look around and count them all hurriedly. There's the usual seven of us, not including Ethan, no one's on Leave or in danger. Are they perhaps introducing some new therapy and form of treatment? If so, then why have we been called away from the Education Room so early, and why is everything so quiet?

Karen comes out of the Nurse's Office and sees us all grouped together in the corridor, uncertain of where to go in relation to what has brought us here. "Can you all sit down in the lounge please," she says slowly, weighing each word carefully on her tongue. "There's something we need to tell you."

Karen's eyes are slightly red and puffy, and when she speaks it sounds like she's suffering from a very bad head cold. I'm confused, and now incredibly concerned. My heart beats rapidly in my chest and I feel as my palms begin to perspire slightly with nerves. I have the urge to turn around and hide from whatever it is that she's about to tell us, I'm certain it's something we don't want to know. "Can you take a seat in the lounge please," she says.

We sit rather closer together than we would normally have done upon the sofa, our arms and hips pressed against each other's, huddling together for support and safety in numbers as any previous arguments and disagreements evaporate into the air. Karen shuts the door firmly behind her before dragging one of the chairs into the centre of the room so that she can address us all collectively. We sit in silence for a minute, and I feel Jacob's leg begin to tremble alongside my own. The staff always maintain a level of control and professionalism. What's happened to cause such a reaction as this? Karen looks at each of us in turn before addressing the room at large. "I'm really sorry to have to tell you, but we've received some terrible news today. We wanted to tell you as soon as we found out, which is why you've been brought from the Education Room early," she begins.

We collectively hold our breath in anticipation of the shock and the pain that's sure to follow.

"I think it would be best if we're open and honest with each other, that way we can effectively support you throughout this

difficult time. I know this is going to come as a shock to you,
especially as I know that some of you kept in contact with
Imogen after her discharge almost a year ago now." Karen takes
a deep breath before she continues, drawing words from the air
that were never meant to be spoken.
"I'm sorry to tell you, but Imogen sadly passed away last night.
We don't know anything other than that at the moment, and we
don't think we'll be giving you any other details should we find
out. Imogen should be remembered for the life she lived rather
than how she died."
The world comes to a complete standstill as my mind floods with
ice.
Poppy lets out a cry like a banshee, but the rest of us remain
silent, too shocked to process what we're being told, because this
couldn't be true, it just couldn't.
"We want to make it clear that Imogen didn't die from anything
illness related, but instead lost her life in a tragic incident." Karen
takes a deep, steadying breath before she continues. "Staff will be
available to give 1:1 support for the near future, and you will be
excused from attending the Education Room for the rest of the
week. Your parents will all be called this afternoon to alert them
to the incident so that they may support you as well." I lean
sideways and seem to collapse onto Jacob next to me. We all
seem to fold into ourselves as we're crushed by the devastation
that Karen's words have brought into our lives.
I had been wrong beforehand in saying that we all assumed the
worst. There's no need to assume, it is the worst.

~ Let Me Go ~

Dear Friend,

Whether staff later found out how Imogen died I don't know, none of us were ever told. She may have died from something illness related, she could have been battling some other illness we knew nothing of, or she could have lost her life in some freak accident. I wasn't sure whether I should even mention her death to you, whether it would be kinder to write that she lived a long and happy life, free from illness and harm – but I wouldn't be honest if I did so. I owe it to Imogen to tell you the truth.

Imogen's death shook me to my core, never before had I personally known someone so young to have lost their life, especially considering she had only been out of hospital for less than a year. Karen released words that day that should never have been thought about, let alone spoken, words that couldn't be retrieved or remedied once past her lips, words that will forever be within our world. I questioned at the time why the world itself and the people within it had not stopped indefinitely. Why, although I perceived it as an ending from my perspective, people still drove in their cars, picked children up from school and held a casual conversation. Why hadn't everyone stopped what they were doing and mourned the loss that had shaken the very world to its core? Yet life continued to pass, the clock continued to tick and the world continued to turn, although this time out of sync because one of its integral parts was missing. I shuddered at the mere thought of what her family must be going through. If this is how I am feeling what must it be like for them? I don't think I'd like to know, it's not something you can appreciate until it's happened to you personally. It was strange when I spoke to my family over the phone that evening and they said how sorry they were for my loss. I didn't understand. I haven't lost her, and neither have any of the others. We know exactly where she is, she's resting now above us, in a little niche in Heaven that has been especially reserved. Imogen will forever live in our hearts and in our memories; no tragic incident can ever take that away.

~ Let Me Go ~

As you're aware, dear Friend, Imogen's death changed me. It made me address things that I had previously brushed under the rug, convinced that if I ignored their presence for long enough then they'd simply cease to exist. It made me realise how temperamental and fleeting our lives really are, how you can be here one minute and yet gone the next. Imogen didn't get the chance to make a full recovery and experience life without the illness, she didn't have the opportunity to achieve her dreams, nor to have children and grow old with the one she loved. Imogen didn't get to live, but I do and now I live for the both of us. All we have left of her is her blue handprint upon the wall, a final reminder that she was here and that she fought so bravely to defeat what had caused her such prolonged suffering. That's all we are. When the time comes, aren't we all just the memory of a handprint on the wall?

Chapter Thirty-Five

It's a relief when Dad comes to get me on Saturday morning to take me on my Home-Leave, I don't even think about going back to school on Monday. It's good to get away from the ward and the depressive, mournful atmosphere that pervades the ward and all those within it like a haze. I'm quiet and subdued over the weekend, and find it more difficult than usual to manage my required meals and snacks. The death of Imogen hangs like a permanent dark cloud above me, and any fleeting moments of joy I do have are short-lived considering I feel I'm doing her an injustice by enjoying life when she no longer can. The weekend seemingly passes within the blink of an eye, so that I'm going to sleep on my first night and then waking up on my last to begin my morning at school. It's strange packing my bag. To be completely honest, I'm not sure if I even need one considering I'm only going to one lesson and so only require a pen, some paper and the set text, but I take one in the hopes that it helps me to blend in with the crowd. The thought of the inevitable crowd of students and accompanying noise only makes me more anxious. I pull nervously at the ends of my hair and feel faintly nauseous. I'm worrying that they're all going to stare at me, what with me joining their class towards the very end of the year, that they'll ask me questions that I can't answer and make fun of the way I look and the behaviours I display. Despite the fact we've all sat our As-Levels (although they don't actually count towards our final grades at the end of next summer) we're beginning to start our coursework which is to be completed over the summer holidays – assuming I remain in the year group, of course. I can't help my behaviours, they're a part of me that has come as a result of my experiences, and I don't want to have to try and change in order for others to approve of me. For example, I can't sit still and instead jiggle my legs rapidly beneath the table at all times and, during periods of extreme anxiety; I twitch my head rapidly from side to side as a means of coping with what's happening to me. Dad takes Natalie to school at eight o'clock whilst Mum takes me to Wellbrook in the adjacent town. She told me she's coming in for the meeting with Mrs Brennan and will then wait in the reception area until my lesson is finished.

I'm nervous about seeing Mrs Hooch again, but even more so at the prospect of meeting another lady and attending class with my peers. I've never met anyone here before; I'm the only one from my previous secondary who transferred to Wellbrook's Sixth Form. On one hand, this does inevitably only add to my nerves at the prospect of not having anyone to sit with or talk to, but on the other it's a relief to have a fresh start. I don't want to be remembered as an illness.

I wait with Mum in the car until I hear the blaring of the siren announcing that tutor-time has ended and that first lesson will be starting in five minutes. I get out of the car nervously, my legs shaking slightly beneath me and my bag feeling profoundly alien as it rests against my back. I follow Mum into the main reception where we sign in once more and wait for Mrs Hooch. As with before, it isn't long before the doors to the cafeteria swing wide and Mrs Hooch comes over to shake Mum's hand and smile warmly at me.

"Alright?" she asks kindly.

"We're ok, aren't we Beth?" replies Mum. I nod shakily and, from the way Mrs Hooch's expression turns to one of concern, I know that she recognises my anxiety at being on the school grounds.

"Are you going back up to the Unit today?" asks Mrs Hooch conversationally as she leads us back through the cafeteria. I automatically hold my breath and clamp my sleeve firmly over my mouth and nose.

"Yes," replies Mum. "We're going up as soon as Beth's had her English Literature lesson." Mrs Hooch leads us further along until we're in the Sixth Form common room once more. There are students sat around the tables on their frees, some are evidently engrossed with their studying with their headphones on and open books in their laps, whilst others are laughing and playing on their phones. I seem to shrink in on myself as we pass through the room, as if I'm trying to become as indistinguishable and unnoticeable as the pale blue walls behind me. We weave through clumps of chairs and tables, each one with possessions strewn across it. I have a brief flash of panic at the thought of what this room must be like when it's full during break and lunch times. Will Mrs Hooch expect me to sit in here with everyone else once the Autumn Term starts? I can't do that. I know I can't. My legs begin to tremble and shake so much that I fear I'm going to trip over my own feet or a chair leg and end up sprawled on the ground. I'll be giving them all ammunition to bully me with and it's not even my first day. Mrs Hooch stops suddenly to tell off a group of boys who have fashioned paper aeroplanes out of A3 paper. "That's not a productive use of your time, is it?" she asks.

"Yeah," begins the boy with sandy hair. He raises the aeroplane dramatically and nods his head in satisfaction.

"It's for physics; we're investigating the velocity of paper planes." He throws it hard, and it twists gently through the air before coming to a landing on the other side of the room.

~ Let Me Go ~

"It's also P.E," says another boy as he leaves to get it. Mrs Hooch shakes her head and I can tell that she's trying really hard to suppress the hint of a smile playing over her lips. She leads us through the common room, leaving the laughter of the group of boys behind us, before she opens the door to the same meeting room we used last time. There's already another lady inside. I sit down awkwardly opposite Mrs Hooch and the other lady, and Mum takes the seat by my side. "This is Mrs Brennan," says Mrs Hooch as she motions to the lady next to her. She smiles at me warmly and reaches across the table to shake both mine and Mum's hands. She has shoulder length brown hair, bright blue eyes and a kind smile. She adjusts the skirt of her dress, which is patterned with prints of pale red and blue flowers before twisting to retrieve a notebook from the pocket of the lab coat draped over the back of her chair.

"Hello, Beth," she says with a wide smile. "It's lovely to finally meet you!" I nod to show that I'm listening and attempt my own smile in return, although I'm not sure how successful this is considering my gradually increasing nerves as the prospect of my English Literature lesson approaches.

Mrs Hooch clears her throat. "Mrs Brennan is the current Head of Year Thirteen, but she's going to go back to Year Twelve next term." I nod again, my eyes trained nervously on the clock above their heads.

"I know it's your choice, and you'll probably want to wait until you've seen your exam results, but we think it might be a good idea if you re-sat Year Twelve when you come to us in autumn," she says. Mrs Brennan murmurs an agreement and I can see Mum nodding slightly in the periphery of my vision.

"We think it would make integrating back into school easier for you, without the stress of learning new content and preparing for the actual exams in the summer," says Mrs Brennan. "We'll support whichever decision you make, of course, but we all just want what's best for you and for your time with us to be as easy as possible."

I nod once more to show that I understand.

"I'll still be around to help you too," says Mrs Hooch reassuringly. "Like I said last week, I've taken you under my wing. I also thought it might be a good idea if you and Mum come into the school again over the holidays, I'll be coming in at some point to organise my area for next year, so I could give you another tour around the school when there's no one in it so that you'll still be familiar with it when you come back in September."

"Thank you," I say quietly. It's strange having all of these people trying to help me, especially considering I've only really just met them. I struggle to understand why they'd want to go out of their ways to help me. They don't even know me. Mrs Hooch turns and glances at the clock behind her. "I think it'll be a good idea if I walk you over to your English lesson now," she says thoughtfully. "It's almost halfway through, so that way you won't have to stay for the whole lesson if you don't want to."

I nod. My voice is stuck somewhere in my throat, and even if I could speak I don't know what to say anyway. "I'm not going to see you before you leave," says Mrs Hooch. "Both myself and Mrs Brennan have to go to a meeting. I've told your teacher that you can get up and leave at any point during the lesson. You don't need to raise your hand or speak if you don't want to. If you leave then the teacher will email Mrs Knight, our Sixth Form Support, and she'll come and collect you from the corridor and take you back to Mum. Alright?"

I nod stiffly, although it doesn't feel alright at all if I'm to be honest. I'd much rather skip going into class and go back to the car with Mum now, even if it means I'll be back on Intensive sooner. "If I take you back to reception, then Mrs Hooch can take Beth to her lesson," says Mrs Brennan.

"Thank you," says Mum empathetically. "It means a lot that you're both doing so much to support Beth."

"It's not a problem," replies Mrs Hooch with a smile. "We're always going to be here to help, so please don't worry about the following year, we'll take each step as it comes," says Mrs Brennan warmly. "It was lovely meeting you, Beth," she says as

he turns to face me once more. "We're all very excited to have
ou here with us next term so that we can get to know each other
a bit better!"

mumble a quiet thank you to her as she leads Mum from the
oom. I follow Mrs Hooch back through the common room and
out into the corridor. I feel strange being with this lady on my
own, I'm not sure what to say or do. We pass numerous
classrooms and Mrs Hooch explains the general layout of the
school again as we go, but I'm so nervous that anything she tells
me is instantly forgotten. I can't stop worrying about what it's
going to be like in my lesson. She holds open the door for me to a
building marked with the glossy sign 'English Department' over
he door. My breath catches in my throat and my hands being to
remble slightly with the knowledge that we've almost reached
our destination. She leads me down the corridor, and I can hear
other lessons being given in the rooms alongside. We stop
outside a door marked with the number six and I hesitate.
"Alright?" asks Mrs Hooch with genuine sympathy and care.

give a jerky nod, despite the fact that I'm not feeling alright at
all. She motions for me to look through the glass window in the
door as she points towards the chair nearest. "I thought it'd be
easier for you to sit by yourself for the first time, that way you
don't have to worry about speaking to the others if you don't
want to." I look at my peers as they diligently scribble into their
notepads, occasionally referring to their copy of the set text
before them. I gulp nervously.

"You don't have to do any of the work if you don't want to, it's a
big achievement that you're going to try and be in the lesson.
You are more than welcome to leave whenever you want to and
Mrs Knight will come and get you. There's nothing to worry
about," she adds reassuringly. "You're more than welcome to
email me afterwards if you'd like to, or Mum could if that'd be
easier. Other than that, I won't be seeing you until the summer
holidays!" She smiles at me once more before opening the door
slightly and motioning for me to take my seat.

sit down nervously, instantly feeling the curious prickle of so many pairs of eyes on my back. I don't whether I imagine it or not, but I think I hear a slight murmur of confusion snaking through the class. The teacher smiles at me briefly in welcome and carries on her lesson without making a break in speech, something which I'm indubitably glad about.

I jiggle my legs up and down rapidly in agitation and can see the silhouette of Mrs Hooch through the window in the door before she turns and moves away. I feel alone, despite the fact I'm in a room with at least thirty others. "Right," says the teacher as she pulls the attention away from me and back to the task at hand. "I'd like you all to make a list about features you think are common of texts in the gothic era. We'll feedback in five minutes. Go!" There's the sound of numerous pages being turned and pens scribbling furtively as they begin the next task. I stare down at the desk in front of me, studying each chip and grain of wood as if my life depends on it.

I know it's bad when my head starts to twitch and I begin to wring my hands with such an intensity that I'm worried that my fingers are going to break. My breath begins to come in shallow gasps as I struggle to stay seated. I want to run out of this room without looking back. I want to leave this school and go back to Mum in the car. I can't do this; someone like me shouldn't be here. I glance at my watch, I've been in here for fifteen minutes, if I can only manage another fifteen more then I'll have done half a lesson. I pick at the cuticles of my nails anxiously, until they split and begin to bleed, the pain helps to steady me. I focus on my breathing, and not on the movement and speech of those around me. The teacher meanders around the tables, stopping occasionally to offer support or comment on someone's work. The volume inside the room gets louder, and my anxiety deepens. I can't breathe. I stand up suddenly and pick up my bag from beneath the table before hurrying out of the room. I press my back against the coolness of the wall to steady myself and train all of my focus onto regularising my breathing. I can't have a panic attack here.

I'm outside on my own for barely three minutes before a lady appears at the end of the corridor. She's dressed in a floral skirt and cream blouse, her hair hanging in loose waves about her face and she has an efficient yet friendly look about her. She smiles at me broadly when she sees me waiting in the corridor.

"Alright, Beth?" she asks kindly. "I'm Mrs Knight. Mrs Hooch told you I was coming to get you, didn't she?" I nod my head shakily in response.

"Come on then, love, let's go back to reception and find Mum," she says. She leads back through the corridors, telling me all the while how brave I am and how much they're all looking forward to working with me next term.

***

I can't do this any more. I'm sitting alone in my room, Rachel is on Home-Leave and the others are all watching some kind of action film in the lounge. They asked if I wanted to join them, but I declined. I press my hands painfully against my head, wishing for the thoughts to slow and quieten down, but I can't stop thinking about my discharge. Dr Ilona and Dr Sergei had come to see me within fifteen minutes of me arriving back from Leave. They had sat me down in the dining room and told me that I'm going to be discharged within a few weeks' time. They told me how pleased they are and how proud everyone is of me. I didn't feel pleased or proud, despite how many times I've yearned and dreamt about the day I'd leave the hospital.

I'm going to go back into the community, and the monster is going to get me again.

I can't do this. I don't want to go home and hurt everyone all over again, I don't want them to have to live with someone like me tainting their existence and ruining their lives. I don't want to go to Wellbrook and have to drop out again when it all becomes too much. There's no place for me in this world.

Truth no.30 – A hospital is a protected environment, there aren't any mentions of calories, weight or anything else deemed 'unhelpful' to contend with. In the real world, however, there are triggers around every corner.

I reach under my pillow and draw out the cord I've managed to keep hidden for so long, even when they searched the room after Simon's attempt it remained unnoticed. I hold it delicately in my hands, feeling as they tremble slightly against the woven material. I don't think about what my hands are doing, it's as if they're doing things of their own accord as if they're doing what was meant to happen all along. The cord becomes a noose. I test it, pulling at the ends to ensure they'll hold. My hands have stopped shaking and a clear mist has fogged my brain. I am calm. I cannot feel anything at all. I slip the cord around my throat before standing and looking for something to hang it from, despite the fact that the whole ward is designed to leave nothing hanging for that very purpose.

Steph finds me like that, with the noose around my neck and my eyes trained on the ceiling, looking for something that's not there in the hope that it will all go away.

~ Let Me Go ~

Dear Friend,

I'm not going to apologise for my actions, and nor do I ever think I will. It was an act of desperation, and there's nothing more to it. I was so profoundly terrified at the prospect of stepping back into the world I no longer felt a part of that I was willing to take my own life. Many people say that your cognitions prior to suicide are irrational and disjointed, that you never truly consider the repercussions of your actions, both in regards to yourself and those who care about you. The strange this is, my Friend, is that I was completely aware of what I was doing and why. Throughout the whole process of fashioning the noose my mind was clear, rational and reasonably calm. I was put on 1:1 once more for a few weeks, and my Home-Leave was stopped. I lost all of my bathroom and toilet privacy with a click of their fingers. They started discussing the possibility of transferring me to an adult Psychiatric Unit, as I had to go somewhere considering I was nearing adulthood faster than anyone would have liked. Despite seeing it as a threat, although it was more of a reality, I was pushed to change. I came to the realisation that if I were to give in to my illness for the rest of my life, then I would be spending the vast majority of it either in a hospital or deteriorating until admission became necessary.
That's not really living at all.
I think the vast majority of what concerned me to such an intensity that I tried to take my own life was my fear of the unknown. But even now, my Friend, I am still profoundly terrified of the future, and yet I am here and writing to you. I was daunted by the prospect of starting at Wellbrook, despite the fact that you couldn't find nicer people like Mrs Hooch, Mrs Brennan and Mrs Knight anywhere. I felt sick with fear at the thought of having so much freedom to myself once more, despite having spent just over a year complaining at my lack of it. I knew, as most people recovering are, that the boundaries between 'managing' and 'relapsing' are so minute that they're virtually indistinguishable from each other.

There are so many options to relapse, it's practically limitless, and yet there is only one option for recovery, and that's staying strong and following your care-plan. As one of the inspirational messages read on the wall of the lounge, 'Listen to your eating disorder, and then do the opposite.' I'll admit, however, the thing that frightened me most wasn't the prospect of starting school or managing indefinitely in the community, it was the fact that I could go through all of this again. But, as Jacob told me on my discharge day, you only go through it if you put yourself through it.

As summer progressed I fought with all of my might, something which I'll be honest in saying I hadn't done beforehand. As you well know, I was still terrified at the prospect of discharge, but things began to settle for me once I'd had some time to come to terms with it and plans had been put in place in my community to support me.

I steadily earnt back my privacy and my leave, I managed all of my meals in the dining room and I took my required medication without causing any difficulty. As was arranged prior to the end of summer term, I met Mrs Hooch towards the end of the holidays where she showed me around Wellbrook once more so that I could remain familiar with it when I started my integration in the following term. Due to the fact I failed my Biology and Music (due to circumstances) and only just scraped a pass with my English Literature, I made the decision to go back and re-sit Year Twelve with the support of my team behind me. I tried not to think about whether I'd fit in or not, or whether I'd have comments made about my behaviours, they're all a part of me and my past and I know I shouldn't have to change them if they help me manage. I don't need to fit in with the crowd; I can live life to my own beat.

My discharge date became fixed for the twenty-first of September, and any mention of transferral became long forgotten. As the day ticked closer, I began to form more substantial plans at school. I would be attending for an hour on my first week, and would then gradually increase this depending on how well I coped and meal times and snacks would be steadily integrated with support from both Mrs Hooch and Mrs Brennan. Although the whole prospect was undeniably daunting and profoundly terrifying at times, I began to accept that things had to change if I wanted live.

Chapter Thirty-Six

The sun streams brightly through the blinds so that the walls are lit by the reflected iridescent glow from the motivational quotes on the walls. The handprints seem bolder than usual, the dates beneath them jumping out in the room and shouting their praise. I am going home for the last time today.

I know they're planning a party, it's hard to keep a secret for long on a locked ward, and that they're all down there now, putting the final touches to the decorations they've meticulously handmade. I have the ward to myself, apart from Karen in the office who must be left to supervise me whilst I'm still a patient, even Ethan has been taken down to oversee the activities. Whilst I have the ward to myself, I use the time to reflect on all of the things that happened on it; from the day of my admission when I crumbled to the floor in my new room, to the day when I was told about Imo and decided to try and live for the both of us. As much as I hate this place from keeping me away from those I love, there's no doubting that it's saved my life and changed my outlook on the world. It feels strange to be on Intensive for the last time and to know that, once I go back into the lift to the Games Room, there will be no coming back. For months upon months I have dreamt of this day, but now that it's here it feels incredibly surreal. Life is waiting for me on the other side of those walls, and in less than an hour I will be out there to embrace it.

***

I stand nervously next to my parents and hold the piece of paper before me in my hands, the slight tremble of nerves causing the words to dance slightly before my eyes what with so many people staring at me. I clear my throat. My mouth feels dry and I worry whether I'll even be able to speak at all, but I must. I am not leaving here without saying what I want to say first. Despite leaving my handprint on the wall with my dates of admission and discharge amongst all the other survivors, I want to leave them with one last message, something which I hope they'll hold within their hearts and something which I pray will make this whole ordeal easier for them. "I would like to start by saying a massive thank you to my parents and my sister Natalie," I pause and glance at my family by my side, where they've remained without faltering throughout this whole process. "They have been here for me every step of the way and I honestly wouldn't be where I am if it wasn't for their tremendous love and support (although sisters can be annoying!)" I get a few chuckles at this, and I hear Jacob call 'here, here!' in agreement.

"My father would wake up every Saturday morning at 4 a.m. to come and get me from here, what can say dedication better than that?" I take another deep breath to settle my nerves, feeling as the words flow from my lips as if they've been waiting there all along. "I would also like to thank the staff here at Birchmoor, particularly Karen and Steph, they have given me numerous 1:1 discussions and have always been able to make me smile when I wasn't feeling the best. Also a massive thank you to my consultant Dr Sergei who has always listened to my views and has always had my best interests at heart. Than you to Dr Ilona how has literally been there for me every step of the way. Thank you for helping me get my life back." I turn towards her and give her a smile, and watch as she wipes a straying tear from the corner of her eye. Dr Sergei beams at me proudly.

"And most importantly," I continue, "thank you to all of the young people. You have been ever so kind to me and have become more like a second family than friends. You have all made this experience so much more bearable and I wouldn't be where I am today if it wasn't for you guys." I look each of them in the eyes, silently thanking them for their contribution to saving me. Rachel stands and takes a bow, before Jacob pulls her back down, saying jokingly that I didn't mean her. Rachel swears at him and is only half-heartedly reprimanded for her choice of language.

"Coming into hospital is scary and it isn't exactly the most pleasant of experiences, but things can change. Coming to Birchmoor has helped me to realise that there are more important things in life than the numbers you see on a scale or the size of dress that you wear. Deep down the only thing that matters are the people who love you. Even if I could take back this year and a half I've spent at Birchmoor, I wouldn't want to. It has taught me so much about what really matters, and has helped me to understand that I can live a happy life outside of hospital." I pause and blink rapidly to clear the moisture in my eyes. I am not going to cry.

"I am still on my recovery journey, but I feel a lot more positive about the outcome than I ever did before. I wish for all of you here to live a beautiful life. The thing is that you will only live once, so make sure that you live your lives with no regrets. You are all so special in your own ways and your lives are worth so much more than this illness and spending your a lifetime stuck in hospital. This illness is not your friend, it will take away everything that you love and will make you into someone that you're not. You are all perfect just the way you are." I stop to let my words sink in, and to give my voice a brief rest as it's beginning to struggle after being used to say so much. I mean every word that I'm saying.

"I couldn't make a leaving speech without mentioning *Harry Potter*, could I? As said by *Albus Dumbledore* 'Happiness can be found even in the darkest of places, if one only remembers to turn on the light'. Please remember that you can all do this, there is a life outside of Birchmoor. I wish you all the best and hope that you achieve your dreams. Thank you for everything, and in the words of my Grandpa, 'you is what you is'.

My ending words are greeted with a loud round of applause and I find myself blushing. I'm finally being rewarded for something I've done that's right rather than what my illness tells me to do. My parents wrap their arms around me and squeeze me tightly with pride; never did they think they'd see the day when they brought their daughter back home indefinitely. They release me as I'm swarmed by the others. I'm trapped in the middle of a group hug, the people who've supported me throughout it all standing around me and celebrating with me on my discharge day. I tell each of them how much I'll miss them, and thank them personally for all of the things they've done for me. I draw Dr Ilona, Dr Sergei, Karen and Steph into tight hugs, murmuring into their shoulders my gratitude for saving my life when I thought I was too far gone to be saved.

Goodbyes are always the hardest, as is proven when nearly everyone ends up crying when the time comes for me to leave the hospital completely. Dr Sergei hands Dad my discharge letter, before repeating that he's sent a copy to both my GP and mental health nurse in adult services. I am no longer a patient. Dr Ilona leads us back through to reception and taps her fob to the black box beside the door to let us out. I give her one last hug before the doors swing shut behind me. I inhale deeply and release all of the pent-up worry and anxiety within me. I'm not going to worry about the future, the future will happen when it happens; right now I'm content with my freedom. Dad drives the car back out of the gates, but I want to walk through them by myself. I came through these gates almost a year and a half ago. I

~ Let Me Go ~

was driven in and under Section because I was so adamant about refusing all forms of treatment. I arrived at the hospital in a very unstable and weak condition, only a few weeks beforehand I had come so close to dying of heart failure. But now things are different.

I walk up to the gates on my own two feet. I am unsupported and strong. My heart doesn't flutter with the increased activity but remains firm and constant. I am alive and I'm not looking back. I take a deep breath and step out into the world beyond.

~ Let Me Go ~

Dear Anorexia,

You are not my friend. I believed wholeheartedly for so many years that you were on my side, that you were right whilst all the others were wrong, but you lied to me. You offered me a better life, and for all of my problems to disappear in the blink of an eye as long as I listened to you and meticulously followed your rules. At first, I'll admit that I did think it was helping, that I was becoming a better person, but then reality hit and all the problems I had suppressed came rolling back with such a force that I was knocked down. You lied to me. You told me that dieting would make my life easier for me, that it would make others proud, but all it ever succeeded in doing was worrying the ones who love me and rather than making things easier I came very close to death.

You're not going to like hearing this, Anorexia, but quite frankly I don't care. I have built a life outside of you and the monster. I integrated back into Sixth Form successfully, thanks to the extensive support of Mrs Hooch, Mrs Brennan and Mrs Knight who have assisted me with mealtimes and other anxiety-provoking situations throughout my entire time at Wellbrook. They've been by my side no matter what, something which you never did for me.

Things are not perfect, and I doubt they ever will be. I am not by any means recovered, but Birchmoor gave me the skills I so desperately needed to fight back, and I know who the true enemies are now, and it's not me. There are still days when I wake up, so consumed with the thoughts of my illness that I stop fighting, that I lie down and give up, but I always have the strength to regain my balance and try again. My recovery journey is a battle, and I make the conscious decision to fight each morning I get out of bed, each meal time I'm faced with and each day I walk through the gates of my school.

I removed the mirror from my wall.

You're probably asking why I'd ever choose to fight at all. I am a survivor, and that means more to me than you ever will.

I wasn't sure whether to include this, but if I didn't I'd be lying to myself, and I know deep down that's a sure way for you to get back into my head again. My recovery journey has not been smooth; there have been many dips in the road which have taken me some time to overcome. My physical health is not what it was; my weight did drop in the months after my discharge, but not to an extent that I'm dying from you and your influences again. I am fighting back and will continue to do so until the last breath leaves my lungs.

You took away my teenage years and made me something that I'm not. You made me hate life and myself with such an all-consuming intensity that I was willing to leave it all behind. You caused my family to suffer and you took away my personality. You have ruled my life and controlled my thoughts for so long, and I've had enough. This is my life, and I want to live it. One day I will be free of you, but until then, my fight continues. I have one final thing to say to you:

Let

Me

Go...

~ Let Me Go ~

~ Let Me Go ~

Printed in Great Britain
by Amazon